WHO KNOWS GOD?

A Novel by Leonard Smith

Copyright 2009
ONTHEBOOKS ENTERTAINMENT®
www.onthebooksent.com
ISBN: 978-1-4414950-9-9
Edited by: Bernard A. Blake
Cover Design by: Leonard Smith

1

SOUNDTRACK

Executive Producer: M. Moe Betta Bowles

Courtesy of Yeahmann Music

Mix & Mastered by: Spyda Tek; Orbit Studio
Bronx, N.Y

[1] INTRO (3:13) by: Author Leonard Smith

[2] THE QUEEN & THE DREAD (3:02)

Written by: Leonard Smith

Performed by: Leonard Smith as *Architekk* and
April Elisabeth Laronda

Produced by: M. Moe Betta Bowles courtesy of
Yeahmann Records

[3] PRAISE IS THE KEY (3:42)

Written by: Leonard Smith

Performed by: Leonard Smith as *Architekk* and
April Elisabeth and Laronda

Produced by: M. Moe Betta Bowles

[4] CLASH OF THE TITANS (4:03)

.   3

Written by: Leonard Smith and M. *Moe Betta* Bowles

Performed by: Leonard Smith as Architekk, M. *Moe Betta* Bowles as J3 and Treniece Moore as Laronda

Produced by: Maurice Moe Betta Bowles courtesy of *Yeahmann* Records

[5] CAN'T WALK AWAY NOW (3:46)

Written by: Leonard Smith

Performed by: Leonard Smith, D'asia Brunson and Adrienne Williams

Produced by: M. *Moe Betta* Bowles courtesy of *Yeahmann* Records

TABLE OF CONTENTS

COMING SOON FROM ONTHEBOOKS ENT ®

- *THE ART OF PEACE*: The 3RD novel from Author Leonard Smith

- *TRUST ME I'M A DOCTOR*: The biography of Dr. Norman McCulloach

- WE GOT NEXT MAGAZINE

- **ONTHEBOOKS FILMS** *49%This, 49%That & 2% Other* THE MOVIE

THE DREAD

THE DEBUT ALBUM FROM ARCHITEKK

LATE 2009

WWW.ONTHEBOOKSENT.COM

- *MOVIN' WEIGHT*: PERSONAL TRAINING BOOKLET

- **THE RAMADAN DIARIES**

- **WHO KNOWS GOD? PART II**

Also from Author Leonard Smith:

49% THIS, 49% THAT & 2% OTHER

VISIT **WWW.ONTHEBOOKSENT.COM**
DAILY FOR CLASSIC HIP-HOP AND R&B
VIDEOS, NEWS HEADLINES AND HOLY
SCRIPTURE! ALSO MAKE SURE TO
TUNE IN ON FRIDAYS FOR OUR TOP 4
OF THE WEEK COUNTDOWN AND THE
WAR REPORT ARTICLE.

FOREWORD

"You, dear children, are from GOD and have overcome them, because the one who is in you is greater than the one who is in the world. They are from the world and therefore speak from the viewpoint of the world, and the world listens to them. We are from GOD, and whoever knows GOD listens to us…"

1JOHN 4:4-6

GOD: The creator of the heavens and the earth, The most high, The infinite, The compassionate, most merciful, The sovereign, The true King, The holy one, one who is free from all blemishes, The giver of peace, one who is immune from all distress, The giver of protection, The mighty, The overpowering Lord, The self glorious, The creator, one who gives life, The fashioner of shapes, one who has control over all things, The all knowing, The all-hearing, The just, The caretaker, The benevolent, The Lenient, The wise, The resurrector of the dead, The omnipresent, The almighty, The invincible, The keeper of counts, The originator, The giver of death, The everlasting, The all perfect, The one unequalled, The assembler, The light, The deviser, The eternal, The most forbearing, The first, The last, The truth!

PREFACE

3.5

"They gone call us some niggas… some crazy ass niggas."

Date: December 18TH 2008

"Here's to family, unity, and never having to sell a dime bag of anything ever again."

Stump raised his paper cup of coffee and took a sip with the intent of warming his body from the chill of old man winter. Jason rose from his seat atop a newspaper on the steps. He patted his good friend gently on his shoulders before sneaking past him to look out of the staircase window onto Madison Avenue; "GOD's green earth."

Stump chuckled to himself, "Green? All I see around here is black and brown."

Jason shoved his hands in his pocket and remained silent for a Moment, still looking out of the window. "…That's crazy right?"

"Yeah; but after tonight, you can walk away from all this good ole ghetto Project shit. You are done here Brother, victorious."

Jason laughed privately yet again as he massaged his newly grown beard; "Run and hide huh?"

Stump tried to rejuvenate Jason's lackluster mood, although he knew he'd be fine sooner than later. "I wouldn't call it hiding. You worked hard for what you wanted, Brother. Nobody can deny you that; especially none of these judgmental fucks out here."

"Remember that scene in Scarface when Tony was barking on the people at the dinner table? *You need people like me. So you can point your fucking fingers & say that's the bad guy.*"

Stump smiled in familiarity, he employed a phony Cuban accent and played along; *"What that make you?"*

"Good?"

- *"Good?"*

The two shared in a Moment of laughter and contemplation before Jason picked up on a sharp vibration quivering through the air. "That's probably Margz calling."

Stump leisurely removed his cell phone from the leather holster attached to his belt; *"Peace."* He said into the receiver.

Jason lent an ear to Stump's conversation while staring at the other side of the Projects through the staircase window. Things certainly changed since he was a kid running around down there, but most of it was the same.

"Bet, bet we leaving right now then."

Stump flipped his phone close then turned to his friend, "We good Tekk." Before he could place his phone back on his side Jason started down the steps. The large man posted at the break in the flight of steps below saw them coming and began descending into the building as well.

"What about us?" Stump asked as he dipped around a puddle of urine trying to keep pace.

"What about us?" Jason asked moving as if he were racing against time.

"What you think they gone say about us? I mean…people damn sure ain't gone call us good, we're Black and we're Muslims in America."

Jason looked back at Stump and in doing so he caught a glance at the face under the hood of the man who was trailing Stump closely. "They gone call us some niggas, Bro..." Jason got to the fourth floor landing and to Stump's dismay he showed no signs of slowing down, "…Some crazy ass niggers."

12:16AM; THE SAME NIGHT

"You can get out of here baby." Jason said to his wife in the driver's seat as he slammed his door shut and got situated in his seat.

"What about Gwinn?"

"She said she not ready to come."

She looked at him strangely. Jason shrugged it off as if he didn't feel like getting into it. He turned back toward Stump who was sitting next to him; "I heard ya man Iron Mike say one time; He was talking about Tupac in an interview for a documentary. He was like; most people aren't good they're just well behaved."

- *"So you want me to drive to the house now?"*

"Yes." Jason answered the question from the front of the car.

"Without Gwinn?"

"Yes Laronda. She don't wanna come right now what you want me to do?" He answered in a state of frustration.

"Alright." Laronda shook her head as if she had more to say but declined, as there was company present.

"See Tupac, I ain't know the man, but I would assume he was a good dude. If you listen to most of the content of most of his music, you see he speaks at least some degree of truth; the Black man's plight, wide spread poverty, Police brutality, things that if you ask me, ultimately cost him his life."

Stump caught a glance of Architekk's debut album lying in the compartment behind the gear shifter just as Mrs. Jason Jordan began to roll the luxury sedan from the curb. "You forgot to give Gwinn her CD."

"Oh shit; I need to give that to her before we leave." Jason yelled over the Papoose mix tape blasting from the stereo, *"Hold on baby, don't leave yet."* He pulled out his phone and keyed up Margo, who was in the car behind them. *"Step out. I gotta go back in the building."* Jason flipped his phone close then turned to look back at Stump, "What you thinking about?"

"One's path… Whether it will ultimately cost one their life?"

"Well that's a good thing right? The Holy Bible instructs us that to be absent from the body is to be present with the Lord." Jason looked back at his security personnel filing out behind him and readjusted the pistol in his waistline. "But we damn sure gone find out Brother; we damn sure gone find out…Stay here, I'll be right back."

Jason stepped out of the cozy S80 interior into the frigid Harlem night and addressed his squad like a Lieutenant. "You stay here. You come with me." He said to the 6' 4", 300 plus pounder known as Big Easy before they headed up the walkway.

Jason noticed a familiar sports car parked in the lot in front of building 1694 that incited question after question in his head.

"Peace Black man!"

"Peace." Jason reached out to embrace Hakeem who was smiling from ear to ear as he squeezed Jason's hand and brought him in for a semi-hug. Hakeem spoke in a private tone, *"I just heard the album Brother. Al-Hamdulla; that was a mighty blow you stuck."*

Jason smiled and turned away in an attempt to be modest. Hakeem pulled him closer and forced him to look into his eyes, "You hear me Bro, a mighty blow? But you know Babylon is gone take interest now… You know that?"

"I know."

"Well then, peace be with you Brother, peace be with you."

Hakeem tossed his hood back over his head and kept stepping, as did Jason and Big Easy. Jason had thought after thought racing across his brain. The most pressing issue on his mind was the talk he just had with Stump in the car. He was eager to get back so he could bring the abstract random thoughts he put forward to a complete circle of knowledge for his good friend. His nerves wouldn't allow him to remain silent any longer and he placed the information in Big Easy for whatever it was worth.

"The path back to Allah is the supreme achievement…the struggle of life is so that GOD, your creator, may test you to see how close back to him you could get. If you so choose."

Big Easy looked at him strangely as Jason carried on.

"Satan…" Jason chuckled to himself; "Satin after GOD gave him respite until judgment day, promised to fuck with us men while we were here on earth. Remember Satin refused to bow before Adam cause he felt like he was better than him?"

Big Easy didn't bother responding as they scaled the few steps in front of the building.

"…And by and by, here the fuck we are."

"Thanks for letting me know that." Big Easy said uninterested.

When they entered the building Jason headed straight for the B staircase and waived the former amateur bodybuilder over. "Come on man, I wanna see what your wind is looking like. You're security; you can't just look tough, you know?"

They pushed and shoved one another as they raced up the first flight of stairs. At the first landing, Jason began to separate himself in an all out sprint to the 7th floor. Jason hunched over in the hallway of the 7th floor and grabbed his knees, thoroughly depleted as he waited for Big Easy to arrive.

"I ain't…" Big Easy gasped for air as he came to a halt, "…I ain't no damn Usain Bolt."

Jason tried to make small talk as he got himself together, "…Inshallah, we'll be home before the sun rise." He was still folded over trying to catch his breath. "Press the elevator; I ain't gone be long."

Big Easy monotonously pulled at the door handle to the A elevator on his right, "I think this one is still out from earlier."

Jason hadn't moved on yet, although he did stand erect to rub on his chest. "I gotta stop smoking; Hollis already leaving my ass in the dust."

The transparent glass on the elevator door illuminated as the elevator car arrived to the tone of a light ring. Jason began walking up the hallway to Ms. Ruiz's apartment.

"Oh shit!"

Big Easy instinctively drew his firearm. Jason turned quickly and did the same, pointing into the open elevator.

"Oh shit!"

"Let's get out of here." Big Easy insisted.

A young man's corpse lay facedown on the elevator floor engulfed in a pool of its' own blood. Two gunshot wounds to the near side of the boy's hood were prevalent. Jason stood in a trance. Big Easy scanned the hallway with his weapon still drawn; "Tekk we gotta go."

Jason was frozen, in a state to which he was clearly at a lost for words.

"You know this nigga?"

UNIT 1

Jason *Architekk* Jordan

28

"Daddy I'm not playing! It's very important to me."

Date: June 29TH 2005

"Look lady, you gone have to borrow the money from a family member, your boyfriend, or something but we not playing no more. Our client need they money today."

"Oh, oh no speaky no en'gles."

"No speaky no damn en'gles?"

Jason became so riled that he was dangerously close to cursing the caller out. "Miss you was just speaking the Queens' English when I told you my name was Dwayne." He said as he reached in his top drawer for a pen to cross her name off of his *prospects* list. "Come on now, cut it out. We need a payment from you!"

"No, no en'gles."

Jason threw his hands up in surrender, "No en'gles huh? That's your story and you're sticking to it?"

"Si."

"Alright *Crystal*, from friggin' *Chicago*, who don't speak no damn english. I'll update my files that you are refusing to cooperate with my client regarding this matter, and I-"

"Thank you, bye." She disconnected the call.

Jason notated the account then looked over to the cubical beside his. "Was you listening to that one?"

"Yeah; deadbeat. You should've let me do a second voice for you. *Hello ma-am this is Jason's supervisor, I understand you were looking to resolve this issue before the Judge.*"

Jason sat back in his chair and flipped through his audio electronics magazine. "We can't take these people to court man, you know that."

"Yeah but the Debtor doesn't. Quality Assurance isn't even listening half of the morning. You can tell these people you're gone a take them to Jail for Christ's sake, repo their cars. Fair Debt Collections Practices Act my ass; we're here to get bonus checks."

Josh stood to look at the payment board at the front of their *Payday loans* department. "You need to at least get a payment on the board Jason. Management is not gonna keep you here much longer if you ain't putting numbers on the board everyday."

Jason placed his headset on mute and stood from his chair to relieve his legs from the sting of inactivity. "Fuck that board." He said as he stretched out his upper-body. Jason caught eyes with Ebony from the Autos department who was looking in their direction.

"She's got the hots for you Bro." Josh said smirking and reeking of immaturity.

A tall, sharply dressed man stepped onto the collections floor and walked directly up to Terry, the Payday loans supervisor, whispering something in his ear before entering Jason's aisle.

"These punks got the hots for me too." Jason said to Josh before the gentleman reached his cubical. "Hi Mr. Jordan, you wanna put your phone in *after call* and come with me for a second?"

Jason tossed his headset on the side of his computer monitor near his training manual. "What yall want?" He asked as he turned around with a hard grill.

"Uh, yeah, we need to speak with you about your performance."

5:38PM; THE SAME DAY

Building 55, apartment 16M; it was in the
Projects but it was home. When Jason and
Denise exchanged vowels in 1996 his Mother
expressed her drunken sentiments to the dismay
of nearly everyone in attendance; *"They ain't no
damn soul mates; they just going half on the
rent. My son's soul is in the Projects. I don't
know about that wanna be prissy bitch."*

Jason turned 33 this year. His had been a long
and painful life thus far; two near death
experiences and years of going around in circles.
All of which rendered the man known around
NYC as Arechitekk primarily and exclusively on
GOD's side. The more he got into his religious
studies, the wider his eyes were opened, the
more Jason got settled into Grant Projects. The
poor are rich in spirit, and there's plenty poor in
Harlem. Hollis was protected and respected in
the neighborhood, and the same held true on the
other side of town with his other children. Jason
decided that if it were intended for him to leave
the hood, GOD would show him the way.

Denise was woman a on a career tract. She was
hired by her alma mater, Hunter University as a
temporary advisor for the office of admissions in
2003. Two years and as many pay raises later,
Denise now had her sights set outside of the
concrete jungle, as her dedication to the job and

sista swagger was something the institution had been looking for.

Jason threw his keys on the kitchen counter and walked into the living room. He flopped on the couch and enjoyed a rare Moment of silence before pulling himself up and into the bathroom to cleanse himself for a prayer.

It was a childish and extensive battle, but Jason got the house vote to utilize the extra room in the back of the apartment as a recording studio. Denise wanted to use the space as a Study, suggesting that it would add class and substance to the home. Jason based his argument, which was brought before their daughter Hollis on the fact that a studio would give him at least some piece of mind, as well as increase his chances of staying the hell out of their busy lives. Two month later he was in his home studio recording his first album.

Jason removed his prayer mat from between his subwoofer and the edge of the track-board. He dried his feet with a designated towel then prostrated himself before the Lord. When he walked out of the *Debt Collections Inc.* high-rise downtown, he did so with a final warning notice in his hand and uncertainty in his heart. He was stressed out, but his faith and belief that GOD had him on a particular path for a particular reason rendered him to his knees anyway. After the prayer, Jason opened his eyes to what seemed like a new day; renewed inspiration. The first thing he saw was the activated screen saver message on the computer monitor:

PATIENTLY PERSERVERE

He stood to his feet, walked over to the track-board and wiggled the computer mouse to expose his electronic desktop. He clicked on the play icon then turned around to find his wife waving her hands, apparently for his attention.

"How long you been there?"

"I know you heard me. What are you doing home so early?" Denise asked.

Jason gave her a faint head nod to acknowledge her and nothing further. Any other response he would've had to her questioning him as if he was their sixteen-year-old daughter would've been the precursor to an argument. His words and actions were the only thing that Jason seemed to have control over nowadays and he came to understand that there were tremendous benefits to keeping them in check.

"I told you, you need to leave that voodoo stuff alone Jay."

"How 'bout hello?" Jason exploded. "How you doing or some shit like that before you get into full bitch mode when you get home Denise."

She responded with feigned amusement, "Bitch? Hmm, that's nice. I see you've been working on your vocabulary for your music's sake." She left the room and went into the bathroom adjacent to the studio. *"And my day was great thanks for asking!"* She said staring into the mirror on the medicine cabinet. *"I found out today that over 90% of my students finished this semester with a 2.5 or better. That's considered good academic standing."*

Jason began closing all of the applications on his computer and he shut off his recording equipment. He planned on recording a song that he was working on in his head since last night, but that inspiration was dead. All he wanted now was to get as far away from his wife as possible.

"I'm going to the store, you want something?"

"Oh, you trying to get away from me now?"

"You came to that conclusion pretty swiftly; you just a plain ole genius ain't you?"

Denise didn't bother responding. She continued to apply her make-up with a secret smile across her face. Jason grabbed his wallet and lighter off the track-board; "And I know what good academic standing is Nesie. You forgot I went to college too?"

"Well the way you play around with all that silly little music crap all day one would never know."

6:13PM; THE SAME NIGHT

Jason picked up a two-gallon bottle of water and a bag of peanuts before he reached the counter at the front of the store. "Peace; and let me get two vanilla Dutches and a bottle of Aspirin please, Mohammad."

-"And let me get four Dutches, Ak."

A young female demanded as she got to the counter. She looked over at Jason; "What up Tekk?" Her instincts rendered a shake of her head in self correction, "I mean, Mr. J."

"You got my album from M.S.G yet?" Jason asked as he ripped open his .50 cent bag of peanuts.

"That's word to Andre; I was just listening to it before I came downstairs."

"That's peace, that's peace. Well then call me Tekk." He said smiling.

Laronda was wearing gaudy gold doorknocker earrings, white leggings and a Michael Jordan college jersey that was stretched out from the bottom over her broad hips. The two of them left the store and walked up the block together as Laronda was going to her meet her girls in front of Jason's building.

"So…What's your favorite track on the album?"

"It's between *The Light* and *The Truth and The Proof*. It depends on how I'm feeling when I press play. But everything on there is tough. I don't skip no tracks."

It was a hot Friday eve in Harlem, groups of kids were creeping all about, NYPD sirens were screaming and Harlemites were dressed-up to go out. Through their short conversation Laronda had proven to be a listener with a common ear, which came to Jason's surprise as he had prejudged her by the company she kept. He assumed, with good measure that she was a member of the J.E.S.I.C.A street gang. She was often with Connie, Grant Projects' J.E.S.I.C.A superior, and Laronda wore more Carolina blue than a little bit, the crew's color.

"Whatever verse where he said; *back when I was nothin' you, made a Brother feel like he was somethin'. That's why I'm with you till the day, boo no frontin'…*"

Buck joined Stump reciting his favorite Hip-Hop verse in front of the building, *"Even when the skies were gray, you would rub me on my back & say baby it'll be ok.* Yeah, that was the first verse. That was tuff."

The entire N.Y.C.M.C crew was out and one could tell by the cars double parked at the curb. Stump, who got his name from his short, linebacker like physique, was a top-notch producer and audio engineer. Buck was an in-house writer for the music group and a local hustler. Jason's memory was selective but one thing he kept with him was Buck's response when he asked if he would join the music group; *"I don't know what they teaching these lil young niggas round here today. But when we was coming up they taught us that life is what you make it; so we gone make something of it. "*

-"A child is born with no state of mind, blind by the ways of mankind. GOD's smiling on you but he's frowning too, because only GOD knows what you'll go through…"

Stump, Stacky and Buck produced a lackluster response to Margo's choice.

"Margz you always gotta say some wild old shit. Go head wit' all that."

"That's cause I'm a older, smarter Motherfucker, Motherfucker!" Margo turned to Jason who was leaning against the railing, rhyming under his breath. "These young boys don't know nothin'."

Seemingly agitated Com interjected, "Yeah; that was the shit. Don't matter if it's old."

Stacky returned to the world after five straight minutes of texting on his phone, "Margo could completely make some shit up & you'll say that's that shit. Get outta here. The hottest Hip-Hop verse of all time is the last verse of *It Aint Hard to Tell.*"

-"Second verse of *Girls, Girls, Girls.*"

- "Beans; *The Truth.*"

This particular crew went all the way back to the beginning. Before the parks in the Projects were reconstructed, before the current Mayoral administration, and before gentrification changed the face of Harlem, there was their affiliation. The name *New York City Music Cartel* was Stacky's brainchild, it came to him after he heard the unmastered copy of Buck's first mix-tape, which three weeks worth of trap money went to fund.

The lyrics blasting from Buck's Audi commanded a tentative ear. Laronda became annexed into a crowd of young ladies when she and Jason got back to 126th street. Jason could

33

see her a few feet away nodding her head to the
flow and pointing him out to one of her friends.
"That's him" He read her lips.

Respect, one of the things that Jason Jordan was
in search of from the time he recorded his first
song in Stumps' old studio in the Bronx, and
here it was on a silver platter... respect. The
crew was on their way to Club Barrel to party
and bullshit for the next five or so hours. Jason
didn't go out much; consequently his music
wasn't built for nightclubs, but rather for the
streets, and the individual listeners. A track that
he recorded less than a week ago bumping in the
Projects on a night like this was a small victory
in his cause.

-*"What up, you broke ass nigga?"* Buck yelled
to the driver of the black Altima that pulled up
and parked beside his car. *"Why don't you go
get that bum ass car washed or waxed or
something? That shit looking bad."*

Laronda and her girl started walking towards
Jason. He grew uneasy, as he knew they were
probably coming over to discuss his music,
which was something he tried to avoid at all
cost.

*"Nigga who you calling broke? I just lost three
stacks in a dice game & I'm still buying out the*

Bar tonight. Everything getting shut down when I walk in the spot; matter of fact, hold on..."

-"Tekk my Sister wanna get your CD, you got a copy on you?" Laronda asked she reached Jason.

"Na, I don't. But you should go to Margo's though and get that." He said as he handed her a business card from his wallet. "He still got copies in his shop."

"Alright, bet, bet." She dapped his hand as if he were one of the Sisters, keeping her two middle fingers folded in their ritualistic form.

"Don't be peacing him up like that. You don't have no fucking discretion! Go back over there."

Laronda barked at her younger set Sister then turned back to Jason as peaceful as can be. "I'm sorry, these little girls are so stupid sometimes."

The young man who arrived in the Altima walked back to his car and reached through the open window to turn the volume on his stereo up. *"You hear that boy? That's that good Bose shit right there; I just got these put in. This ain't that trash you call a system. Turn that shit off."*

Laronda looked at Jason with a different level of comfort, "See, I was trying to get you that extra sale. You need to put me on payroll." She said, popping the gum in her mouth just about the whole time.

-*"Yo chill that's my man Tekk shit playing. Don't disrespect like that."*

"So what that's your man? Stop being a lil bitch."

"Yo homie didn't I said cool out?"

Jason let Buck handle the politics of that situation. He didn't have any reaction toward the young man's comments, as the only disrespect that he intended was towards Buck's stereo. He continued conversing with Laronda. "You going out with them tonight?"

"Na I don't do the whole Club scene thing." She answered.

-*"Buck, I wasn't even talking 'bout your man music. Ain't nobody thinking' bout that nigga."*

Before he could understand what kind of trouble he dug himself into by appearing to disrespect a Grant native, Buck squared him up and swallowed him in a hail of body blows.

*"Oh shit! Fuck that nigga up! That's right,
fuck him up!"*

Com, Margo's right hand man hopped off the
hood of the Jeep he was sitting on and ran over
to apply a vicious headlock and he did so
without disturbing the cigarette wedged between
his lips. Applying crushing pressure, Com
dropped his bodyweight on his victim, folding
him to the ground. Margo flashed from around
the Jeep running relentlessly towards his target,
catching him with a right hook as he arrived,
forcing Com to release him to the concrete.

- *"Yeah fuck him up!"*

- *"Check his pockets."*

It was all construction boots and the bottom of
basketball sneakers from there. They stomped
him until he was motionless then seemingly on
queue, everyone evacuating the scene; Buck to
his Audi, Stacky to his Beamer, Margo and Com
hopped in a black Durango, some of the girls
were packed in a beige Jetta and everyone else
scattered throughout the Projects. T-Rock from
135th street drove off in the Altima that the
unlucky, unconscious fellow on the ground
pulled up in.

11:32 PM; THE SAME NIGHT

For the past six years Jason's Friday nights were designated for his music. Facing unemployment for the second time in as many years rendered this Friday's studio session all the more critical. Jason was a Muslim by faith, by the inspiration of the Holy Qur'an, which among many things teaches that GOD created the earth for equality and just ends. Once Jason fully understood that particular lesson, he began to view his craft differently. GOD inspired the music, and the Artist known as Architekk was charged with capturing as much of it as possible and sending it through the microphone. Jason felt in his heart that GOD's music never stopped but rather, GOD provided periods of enlightment, an open ear to his never ending party, or a window of opportunity. This was one of those nights when that window was wide open. Inspired by the things he'd seen on the block, at his place of employment, inspired by his life, Jason entered his studio in the back room of his apartment, closed the door and found a flow.

JULY 10ᵀᴴ 2005

"Aight, you ready to do this?"

Hollis was gasping for air with both her hands planted on her hips, walking aimlessly about the track. "Daddy...you got a give me another minute."

"Come on Honey you gotta get in them blocks. I need you to be able to do this now. You ain't gone have time to rest like that at the next level." Jason said forcing the issue.

Hollis turned and walked away still fighting to catch her breath. "I need another minute."

"Aight take your time, we got all day... Nope, nothing's at stake here."

Hollis had her buttons, and her Father knew exactly how to push them. She inhaled deeply and loosened her body by shaking out her hands from the wrist and bouncing from side to side; "Let's go."

"You ready?"

She focused on the damp vast path ahead of her as it had been drizzling all morning. "Let's do it!" She said stretching her neck to either side. Jason held the stop-clock suspended from his neck to his line of sight and extended his left arm toward the sky. "On your mark... Go!"

9:20 AM; THE SAME DAY

"What, you and Mommy just completely stopped talking to each other?"

Hollis ascertained as she navigated the family sedan away from their designated practice track on Randall's Island. Jason tried to raise his kids to speak their mind at all times, and to be as straightforward as possible. On this particular day he wished his oldest daughter had been a little more subtle as he didn't have an easy response to her question.

"…Your Mother and I are going in two different directions with our lives sweetie."

"Go ahead stupid!" Hollis yelled at a vehicle trying to cut in front of her.

"Relax Honey; what's wrong with you?"

She pumped her breaks as the light on 8th Ave turned from yellow to red; "Stupid ass immigrants!"

"Yo watch your mouth! You got some damned nerves talking bout immigrants. I gotta get you your own Koran. It's about time for you now anyway."

"Daddy what; you just gone sit back and work on your music and not work on your marriage?"

Jason turned in his seat and looked her up and down abruptly; "Excuse me?"

"Yall not even sleeping in the same bed no more; I know that can't be the *way*."

"Hollis you better watch your damn mouth. I'll still pop ya lil ass."

"Daddy I'm not playing! It's very important to me."

JULY 18th 2005

"Hi, Mr. Jamison?"

"Mr. Jamison is not here. Who's this?"

"This John from up the block, what's going on?"

"John from, - oh; what's up man, I thought you was one of them damned bill collectors."

"*Sir we are going to take you to Jail!* This is Mr. Jordan with *Debt Collections Inc.* You pay my client the balance in full for this loan or I'm a have the Sheriff at your door the first thing in the morning! Keep playing with me."

Jason could hear the shock in the gentleman's voice. He was hesitant as he spoke, "Mister I know I said I was gone pay yall but I need to

pay my light bill. My kids ain't gone have no
lights!"

Jason's instincts told him to ease up, but it was
closeout week and he was one of the few reps in
his department who hadn't reached his
collections goal for the month. "Sir, that's not
my client's problem. You should've thought
about that before you took that credit card &
went berserk at the mall."

"Oh my GOD!"

"GOD ain't do this; yo' ass did! *Pay this bill or
we taking you to jail*!"

He knew the longer he allowed the Debtor to sit
in silence, the smaller his chances of turning this
into a cash call were. "Okay Sir, me and the
Sheriff gone see you in the morning. Kiss your
Grandkids goodbye tonight cause you're going
to get processed as soon as you finish seeing the
Judge-"

"Okay mister, I'll pay the bill."

Jason was Momentarily shocked. He hadn't
gotten a payment in so long that he forgot how
to go in for the hard close; "You gone pay it?
Alright, hold on let me see how my supervisor is
willing to accept that payment at this point."

He placed the call on hold and looked to his side, "Josh, close this guy out for me please."

Josh scooted his chair to Jason's cubical and plugged in his headset. "What's the situation?"

"Try to get the balance in full or a check series. But I need a certified payment today one way or the other."

-"Mr. Jordan, may I have a word with you?"

A rep from Human Resources snuck up behind Jason. The rep was staring into Jason's computer monitor and he looked over his workstation before escorting him to the training room at the back of the 17th floor.

"Hi Jason this is Pete with *Bet it Credit*; our client. Pete and his team are in this week randomly screening phone calls to make sure that we are complying with their standards as well as abiding by the F.D.C.P.A."

Pete interjected, "Jason we were listening to the call that you were just on. You want to tell us what that was about?"

"What you mean, what it was about? I was going hard to try to hit my goal."

"You do understand that you violated several laws outlined by the Fair Debt Collections Practices Act?" The HR rep asked condescendingly.

"Mr. Jordan, I'm not sure that we should maintain our affiliation. That one phone call can cost *Bet it Credit* big bucks if that man decided to press charges."

"My man, your top reps on the floor break the law on every call that they're fortunate enough to get an actual live person on. Yall just gone single me out?"

"I'm sorry Jason, we've been listening to calls all morning and yours' has been by far the most offensive we've come across."

11:58 AM; THE SAME DAY

Stump mashed his hefty fingers into his wireless joystick as he jolted to either side of his Mother's worn out leather couch. "Kobe advances up court. Kobe shakes this bum out his shoes. Kobe pulls up..."

Jason sat in the corner trying to appear as interested in the video game as possible for the sake of blending in. Normally he would be sitting at his desk waiting for the dialer to send a call through or working his East coast accounts, but it was a new day.

"Kobe scores! *That's my son! That's my, son!!!*"

Buck flicked his controller at the television in frustration as he had just lost to Stump for the third time today.

"That's my son right there. Gimme my money." Stump demanded.

They hadn't even had breakfast yet and some of them were down a day's worth of trap money gambling on video games. The neighborhood stars, the hustlers. The products they were slinging sold themselves; there were just playing pitch and catch. They all worked off of their phones, had steady clientele and they all liked to gamble. The hustlers had the luxury of time that the average working person didn't; that's why they looked so good and laughed at seemingly anything. Jason hadn't exactly shaken his workingman demeanor yet. He was wearing an old Echo sweater and a pair of gray sweatpants that Denise got him from V.I.M. He was quiet, hunched over in his seat with a serious rigor across his face.

"What's good Tekk; why you look so tense my nig?" Stacky asked while checking a message on his cell phone.

"I'm good fam. I'm just running through math in my head, that's all."

Jason Jordan was through with the straight and narrow. He'd been through job after job since leaving college after two years. There was nothing there for a man of his sort, no sense of peace or true productivity. Even when he landed what most people in his neck of the woods considered a good job, he felt trapped. There was never quite enough money to make him feel a sense of security, and there was no time to do besides work. The co-workers, the commute, routines, he was leaving it all behind for good. Today Jason was waiting on Com to return with a quarter-pound of lime green Arizona weed. He had a new plan.

Jason paid $250 for the weed, he had $423 cash remaining from his last paycheck and over $2,000 coming back from his 401K, which he thought long and hard about but was cashing in. He was taking things into his own hands, putting up his very last to bring his second album to life and building on the music group that he created alongside the release of the first album.

"So what's the plan; how you gone get that money boy-boy?" Stacky asked as he finally put his phone away.

"I'm a bring that quarter-pound back to 640 real quick; bring each ounce back at 160 and re-up. I'll have $190 left, I'm a put 110 to that and holler at yall for an ounce of Piff. Bring that ounce back to 700."

Stacky employed the ambient air as a chalk board, "That's $1,340 from $250." Stack slapped his diamond-studded fist into his open hand, "Boom!"

"Boom!"

AUGUST 9ᵀᴴ 2005

A woman draped in rags kindly opened the front door to M.S.G for Jason. "Come on Tekk I know you got something for me today."

"Let me go get my lesson and I'll holler at you when I come out." Jason said as he entered his friend's small retail store on 113th street. He could hear Margo running a session behind the stacked piles of sweaters on the clearance table toward the back.

"It don't matter? How he gone tell you it don't matter? What in the fuck is that beloved? ... *It don't matter.*"

"That's what he said." Darrel, Margo's thirteen-year-old nephew said as he shrugged his shoulders.

"What yall talking about?" Jason asked to get caught up to speed on the politics of the day. Margo, Com, Darrel and one of Darrel's friends from school were sprawled about in a semicircle.

"Preacher man gone tell my nephew that Jesus' childhood is missing from the Bible cause it don't matter. I should a go down there and give his lying ass a piece of my mind." Margo refocused on Jason as if he remembered something; "Matter of fact, Tekk, tell my nephew why Jesus' childhood is missing from our Holy Bible."

Without hesitation Jason got right to it, "The Church rewrote and recomposed the Bible, removing all information that would make Jesus look like a human being. They ain't want you to overstand that Jesus was just a man, just like Moses, just like Abraham, Noah, Mohammad, David, Jacob... just like you young blood. The Holy Bible is for you!" Jason took hold of the Bible that Margo was holding. "This is your

history, the history of your Bothers and Sisters."
He grew more excited by the Moment as he
moved to the center of the circle. "If you know
your history, get knowledge of yourself and your
black ass is still alive to process that shit, you'll
understand life, nature, your positioning and
relation to that nature; you will understand that
GOD is with *you*, and you move accordingly."

Darrel sat forward and engaged himself,
reassuring Jason that he was being clear with the
youth.

"Well, what I'm a do? I mean, what GOD want
from me?"

"Anything you do in Allah's name is acceptable.
There's seven firmaments, ranks and order given
to all things, you gone land somewhere. Yes,
there is an active Holy war and GOD need
Soldiers; but he also needs Nurses, he need
water boys and fans. You know, shit like that."

"Least you should be a pussy beloved." Margo
interjected.

The group exploded with laughter, all except for
Margo who brandished a hard, obscure grin that
could only be manufactured in Harlem. Margo
usually fueled himself with energy drinks and
cigarettes during the day, as he usually worked
on developing and expanding his business at

night, and one could see the lack of rest in his red eyes. Through the aura of jubilation Margo hammered his point home. "True righteousness takes courage. Don't walk through this Earth for all your days like a bitch."

Jason left the store and dropped a dollar into the homeless woman's cup that opened the door for him.

"What's the word for today Tekk? I see you got something good; you glowing."

Jason stayed put for a Moment, posting his back to one of the windows of the storefront. He looked up Madison Avenue in search of beat walking cops and other potential hazards to his lifestyle. "The word for today is fight. Whether heavily or lightly armed, one must fight evil in the name of the Lord." He said before stepping off.

AUGUST 22ND 2005

"Jason I'm leaving you."

"Yeah?" Jason asked carelessly while counting out the crumbled five and ten dollar bills that he pulled out his pocket onto the track-board. "What you waiting for?" He smiled at her with hazy, half closed eyes. Denise walked over, wearing a silk pullover garment that stretched just below her waist, revealing her long, healthy legs. Her deep brown hair was tied down with a silk scarf. Denise was 5' 5" and brown toned, with well-endowed breast that Jason still liked to taste every now and then. She sat on his lap and looked tenderly yet seductively into his eyes. "You don't care if I leave you?" She asked as she wrapped her legs around him. Jason looked away as he was beginning to rise in his pants and he knew the significance of their conversation would be lost if he let passion take over.

"If you feel like you can do better, you gotta make your moves right?"

Denise tried unsuccessfully to read his face. She kissed her husband softly on his lips and grazed her soft vagina along his stomach where it was resting. Jason could smell her sweet body. She planted a softer, sweeter kiss and he began to reciprocate. She leaned back across the track-board and waited for her husband to take her in anyway he saw fit. He removed his shirt like it had suddenly got in his way. He spread her legs and buried his head beneath her garment using brute strength to pull her closer to his face. Jason slithered his tongue around the slide of her panties and licked whatever he could to his wife's delight. She grabbed either side of his head and pulled his hair uncontrollably, squeezing the side of his face with her thighs.

When Jason finally left his zone he realized that he had forced Denise to explode in his hands. He looked up to find her looking down at him sweating from her forehead still trying to catch her breath. She dropped her legs from his shoulders and grabbed at the crouch of his Jeans; "You don't wanna finish?"

Jason rubbed his face and wrung his wife's juices out of his mustache and bread as he stood to his feet, "Na I'm good. I'm a go wash up."

He went into the bathroom and ran water from the sink as he stared in the mirror and tried to figure the reality of himself; where he was and what he had become. He was having a good run on the streets. He was recording music with ease and taking care of business at home. As he wiped the last of his wife off of his face, he was reminded of the different facets of what business was at home and the promises that he made to Hollis. He reached inside his jeans and pulled out the quarter-pound of Purple Haze that he picked up from Stacky earlier and numbers began racing through his head. The $2,800 that the Purp was going to bring back was going be the new set point for his re-up. He had nearly a half of pound of Arizona in the safe and well over fifty dime bags that he accumulated by re-upping quickly. He was sending Bernadette the same amount on a bi-weekly basis that he had been when he was working and he was handling his bills the same as always. He rubbed his forehead and tried to figure it out, how many bags, ounces, pounds he needed to flip to walk away from the game as an independent man and a winner. He kept searching.

10:33 PM; THE SAME NIGHT

"Who is it?"

"Your Father."

"...Hold on a second."

Jason wondered what they could be doing that would warrant his daughter to have him waiting at the door. He could hear Bernadette on the other side instruct Gwinn to open up.

"What's up?"

Jason tried to catch Gwinn's eyes but she chose to keep them to herself, "Hi Daddy."

"How you doing?"

"Fine."

She was as blunt as can be; wearing a pair of blue Frankie B jeans and new white Nikes. Jason made his way to the living room a few feet away and turned to find his Daughter walking in the other direction. "Yo where's your Mother?"

"She comin'."

Jason took a seat on the couch and looked around his former home. He was so anxious to get here just minutes earlier now there was a side of him that wanted to be anywhere else. Gwinn couldn't have been any less interested in speaking to him, leaving him feeling out of place, with the strangest urge to get back to his music. He could hear the deep rumble of Bernadette's company from the master bedroom. A dark feeling of emptiness seized him and he was reminded of why things didn't work the first two times he and Bernadette tried to play house. He stood to his feet, removed his wallet from his back pocket and counted out two hundred dollars.

"What's up Jay?"

Bernadette asked from the other side of the wall in the kitchen. Jason could hear her drop a load of dishes in the sink; he walked over.

"I'm good. What's up with you?"

Bernadette looked like she had been smoking, she had a mysterious satisfaction across her face and her hair was a mess. "I can't complain." She answered.

Jason dropped the money on the washing machine and humbled his demeanor, "Aight well there's two hundred dollars. I'm a see you as soon as I get some more." He crept past her protruding, ever tempting backside on his way to the front door. "Can you let Gwinn know I got her a pair of sneakers? I'll bring them by the next time I come."

Jason left the apartment in a daze, unsure of his own emotions. Before pressing for the elevator, he wandered onto the seventh floor terrace and stared past the metal fence separating the project building from the world. The drama going on downstairs had a calming effect on his nerves. He felt alone but he felt strong, as if the Lord was with him and watching to see if he was going to feel sorry for himself or if he was going to get busy. If it was truly about the music, if that was truly his calling, then he was going to need to turn it up; better production, tighter more conscience lyrics, and the hardest part, he had to sell. The music was partially about the money, and the money was about Fatherhood, or so it seemed at the time... Jason was getting lost in the numbers and the transactions, and the bullshit. The money was coming in but the love wasn't, other than from his customers, who were getting more product per dollar from him than with any other weed-man. He hung his head; *"...Father please forgive me for my sins. Please understand-"*

"Yoooo?"

A voice coming through the walkie-talkie on his phone broke the silence on the terrace. Jason removed his phone from his hip and pressed the direct connect button, *"Yo?"*

"Tekk I need a two piece."

"Two of them fluffy pillows or two of them smaller things?"

"What ever you can do for twenty my dude."

"Aight, I'm on my way."

56

"...don't want to stay here with your irresponsible, dangerous ass. "

Date: October 3RD 2005

"Baby, don't leave me; don't ever, desert me..."

Jason could hear an angelic voice through the steel and concrete of the building. The first floor staircase door was cracked open just enough for the melody to seep through from the lobby.

"...I promised my life to you and I'll love you always..."

Jason, Stacky and Stump had just finished meeting in Stump's third floor apartment to discuss the possibility of doing a N.Y.C.M.C tour and they trotted down the B staircase to the first floor. Jason looked around a brick pillar in the lobby to see Laronda soulfully grooving to one of his favorite old school tunes on her MP3 player.

"This bitch." Stacky said as he made his way out the front door.

Laronda was sporting a Carolina blue Pelle' leather with rhinestones in the back, and tight blue jeans. Her hair was pinned in a wrap and she was looking out the window to the front of building 55. Jason stopped breathless as she hit a high note that forced him to put both his hands across his chest in admiration.

"Yo Tekk come on."

Laronda turned to discover that she had a listener and smiled as she rarely did, "You like that?"

"Oh, I love it." Jason extended his arms playfully to embrace her and she reciprocated smiling all the more brighter. "I love it." He proclaimed.

"Tekk come on man!" Stack pulled back the front door and hollered.

"You better catch up to your boys."

He pulled away from her still visibly delighted at her ability, "Don't nobody control me, sweetie. I move when me or the Lord says so."

She stepped back and gestured as if impressed, "I heard that."

"You ever been in the studio?"

"Na." She answered apparently regretfully.

Through the side of his visual field Jason could see Stack release his grip on the front door. He looked deeper into Laronda, "I could use a voice like that." He rubbed his goatee in mellow contemplation, "That could open some things up for me."

"Well what's up; what you trying to do?"

10:41PM; THE SAME NIGHT

"I can't hear you; you gotta turn your mic on." Jason yelled at Stump through the soundproof glass from the vocal booth. Stump activated his microphone then continued to locate the point on the track were Jason wanted to begin recording.

"I said the Holy month begins tomorrow. You ready to do this?"

Stump and Jason were the only people in Stump's 57th street studio. For the past five Wednesday nights Stump reserved the A block of the studio to finish Jason's second album.

"I'm ready; I need it... I don't believe it's October already." Jason said as he adjusted his headphones for a better fit. He'd been so buried in his recording and running bags of marijuana from point A to point B that he had been slacking on his prayer routines, his side of the

59

house chores, and he hadn't called Gwinn or Junior in a few weeks. Thirty one days of manifest self restraint, putting GOD first and disciplining his life was exactly what he needed to put things back into perspective...seedtime.

"I been looking forward to Ramadan this year man; I got a good feeling about it." Stump was smiling like a child at the track-board. Since they were kids Stump always embraced a good challenge. "I feel like, like magic could happen during Ramadan 05 Bro; like we could do anything."

Jason took a sharp mental note of what Stump was saying as he could tell that GOD felt like being mysterious this evening.

"Aight yo, I found the spot. You ready?"

"Let's go."

Stump dropped the beat and leaned his thick, solid forearms across the track-board and nodded his head to the track. Jason could hear his powerful voice through the headphones spitting the lyrics that he just recorded. He waited for the break where he would jump back in to punch in a line where he misspoke. Stump raised his hand and began counting down with his fingers; 4,3,2,1...

OCTOBER 13TH 2005

*"Will the first heap of the girls' 200 meter relay,
please check in at the Scorers 'table. "*

Jason stood a few yards away from Hollis in a
secluded tunnel in the basement of the Amory.
For nearly ten minutes he'd been glancing back
and forth at her as she sat with her head hung
and her back against a wall. It was ritualistic for
Hollis to steal time for herself before a race.
Still, Saturday after Saturday Jason couldn't help
but wonder what ran through her head during
these Moments.

They practiced rigorously for this Moment all
summer, the first week of the indoor track
season. Hollis was now a senior Frederick
Douglas Academy and one of the highest ranked
sprinters in the city. There wasn't anyone that
could seriously contend with F.D.A in the 4 X
200 out there; now it was time to prove it.

Hollis still hadn't budged after the public
announcement several Moments ago. Jason held
back for as long as he could, but he couldn't help
himself. "You heard the call baby?"

Hollis fired herself to soles of her New Balance
warm up sneakers and clapped her hands with

firm enthusiasm. "I'm ready!" Her break in
silence was Jason's green light to say everything
he'd been holding back for the past few
Moments. "See it, do it, *bam!* Don't take no shit
out there. Secure that stick before you really
take off. Hug them turns like you missed the
hell out of em; low, then high, then long. Open
that stride up and keep it open, ya heard?"

Hollis nodded in comprehension as her Father
gave her final instructions face to face, their
foreheads pressed ruggedly against one another
and their eyes were locked. "It's time for some
truth & proof out here. Give a good testament.
I love you alright?"

"I love you too."

Jason kissed his girl on her cheek and watched
her join her relay team on the track. He knew
he'd put enough energy in her for her to mess
around and lap somebody. He went back
upstairs and sat beside Denise to watch the main
event.

8:09 PM; THE SAME NIGHT

Hollis patted down the metallic pins in her
Father's hair before grabbing another one of his
locks to re-twist it. "Turn your head Daddy."

62

Jason hadn't been to sleep since Thursday night and could barely keep his head stable. Hollis was rushing to finish manicuring his locks so she could join her teammates who were celebrating their team and individual victories at 1 Fish-2 Fish Restaurant on Madison Ave.

"Jason!"

Hollis tapped her Dad on the shoulder, "Ma calling you."

"Jason, Danny is at the door for you!"

He stood up; Hollis picked up her phone and checked the messages she'd gotten since the last time she checked five minutes ago.

"I hope he not coming here to buy no weed from my house Jason." Denise said from over the sink while washing dishes.

"Relax wit' all that. Danny told me he wanted to ask me something." He dismissed his wife and stepped through the front door closing it smoothly behind him.

"What up, what you need?"

"Yo Tekk I got thirty dollars, see what you can do for me fam."

"Aight give me one minute, go wait in the terrace for me. I told your ass don't come up here. From now on, call me and I'll meet you downstairs."

Hollis was still glued to her phone, texting frantically and laughing to herself. Jason went into the closet and dug into the stash in his leather coat. "Who you talking to on that damned thing?"

"Reggie, Kishma, Renee, Taneisha, and Gwinn." She released her legs from their folded position and took a swig from the glass of Kool-Aid resting on the floor.

"Tell Gwinn I said what's up. What she doing?"

"Yo, G is a little thug Daddy."

They both laughed as Jason got Danny's order together on the sneak-tip.

"She stay about to pop off on somebody, that's my girl."

Jason smiled, pleased that his youngest showed signs of being his strongest. "Try to get her to chill out though, that ain't the way."

"I be trying to tell her. Especially since them JESICA bitc-" She covered her mouth to excuse her potential fowl language, "Sorry, chicks, be out their wilding on the eastside."

"Yeah I know." Jason said as he shoved his fist into his pockets and excusing himself. "I'll be right back."

DECEMBER 4ᵀᴴ 2005

Jason carefully navigated his way through the dark Harlem streets. He had to make a drop off to a customer in the Columbia dorms on 117ᵗʰ. Then he needed to drop off a quarter ounce to Big Rich on Morningside. When he got to 117ᵗʰ Jason made the transaction with the Columbia College foreign exchange student at her door and engaged in a little small talk, as to remain civil in business. As he turned to walk away the girl called out to him in her heavy Indian accent, *"Hey Tekk want to smoke?"* He pulled out his cell phone to check the time. He was going to be a few minutes late for the second drop off, but a free blunt meant pinching his personal stash less and a more enjoyable hike to Morningside. He turned around and shrugged his shoulders.

"Hey, why not?"

Jason sold two CDs on credit and made four new acquaintances before dipping out. He hadn't walked but 3 blocks before his hands became numb from the temperature. He kept his legs moving, the thoughts flashing through his mind was his only form of entertainment. This is where he was tested foremost, the long lonely walks through the night in search of the Lord's bounty. Last year at this time of night he would've been showered, fed and laying beside his wife. He was now playing a game where he didn't know what laid around the next corner, he didn't know who was listening to or watching him, but it didn't matter, he had to keep playing.

Jason knew GOD was watching, GOD put him here; and Jason knew that GOD knew that he knew GOD was watching... So he forfeited speaking the words. He fought the feelings of ingratitude that used to get him in trouble with GOD, although he had some questions in the depths of his soul for the creator, who could put him and his kids in a big house with wealth and abundance just by declaring it. Jason just walked, he just pushed on, across his face was the rigor of his test, not despair but a focused grit. He could but only hope that somehow, through the burdens he took on his shoulders that his children would stay warm, because outside, it was freezing.

He cut down 121st and completely lost his cool as he saw three beat walking cops coming towards his direction. He pulled his Yankee fitted lower and sunk his hands into the chest pockets of his ski coat. As Jason neared the trio he noticed the heavyset Black Officer staring him down. He wanted to stare back but the contraband he was toting made that a bad idea. He walked past and figured the joke was on them until; *"Yo come here man."*

Jason turned around and checked the Officer; "Who you talking to? I ain't no little fucking kid."

The other male Officer stepped up and into Jason's personal space and the female reached for her utility belt.

"What you want?" Jason asked in a tamed roar.

"You smell like weed. You carrying drugs on you?"

Jason grew nervous and began speaking without thinking. "No I ain't carrying no drugs on me. Get outta my face."

Without the slightest hesitation all three Officers began closing in.

"Do me a favor. Put you hands up against that wall and spread your legs for me."

"For what?"

"Do it now!" One of the Officers yelled before drawing his weapon.

2:13PM; THE NEXT DAY

Jason could see Margo and Com sitting in Margo's Durango when he got out of Central Bookings. Jason took a second to secure his belt, which he got back after being processed, then walked over.

Margo lowered the stereo and pulled from his cigarette as if it were essential before he addressed Jason who was slouched back in exhaustion.

"Ah Black man, how long you gone be doing this weed shit for?"

"I can't call it right now Margz." Jason answered annoyed at the fact that he knew his plans were going to look silly after this. He didn't bother looking at his one time mentor as he elaborated; "I need to at least get this album finished, so I can shop this shit to the Record Labels." Jason leaned his head against the frost bit window and gazed at the heavy snowfall. "I don't know man… if something don't develop soon, I'll go get a job wherever I can, I guess."

"Well, why's the album taking so long?" Margo asked as he started the engine.

Jason smiled, finding a degree of calm therein. "Margo trust me, at this point, nobody want this project to be done more than me Brother."

Margo looked at Jason through the rearview mirror, "I got people coming in the shop all the time, all the time, asking for your shit; your CD! That's respect, that's love. Harlem need you as a voice, a stand up shining testament. They don't need another fucking weed-man. You need to put the same energy and commitment into your music as you do with hustling some shit that's gone have your freedom snatched from you."

Jason didn't bother responding, he sat in thought as the jeep made its way back to Harlem world.

"You know M.S.G about to close down? ...Yep; after six years, the man done finally caught up with me."

"The man got his foot in all of our asses don't he?" Com asked in a barely legible grumble. The fellas sat in silence for the rest of the ride, each person in his own head, each one trying to figure it out.

"You're not a Muslim."

Jason didn't feel like entertaining any foolery after such a busy day; "Okay." He placed the

Holy Qur'an in his hand on the counter and pulled out his wallet to pay for the turkey and cheese sandwiches, sodas and cigars for him, Stump and Laronda. The small, brown skinned Brother seated on the deep freezer pushed on. "I seen you on the train reading the Bible."

Jason dropped his head back and took a second to breathe before he turned to engage his Brother, who felt the need to judge him. "You know your Qur'an Bro? Don't bullshit me either cause I've read it from cover to cover several times." Jason asked growing intense.

"What do you mean, do I know it? I can recite most surahs word for word in Arabic."

"Yeah and many Christians can recite many Bible verses. Many Jews can recite from the Torah..." He pointed to Stump, "And many niggas like me and him can recite whole Tupac albums word for word. But have you processed the word of Allah, have you lived by and alongside it, demonstrating utmost faith therein? Have you grown with the word so you can testify to its' authenticity? The Holy Qur'an is a history book *of*, and guidance *for* man. The Torah and new testament are more ancient accounts of our history."

"Preach Brother!" Stump yelled facetiously as he took a seat on the egg crate in front of the store.

Jason turned to him, "No I gotta testify Brother; no bullshit. GOD has been too kind. He's been too magnificent; he's been too solid in his promises to me for me to not testify." Jason caught a glance of Laronda and noticed that she was no longer lost in the electronic conversation on her cell phone. He continued, "You show a lack of faith in the Lord when you do shit like this Ak. The Holy Qur'an confirms the previous scriptures; the Bible, the Holy Torah, and the prophethood of the Brothers; Moses, David, Joseph, Jesus, Abraham, Noah. The Holy Qur'an is a book that leads to peace in ones' life. But you can't have a disposition; you can't go into it thinking that you know what peace is, that's how men end up restricting things from their lives that GOD never intend to be restricted. That's how men end up befriending vowed enemies and creating static between their natural Brothers and Sisters. I walk a path that the Lord made. Through my music I actively engaged the enemy, the Devil. But you see me, my hair, my clothes, my Qur'an, my Bible and parts of my actions, and you don't trust me..."

Mohammad chuckled and looked as if he just wanted Jason to pay for his goods and go on about his business, but he carried on. "But know that I am watching you also, and know that I don't trust your ass either. That's why I stand on the front lines of the battle. Cause they killing us out there. Police is shooting my Brothers fifty times cause they seeing shit on them that looks like guns. They been in Iraq killing your Brothers and Sisters in the Middle East because they supposedly saw these weapons." Jason reached in his back pocket and removed the miniature version of the New Testament Bible therein and placed it atop his Qur'an on counter. "These are my weapons right here Brother, so you shouldn't feel threatened by me. What I'm looking for in life can not be achieved by hurting you."

When Jason walked out of the store he lent an open ear to the stark silence behind him. Second Avenue was in front of him and it, the streets, seemed to embrace him better. Stump, Jason and Laronda were coming from one of Stump's friendly studios in the Stanley Isaacs Projects on 93rd street, where the three of them just recorded their first track together. When they were leaving Isaacs' Laronda ran into several J.E.S.I.C.A Sisters who brought a few dimes bags off of Jason and one of them purchased his first CD which he was now carrying with him everywhere he went. After the studio session Jason convinced Stump to walk with him to 110th to take Laronda home, from there they caught a cab back to Grant.

Jason's second album, which was appropriately titled The New Testament, was just about halfway complete. He was going to redo the vocals for the album's sixth track at Stumps apartment studio. The two decided to knock out a quick prayer before recording. Stump was in the bathroom making wudu.

Jason's eyes caught hold of a picture of himself from before he was saved. He smiled as he pulled the *We Got Next* magazine from Stump's box of old mix-tapes near the couch. A skinny, angry, perpetually lost soul he was. In the picture he wore a dark wavy haircut, a white gold chain and he projected a menacing aura. Jason read the caption across the front:

I AINT DEAD YET

THE PRODIGAL SON BACK IN THE BOOTH AFTER SUFFERING

MULTIPLE GUNSOT WOUNDS.

"Get out the Motherfucking car!"

Jason recalled riding down Fifth Avenue with 125 grams of soft white in the trunk. He was planning on getting ten grams off of Stacky at $35 per and jumping into the game full throttle, and risking it all. That plan flew out the window when a robber crew stuck their machineguns barrels in Stacky's E class.

"Hurry up, or I'm a blow your shit smooth the fuck off! Oh you think I'm bullshittin!"

Jason could hear Stump leaving the bathroom and he placed the magazine back in the box that he removed it from. They passed each other in the living room; it was Jason's turn to cleanse himself for the Lord.

From his reflection in the medicine cabinet mirror Jason found amusement and a sort of ticklish humor. He hung his head and shook the front row of dreads suspended from his scalp. He looked back in the mirror smiling all the more; *"...Knotty dread locks."* His content and peace seemed too surreal, too right, and for some reason he forced himself to continue reminiscing on the night he and Stacky almost had their lives snatched from them.

Jason awoke from his coma in Mt. Sinai hospital. He took a series of catnaps before recollecting on where he was and how he got there. When he finally awoke for good Hollis was applying a coat of vaseline across his lips.

"What you doing?"

"Your lips were dry." She said as she backed away. Frail and weak, Jason slid into the slippers at the foot of his bed and he made his way into the bathroom. He caught a glance of himself in the mirror and became lost in the image. He had a full, rugged beard and his wavy hair was now a small, untamed afro. *"Oh my GOD, what happened to me?"*

Jason swung his locks to the back of his head so he could scrub his face. He thoroughly rinsed his right arm from wrist to elbow and squeezed blood through his veins, flexing the muscles in his forearm. He washed behind his ears, neck and his feet, then went to join his Brother in prayer. By the time Jason got to his prayer mat, Stump was standing upright before the Lord on his respective mat. He lined his left foot with Stump's right foot and Stump made the call to prayer; *"Allahu Akbar…"*

Stump needed to complete a makeup prayer and therefore he stayed in the cut after their joint prayer was complete. Jason sat patiently and waited for him to finish before disturbing the peace. When Stump began twirling his prayer beads through his fingers, indicating that he was just about done, Jason stood up and crept over to the computer. He pulled up Protools to queue up the music.

"Yes sir!" Stump said enthusiastically as he stood to his feet and folded his mat; "Drop that beat!" Jason press play then went into his creative zone, wondering off, piecing lyrics together in his mental. Stump walked over to the speakers and turned the volume to a deafening blast. *"Lets go!"*

8:25PM; THE SAME NIGHT

"Did you get arrested last week?"

Jason became instantly agitated, he turned away from Denise and walked further into the bedroom. "You obviously already know the answer to that question Denise, you not just asking me that for no reason."

"I'm-I'm- You know what?" She slammed a tandem of blouses into an open suitcase on the bed. Jason laughed finding amusement in his wife's unfolding befuddlement.

"I'm glad everything is such a big fucking joke to you! We'll see how funny things are when your ass is fifty and alone."

"I'm a be alone when I'm fifty?" He asked inquisitively as he continued to watch her frantically pack her belongings.

76

"Do you know two of my co-workers saw the Police arresting you? Do you have any idea how embarrassed I was trying to explain that shit?"

"So what? Fuck them bitches; they opinion gone matter if I don't come up with my half of the rent?"

"I'm not sticking around long enough to find out the answer to that question."

"What?"

His broad chest and powerful voice weren't enough to shake her; she knew he wasn't going to lay a hand on her. Consequently, he quickly employed a different approach and a much softer tone as he took a seat on the bed. "Denise I got knocked for a couple of bags of weed, you acting like the Feds looking for me or something. Where you going?"

"You got fired from your job and didn't tell me. You start selling weed out of my house. You got that big ass gun in here that I've been asking you to get rid of for years!" She filled with a wave of frustration; Jason could tell by the way she let it out that she seriously had had enough. "I'm leaving Jason."

"And where's my Daughter going?" He rose and demanded.

"My Daughter is coming with me!"

Jason's adrenaline boiled, his face became a canvas of terror. *"Bitch you not taking my Daughter away from me!"*

- *"Daddy!"* Hollis stepped into the room from her eavesdropping post in the hallway.

"She don't want to stay here with your crazy, irresponsible, dangerous ass. You have completely lost your mind!"

"What?"

"Daddy I'm a come see you on the weekends, and we'll talk on the phone."

Hollis pushed on in attempt to pacify him. Jason tried to look his Daughter in her eyes but couldn't due to pending tears, "Hollis you can't leave me. You….you have to finish your training. She can't teach you the way I can. She don't…she don't-"

Denise laughed as Jason tried to gather his thoughts. Hollis held her hands out trying to calm her Father down which broke him, and forced tears from his eyes. He took a look around; on Denise's face was the tale of his defeated cause. He knew, he just knew that this particular battle was already lost. In some small way, he released his need for physicality through the holler in his voice, *"Go then!"* He made his way toward the studio in the next room. *"Get the fuck out of here!"* he said before slamming the door.

Jason remained in his studio for the following seventeen hours. When he came out he found his family, the stability in his life, gone. He didn't leave the apartment for the next three days. No drop offs, no sunlight, and no piece of mind. Vexed and depressed he was, but the word…the word went forth.

"You come in right there; *Faith is the key, for you and for me. Faith is the keeey for peace and harmony.*"

Laronda laughed at Jason as he tried to mimic her refined voice. "Aight so you want me to like, fill it in or just straight like that?"

"Yo, however you're most comfortable, rock out like that."

"Alright."

She clapped her hands and sassed into a Harlem songstress as she left the engineer room for the vocal booth.

"Give me a mic check." Stump asked Laronda while adjusting all the levels he needed to create the sound he was looking for. She smoothed her voice into the microphone, confirming that she was wired up and ready to go. Jason looked at Stump and grinned with the highest degree of content as she brought her note to a soulful end.

"You ready?"

"I'm ready."

A few weeks back Jason humbled himself enough to ask Margo to loan him money for a month's worth of studio sessions. He'd been keeping Laronda within arms reach for a creative edge and Stump handled the production. Margo's Sporting Goods closed its doors during the first week of November. Margo was now running his business via the internet and doing odd jobs here and there to make ends meet. He agreed to tag along when the crew pulled out for their N.Y.C.M.C promo tour as a driver, security staff, Assistant and in his own words *whatever the hell else needed to be done.*

Stacky and Buck released a Mix-tape together and the both of them were still hustling uptown to keep their pockets hefty. Stacky was starting to build a buzz around the city as perhaps one of the best hardcore Rappers coming out of N.Y. Buck was still writing tight hooks and partaking in his fair share of drama at the nightclubs. His girlfriend of two years gave birth to his first child the day before Halloween, and Buck was relentless in buying his son the best of everything.

Jason grew spiritually throughout the Holy month, degree after degree. He sold enough weed to send Bernadette something every other week, give Hollis her allowance and hit the Chinese food restaurant every night. He had more savings in his shoebox now than he had in the bank when he was working and the extra time he put in at the studio was evident in the melodic, swift flows he was lacing his second album with. *The New Testament* was initially scheduled to release over a month and a half ago, but it simply wasn't ready. And by the way Jason was starting to see things, there was no sense in rushing since the longer he waited meant the more money he could dump into the project.

Jason used some of the profit from last week's sales to print window posters and flyers. His eyes were glued on one of the posters so sharply that he became lost somewhere in it. He mentally zoned out from his surroundings to contemplate on whatever he chose. He wondered if GOD was going to continue to make his path smooth. He wondered if his kids would understand and appreciate his sacrifice.

He wondered if Laronda was trustworthy enough to begin confiding in her. He kicked back even further as he began to look at the same poster with renewed enthusiasm. He smiled, finding joy in the mere fact that he was still here, still among the living and still getting it in. The Lord still had him on the earth for a reason; so until the cops came knocking, until he was killed in action… until he was done, he was going to give life all that he had, starting with the music. As he stood up, the ashes piled on the tip of his blunt fell to the surface of the poster, he gently brushed it aside and smiled again as he looked down.

ARCHITEKK

THE NEW TESTAMENT

01/15/06

www.ONTHEBOOKSENT.com

N.Y.C.M.C RECORDS

DECEMBER 30ST 2005

"What's up yall; it's your girl Tricky out here on the Red Carpet with the three time nominee J-Bzy…"

Jason sat in his nearly empty living room reading over a few company documents and occasionally checking out the BET pre New Years Awards Special on channel 43.

-*"I just wanna thank Atlanta, my hometown for showing so much love. Ah, we runnin' this Hip-Hop thang right now shawty."*

Jason grinned as he saw J-Bzy hold his *Mouth of the Deep South Records* platinum chain up for the cameras. He picked up the proof copy of his second album, which by the grace of GOD was complete and in printing, and held it in his hands as he smiled from the inside with Yankee pride and confidence. He took another lonely sip of his cheap champagne and fell asleep somewhere between J-Bzy's acceptance speech and realizing that he forgot to put his Aunt Jennifer's name in his *thank-you's* in the album jacket. He awoke to an abrupt and menacing pounding at the front door.

"Who is it?" He yelled from his chair through the hallway.

"U.S Marshall. You are being evicted."

Jason almost fell out of his seat, frightened manifest. He knew they were coming, he just didn't know when, and not knowing when sort of gave him the hope that he would be able to sit in the living room with his television and rhyme book and chill until.

Jason gathered himself in his head; *GOD is trying you. GOD is trying you.* He spoke to himself and calmed his nerves. The majority of his bags were already at Stump's, save for one of Hollis' old track totes which he packed with two pairs of jeans, underwear, his electric trimmers, socks, his toothbrush and deodorant. He had already prayed about this and he could feel the Lord answering his prayers simply by removing his fear.

"Aight yo, give me two minutes to put something on."

"No Mr. Jordan, we need you out of that apartment now."

"I'm butt ass naked in here; yall gone have to wait!"

He picked up his bag and unplugged his small television set and scooped it under his arm. He didn't want to go through the drama of looking back so he looked down. The Marshals banged at the door once again while Jason was in route to open it. When he opened up he looked the Agents straight in their eyes. One of them reached to pull him by the arm and he pushed his hand away with might and main. "Keep your damned hands to yourself."

The Supervisor stepped between them; "Hey come on. Everybody just relax, take it easy." He looked at Jason and handed him an official notice, "Mr. Jordan…"

Jason snatched the paper and went about his business.

Jason sat in the park out front for a while. As driven and as determined as he was to keep going, at this particular Moment there was nowhere for him to go. He planned on spending a large amount of time at Stump's, but he and his Mother were both at work. He tried thinking of another place he could go but there was no one else, nothing. He sat alone and tried to figure something out, and then his cell phone rang.

"What you doing?"

"I'm…" Jason looked around at the buildings of Grant Projects and chuckled into the phone, *"I'm…I don't know."*

"I need somebody to talk to. You got some time?"

2:44 AM; THE SAME NIGHT

"You know I'm originally from here?"

"Where?"

Jason laughed, as it should've been obvious,
"From Taft; I lived here for nineteen years." He
said as he closed his carton of chicken wings
and fried rice and took a swig of soda. "Went to
college... thought I was gone set the corporate
world on fire." He shook his head smiling while
wiping his hands with napkins from the Chinese
restaurant as he seemingly gave up on whatever
he wanted to say.

"Why didn't you?" Laronda asked innocently.

"...When was I gone get to come back and see
all this beautiful shit here?" Jason said looking
off the terrace. Laronda wasn't sure what he
meant by that, or if he was even being serious.
He blew out a cloud of smoke and sat back on
his flimsy chair giving no further intimation.
Laronda sat back as well and stared at her
building which was visible through the curious
Spanish Harlem night air, to the right, "Dang,
we lived across the street from each other for my
whole life and never knew it."

Jason turned and looked her in her eyes. A stark
gust of wind broke their intimacy. Laronda
shivered and wrapped her arms around her
upper-body. Jason reached in his pocket and put

on a pair of black mittens and untied his hair, allowing his dreads to fall and protect his ears and part of his face from the chill. He looked over at Laronda and simply couldn't let her fight her battle against the night alone, especially since her sheer presence was making his fight tremendously easier, at least for tonight. He reached out for her with his right arm. "Come here."

84

"Oh boy, this nigga on his Malcolm X-Tupac shit today."

Date: February 1ST 2006

"…Alright, so for the next two weeks we need to all focus on not spending any unnecessary money. We gone have to make some sacrifices and discipline ourselves so we can do what we gotta do. The Wednesday after next, we gone pool our money and print copies of all the CDs in bulk."

Jason had a black and white turban wrapped around his locks, a matching black and white camouflage coat and fresh construction Tims. His mind and eyes were sharp as he sat in full command of a N.Y.C.M.C meeting in a Hotel room that he rented for the weekend.

"At the price we getting them at, we can sell the CDs at $7 a whop and be good. We gone keep that money on reserve, and there it is…" he extended his strong, capable hands, "The tour money."

The whole team stayed busy throughout the winter. Tekk trekked across GOD's green earth in search of his piece of the Lord's bounty, creating ear catching, mind grinding music every step of the way. He molded and formed most of his songs in his head. His rhyme book, which he carried in a messenger-bag along with copies of his albums, served as a recording devise for random lines, hooks or verses for him to put into context when the time permitted.

The dime bags sold. The quarters sold, the halves, the ounces, they all sold. But in just a few months the game got old. There was too much traffic and trafficking for little in profit. Jason found himself petrified of the possibility of going back to jail, so he switched his phone and his routes, and his aliases and even his clothes. He found himself submerged in a circle of men and woman who indulged in lies and drama all day, GOD for some reason hadn't put them on any particular path, so they spent most of their time making things up and looking to be entertained. Jason found himself missing his wife from time to time. He was lonely, but he found comfort, shelter and great joy in the Lord, and that's what kept him moving forward.

The off the books money went to the kids and getting by. The money made on the books went toward building N.Y.C.M.C. Laronda was making extra money pushing Tekk's Albums, running errands and rolling the blunts. Stump was calling the prayers and creating the beats. Stacky and Buck were getting rich in the Project lobbies and spending half of their studio time shooting dice and getting intimate with groupies in the back room. Margo was still running his internet business, but the slow revenue put him in a position where he was going to have to make another move in order to keep his head above water.

"Why would we cut the price down to $7, when they been moving at $12?" Stack asked as he wedged his hands in the pockets of his BAPE hoody.

"Right now I think it'll be best if we find and equilibrium between making a profit and expanding on what we're doing. More people will buy at $7, so more people will listen. In turn, we get more exposure and build a bigger fan base; get a nice buzz in N.Y before we start the tour."

Stacky sat upright on the edge of the bed, gravity pulled his diamond pendent to the mattress. "Fuck a buzz, I'm trying to get as much dough as possible, ya dig? My V12 don't run off of exposure."

"My dude, $12 per takes twice as long to sell. The game ain't always about collecting every fuckin' dime you can. While we still in New York, we need to get our shit into the peoples hands."

"The people? Oh boy, this nigga on his
Malcolm X-Tupac shit today."

Jason began squeezing his triceps and back
muscles to make sure they were still with him.
"Yo yall niggas sit around Harlem selling crack
and shit to people all day and yall ain't never got
no money to do nothing besides be cute while
you selling the crack. *We got a goal!*"

Stack laughed at Jason's fiery seriousness.
Jason lunged a fist at his face, and the word
went forth...

As the 6 train ripped through Manhattan, Jason
flipped through his Qur'an in search of an
applicable surah for Laronda for when they got
back to her Aunt's apartment.

"Sister! What's good?"

Jason looked up and saw two J.E.S.I.C.A Sisters
walking through the train car. One had sky blue
bandannas hanging from her jeans and dark
sunglasses on, the other girl who was yelling
across the train had the same bandannas flagging
from under her ski hat and draped around her
neck. Laronda didn't even look up, she was still
completely drained, mentally in another place.

"Sis-ter!" She stood directly in front of Laronda with her hand out waiting for her acknowledgement. Laronda looked up uninterested to the utmost, "Do I know you?"

"Na Big Sis; I was a freshmen at Manhattan Center when you were there though. They call me Bladder; Isaacs' set, fourth round." She introduced herself then motioned toward her partner, "This T-True Blue; East River, fourth round also."

Laronda looked Bladder in the eye and toughed up a tad, "I'm a first rounder, but I'm sure you already know that. And I hate to pull rank, but get the fuck out of my face right now."

The girls walked away preserving their gangster strolls and intimidating whoever they could. Jason wrapped his arm around Laronda to comfort her, the instant he did she broke down crying for the third time since they left the hospital.

12:06 PM; THE SAME DAY

Jason laid across Laronda's lower half of her bunk bed and watched her walk from point to point aimlessly trying to keep her mind occupied. She eventually ran out of gas and walked over to the bed and laid her entire body on Jason.

"I don't know what I'm going to do without her."

"Just know that your Sister is in a better place sweetie. Trust in that."

"Thank you for coming with me, and spend-."

"That's nothing." He interjected.

She looked up into his eyes. He could feel her relax to another degree as she exhaled from the pit of her stomach. She scooted up and planted a tender kiss on his collarbone. When he looked down at her she kissed him again on his face. He laid back, not looking to initiate anything, at least for the Moment.

"You probably want to convert me to a Muslim or something."

She framed her question in a manner that put Jason in a spot were it was simpler to just go along with her agenda, although he desired to straighten her out.

"I'm not an imperialistic person. I'm not trying to convert you to anything."

She placed a hand on his chest and squeezed his pectoral muscle. She propped herself further along his body and kissed him on the lips. "I wanna feel you inside of me."

Jason watched without words as she raised her upper body and removed her blue sweater. She had a body that easily excited him; tender, curvy, brown.

"Tekk I just need you right now, okay?" She shook her head in agreement with her own sentiments and Jason joined her, not needing to be forced in the least.

"Okay."

"...pregnant women are crazy. It's like she's running things now." Junior said to Stump as he joined his Father on bench in front of building 55. Jason was outside trying to pick up a few extra sales, as his cell phone activity was slow, when he saw his son Junior enter the Projects.

"Yeah I know." Stump responded to let Junior know that they were listening, as Jason was being curiously quiet.

"But I'm a be a man though, stick it out."

Jason glanced at Stump as if he needed Stump to stop him from speaking his mind.

"How's your Mother doing? Wit' her fine ass."
Stump asked Junior.

Jason casually stood up and stepped into
Stump's personal space; "Don't be talking 'bout
my kids' Mother, punk. I'll bust that ass."

"You ain't gone do shit."

Stump backed up and threw up his hands and
Jason reciprocated. "Boom! See I could a
caught you right there," Jason said after feigning
a kick to Stump's leg then quickly bringing his
fist inches away from his jaw via a right hook.

Junior laughed, answering Stump question after
he and his Father stopped playfully staring each
other down. "My Moms is aight. She messing
around with some new dude, so she been
walking round glowing whatnot."

Jason noticed that Junior had gotten bigger since
the last time he saw him. He was growing into a
man. His girlfriend was in her second trimester
of pregnancy and by Junior's appearance and
from the bouquet of flowers in his hands, Jason
could tell that his son was doing the right thing.

"I thought I heard some nigga in there the last
time I was there. They was in the back though."
Jason said as he pulled his baggy jeans up
looking through the block.

"Yeah; he some tall light skinned nigga named Rodney."

Jason eye balled Stump to see if the name rung a bell, *"Rodney?"*

"Rodney? I don't know no Rodney."

"Where he from?" Jason asked as he positioned himself to do another set of chair dips on the edge of the bench.

Junior shrugged his shoulders, "I don't know." He stood up after glancing at his wrist watch and seeing how much time had passed by; "Hollis upstairs?"

Stump's eyes shot open in shock as he turned and looked at Jason.

"Na they not here now." Jason replied.

"Oh, aight. Can you give her these for me?" Junior handed his Father the flowers in his hand. "Tell her I said I'm sorry."

"Sorry for what?"

Junior looked at him as if puzzled, "For the indoor championships. I saw the coverage on New York 6 News. She almost pulled it off though."

Jason spaced out in thought for a second. Stump jumped to his feet after his set of dips, once again speaking in place of his friend who was at a loss for words. "Alright boy, you getting out of here?" Stump gave Junior a five; "Be good out there. Keep in touch and stay out of trouble."

As Junior walked off Stump called out to him, *"Yo what's good wit' your boy Red Out, he came home yet?"*

Jason walked off unannounced as Stump and Junior got into a quick conversation about the underground rap game on the other side of town. Stump met Jason in the staircase where Jason had spent numerous nights since being evicted. He pulled up the egg crate that Jason used as storage bin and footrest, and sat next to his friend. "Your boy is getting big… You know he starting to get a little rep with that mix-tape he put out with that kid Red Out from 119th?"

Stump could see that Jason was uninterested in vain talk, so he cut to the chase. "Just call her Tekk. Call her, call Gwinn, you know? Just do it. You ain't gotta be rich, or sell a million records for them to be happy with you."

Jason had rage contained within his face; hurting inside for not seeing or speaking to his kids like he wanted to. It hurt too much for him to think about them while he still wasn't in position to be the Father that he wanted to be, so he came to stop thinking about them, with the hope that one day GOD would perfect his inner concerns. He was moving along the path that he was sure the Lord ordained for him. There were high times; the sales, the women who found attraction to him because they felt his style, the spins on the local radio stations. Then there were the hard times, what Curtis Blow so eloquently described as the brakes.

It wasn't easy or pretty for that matter, but N.Y.C.M.C continued to grow. They had Uptown buzzing and they had the attention of most of the local DJs who mattered. Architekk was featured on several mix-tapes over the past few months. Most notably, he did a track with Roc-O-Pop of the *Cell Block Hell* crew from Yonkers. They shot the video in Whitney Young Projects, the Polo Grounds and Grant. Jason and Roc-O-Pop went to 125th to get some shots but were shut down quickly after a J.E.S.I.C.A Sister spit in a Police Officer's face inciting a small riot.

Jason took things as they came, the hype surrounding his ventures added value to his second album, which at the time had sold close to 1,000 copies. Jason put that money into the business to establish a credit history and a solid reputation as a music publisher and legitimate

98

organization. Between Buck and Stacky's mix-
tapes and Tekk's two albums, the crew needed
to only sell an additional 200 units to raise
enough money to go on an independent promo
tour, which would catapult the whole movement
to a new level.

Now of course there were people who didn't see
things as Jason did. Some saw a man confused
in his ways, chasing a dream that he should have
given up on many moons ago. Some saw his
locks as dreadful and perceived evil in his ways
even without merit. When Jason cut off lines of
communication with negative people to keep
peace, they ascribed terrible false attributes to
him and his mission.

5 MINUTES LATER

"...I got your back Bro. I see you. You been
working hard, you've persevered." Stump
looked around, along the monotony of the
concrete staircase walls and continued to try to
inflict the inspiration in Jason that Jason so often
put in him. "Not many people can hold on, let
alone grow under these circumstances Bro." He
could see Jason's frown on the verge of turning
in a loosing battle to fight his pending smile off.
"Go 'head nigga let it out." Stump pushed him
at his side, they both laughed like they used to
when they were kids. "Relax...I'm your
witness. I fasted and prayed beside you five

times a day for thirty one days straight last month. We sacrificed in the name of the Lord, we spoke kindly to the people, we gave glad tidings and fair warnings. We gone win."

Jason stopped nodding his head and he began to stretch his neck muscles. He stood to his feet and began mentally plotting on whatever he was about to do.

"Don't come up here and falsely accuse Allah, Tekk. He's been good to us. We gotta bag the rest of that pound up and re-record that track from last night. You ready?"

And it came to pass that Jason awoke on the terrace to find a rat eating off a chicken wing bone a few feet away and he became frightened. Then sayth the Lord unto him; *Shouldst thou be among the ignorant; who when he sees a single rat out and about, becomes frightened? But if We reveal to Thee that there are hundreds of Rats living beneath the surface of these walls; Ye muster the piece of mind to return back to sleep. Who speared your life and endowed you with degrees of knowledge and wisdom? Your Lord! For I am your constant protector and only sustainer, fear not!*

Jason laid his head back to rest and the word went forth. Minutes later he was awoke yet again by the endeavoring rodent. This time Jason could see his long coarse tail hanging out the opening of a bag of cheese doodles. He pulled out his cell phone to check the time.

3:52 AM APRIL 1 2006

He pulled his clipped off blunt from his duffel bag and sparked it. It was still creeping and crawling out there; Harlem still hadn't gone to sleep. He watched the over sized rat slither through the opening of the terrace door and he quickly got up to shut the door. His mind was still fixated on his role as a Father; thinking about his livelihood and the direction he was headed in. He wondered what the Lord had in store for him; if he'd be sleeping on the terrace this time next year. Jason Jordan asked himself one last question before he stood from his makeshift bed to which he had been seated for the past five minutes in a daze; *where is my faith?*

He took out his Bible and read Psalms 23, after which he stayed up until five AM writing what would became one of his best songs, *The Super Life.*

"...and Satin was with them. And Allah asked him; wh-wh-what's going on, where you coming from?" Margo sat back and folded his hands across his large belly before continuing, "And Satin replied; *from the earth, wondering to and fro, fucking wit' man, leading them from their righteous path.* And Allah said, well did you try my servant Job? Truly Job is among the righteous, he will not loose faith..."

Jason had been running errands all over Manhattan since early this morning. He got to the circle discussion at Margo's apartment minutes before Margo was finishing his weekly testament. Afterwards, Margo pulled Jason aside and expressed some concerns about Jason's public image and the promotion of *The New Testament*. Margo explained to him that he was beginning to exemplify all of the characteristics of a typical hustler and that he was going to have loads of trouble convincing people that he was a agent of the Lord looking like he just got out of jail. Jason took the constructive criticism for what it was, although he gave Margo a piece of his mind before walking out the door; *"My music is all I'm ever gonna give the people from here on out Margz. I'm a keep my look; I'm a keep everything else actually. I'm not no fucking commodity. What you want me to wear a suite and a tie? You know what? Don't even answer that, cause it don't matter. What I need you to do is, I need*

you to be ready to go on tour next month. Can
you do that? Good, you get ready for the tour,
I'll make the music, and we'll all dress however
the fuck we wanna dress; how bout that?"

After confusing the shit out of Margo, Jason
went downstairs and gave a man in need a dollar
before climbing into the car that he rented for
the week.

"Allah don't put nothing on your shoulders you
can handle. But there is a prescribed period;
seedtime and harvest. You can rise above your
circumstances homeboy." Jason figured if he
was going to give up his hard earned money the
least the desperate Brother could do was hear
some truth along with that. He started the car
and the stereo exploded, welcoming him back.
Architekk was vibing to his own music. He
stashed the twenty dimes he had on him in his
underwear, buckled himself in and unrolled the
window.

"All praise be to Allah!" He testified to all that
could hear before pealing off.

When the money and situation permitted Jason
rented a room out at the Burlington on the
Westside overlooking Central Park. Indulging
in some degree of luxury was his secret to

creating music that the kids on the corner simply couldn't. He had his pen in his notebook for what seemed like the entire weekend as he was outlining a list of the Community Centers and nightclubs that the crew had contracts to perform at. He also worked extensively crunching numbers to accurately project how much June's tour was going to cost. The only time he went outside was to get something to eat or to get blunts from the store.

The weather was changing. Jason took breaks from working by sitting on the patio, soaking up the sun while watching New York go round. He was working on the final verse of a new song which was somehow unfolding as he bore witness to the life of Manhattan. As he swatted an insect away Jason picked up on Laronda swaying her body, apparently singing, through the glass screen door.

"...I-can- see- you. Tell me what you-want-to-do..."

She was singing along to her mp3 player. Between the high glare from the sun and her mood, an alluring energy was produced. Jason smiled and leaned against the wall, finding delight in watching her be herself. She smiled and extended her arms. *"I-know-who-you are. You're my superstar..."* She hit a note that sent Jason's soul into orbit. He was taken aback in bliss, "Oh, brilliant. Fucking brilliant!" He said while clapping lightly.

Laronda snapped her fingers in a groove of her own. "I sold seventy two copies of your album today." Jason's surprise and content was written all over his face. He folded his arms and continued to watch her as she playfully performed for him. Her tender, renewed smile was unrelenting. She had a graceful command of her body, her skin was illuminated; hips swinging, and the sweetest scent of a woman.

"...My love has always been always been true and I could prove it babe..." She removed her headphones still glowing.

"What you know about Floetry?" He asked.

"No, what you know about Floetry?" She shot back, "That's new school music there."

Jason confiscated her device and removed the earphones. He went to the large wooden desk in the center of the room and plugged her ipod into the speaker depot he had set up.

"So I got $303 for you and $201 for me."

Laronda said as Jason searched through her library of songs. "And I passed your info to some chump who was trying to talk to me on the

1 train. He said he work for Def Jam... We'll see."

"Can you sing this for me?"

Jason pressed play and grabbed a seat on the edge of the bed. He gave Laronda the attention of her own private audience. She had not the slightest problem getting into character. *"Ooooooooooh baby..."* She playfully turned away, revealing her wide, curvy backside bulging through her denim dress; *"Ooooooooooh baby..."* She began to undress him starting with his tank top. She was halfway undressed herself when she dropped to her knees and grabbed and pulled at his manhood. *"I'd rather be with you cause I love the way you scream my name..."*

"Yo where yall at?" Jason yelled into his cell phone. Margo and Com were looking at the end of the Spurs/Lakers game. Laronda was unloading the food Jason brought for the group onto the table.

"Aight, hurry up. Yall close to twenty minutes late for this meeting."

Jason flipped his phone close then stepped out onto the patio to let his head cool off. Laronda finished dressing her fried rice with soy and duck sauce and she brought her and Jason's food outside. "I got a question for you." She said as she placed his carton of food in front of him, "What happen that night you and Stacky got shot?"

Jason sat down and massaged the stress around his forehead, "...Living too fast...Allah had to get at me."

She looked at him as if expecting him to elaborate but he didn't. "When's the last time you spoke to Stack?"

"It's been over a month." He answered as he checked on Margo and Com behind him. "But that's my Brother...Why you don't think he gone show up?"

Laronda didn't have an answer for him and therefore she didn't say anything, she just looked out at the city, but Jason understood her.

"I have a question for you as well." Jason performed a balancing act between laughing and swallowing the chicken in his mouth, "Why is your crew named J.E.S.I.C.A?"

She smiled as if she'd prefer shying away from answering, "Jefferson, East River, Schaumburg, Isaacs, Clinton, Abraham Lincoln; those are the housing Projects our founders were from."

Margo and Com waited another fifteen minutes
for Stack and Buck who never showed up.
Jason walked them downstairs to Margo's jeep
and leaned his forearm against in the driver side
window.

"Ah beloved, you trust that girl?" Margo asked
as he got situated in his seat. Jason leaned his
hard, tattoo covered arms in the car window.
"Let's cut the bullshit Margo. You know
something about her I don't?"

"Not necessarily. I see yall been hanging around
each other a lot lately. You gotta have people
around you that you can trust, right?" Margo
stuck his hand out and Jason dabbed it with a
closed fist. "I got you."

Jason went back upstairs and reviewed the game
plan alone at his desk. Laronda found interest in
a movie on channel 7 and tried to stay out of his
way, as she saw Jason was mentally involved in
whatever he was doing.

"I'm not gonna have enough." Jason said aloud
as he slammed his calculator to the desk.

"What's that?" Laronda asked sunk in the lush
mattress while snacking on chocolate candy.

"I was trying to see if I could do this tour without them, but I'm not gone be able to get up that kind of money."

Sitting up, she asked, "How much are you short?"

"I don't know exactly, it don't matter. I couldn't do this alone."

"Well you don't have to do it alone. Margz and Com obviously got your back. Well Margz do at least... Com is kind of out to lunch." She laughed and noticed no visible change in Jason's defeated demeanor. "...And what you think I'm here for?"

He looked up at her and smiled as if to pacify her, little authenticity therein.

"Will thirteen hundred get it? I got about thirteen hundred saved up, and I can help you with whatever you need on a personal level." Laronda had sincerity and optimism all over her face. "We would have to make some sacrifices and discipline ourselves." She said regurgitating Jason's own instructions back to him. "But we can do it... We can take the weed on the road with us and have another source of income if need be."

He looked over at her as if he were slapped with the reality that everything was going to be alright. He shut his composition notebook in relief that he could finally call it quits for the night. He stood to his feet and stretched out in exhaustion. "You ready to hit the road?"

Laronda's eyes lit-up with optimism, she sat up in the bed; "Yeah lets do it."

"Aight. I'm a get on the phones Monday and start confirming our show dates."

"Good, now would you come over here and relax?"

Jason fell across her lap and picked up the remote to cut the television off.

"So…" She asked as she began twisting his hair, "Tell me about the Koran."

Jason's grin widened from ear to ear, "That's my saving grace right there." He turned and looked into her, "And it can easily be yours as well."

"Really?" She questioned cynically as she rolled her neck.

"Islam is the truth and proof, so look at actualities and pay no attention to the hype."

Jason pointed, "That's why I cut the TV off." He turned around to look at her exclusively. "You've been smiling a lot more lately, and I could look at you and tell those smiles are coming from within. I can see you've been embracing your more graceful, articulate qualities, and sort of pumped the breaks on the...the hate and the negativity."

She contemplated for a Moment then commenced fondling Jason's hair again. "And you're saying that's because of Islam?"

"Allah reaches us by way of his wondrous signs and by inspiration. So either of the two is causing you to live better, to feel better and be better." He said before rising from the bed.

"And what does that have to do with the Koran?"

"Well... what if that inspiration is me?"

"Then..."

He reached out for her, "Come here." She stood to her feet. Jason stood behind her and held her by the shoulders then caught eyes with her through the mirror mounted on the dresser in front of them. "GOD designed this..." He graced his hands along the length of her tender arms as he spoke softly into her right ear. "Each muscle group is a facility, to either be mastered and understood or neglected and left to rot." He raised her arm with a firm grip on her wrist, "The biceps muscles are a facility, the triceps…" He soothed the surface of her skin as he worked his way down her arm. "The muscles of the forearm are a separate facility..." They locked fingers and Jason turned her around, "The pectorals..." He said as he massaged her breast. "They are all separate facilities that work together in unity for a common cause."

"Stop."

Laronda whispered as she scooted back and closed her eyes looking for more. Jason did stop, as he knew a day was coming when he would have to explain to GOD why he squandered this opportunity to make a believer out of her because his dick was hard. He pulled back; "This is how we have to look at our individual roles in society; parts to a whole. You my Sister have been brainwashed to believe that the whole you're supposed to be apart of is your country, or your school, your Projects or some fucking gang. But if it's not a facility of GOD, then the works of that institution or that facility will be fruitless, they are in manifest error and they will have to answer for their bullshit on the day when the trumpets will sound."

"The trumpets?" She asked hot, bothered and confused.

"How well do you know your Bible?"

She frowned in frustration as she watched him walk away, lost in his own thoughts yet again. "You need to know your Bible before you start messing with the Holy Koran. The Holy Bible gives the Holy Koran precedent. You need to know the story of Abraham and Moses; what those men went through and why. You need to know the covenant that Allah made with Noah and Abraham. You need to know how and why Jesus was crucified, what his message was… Jesus never said that he was GOD. When the people came up to him they said; *Oh Rabbi, teach us how to pray.* And they joined hands and Jesus said the Lord's Prayer."

"Our Father, who art in Heaven-"

"Right! *Our* Father, who are in *Heaven*; hallowed by *thy* name…Jesus was a righteous man, our Brother not our Father. The significance in that is of vital importance to you."

"So what, any of us can be like Jesus?"

"Well I don't know if I'd take it that far, personally. Jesus was in his thirties when he

began his prophecy, so he lived, he saw and
tried things. So when he was baptized in the
Jordan River and he could see clearly, he could
testify from a particular vantage point, he knew
GOD." Jason pulled the good book from his
duffel bag and tossed it on the bed, "You're
welcome to check the word yourself." He began
removing the contents from his pockets, placing
them in a drawer of the nightstand. "Eventually
you're gone a have to, cause I'm just a man;
your teachers, Priest, they are all just men and
women. We will all lead you astray if you listen
to us long enough."

Jason slipped out of his shirt, apparently getting
ready for a shower. "We're Humans, we ate that
damn apple…we all have this thing deep down
in our core that makes us think we can fuck with
Allah. Like the wisdom that is in us or within
our fellow Humans heads is the end all to be all.
So eventually we gone sneak some of our own
biases and prejudice into our teachings, therein
lays the potential to lead our followers away
from the path of their Lord. But it's not about
me, it's not about you, and it's not about Jesus,
or any other piece, it's about the whole, GOD is
the whole. GOD is able to reach all of us all of
the time because he is the whole, he is
everything, not to be captured by an idea, a
name; he is everything, the infinite. That's why
in Islam we say Al-Ham-dulillah; All praise be

to GOD." Jason went into the bathroom and
shut the door behind him.

112

"No Brother, this is a beautiful morning."

Date: June 13TH 2006

"What's up Rasta?" A young man walking down the street with his lady friend greeted Jason as he walked by.

"I'm not a Rasta, Bro." Jason propped the kickstand on the R3 Ninja he rented, climbed off the side and handed his helmet to Laronda. He approached the couple with a curious grin and pep in his step.

And so it came to pass that GOD kept his promises with Jason, every single one. Jason fought and preserved while planting seeds in the field that was he and his kids' future, and the spring of 2006 most certainly welcomed a harvest. Jason found a degree of inner peace that seemed to attract people to his music and message from city to city and town to town, yielding solid turnouts in the public appearances and keeping the N.Y.C.M.C machine moving when it was expected to falter.

"...GOD is your only sustainer; submit to him and do it in a true state of humility, he'll forgive you…" Jason turned and eye balled the young lady who was sporting from what he could tell had to be an 18-piece wig. He continued bringing glad tidings; "And if you repent your sins and work righteous deeds then he will put you on a path that leads to an understanding of his laws and his creation; which is direction, guidance manifest. You think your Father would create you and not leave you directions or signs to analyze? You bugging Black man, bugging; far, far above he, as what we ascribe to him."

A group of fellas walking by slowed down to check out Laronda, who was wearing tight Burberry plaid shorts, a white tee shirt that she tied up on her back and a pair of white on white Air Max.

"Yo I got them dimes of Dro, you heard? And I got the boy Architekk first two albums for sale ten dollars a whop. Get right." Laronda was sharp, not lost in their stares but focused on the business as she pitched the products.

-"So let me give you my information. I don't be picking up my phone cause, you know Babylon be listening, but leave a message. I'll call back." Jason gave the fellow Dread a pound and dapped him on the back.

-"Yo instead of me giving you $10 change back, why don't you let me brake you off a fat dime of Dro. I know yall boys light up."

Jason already had the engine roaring in idle when Laronda mounted on his back. He threw up a peace sign to the fellas who'd just supported the movement and walked the motorcycle a few feet from the curb. Margo, Com, Force and Tracy were racing up the other direction of Peachtree on their bikes at high speed and they flew right by them. Jason rocked and leaned the Kawasaki, curling into a U turn as he switched into second gear. He ripped the throttle and sent the bike exploding off. Laronda wrapped her arms around him and held on tightly.

1:20 PM; THE SAME DAY

"19, 29, 39…" Margo finished counting out the money on the Hotel bed. "So that's $1,139."

"How the fuck we get thirty nine?"

Tracy blew a cloud of smoke and passed her cigarette to Com, "Oh… I used a dollar to go get a blunt wrap."

Laronda looked at her Sister who she drove out of the Projects for the week and checked her quickly. "Yo clean that shit up! Everybody get paid out at the end of the day. What the hell is wrong with you?"

The crew breezed through Atlanta for the weekend. They were preparing to go to Margo's Mother's home in South Carolina, which was going to serve somewhat as their base throughout their traveling. They had yet to reach their break-even point from what was initially put up for the monthly car rental, gas, studio time, radio commercials, hotel rooms, and their investment in two pounds of hydroponic weed, but the numbers were turning in their favor more and more everyday.

Architekk designed the promo tour to go up along the east coast, starting with their furthest location then working their way back up to New York. He and Laronda performed at Club Wreck in Miami last Friday. The next night they preformed three hours away in Orlando and did a radio interview at W.L.O.W 102.4. The entire N.Y.C.M.C crew was coming full force in a few days when Jason and his party joined Stacky, Buck and Flo who were driving down from New York as Jason and Stacky finally reconciled their differences.

A quick tooth brushing, wash-up and a quick prayer; Jason was so tired and smoked out that he just wanted to kick off his sneakers and lay down when he got out of Margo's Mother's guest bathroom on the main level of her home. Tracy was curled into her jacket across the couch in the living room. Com was flipping through the channels on the television and Laronda was texting on her phone from the loveseat. Jason looked to his right and saw Margo scrolling through the cabinets in the kitchen.

"We got some cans of chilly in here, some cereal… Yall can make some hot dogs if yall want." Margo said to Jason as he opened the refrigerator.

"I ain't thinking about no hot dogs right now. Let me get a sheet and show me where to crash."

Margo lowered his voice to a whisper, *"You can go upstairs. We got an extra bed that you can have. They gone have to stay out here though."*

"Let me bring Laronda up there with me."

"Come on Tekk." Margo scrunched his face as if he preferred he didn't ask that question. *"What my Mother gone say when she wake up?"*

"We'll creep out at different times. Come on Margz you know that ass be calling me."

"Yall can't have sex on my Mother's sheets!"
Margo said before looking back toward the
living room to see if anyone heard him.

*"Aight we won't have sex. Let me just bring her
up there with me to talk."* Jason said as he tried
to keep a straight face.

"Go 'head nigga." He looked at him as if
ashamed; "Fornicating Motherfucker."

Margo started for the stairs and Jason followed
in his wake. Jason could hear Laronda's phone
shutting down over the creaking of the old
wooden steps as he looked in her direction and
motioned for her to follow him.

3:47 AM; THE SAME NIGHT

Jason opened his eyes to find Laronda staring at
him with a faint smirk on her face.

"What you looking at?"

She smiled and turned her away. She had one of
Jason's turbans wrapped around her head and a
long gray t-shirt on.

"How long I been sleep?"

"Only a few minutes." She looked back into his
face, "...It's like... if I could say everything that

121

I wanted to say to you…I would have you in the bag-" She snapped her fingers in absolute certainty, "Like *that.*"

"Oh really?"

Looking at him with nineteen year old confidence and conviction in her eyes she snapped once again; "like that."

"I don't know; I already got you reading the Koran, giving me ass all over the place and trying to check my phone & shit."

She struck pointlessly into his brawny shoulder; "Shut up…I hate you."

"*Stop yelling*, his Moms is in there sleep."

Her eyes opened wide, yet still saturated with exhaustion. "You want some chilly dogs?"

Jason smiled like a child at the promise of a tasty treat. "Hell yeah."

"I'm a make you the best chilly dogs you ever had in your life."

Architekk wrapped a Nike headband around his vivacious dreadlocks and slipped a pair of Ray

Ban's over his hazy eyes then checked himself in the mirror. The banging at the dressing room door let him know it was just about time to go on stage.

"Yo Tekk you ready?"

He seriously considered the question. Laronda was sitting on the shut toilet braking marijuana into a split blunt inches away from him.

"Yeah I'm coming!" He hollered.

Jason removed the heavy rose gold chain from around his neck and placed it on the basin and took off the sunglasses he just put on. "You gone have that ready for me right?" He asked Laronda while still analyzing himself in the mirror. Laronda responded with overt confidence as she sealed the blunt with her plump glossed lips. "I got this. You go handle that."

He left the dressing room; Margo, Com, Force, Stacky, Buck, Flo and Tracy followed suite. Jason loosened his neck and stretched his back muscles with a laser sharp focus on his clear path to the stage. Stump dropped the beat and yelled into the microphone in his DJ coffin. *"What's the deal South Carolina? Yall know we bout to get down right? Yall know how the N.Y.C.M.C. camp put it down right? Put your*

*Motherfuckin' hands together for my Brother
from Harlem World! New York is in the
building! And we gone do it like this…"*

JULY 20ᵀᴴ 2006

"Oh my GOD! Shake that shit! Shake it!" Force
yelled while smacking the Stripper's ass on his
lap. Buck sprinkled a stack of singles over her
body, clutching a bottle of Clicquot in his other
hand. Deep southern bass patterns dominated
the Club atmosphere. They appeared to be
having the time of their lives.

*"How much it's gone cost me to take you home
baby?"*

JULY 20ᵀᴴ 2006

"Yeah Motherfucker!"

Jason dropped from another set of pull-ups and
took a swig from the gallon of water he brought
from the convenient store on Memorial
Boulevard. *"That's what the fuck I'm talkin'
bout."* He growled as he handed Stump the
lifting gloves. "So what you saying Stump, you
think I'm a have to go through a Bank no matter
what?"

124

"I mean, it's whatever Allah wills. We'll see."
Stump said while placing his water jug on the
concrete. He took a deep breath. "…I mean
who knows? You walk into the room with a
hundred grand cash, somebody'll sell you a
house." He added before jumping up to grab the
street signal to do his set of pull-ups.

JULY 20ᵀᴴ 2006

"Don't let that nigga control your mind. I see
you trying to play the housewife role & shit.
You better slow that shit up." Tracy took
another sip of Hennessey and re-propped herself
up on the hood of the car she was sitting on.

"You know you want what I got." Laronda said,
pushing Tracy's buttons simply because she
could.

"Oh no bitch, and what is that?"

"Piece of mind; I feel good. I'm happy, I'm not
in need, I'm not in want."

Tracy laughed all over herself, "Not in need, *not
in want*? Bitch you getting a little too
comfortable with your life on the road. Beef is
still cooking in the hood. You gone have to

bring your happy, little ghetto ass back to
Harlem sooner or later."

JULY 20ᵀᴴ 2006

"Go head bitch, take me to court!" Margo
yelled into his cell phone. He pulled out a
cigarette and Com quickly reached across the
table to light it for him. Com reclaimed his seat
and began flexing and stretching his prison built
muscles while listening to Margo continue to
blow a gasket. *"Tell me what 17% of nothing is
bitch!"*

JULY 20ᵀᴴ 2006

*"I got that white. $175 for a 8ᵗʰ of that good,
good; holler at me baby."* Stacky said to a local
hustler who walked by him into the convenient
store on the corner.

JULY 31ˢᵀ 2006

*"Thank you for dinner. That was excellent,
baby."*

"Why don't you eat your salad Jay? It's good for you."

"Aight, leave it there. I'm a eat it."

"No you're not Jason. You got food all over the place that you supposedly gone eat…" Denise placed her hands on her protruding belly and took a seat at the dinning room table. *"…And what happens? I end up having to throw it out. Ouch-"* She squinted in pain and hunched over.

"You alright, Ma?"

"I think I can feel the baby kicking."

"Nesie your ass is only four months pregnant. You don't feel no damn baby kicking."

She laughed and playfully frowned; knowing she was in her newly acquired brat mode, as she knew she could get away with being a baby until the real baby arrived. She stole a lick from Jason's chocolate birthday cake on the table and continued to caress her stomach.

"Go lay down beautiful, I got the dishes."

Denise lifted her heavier self from her chair and covered the cake she baked for him.

"I love you… I got the best Baby Daddy in the world!" She said as she graced off.

Jason could feel a poking in his back through the sheets.

"Stop Nesie, I'm up!" Jason turned around to Laronda's steaming face. She threw his stage outfit at him. "I'm not fucking Denise!" She yelled before storming out of the room. Jason rolled over and grabbed his phone off the nightstand.

12 MISSED CALLS

He dropped his head back to his pillow. *It's about to be August,* he thought to himself; coming up on a year since Denise left. The presence of GOD wasn't so evident as the sun had set a few hours ago. He knew that he needed to get ready to head to the venue, but his energy had forsaken him.

"Oh shit!" He slapped his forehead then picked his phone back up and quickly called the first number in the speed-dial. He was still trying to shake his drowsiness, regretful he didn't call in the morning because he figured it was too early.

"Hi Daddy."

"Happy birthday Honey."

128

"Thank you."

Jason began stretching his aching muscles as he waited to see if Hollis would give him anything else to work with. "...How was your day?"

"It was good. I went to the movies with Renee and Dominique; then we went out to eat."

"That's peace, that's peace."

Jason could hear loud dancing music through the receiver, as if she were in a nightclub.

"I see you waited till the last minute to call."

"I was knocked out baby. But you know I wouldn't forget your birthday."

"Okay."

"You got the package I sent you?"

"Yeah I got it. Daddy, let me call you when I get home alright? I can barely hear you."

-*"Yo Tekk lets go!"* Buck yelled as he banged rapidly on the hotel room door.

"Aight Honey. I'll talk to you later."

-"Our ride gone be here in ten minutes; ya heard?"

Jason sat perfectly still with hopes of swindling Buck into thinking that he wasn't there. There were no lights on and there wasn't a sound coming from inside the King suite.

"Ah yo?" After another round of knocking and a few more Moments, Jason heard the swagger of Buck's heavy chain moving further away from the door. Jason could feel himself slipping emotionally. His religion permits certain exemptions from prayer when traveling, and Jason had been using his free pass since the commencement of the tour. Consequently, the source of his power was diminishing. It was still so early in the game that he didn't even realize he was already on the board. Yet and still, his wild oats were already just about sown. He had gotten respect, admiration and groupie love up and down the I95; but there remained a void and he could feel that void widening.

Jason decided that he was going to steal tonight and use it to restrengthen his spirits, to refocus his perspective and to build. With all the rapping he'd been doing over the past two months, he found himself talking too much and lacking the substance that defined him.

He cut off his phone and walked to the other side of the room and shut the venetian blinds. He went into the bathroom and washed his hands then ran them across his face. "Father please forgive me my sins..."

"Yo, how yall make yall apple pies?"

"Apple pies?" The counterperson asked in a deep middle-eastern accent. Stack looked down at his ringing phone and absentmindedly placed a wad of money on the counter.

"What do you want my friend?"

"Hello?" Stack answered his cell phone.

"My friend what do you want?"

"Hold on."

Stack yelled through the bulletproof glass window, *"Some Motherfucking pie!"* He finally noticed the stack of money he put down. "Give me my money back nigga." He snatched his cash and tried to shove it into his pocket spilling crumbled bills on to the floor.

"Apple pies one dollar my friend." The clerk insisted, growing inpatient and agitated.

- *"Ah! Free money over here!"* Flo playfully yelled out.

As he reached down, Stacky pushed him to the seat of his pants. "Fuck outta here."

- *"Oooooo."* The on looking members of the entourage instigated from the sit-in booths.

"Stacky you fake ass Jay-Z. I'd bust ya ass if I was a man, you know that?"

"Get off my dick." Stacky fired, obviously in no mood to joke with Laronda.

"You wish you had one faggot."

"Fuck you; fuckin' bird."

Laronda threw a ketchup drenched French fry from her table, hitting Stacky on the shoulder of his Evisu tee. Stacky looked down, Jason could see a certain seriousness mounting on his face. Jason grabbed the pie that the clerk put on the countertop, broke it in half and flung it across the room at Laronda.

"Look out!" Tracy covered Laronda then dug into her snack basket and whizzed a piece of chicken at Jason. *"Don't be throwing shit at my Sister!"*

Stacky snatched the other half of the pie from Jason and shot it at Tracy. She ducked, and the stray pie slapped Buck on the side of his face. *"Ah yo, yall niggas play too much B!"*

Stump and Tracy laughed hysterically from the booth in front of Buck's. Laronda was eyeballing Jason as if she were contemplating throwing something else. Stacky turned to Jason laughing and slapped him five.

"Oh word, yall think that shit is funny?" Buck demanded, still livid. Stacky turned back to the counterman as he saw Buck loading up, "Yo Ak, let me get some chicken, hurry up."

"Please, you can't do that here!"

Buck rapidly tossed all the fries that he could at Stacky and Jason. Laronda joined Buck bombarding them.

"Ak, give me some damn chicken!" Stacky yelled.

Flo jumped in on Buck and Laronda's side, sending Jason and Stacky retreating out the front door.

"You can't do that here!"

Jason ran to the BMW parked out front and grabbed the jug of water that he left in the passenger seat. Laronda ran behind him tossing the remains from a tub of sauerkraut on his white t-shirt.

"Oh shit! Get back! Get back!" Laronda yelled and about-faced as Jason raised the bottle of water in his hand. As she ran away he caught and drenched her as she tried unsuccessfully to use Flo as a barrier. The clerk came busting out of the store with a baseball bat in one hand and his cell phone in the other, *"I'm calling the Police! You can't do that here!"*

The crew had been rolling nonstop for over six hours straight along the 99 Interstate. Laronda was struggling to keep up with Stacky as he raced his luxury sedan through the hills of Northern Pennsylvania. Margo trailed Laronda's Volvo and Buck was behind Margo. The music no longer dictated the mood. Nas' *It was Written* was blasting from the stereo yet Jason could barely keep his eyes open, Stump was in the back passed out and Laronda was fighting emerging slumber.

Stacky activated his turn signal and decelerated to a halt on the shoulder of the highway; every succeeding car followed. Laronda put on her hazard lights and stepped out. Jason got out of the car and was absolutely besieged by GOD's creation as he looked out at the scenery. They were atop a dark, grand mountain in a vast mountain range, too much to take in with the naked eye. Laronda walked up to Stacky's car to see what was going on.

Jason wandered toward the side of the mountain and spread his arms as wide as he could. He pulled his head far back and turned his elated face to the sky. His eyes were shut, but he was in great harmony with the world around him. His inner vision became fantastically vivid, fantastically clear.

"Tekk you alright? We gone get a Hotel for the night...Tekk?"

Without any intimation Jason fell to his knees in a state of smooth astonishment. His peers couldn't begin to describe what they were seeing and therefore they grew apprehensive.

"Yo son we getting the fuck outta here. It's Deers out here & shit."

When Jason opened his eyes he could feel the energy around him begin to level off. He dropped to his backside and gazed out at the earth in deep, blissful contemplation. When he finally turned around minutes later, Laronda was waiting for him on the hood of the silver S80. They acknowledged one another with a brief stare and the word went forth.

7:53 AM; THE NEXT MORNING

Jason slid his plastic key into the access slot for the hotel gym and pushed the door open. He was welcomed by the sound of track sneakers slamming into the bed of the treadmill in the corner. Jason placed his towel alongside a pillar in the middle of the room, waived hello to the woman on the treadmill then commenced a stretch routine. He was preparing his body for the turmoil he was about to put it through as he thought about the day ahead of him. They had to stop in Buffalo New York to stash the contraband that they were traveling with before hitting the Canadian border, a show in Toronto, promotional efforts in Niagara Falls, drop offs, pick ups... N.Y.C.M.C. was getting out there today.

"Hey aren't you that Rapper guy?" The woman asked as she stepped off the treadmill.

Jason unfolded his body and looked up with a sincere smile on his face. He extended a hand and introduced himself, "Jason."

"Yeah, but what's your stage name again?"

"Tekk; Architekk."

"Right Architekk; the Muslim Rapper from Harlem." She smiled and tried to figure him out with her eyes. Jason continued stretching, not particularly looking for a conversation. She stayed put, as if there were something else she was looking for.

"I wish you would show me how to pray." She chuckled, unsure of herself. "I sure need it."

"Yeah?" He asked as he released his grip from around his ankles. He took hold of one of her soft hands; "There's no better time to pray than the present."

"Now?" She questioned as she gave him the other hand that he was reaching for. They bowed their heads. "Father please accept this offering. For you said that when two or more of us are gathered in your name that you are present with us and we thank you for keeping your word Father; I can feel you." The woman gripped Jason's hands firmly, with more confidence and closed her eyes tighter. "Please Father forgive us our sins. For we are man and woman created weak in the flesh, transgressors in our ways and ever ungrateful of your *unrelenting* mercy and countless blessings. Father we come to you today in search of peace and we ask that you open our hearts to your glorious ways, your universal laws, that we may achieve our peace. Father we ask you for the strength to do right instead of wrong, the vision to see clear and the fortitude to live righteous lives according to your liking. Father I ask that you endow my Sister with knowledge, wisdom, and understanding. I ask you to strengthen her faith Father, that she may see the value in her relationship with you, that she may keep an open and honest line of communication with you."

Jason's cell phone vibrated as a text message was coming through. "In your *mighty*, holy name, and only in your name do we pray, aminah."

The woman opened her eyes which Jason noticed had become foggy and spaced out.

"You good?" He asked.

"Yes."

"Good." He politely took his hands back and checked the text message that came in on his cell phone.

Lakrisha Fwd: Praise the Lord! Today J3 and I gave birth to Anthony Jordan.

He weighs 7 lbs. And 11 ounces and is a little angel!!

"Is everything okay?" The woman asked Jason as if it were somehow her business.

"Oh, shit, oh shit," Jason took a step back "... I'm a GrandFather!"

Hang the sign up on the door, that says don't disturb this groo-ooo--oove...

"That's my shit right there. Turn that up!"

Jason and Buck were sitting on the hood on Buck's Audi. Stacky was a few feet away talking to a female that he stopped from walking down the street.

Pay attention; are ya listening? Hey you're my favorite girl... Excuse me for a Moment I'm in another world...

Com and Margo were playing a high stakes game of Tunk in front of Stacky's building on the other side of Grant Projects. Stump and Buck were sporting the latest Jordan's, military inspired t-shirts and pounds of jewelry. Jason was wearing a new Yankee fitted, a yellow Polo shirt and a flashy Raymond Weil watch courtesy of the game. Laronda was sitting in the driver seat singing to the radio along with Buck.

Tracy just got back from 119th handling some personal business. Now they were just waiting on Chauncey, who was tagging along on the tour, to come out of building 63 before they rolled out to their photo shoot in midtown. The elevator dropped another load of residents in the lobby. Jason looked through the crowd with hopes of spotting Chauncey and caught eyes with Mr. Garret as he came trotting out of the building pushing an old metal shopping cart.

"Good morning." Mr. Garret greeted politely as he passed by.

"No Brother, this is a beautiful morning! Allahu Akbar!" Jason said before flopping to the car seat and reclining all the way back to light a blunt.

5:08PM; THE SAME DAY

"…Bush steals the election in 04, the country is still involved in this stupid ass war, still! I thought this shit was about 9/11 and Bin Ladin; I mean what the fuck? It does not end, the bullshit does not end with this Country." Jason tried to stop talking but he couldn't until he was absolutely certain he hammered his point home, "That's what the News is about, the nightly News; it's like, here's the update on the bullshit. So don't go throw the President out of the fucking White House, because the system is unfolding, your victory is coming, shit is working itself out...Bullshit!" He took another gulp of Moet and slammed the bottle to the floor of the terrace they were sitting in.

Jason was back on Madison Avenue, back in Taft Projects and he was having a friendly but heated discussion with a group of residents who were also former Marines about the current state of the nation.

"Alright now wait a minute Jason. We fought proud for our country. You sitting up here talking all this, fuck America this, fuck America that. Your Black ass wouldn't have the freedom to do that in other countries. Government'll come to your house & snatch yo' ass right out your bed."

"Well that's gay to even think along those lines."

Mr. Johnson looked at Jason as if he had seen a ghost, his patience was being pushed to the limit.

"What I'm saying is the truth, fuck what the government think. They got they own agenda; and the history of *our* people in America is a testament to that agenda not having the slightest bit to do with us. That's the truth. If a man can't speak and deal with truth then what is he doing? He's walking around pretending his whole life; lying, and not dealing with reality, that's gay."

"Ah young fella, I done had about all the gays out of you I'm gone take."

"What you wanna fight now? I want to help you break that mental slavery thing you got going on, not fight. But don't think I'm scared of you." Jason looked derogatorily at the patches on Mr. Johnson's old service jacket. "Yall ain't tough in my eyes. If you was tough you would've fought against the oppressor, not with them. America stole your Great, Great, Great Grandparents, raped and oppressed them, put them in chains and shackles, and historically denied you your natural rights as a man. You know the Holy Koran instructs us that turmoil and oppression is worse than death? You know why? Cause it's the truth!"

Mr. Johnson waived his hands with ignorance, the group as a whole became unsettled.

"Alright you don't got a trust in that but let me ask you this; you put your life up for them, what did they give you? What did your team win?"

Mr. Johnson had no response ready, so Jason continued, "That's why the suicide rate among U.S soldiers is at an all time high. Cause

there's no answers to the real questions, too used
to dealing with the bullshit to make it even make
sense to yourself. You know, I studied this in a
course in college..." A group J.E.S.I.C.A.
Sisters walking out of the building caught
Jason's attention. He paused for a Moment and
watched them walk to the parking lot in front
and gather around a car.

"...The harder someone is initiated for
something, the higher allegiance they pledge to
it... I would've went AWOL on they asses.
Excuse me." Jason suddenly left the terrace and
ran down the staircase.

"Yo!" He yelled as he busted through the lobby.
He could see some of the girls trying to hide
their plastic cups of liquor when they saw him.
The Sisters seated in the car continued smoking
and listening to their trunk rattling music.

"Yo Gwinn what the fuck you doing?"

UNIT 2

Jayson *J3* Jordan Junior

140

***"Fucking faggots gone wanna talk to me
soon enough."***

Date: August 17TH 2006

"I need more, I need, something more!"

Junior tried not to yell out loud but his
frustration surpassed his restraint. He stepped
between two parked cars then hopped over the
curb as he crossed onto Needham Avenue.

"I need more to work with GOD."

Junior examined all that he could lay his eyes
upon, ensuring himself that no one was watching
him. He was looking into the windows of
vacant Spellman High School across the street
when his cell phone rang.

((INCOMING LAKRISHA))

"Yes baby?"

"Where you at?"

"At the store. What up?"

"Bring the baby some more wipes."

"We finished all those wipes we got from Target the other day?"

"Yeah, and can you bring some bleach too."

When Junior disconnected the call he could only look up to the sky and express his discontent, *"...This can't be what it is GOD; this can't be life. I need this music thing to work. I need...I need, something...I need more for my family, damn."* He was so upset and defeated that he was on the verge of tears.

Junior had been going back and forth to court for the past two months dealing with traffic tickets that he got while driving to Lakrisha's baby shower in April. His cell phone was about to get cut off and most of the money he'd saved from joining the work force fulltime last year was drying up. Lakrisha just returned to work from her maternity leave and hadn't seen a full paycheck yet and Anthony was running through diapers like they were going out of style. All of which had the completion of his demo and his music in general, on ice and had him feeling like he'd be stuck at his crappy job parking cars and taking orders, forever.

Junior turned around and headed back to his 234th street apartment. He usually didn't walk this far when he took his late night walks to clear his mind, but he'd been feeling increased pressure lately and the two miles he strolled may have been the reason he didn't burst.

9:36PM; THE SAME NIGHT

"...little star, how I wonder what you are..."

Junior stopped his forward Momentum as he realized Lakrisha had gotten Anthony to go to sleep. He stuck his head through the cracked room door and checked on his new family. Lakrisha's full, round breasts were exposed and Anthony's open mouth was still touching her erect nipple. She smiled to acknowledge Junior, though neither of them uttered a word with mutual desire to keep the baby sleep.

He crept back, and into the hallway closet and began getting his clothes ready for work tomorrow. He plugged in the iron and cut on the Sports Network to check out the highlights while the iron warmed up. Then he went into the kitchen and took a spoon to the pot of soup from the night before that Lakrisha heated up.

"Greedy."

Lakrisha said standing behind him adjusting her maternity bar. Junior placed the spoon in his hand into the sink and walked over to her and caressed one of her breast. "I'm still hungry."

"Uh, uh; I'm about to go to sleep."

Junior deflated, "Damn Krish, our lives are getting too boring baby."

"It's called growing up. Tomorrow is close out Saturday; I got to be to work early. And speaking of which…" She leaned against the wall and looked Junior in the eyes, "I got this couple to re-fi their home to pay off a high priority account. I maybe getting a fat bonus check next month."

"Yeah, how much?" Junior asked as he covered the pot on the stove.

"It should be enough to get my engagement ring off of lay-a-way." Lakrisha suggested with a hint of a sparkle in her eye. As Junior turned to open the refrigerator he could feel Lakrisha's eyes on his back.

"You know what I'm sayin' Junior?"

"I-hate-this-j-o-o-o-o-b…"

Junior continued tossing an oil-stained softball off of the frail wooden wall in the company trailer. His legs were folded over one another and he'd been singing to himself the past few minutes. *"I-hate-this-job..."*

He saw Michelle roll through the Atlantic Avenue entrance in her red Honda. He removed a used ticket stub from his back pocket and scratched off the previous timestamp.

"What's up Ms. Anderson?"

"Hey hon' how you doing?" Michelle asked as she pulled her handbag and laptop carrying case from her backseat.

"I'm doing good. You looking right today Ms. Anderson." Junior commented in admiration of her personal style and healthy body.

"You think so?" She turned to expose her melodically curvy backside to him, "My butt don't' look too big in this?"

Junior tried to preserve his cool and keep his hormones in check; "Na, na it's good; you good." He placed her ticket in one of her windshield wipers and handed her the stub.

"Thank you." She strutted off and hurried into downtown Brooklyn to start her day.

"You want it washed?"

"Yeah go 'head, you can wash it for me!"

8:14PM; THE SAME NIGHT

"Biggy Smalls; Machinegun Funk."

"Which verse?" Red Out asked as he lit another cigarette from his chair in front of the track-board.

"All of them shits. Them shits was all fire." D answered.

"Shut…" Red Out waived his hands thoroughly frustrated, "the fuck up! We ask what's the hottest verse of all time and you go name a whole fucking song."

"That's a good choice though." Jeff, one of the studio engineers said to pick D up.

"Fuck that nigga & his choice. I should pound you out right now." Red Out said as he cringed his fist and sat forward in his seat. "Say something." He dared D.

-"Chill Red. You be braking on people for no reason."

"What you got Red, best rap verse of all time?" Jeff asked for the sake of not allowing Red Out the chance to work himself up.

Red Out slammed down a strong palm, hitting the track-board with such force that he sent the wireless mouse in front of him airborne; "Nas; It Ain't Hard to Tell, the last verse."

Junior had been sitting on the small couch in the corner listening to the B.X Bombers discuss everyone's business but their own for the past ten minutes. He couldn't continue hanging around talking about the legends in a room full of music producing equipment that could one day make him a legend in his own rite. "Yo, I'm about to hop in the booth; yall bullshittin'."

"Hold up J3. We bout to finish that *Dance with me* track from last week, I'm trying to find it now." Jeff continued searching through the files on the computer monitor he was seated in front of.

"I gotta get back home my dude. I got a new born and Krish waitin' on me. Yall sittin' up here talking & shit." Junior got up and slid open the soundproof screen door to leave the room. He walked through the guys rolling dice in the hallway and into Money Black's office all the way in the back.

Money Black was seated behind his compact wooden desk with Desree, his *Monday chick* sitting on his lap fondling his diamond chain.

"What's up boy? How's the baby?"

Money Black asked as he pushed his gold toned shades back up his nose. Junior smiled, filled with Fatherly pride, "Lil man good; getting bigger & smarter everyday."

"Good, good." He uttered as he returned a kiss from Desree.

"Yeah, no doubt. Yo Black, I was wondering if I could hop in the booth to lay this verse down before I get out of here."

"Yeah boy; Why somebody in there?" He scooted over in his leather chair and peeked through his black venetian blinds.

"Na, wel-"

"Fucking kids!"

Money Black pounded his fist into the desk, rattling his jewelry. He pushed Desree in her back, "Get up."

He made his way to the engineering room where he invested over 20,000 of his hard earned dollars and interrupted the Bombers' conversation. "Yo what's up, what yall niggas doing in here?"

"We bout to work on them joints from last week."

"Well, what the hell yall waiting for?"

"We tryin-"

"Let this man go in there and do what he need to do. Yall can take that talking shit somewhere else. This is a place for making music, making hits. Go 'head." Money Black directed Junior towards the vocal booth. "Go make me a hit."

"...cause, see GOD, is doing a new thing. Can I get a witness? Amen."

Junior sat with his family with secret optimism that Pastor Redding was somehow referring to his music and the apparent industry shift away from the more hardcore content. He hadn't been praying as much as he liked, but he figured he had to be the only aspiring Rapper sitting in a church right now, and therefore if someone were going to get a record deal surely it should be him.

Moments ago Junior was spaced out, letting his mind ponder on anything but the sermon in front, but the Pastor began to grab his attention once again. Unfortunately, just as Junior starting paying closer attention the choir segued into a musical number and Pastor Redding stopped preaching the word to sing and dance yet again.

"You know, they could've paid me to perform the music." Junior whispered into Lakrisha's ear as they continued clapping in the name of the Lord. Lakrisha smiled at him and continued clapping.

5:49PM; THE SAME DAY

Hollis lifted Anthony from Lakrisha's arm as she saw him smiling at her. "Aw, come here lil man." She secured him and began tickling him with a single finger to his stomach. *"That's my little nephew; yes he is, yes he is.* Say Auntie.*"*

The innocence and sincerity of the baby's laugh filled the living room with the peaceful and relaxing vibe that could only be felt on a Sunday.

"Where yall went, to Alabaster?" Hollis asked Junior who was flopped across the couch.

-"Na, Mt. Holyoke on Madison." Lakrisha spoke in place of her man.

"Oh okay." Hollis took a grape from the fruit bowl on the table; "So what's the word of the day?"

Lakrisha once again decided to do the talking, "He was talking about how GOD is gone be doing a new thing. How all these things is changing around us. Yup…" She sucked her teeth and smoothed her ghetto tone before continuing, "How there might be a Black President soon and people are starting to become more environmentally friendly. You know, like, they be thinking about the planet and that kind a stuff. Yup girl."

Though she didn't show it. Hollis found amusement in the way Lakrisha expressed herself. Hollis' peers at school, her teachers and acquaintances would see someone like Lakrisha as lacking in something or in need of, but she spoke passionately, from her soul and Hollis had a certain admiration for that. Hollis wiped Anthony's mouth and continued to keep him entertained. "You dag on right GOD's doing a new thing."

"You want something to drink?"

"Please."

Lakrisha grabbed her and Junior's cups off the table before she got up and went into the kitchen.

"So how you doing?" Junior asked his Sister before turning down the volume on the preseason football game.

"I'm good, can't complain; getting ready for my senior year."

"That's what's up, bust that out… You heard from your crazy ass Father?"

"Yeah, he been coming around lately."

"Yeah, lately…" Junior tried to speak through a deep yawn and deeper stretch of his upper body; "He working yet?"

"Not that I know of; he still working on his music thing."

"What he think he gone rap and not work for the rest of his life?"

"I can't call it. You know Daddy."

-"Here you go." Lakrisha reentered the room and sat Hollis' drink in a coaster on the table.

"I'm tired as hell."

Junior propped his feet up on the table, turned up the volume on the game and closed his eyes. When he awoke the game was coming back from halftime and the living room was empty. He shut his eyes and continued napping.

11:50PM; THE SAME DAY

More often than not, Junior would get lost in his son's face. Anthony's striking similarities, paralleled with his innocence; he took Junior to another place.

"Look at my lil man. What up?"

Anthony's look shifted from obscurity, on the brink of irritation, to delight as he mumbled to his Father.

-*"What yall doing?"*

"Go to sleep Krish; we chilling, bonding." Junior assured her. Lakrisha turned over and buried her face back into her pillows. Junior quietly took his son into the living room and placed him in his powder blue body pillow on the couch.

"You alright, you good?" He asked Anthony before walking away. The baby responded with a faint, sloppy lip smile that ignited his Father's soul. Junior went to the stereo and played his disk of instrumentals and tried to find the right words to rhyme as he watched his son watching him.

"I got us little man, you hear me? I'm a make this happen for us. You not gone have to grow up like I did."

12:02PM; THE NEXT DAY

Red Out trotted fiercely in his loose white tank top and Cincinnati Reds fitted toward the *New City* Parking Lot trailer. His red bandanna and gold chain flew through the humid city air as he made his way. Junior seen him through the window and figured he just came from Court on State Street although he didn't remember him catching any cases in Brooklyn.

"Yo son…" Red Out put out his hand for Junior to dap. "Rhyme & Reason, them hood DVD series niggas; they want you to battle the boy Danger Manger for *Tear the Streets Up* part two." Red Out looked into Junior's surprised face and urged him on; "This could be your ticket fam'."

"Shit, I'm wit' it. When they trying to do it?"

"Now nigga!"

"Now?"

"Now!"

"I'm not ready now. I don't really got no battle raps ready like that."

"My dude, Danger Manger is on his way to the 125th right now. This is a one time offer baby. So if you serious about trying to get on, we need to get uptown to give that man the business."

2:41 PM; THE SAME DAY

"I got bars & I spit em all day like outfielders. In the club deep with the thugs & drug dealers, knife wielders. This boy can't be serious, must be delirious, you cats' squealers, burn your whiskers with the 4-5th. A southern player, diamonds accent my tee like a tilda. Your girl's a horse, Mr. Ed wouldn't grill her. Go 'head sonny before I put your body in your borough, an A.T.L.ien punk, they breed us to be thorough."

The crowd in front of the Magic Johnson Theater was warmed up; some of them hyped up off Danger Manger's verse, some of them weren't moved. The Yung City Boyz crew members slapped each other fives after their headman finished his verse, confident they were taking the crown back down south. Even with the hometown support Danger Manger won the first round. Junior stepped up through the live Harlem crowd and ended the battle.

"...Nigga I'm a N.Y.C banger, microphone cord strangler, wild beast tamer, fuck a nigga named Manger. J3 is eminent danger, you the lamest

of the wanksters. You nameless & a faker, spit
out my razor to shank ya; or click back & bang
ya', send flames at you strangers. Soon enough,
I'll fill Madison Square Garden like the
Rangers. Rearrange ya face like a banger; it's
time I eat your food. This that Northern
hospitality, so pardon the man for being rude.
Never stay in a spot for too long, I'm too strong,
my crew swarm. Not lukewarm, that sucker shit
that you on. I could've just shot you cowards
instead of the Nuke-bomb but yall children gotta
learn. Boy get back in line, it aint your turn."

9:59PM; THE SAME NIGHT

"Yo, I ripped him baby! I'm telling you,
straight ripped him."

Lakrisha smiled, visibly happy that her man was
so happy. She rubbed his shoulders; now
giving half of her attention to a text message that
came through on her phone.

"When I finished my verse the crowd went
crazy, like *oooooh J3 the truth* and all that."

The weather was beginning to change. Junior
was wearing a navy blue hooded sweater and
Lakrisha was keeping warm with a light Baby
Phat jacket. Junior pulled her toward him and
she descended onto his lap resting her head on
the back of one of her hands. He nodded toward
her phone, "Who you was talking to?"

"Amanda; she said Anthony just went to sleep."

Junior now understood why she finally allowed herself to relax and kick her feet up.

"I'm telling you baby, when this rap shit take off, we gone live the good life. We gone get married & all that. Watch…"

Lakrisha remained silent for a Moment before looking up at him with a higher level of sincerity, "When's the last time we came down here Jay?"

"I don't know… We was still in High School-"

"Sophomore year!"

Junior was taken aback by her holler. She busted out laughing, amused at his apprehension. "Sorry."

"You need to calm the hell down. I swear, you need Ritalin some times."

"No but listen…" Lakrisha tried to speak through her schoolgirl laughter; "I know cause I remember when I got to school the next day Mrs. Stockton was riding my ass for not being in P.M homeroom. Cause we cut half of that day."

"Yeah you right." Junior concurred while staring off into Harlem. "Mrs. Stockton, wit' her crazy ass. I remember she used to tell me damn near everyday that I wasn't gone be shit in life."

"Jayson Jordan Junior!" Lakrisha mocked her and Junior's Jamaican homeroom teacher; *"Jayson Jordan Junior, stop rapping in my classroom! Ya don't have nothin' better to do wit' your brain young man?"*

The couple enjoyed a good laugh. Junior admired the fact that after six years of companionship he and Lakrisha could still joke around. Not many things could lighten his mood nowadays; life had taken on a new level of reality since Anthony was born. Junior looked down at his lady and caressed the top of her head and they continued to sit and mutually reminisce.

In High School, Junior's friends often called Lakrisha out her name behind her back, due to her reputation. A reputation which after Junior got to know her, he discovered was ill deserved. Today she was Junior's partner, hand in hand in the most important task of either of their lives, raising their son. She was family; Junior could no longer look at her without somehow seeing himself.

"I see you ain't having no problems fitting into your old clothes." Junior said as he rubbed the palm of his hand along her denim covered thighs.

"You like that?" She asked as she reached up and rubbed his face.

Out of nowhere Junior asked, "Why we need a ring to get married baby?"

"Who said we needed a ring? I told you we could've gone to City Hall last year Junior."

He remained without a response as he did vividly recall. Lakrisha didn't let him off the hook so easily, "What you forgot?" She inquired with a mild roll of her neck at him.

"Na…" Junior admitted, "I do think I remember you saying something to that."

"Mm hmm…Yall men wanna put all that extra shit on yourselves to satisfy yall own egos sometime. I'm a simple chick; I 'on't need much. I don't need much at all."

"I hear that." Junior brandished a proud smirk, as if he was particularly pleased with her this evening. He dropped his head back and continued to take in the quieter side of Harlem.

"We can do it right now." Lakrisha boldly reinforced her statement; "We should do it now."

"Do what?"

"Get married."

"What you mean right now? We don't have rings, vowels, no Pastor, nothing."

"We got everything." She rose from his lap and straightened out her clothes. "Marriage is a union before GOD. We don't need none of that stuff. You a Rapper, you can't bust out some vowels off the top of your head?"

Junior laughed aloud, "You serious?"

She didn't respond, and she didn't break eye contact with him.

"Aight...Aight."

Lakrisha took him by the hand and the couple strolled along one of Mt. Morris Park' many walking paths. She seemed to be glowing every step of the way. This is the park where as High School sweethearts they used to stop at before Junior walked her back to her old apartment on 117th street after school. They were ascending up a hill to which an old Fire Department memorial statue stood; the place where they shared their first kiss. Lakrisha looked to the sky and examined it as if she were trying to locate a particular point. She turned around still searching, "…There it is." She pointed out the bright, full moon that seemed to be looming over Fifth Avenue.

"I'll take my vowels under the moon tonight. You can take yours' tomorrow under the sun… You ready?"

"So, just you going tonight?"

"Yeah," Lakrisha flashed her pearly whites, "Since you're such a punk."

"Okay. Cool."

"Okay... GOD…" She turned back to the moon. "Please understand that I love this man and that I would do anything for him." She looked Junior in his eyes, no longer smiling, "He has given me the greatest gift that I could ever receive in the birth of my son. I…" Her cool and collectiveness escaped her and she began to shed tears, "I am proud of the sort of man that he has become. He's come along way from finger popping girls in the hallway, and cutting class with his boys everyday."

Junior busted out laughing, "You can't say that in front of GOD."

"Why not, you think he don't know?"

Somewhere in Junior's face and gestures Lakrisha saw that he got the point.

"Anyway…"

She turned back to the heavens; "GOD I pray that you strengthen us a unit. I ask that you keep our hearts open and our minds clean; that you may see us through tough times, and guide us as a family to peace and happiness." She took a deep breath and hung her head as if humbled before her Lord. She kept her eyes to the earth beneath, "Please accept my promise to love him in sickness and health, for richer or for poorer, till death do us part. Amen."

Junior noticed the tender changes in her face and he reached out for his best friend. She broke out in tears the instant he wrapped his arms around her. He embraced her as he looked up to the sky where Lakrisha put forth her declaration of love. While caressing her, he mentally reexamined the old adage that GOD doesn't put anything on one's shoulders that they can't handle. He snuck a peep at the moon. *Damn, now I got a wife?*

When they got home, Amanda, the baby sitter, was asleep on the couch with the baby lying on her chest. Lakrisha situated Anthony in his crib and Junior paid Amanda before escorting her out. Lakrisha went in the bathroom to wash up. When she came out she lit an aromatherapy candle and climbed on Junior, reminding him where home was and how that came to be before riding him to sleep.

6:56AM; THE NEXT MORNING

"Good morning."

Junior greeted Lakrisha who was sitting at the kitchen table breastfeeding Anthony.

"What's up baby?"

Junior leaned over the back of her chair and planted a kiss on her cheek then headed for the fridge.

"I'm about to put on a pot of grits."

"Na, don't even worry about it." He shut the fridge and grabbed an apple off of the table. "I gotta handle some business this morning before I go to work."

Lakrisha laid the baby across her shoulder to burp him. "Wasn't you supposed to do something else this morning?" She asked as she patted Anthony on his back.

"What? Oh that's right…"

Junior darted to the back of the apartment to get his *New City Parking* jacket. "I have to pay that traffic ticket today. Shit!" He ran back over to Lakrisha and gave her another kiss and one for the baby. *"Yo baby I gotta talk to you later too. I'm thinking about tagging on to my Father's tour sometime next month as the opening act. But I got a run, I'm a call you."*

Junior squeezed the green softball in his hand with all his might before launching it back off the trailer wall. He had so much he wanted to confide in his friend, so much was running through his head, but there was nothing left to say. Junior knew he was going to have to start doing. He squeezed the softball again and fired it out the door.

"I'm about to go super hard at this music shit fam. I got a kid, and I'm *married*!" Junior added as if he forgot.

Red Out laughed and continued skimming through the We Got Next Magazine in his hand.

"Word, ain't trying to be no Al Bundy ass nigga."

Although he wasn't in a joking mood Junior chuckled. Red Out flipped through his magazine and checked out an eye catching ad before handing the Hip-Hop periodical to Junior; "Didn't you say you was thinking about linking up with them?"

"Who that?" Junior asked as he read the full page advertisement.

New York City Music Cartel

2ND INFANTRY TOUR

FALL 2006

www.ONTHEBOOKSENT.com

"I know you don't fuck with him like that, but call him...See what's up."

"Yeah, yeah, I think I'm a do that."

Red Out handed Junior his cell phone, as he knew he didn't have any daytime minutes on his. "Go 'head."

"Right now?"

"Yes nigga, now. What is it with you and later?"

Junior took the phone and removed his own phone from his pocket to access his Father's number.

"Damn that Beamer is sick. Check that out."

Red Out said to Marven who was returning from parking a car in the back row. Junior stuck a finger in his left ear and stood from his seat. *"What up Pops?"*

He hopped from the trailer to the ground in search of privacy only to look up and see a customer who'd just parked in the far side of the Lot. *"Yo Red, stamp a ticket for me please."*

Red Out slid a parking pass through the time stamp on the desk. "I'm a have your boss put me on payroll, as much as I be in here doing your job."

"Good lookin' out." He snatched the ticket from Red Put and handed it to the customer giving each thing he was doing about half of his attention. "Here you go sir."

The gentleman grilled Junior before walking away as if dissatisfied with his service; Junior wasn't concerned in the least.

"...Chillin' man, working my ass off trying to get by. I'm still trying to get this demo together..."

Business was beginning to pick up at the Lot. Another car pulled in and Marven had just gone on his break.

"...He's doing good man, doing real good. Getting bigger everyday..." Junior remained on the phone as the customer who just pulled in got his briefcase together in his seat.

"...That's actually what I wanted to talk to you about. I see yall doing a second tour. Can, or rather, do you have room for another emcee?"

The patron stepped out from his car and a tall blonde woman in a black skirt emerged from the passenger side.

"Here you go sir."

Junior handed the man his ticket then focused back on his conversation. *"How much can you commit to paying me? Yo hold on one sec Pops."* Junior yelled at the odd couple headed for the State Street exit, *"You want it washed?"*

"No, I don't want it washed. Just park it!"

Junior could see Red Out laughing at him in the trailer door.

-*"Yeah Pops, that sounds good. Right now I just need a chance. We having a hard time making ends meet. So I'm a call you later to work everything out."* Junior flipped the phone close and headed back to the office.

"That nigga played you." Red Out said from his chair in front of the entrance. Junior eye-balled the man through the fence surrounding the Lot; "Fucking faggots gone wanna talk to me soon enough."

"What happen?"

"What you mean, what happen, you ain't hear him try to talk down to me? *Just park it.*"

"Genius, what your Father say? I ain't thinking bout them."

"Oh, It's a go. I'm going on tour."

11:59PM; THE SAME NIGHT

Lakrisha's arms were folded with attitude, staring at Junior as if she was prepared to pounce on him.

172

"Junior I don't think you should be leaving me and the baby right now. I think this can wait."

Junior stood his ground, although he couldn't maintain consistent eye contact with her for some reason. "It can't baby. I need to do this. I feel like less then a fucking man right now. When we go out, all I see is prices; gas, food, if we get desert we can't do something else. I can't live like this! I'm not happy."

"That's just how it is Junior, you can't have it all!"

"Fuck that!" He hollered over her, waking the baby. "I'm not trying to hear that. I'm going, I'm gone a go try. If I fail, I'll be back home. If I succeed..." Junior grabbed both of his wife's hands in attempt to reassure her, "I'll be back home."

168

*"Hurry up. I'm a business woman; I got
things to do, thank you."*

Date: September 9TH 2006

The sun was on the verge of setting. Junior's
pants were beginning to saturate. He tried to
maneuver his umbrella to block as much of the
downpour as possible. He looked over to Stump
who was fully focused on what Junior knew not.
Junior had gotten uncomfortable being the only
person in the entourage asking so many
questions in the week that he'd been aboard, so
he kept his mouth shut and continued to protect
him and Laronda from the rain.

"There it go." Stump said.

"There what go?"

-"Let's go."

Laronda grabbed Junior by his shirt sleeve and
pulled him off the curb to the courtyard of the
Motel across the street. Stump waited outside
while Laronda and Junior went inside.

*"Hi, I have reservations under Ms. Theresa
Byrd."*

Junior casually looked through the heavily reinforced glass that the clerk was behind, then around the office. He spotted a security camera in the upper right corner and stared into the lens Momentarily. He looked into the black car outside at Stacky who was looking back at him through the windshield. It was then that Junior realized that he hadn't seen Buck or Flo in two days.

The clerk dropped a pair of access cards in a single envelop under the opening of his protective shield. *"Come on."* Laronda snatched him yet again. They made their way through the propped exit door to the staircase and up to the second floor. They then walked the entire length of the corridor without exchanging a word. Laronda stopped in front of the last door on the left hand side.

219

She unlocked the door and held it open for Junior. "Wait in here."

8:52PM; THE SAME NIGHT

Junior rolled his lanky body around on the king sized bed. The room had grown completely dark as the sun had set and he fell asleep without lights or the television on. His eyes had trouble adjusting to the high glare from the doorway.

He could make out Force's large body, his Father by his thick, abstract dreads, and Laronda to Jason's right. Junior blocked his face from the light, still trying to shake his slumber.

"Let's go."

2:45AM; THE SAME NIGHT

The three car entourage sped down the 95 Interstate South Carolina bound. Although he was dead tired, Junior couldn't sleep with so much going on around him. There was road kill seemingly every mile of the way. EPMD was blasting from the system; Stump was in the front seat with a pen to his book of rhymes.

"Yo Pops, what's up with this mysterious, mob type shit we on? I feel like I'm ducking the Feds here."

Laronda laughed, still controlling the wheel, navigating through the heavy tropical storm. Stump turned around grinning at Jason who kept his eyes in his Qur'an as if he had no intent of answering Junior's question.

"Hello?"

Jason closed his book using his fingers as a page marker and addressed him, "Hip-Hop task force is on our asses."

"What, why?"

"Forget *why*, all that matters is that they are. Don't worry, you gone be aight though."

-"Excuse your Father Junior." Laronda interjected looking at Junior through the rear view mirror. "He's looking for something and he don't know that he don't have to be such a dick about things in the meantime."

Junior didn't quite understand what she was talking about but he smiled along anyway. Jason looked at Laronda who stuck her tongue out at him from the front seat.

"Anyway, you ready to rock the mic boy?" Jason asked his son as he lightened his mood.

"Yeah; I was born ready."

"Good, cause you going on stage tonight at Club Dodges."

"Tonight?"

"Well, it's after midnight, so…yeah. You ready right?"

"Yeah, I, I guess, I mean a never did a show bef-"

"You better be ready kid. This ain't Motown, we do things a little differently around here."

11:20PM: THE NEXT DAY

Junior had been pacing to and fro backstage since Architekk began spitting the first few lines from the last verse of his new single to the crowd. He and Force were the only crew members not on stage. Buck sang along with Tekk at his leisure, as he drifted from point to point hyping the crowd. Junior cracked a smile watching his Father and Laronda grind on one another as she sang the closing hook. Tekk wrapped one of his perspiring arms around her as she capped the song with a note that the S.C. locals were sure to remember. Stump faded the beat and yelled into his microphone. *"Yeah, yeah that's what it is Columbus. Now check this out, I got my homie straight out the B.X coming to the stage; he murdering the mix tape game in N.Y.C right now. I want yall to show some love. Put ya hands together for my man, J3!"*

3:12AM; THE SAME NIGHT

Junior walked with Laronda to the front desk as the rest of the entourage waited in the large, lavish, International Inn Lobby.

178

"Hi, my name is Laronda Williams; I have reservations for the New York C.M.C Music Group."

Junior squinted in curiosity, as he'd never heard N.Y.C.M.C referred to in that manner. He could hear Laronda using her out of Harlem voice, yet and still, he noticed a genuine change in her. She hadn't been dressing as flashy as he usually saw her. She seemed bright-eyed and bushy tailed and was bending over backwards to help his Father with whatever he needed.

"Yes, please right this way."

The elevator was filled to capacity. Junior felt his phone vibrate in his pocket but couldn't answer it as he was squashed between Buck and a young lady he never met before. Stacky and Margo were tipsy off the champagne they'd been popping since back in the dressing room at Dodges. Junior noticed Stacky staring rudely at the Concierge as the elevator made its way to the top floor. *"Yo what's your name homie?"*

"Mr. James Alexander." The bagman responded with a distinct level of professionalism.

"J.A!" Margo shouted in a drunken abruptness.

-*"Like Jamaica."* An inebriated blonde who followed the crew from the Club threw in her two cents.

-*"Like Jah!"* Buck tagged along for the hell of it.

-*"Lord a mercy!"*

"You Jamaican my nigga?"

The entire elevator saturated with laughter at Mr. Alexander's expense

Ding

The Concierge was clearly uncomfortable being the but of the group's jokes and was saved by the elevator bell. "Ah here we are; the top floor."

The elevator went up and down several times over the next few minutes, dropping party people off to the Royal suite. The Hotel room had become nearly as energetic and loud as the club they'd just left.

3:53AM; THE SAME NIGHT

"Damn shorty, your accent is crazy heavy. Where you from?"

"Richmond Kentucky." The young lady smiled at Stacky holding her champagne flute near her chest with a certain hint of elegance.

"Damn, they producing asses like that in Kentucky?" Stacky asked rhetorically as he peeked at the mound of flesh behind her. He turned to Buck, "That's official tissue. We need to get a couple of cribs down south. Get that exclusive access, ya dig?"

Buck switched the hand he was holding his bottle of vodka in and grabbed a handful of the girl's behind. "What yall doing out here baby?"

She laughed, "Ooo, you got strong hands." She looked at Buck as if she was feeling him, feeling her. She grabbed her friend by her shoulders; "Me and my girls heading to Myrtle Beach tomorrow. Why, yall trying to do something?"

Junior watched from across the room on the sofa as Buck and Stacky walked into a private room with their company. He continued pretending to listen to Com who was sitting beside him.

"...I maxed out on a five to fifteen. Seen parole, got a thirty two month bid, fucked that up; kept shankin' niggas..."

Junior shook his head, barely following Com's line of discussion. He took another sip of

Johnny Walker Red and allowed Com to finish venting.

"...seen Parole again! They said, *inmate has not deterred criminal behavior; inmate has a likelihood to commit the same offense.* I ended up maxing out."

Junior excused himself and walked across the room to the balcony where he figured he was sure to find some Junior time. He rested his forearms on the metal railing and looked out into the night as he contemplated on what Lakrisha and Anthony were doing. A feeling of a deep void crept out from his soul and he hung his head. He wondered how long it would be before he was back home completing the balance in his family, how long before he got the capital he was in search of. He pulled out his cell phone and scrolled through the pictures Lakrisha sent him from her and the baby's outing to Central Park last weekend.

"You miss them huh?"

Junior turned, shocked to see his Father standing behind him.

"Yeah..." He wanted to formulate a more elaborate response to convey just how much his family meant to him, but he was still trying to figure out how he didn't hear Jason walk up.

Jason shut the screen door behind him with great ease and joined Junior overlooking the city.

"Did you miss us all that time you were gone?"

Jason looked down on to busy International Boulevard emotionless. Junior wasn't sure if he heard him or if he just wasn't going to answer his question. He looked at his Father with a hint of compassion, as if he regretted possibly hurting his feelings, "I mean-"

"You don't think I missed you?"

Junior looked away, "Well then why'd you leave?"

"I ain't leave you! Your Mother took you and she left me." Jason said, hardening his face and squeezing his fist. Junior could see he hit a nerve, but he still had questions that needed answers and he pushed the issue. "And forget all that, what about Gwinn? She's growing up with out a Father. That shit ain't cool."

"...It ain't, it ain't...Gwinn is special, she represents when I started trying wit' this whole life shit. I seen you and Honey; you was my little man and that was my little lady... But the world just enveloped yall; it was like, I didn't stand a Motherfucking chance. In the Hospital, there was all these people, pulling you here, taking you there, telling you this shit... Then we got home and there was more Motherfuckers there, and it was like somehow someway, that shit never stopped; the enemy got to you."

Jason looked sharply in another direction as if he were summoned by something Junior could not see. Junior looked in his face and could tell that he was speaking sincerely as he continued. "They wanted you to wear this damn hat, or watch this fucking cartoon. It's like what the fuck? Miserable, unhappy, misguided, all sorts of Motherfuckers, each with their own set of problems, gone try to put you on a path?" Jason employed his hands to further articulate himself; "So if you go this way, you have high blood pressure and...I don't know; you're socially withdrawn. And if you go that way, then you get so much pussy that it destroys your life, and...I don't know, you develop a drug addiction...You gone have this problem or you gone have that problem, you need Allah. That's who you need first, last and always. And it would've been easier to prove that to you the younger you were. Cause now you need proof, all three of yall. Even though the proof is all around you, you still need more ill shit to happen for you to believe."

"Come on," Junior smudged his face, irritated, "What you talking about? How you know that?"

"Cause yo' ass don't put the Lord first. When was the last time you gave thanks, prostrated yourself or gave something to someone less fortunate than you?"

Jason could see his son transcending into a state to which he was only waiting to talk and not listening but he continued to speak over him.

"I don't need to ask those questions." Jason said waving Junior's pending statements off. "I was you. I been were you are. And I wasn't going to bend with Gwinn, I wanted to do certain things with her as a Father, and I was wrong according to your Mother, according to your Grand Father and everyone else that yall swear love yall so fucking much. Them niggas don't love you as much as you think. They're mostly infatuated with the possibility of having another stupid ass, little them running around; misery always did love company." Jason laughed to himself and shook his dreads out with a wiggle of his head. "Shit, you judging me, why'd you leave your family?"

Junior responded quickly and defensively, "That's a completely different situation. I left in search of a better living for us, so my wife and kid could have nice things and we could go to nice places and shit. And I'm going right back. I aint leave cause-"

"Well what the fuck you think I was in search of?"

Junior turned around to the party unfolding behind him. "Looks like you was messing around with your music-"

"Come on son; don't be like the ignorant, who can't see something that's right before their eyes."

Jason said as he turned away in an emotional state that Junior hadn't seen in years. "The music was my particular path son; it made me free and gave me independence. How could I have been a good Father to you without being my own man and having piece of mind, having to depend on other men for my livelihood?"

Junior shrugged his shoulders, not looking to entertain his Father's superficially deep logic any further. He took the seat behind him and hunched over onto himself; "I'm not trying to hear all of that Pops, you should've been there for Gwinn. I don't care."

"You right. You are right... But life is long kid. I'm here now, when you needed me. And I'm a be there for my Daughter, trust me on that. GOD got a path for her life and it's gone run through me in some form at some point. She just gotta decide if she fuck with GOD."

186

Junior's frustrations toppled; his Mother's issues with his Dad started to make more sense as he listened to his Father ramble. "What the hell does GOD have to do with you; what you think you some kind of prophet?"

Laronda opened the screen door and stuck her head through. "Babe come here, I want to introduce you to Max from Wreck House Records. He's very interested in meeting you."

OCTOBER 1ST 2006

But things just get so crazy livin', life get hard to do...

The crew was heading to Jacksonville to kick off a Florida campaign of shows, in store signings and fun in the sun, beginning with a street festival this Wednesday. Maroon 5 was grooving from the speakers as per Jason's request who was sitting next to Junior in the backseat flipping through a folder of documents.

And I would gladly hit the road get up & go if I knew... that someday it would lead me back to you... that someday it would lead me back to you...

187

"You sent Lakrisha money this week?" Jason asked Junior who was checking out the scenery out his window.

"Na, I'm a send her something out the show money from Wednesday though."

Jason reached in his pocket and pull out a wad of manicured bills. He gave Junior $350; "Tell her to give a little something to your Mother out of that."

- *"Ain't this about a bitch!"*

Junior looked at Laronda puzzled. Jason turned around to look out the rear window then shoved all the documents on his lap in the leather briefcase open between his legs. "Don't worry bout it sweetie, we clean right now. What the hell they gone do, give us a ticket?"

Margo sped up, getting parallel with their rented Honda. Laronda rolled down her window.

"What you want me to do?" Margo yelled from the other traffic lane.

Jason scooted up and pointed forward and Margo pulled in front of them. Junior turned to locate Stack and Flo's cars but the flashing lights from the Police cruiser rattled his nerves and he turned back quickly.

"When the last time yall been to church?" Jason folded one of his legs over the other and looked directly at Junior.

"What?"

"We're going to go to Church after this."

- *"Church?"* Laronda asked via the rearview mirror as she pulled the car to the shoulder of the highway.

"The Holy Qur'an instructs that the Christians are among our closet friends. We should go see what they up to."

- *"May I see your license and registration please?"*

Laronda already had her paperwork in her hand, she handed it to the Officer outside her window.

"You know those guys?" The Officer asked pointing to Margo and Stacky's cars parked a few yards ahead of them.

"Yeah; those my peoples."

"Why'd they pull over?"

"Cause we don't play that. What'd you pull me over for Officer?"

"I'll be right back-" He looked down at her license, "Ms. Drexel. I just want to make sure all your information is okay."

"Okay hurry up please. I'm a business woman I got things to do, thank you."

As the Officer turned to walk away he caught a glance of Junior looking at him and Jason on his cell phone. "And who are those guys? And why are both of them sitting in the back?"

"That's my Imam." Laronda responded with her usual sharpness.

"You're Imam?" He questioned. "You're a Muslim?"

"Yes, and I don't want you causing him any trouble. He has a tremendous workload."

The Officer looked down at Jason's briefcase then at the black and gold Qur'an to his side. He looked up the road at Stacky's European luxury car and Margo and Com's ever watchful eyes. "Here." He shoved her documents back through the window. "Start using your turning signal please; this ain't New York girl." He took one last look at the Dread. "Yall have a nice day."

11:27 AM; THE SAME DAY

"I don't believe this nigga got me in church."

"You can't say nigga in church, nigga. Aw we going to hell." Junior slapped his head in confusion; in the process he removed his hat. He saw his Father who was ahead of them with Laronda remove the turban on his head for the first time in over three days. His long, deep brown hair fell freely to either side, somehow making Junior more uncomfortable entering the Lord's house with his present company.

"...And they brought the woman before Jesus, and they told him! This woman has been accused of adultery; that's a crime punishable by death! Under Mosaic law this woman had to be stoned to death!"

The small congregation was gathered in near silence, tuned in to the Pastor. Junior smiled affably with the people who stared at him as he walked along the far left aisle in search of a place to sit. Laronda's cell phone ringer ripped through the air, as it was necessary for her to lower her alert to vibrate, which she did before stuffing the phone back into her Roc-a-Wear purse. *"Sorry."*

Junior could hear her as she turned to his Father, *"They act like they ready to kill us."*

191

"..And Jesus said; let him who is without sin cast the first stone. And the people around him were touched by their own conscience; they were so awaken by this man's words that they all left..."

Junior took a seat next to Stacky and Buck. He lowered his phone alert as well before giving the Pastor his full attention. Stacky raised the two rose gold pendants draped from his neck and dropped them on the other side of his Champion sweater. Margo and Com had taken seats somewhere on the right hand side of the church.

"Did you people come here for service?" The Pastor interrupted the service to address the Hip-Hop foreigners.

"You people?"

-*"You people?"*

"We know where we are Reverend." Jason responded on behalf of the group before locking bitter eyes with the Pastor.

The Pastor filled with a sort of elderly pride and toughness, *"Anyhow, as I was saying; whatever it is that you're looking for, whatever you desire in life, Jesus will provide for you. He has provided time after time without a single failure. Jesus is the-"*

-"GOD!"

The Pastor stopped and looked at Jason who interrupted yet again. "I'm sorry..." He leaned over his podium with a sharp arrogance, "Do you have a problem son?"

"I'm not your son. I was simply correcting you Brother. You said Jesus will provide. I think you meant to say GOD. This is a house of GOD right; all praise be to He?"

Laronda and Stump had visible trouble containing their laughter. Junior buried his face in his hands with hopes that he could just disappear.

"Yeah, yeah that's what I thought too." Margo yelled from the very last row on the right.

"Son, I think it would be best for you and your entourage to excuse yourselves if you came here looking for trouble."

"I'm sorry Rev, I didn't come here looking for trouble. I apologize. I'll be quiet, sorry about that. Go 'head."

One could feel the vibe in the church disturbed; the congregation began whispering among themselves. The Pastor looked into his Holy Bible, which seemed to provide him with the patience he needed to continue to address his followers. After a brief meditative pause, the word went forth.

"When Jesus comes with the power, he will never fail! *He will save you, he will show you the error in your ways, and help to make you a better Mother, a better Father..."*

Junior's heartbeat skipped as his cell phone rang. He was near certain that he switched his alert to vibrate. With the instinct and precision of a Ninja he pulled the phone from its holster and rejected the call, stopping the alert after only a single low toned ring, which no one seemed to notice.

"...See that's because Jesus has power over all things..."

Jason turned to a woman in his pew with a baffled look across his face; "Why does he keep saying Jesus?"

"Oh would you get out of here." The woman said aloud, highly aggravated.

"Young man how bout we do this..." The Preacher man removed his reading glasses and looked at Jason with a rejuvenated cool, "How about you come up here and preach the word

since you can't seem to stop running your mouth in my Church."

Without a second thought Jason clapped his hands and stood to his feet. "Great." He was eager to relieve the elder Preacher who was visibly surprised by his acceptance. When he got to the elevated podium he addressed the people in a somewhat playful mood. "Alright; peace guys!" He raised his right hand smiling like a child. All the N.Y.C.M.C members seemed delighted to see Architekk at the helm save for Junior who wanted no parts of this.

"Alright who in here knows GOD, hmm?" Jason rubbed the palms of his hands together in exceeding confidence before grabbing either side of the wooden podium, aligning himself with the microphone. *"Alright, well I know him; that's my Father. And before I begin, I'm a raise my hand to the sky and ask that my Father please accept this offering, and if I should be so stupid as to lead these people astray, you can go on and take my life right here and now; no sense in procrastinating..."*

There was something in his presence, in his swagger, his glow, that commanded attention. *"...Your Father loves you. But you got a understand that he also loves the person next to you as well. Like, how dare you, when I come to my Father's house, where his children are*

*gathered, supposedly in his name, look at me
and my people some kind of way. Some of my
friends ain't been to church in years, and I
bring them here and yall wanna judge. What if
we wasn't strong enough to handle that?"* Jason
grabbed the mic and began walking along the
stage. *"What if we didn't know GOD and know
that we are welcomed, then what? Then back to
the world we go, to spread mischief; further
astray. That's sowing bad seeds in the earth...
And we all know that we reap what we sow,
right?"* He shook his head concurring with
himself, *"Right?"* He turned to the Pastor, *"So
you cast the first stone, I guess that means you
all are the ones without sin. But luckily, we
ain't even come here to get into all that.
Fortunately for you, we came here in the name
of peace."* Jason said holding his hands out
defenselessly. *"We come bring glad tidings,
truth, and the courageous word of victory to
GOD's beautiful children. My Father is doing a
new thing. Your days of praising men, exalting
men as if they were GOD simply because you
need something you can see to praise, because
of the shakiness in your faith... Your days of
ascribing belittling falsehoods, and demeaning,
demeaning accusations to my Lord! Your days
of hypocrisy and secretly trying to save your
own asses, your days of misused collection plate
funds, your hoard of wealth and greed, getting
fat for the sake of getting fat, mismanagement of
natural resources, mistreatment of woman and*

*children, your days of consuming without
producing is done!"*

The Pastor stood up, *"That's enough!"*

*"My Father has many seeds in the field, and you
can't frustrate his plan in the least. It's chess
not checkers-"*

The Pastor covered the microphone. Jason
looked down at him and smiled as he stepped
down from the alter and up the center aisle, out
of the Church.

Music and free spirits dominated the
atmosphere. Junior stopped jolting to either side
and leaned against the wall behind him to let the
girl he was dancing with do her thing. He
peeped beneath the opening of her gold blouse
and examined her smooth brown skin. She
turned to face him and wrapped her arms around
his shoulders while grinding into his midsection.
They indulged in a lingering stare before Junior
noticed tense commotion at the bar off to the
right.

Junior saw Stacky turn his Yankee fitted to the
back and was certain he could read his lips from
across the room; *what's up nigga?* Stacky was
trying to push his way through a group of people

who were holding him back. *"What up then nigga?"*

Junior pushed his dance partner to the side and tried to make his way through the dense crowd. The man that Stacky was jawing off with was being suppressed between two bar stools. Junior had to walk down a small set of stairs to get to Stacky, who had no backup from what he could see. He tried to sneak around a couple dancing just before the stairs as the tension in the Club rose.

"Yo fuck that!"

Stacky tossed the people in front of him to the side and lunged a punch into his counterparts face, kindling what seemed like the beginning of anarchy.

"Oh shit somebody got a gun!"

People ran frantically. Junior was trampled by a group of ladies on the stairs who were scrambling to get out of harms way and were pushed aside by other fleeing guest looking to do the same. Junior lost his footing and fell along with countless others down the stairs. He got up quickly as to avoid being crushed, and tried to stabilize himself. He reached down to pick up his phone, which he dropped on the floor, and he saw who he assumed was Stacky run past him up the stairs. A group of guys all in white t-shirts pursued.

A separate altercation broke out near the bathroom sending security into an uproar. Junior finally spotted his team near one of the Bars by their matching Yankee hats and leather jackets. He ran up to Force and Jason. *"Yo they chasing Stacky!"* Junior said pressed for air. *"They went that way!"*

They all headed for the exit searching for Stacky. More isolated fights broke out all over the place. Police arrived and fired rounds of pepper spray inside, sending people storming out. Minute after unsuccessful minute of searching around outside, and after a slew of phone calls, they still hadn't located Stacky.

"Yo you sure you seen them leave the Club?"

Jason asked Junior with his eyes scowling through the multitude of people.

"Yeah."

"You positive he not still in there?"

"Yes." He insisted.

After several more Moments Margo purposed to go wait by Stacky's car, knowing that if things

got too crazy he would be sure to head for his
trunk. They made their way to Stacky's new
Saab parked a few blocks away on a quiet side
street. Laronda took Margo's jeep and waited in
front of the Club in case Stacky showed up
there.

"Where the fuck he at?" Buck asked no one in
particular as Stacky's phone went to voicemail
yet again.

Fresh out of ideas, they stood in cluelessness
until a beep from Stacky's alarm system broke
the silence. All eyes turned to the car; the head
and tail lights flashed and one could hear the
latch for the trunk release. Junior looked over to
his Father who just turned away from looking at
him and was now focusing in the direction
where commotion was building.

"Come here Motherfucker!"

-*"Catch that nigga Moe!"*

Stacky darted around the building on the corner
moving as fast as he could. A split second later,
a short heavyset thug in a white t-shirt appeared,
chasing Stacky with all his might with a broken
bottle in his hand. As if he could feel him
closing in, Stacky turned around and threw his
hands up, tagging the man several times with

jabs and weaving his malicious stabbing attempts.

"Fuck him up Stack; that's right!" Margo said as they made their way over from the middle of the street.

"Yeah what's up? Harlem style, bitch."

- *"They right there!"*

Junior took a few steps and peaked around the corner that Stacky emerged from. *"Oh shit!"*

Heavy gunshots ripped through the air. Junior ran and ducked behind an old Buick parked beside Stacky's car. Force pulled his large handgun on the army of advancing, pissed off locals and began firing back. Junior could hear at least two other handguns bussing off and his body froze from the unfolding events. He snuck to the front of the car he was using as a shield and cringed to the earth. From his new position Junior could see his Father reach into Stacky's trunk and pulled out a shotgun.

"Oh GOD!"

More gunfire ensued. Junior peeked around the car to confirm the safety of his location and saw Stacky's body lying dead in street; his eyes were open and a stream of blood flew from the side of his mouth. Junior shed desperate tears as he didn't see any realistic way he was going to walk away alive. Jason was firing his weapon just a few feet away; each distinct round shook the ground to which they stood. Margo was shooting rapidly from across the street, shots were being returned at the same pace. Junior decided that he was going to take off and run, until automatic rounds stopped him and everyone in his range of sight dead in their tracks. Margo's Durango screeched its way around the corner, stopping just before the car Junior was hiding behind.

"Get in!" Laronda hollered as she frantically waived him to her. *"Get the fuck in!"*

OCTOBER 25TH 2006

"...I ain't sign up to do this by myself Junior. I don't never get no sleep, I always feel alone."

"Well you ain't gotta worry about that much longer. I'm bringing my black ass the fuck home."

"For real?" Lakrisha asked considerably surprised.

Although they were on the phone, Junior knew exactly what she looked like, and what expression she brandished across her face. He opened the bathroom door to make sure no one came back into the room then he shut the door again. *"Yeah; I'll be a Parking Attendant for all this shit. These niggas is crazy; they don't even make the majority of their money on the books. Pops and his little girlfriend make they money selling weed. Stack, may he rest in peace was selling cocaine. These niggas is criminals that happen to rap. They may sell a hundred albums in any given city, that's it."*

"Oh yeah? A hundred albums is good though ain't it?"

"Not when you can go to a major label and sell a couple of thousand wherever you go; bigger budget, better advertising, better venues. This shit is smalltime. And Pops about to blow his deal with Wreck House Records, they already told him if he get in any more trouble they wont be able to associate with him. You know I almost got my fucking head blown off the other day?"

11:14AM; THE SAME DAY

...off my physical creation, slip into a hall-u-cin-ation. Situations, got me thinking bout life ser-ious-ly, keep it real con-tin-uous-ly ...

203

Junior walked into the far bedroom on the left and saw his Father sitting on the bed reading the Coco Brothers, *Da Shining* album cover. He looked up at Junior and flashed a skin deep smile; "This is one of my favorite songs of all time."

...Before I slip into blackness, I prepare for combat. Protect my dome cause that's where my home's at...

Junior shut the door behind him and got right to the point. "I'm not going to be rejoining the group when yall resume the tour."

Jason placed his CD on the nightstand and continued packing his scattered articles of clothing into a suitcase on the bed. "Yeah you know what? That's probably the best thing for you."

Junior took a few steps deeper into the room and leaned against a wall. "I mean, I came here to do music; I love music. And yall, yall-"

"Do me a favor," Jason interposed as he slammed a stack of underwear into place, "Go 'head wit' all that Golden girls shit right now, alright."

Junior turned abruptly and flung open the door to leave.

"Yo?"

His Father yelled out; *"I'm on point for this trip tonight*, so I'm not going to see you till we get to New York. So…" He gestured with his hands as if Junior needed to understand what he'd said or forget that he said it.

"What you mean on point?"

Junior tried to keep his tone uninterested in attempt to convey his dismay of being referred to as an old white woman. He did however want to know what his Father was talking about. Jason stopped throwing his clothing about for a Moment and abandoned his usually discreetness.

"Look, we designate one car as the sort of, contraband car. So if things go bad they don't' go but so bad. Okay? Tonight, I'm driving said vehicle."

Junior shook his head and walked out of the room.

10:40PM; THE SAME NIGHT

Junior looked behind him and noticed a gray Mercedes still trailing him and Laronda's car. He turned around and lowered the volume on Ciara CD she was playing; "If that was the Cops following us, they would've pulled us over by now right?"

Laronda peeked in her rearview as she eased on the breaks. "Why; what happen?" She asked checking the speedometer. The Benz sped around them and activated its previously hidden sirens a few feet behind Jason in the trap car.

"Shit." Laronda pounded the top of her steering wheel, "That's them Hip-Hop Task Force sons of bitches." Her mind visibly raced with questions, she pulled over and turned the stereo all the way down.

The plain clothed Officers searched Jason's rental for over thirty minutes before discovering a zip-lock bag full of marijuana stashed in a box of CDs. Junior and Laronda watched helplessly as the Officers cautiously applied the handcuffs. Laronda restrained herself for as long as she could. She unbuckled her seatbelt, stepped out the car and put both her hands up to the sky.

"Get back in that fucking car young lady!"

"I come in peace; I ain't stopping yall from doing yall job." She insisted. *"Yo Tekk tell me what you need."*

Jason yelled through the cracked window from the backseat of the Police cruiser, *"Yo L tell*

Hollis where I'm at. Do something for Gwinn please! Send her something when you can, anything. And make sure she stay away from those fucking girls!"

-*"Young lady get back in that fucking car right now!"* One of the Officers pointed his firearm at Laronda's chest with fatal intent.

"Okay baby I got you. Don't brake, Allah is with you!"

196

"What you doing? You got Mr. Big in your hand?"

Date: December 24TH 2006

And it came to pass that GOD kept his promises with Jayson Jordan Junior. Junior worked hard for the sake of his family, with unrelenting support and encouragement from Mrs. Jordan. He returned to *New City Parking* in Downtown Brooklyn and he eventually completed his demo. Junior and Lakrisha legally married on the twenty first of November at St. Patrick's Cathedral in Manhattan. They had close to $2,000 in their joint account and were caught up on all of their respective bills. One could say that they were doing well.

Since returning to New York, Junior invested time into strengthening his relationship with his Mother. A relationship that had been on the rocks since Junior moved out after Lakrisha got pregnant last year. His Father was still in South Hampton Correctional, serving a year for possession of a controlled substance, and his Sisters were, to his knowledge, doing well.

I can tell you how I feel- about you- night and day...

"Woo-oow..." Ms. Johnson raised her bottle of beer in the air. "That's my jam right there... *How I feel about you. Oo- oo- oo...*"

Junior chuckled as he continued to lace the Christmas tree with garland.

"Where that fine ass Father of yours Junior? Tell him I wanna give him some of the good stuff; *Aow.*"

-*"Aow"* Lakrisha slapped her Mother a feminine five as she returned from the kitchen with another blender full of Pina Coladas.

"I don't know why yall wait to the last minute to decorate the damned tree. Ant don't care about all this Christmas shit no way. Do he?" Ms. Johnson lined her drunken face up with Anthony's who was grinning from ear to ear at his spirited Grandmother. "You a little warrior ain't you? That baby don't need Christmas."

Anthony began jumping around in his walker, banging the plastic platform with his fist.

"*Ah!* That's my little Shaka Zulu nigga right there. *Boom, boom,* look how he bang his spoon. Look Junior, look."

Anthony grew with such excitement that he nearly jumped out of his walker.

"He go bang, bang with his spoon, look. Wit'
his big ass monster hands, look at them hands.
*Lakrisha where the damn refills at? You taking
all day!*"

Lakrisha stuck her head out from the kitchen,
"Mommy I just filled you up."

"So what; what you wanna toast? *Go Lakrisha,
she's so fast.*" Ms. Johnson handed Lakrisha her
empty cup, "Here go get me another drink I'll
toast to that, shit."

The New York City streets were slow, bitterly
cold and covered with slushy snow. The newly
weds invited their families over for dinner and
drinks. Bernadette was sitting on the couch with
her legs crossed trying to vibe to the old school
countdown on W.B.L.S, but she found herself
compelled to speak out about Ms. Johnson's foul
mouth. "You sure you want another drink
Aretha; you don't think you had enough for
tonight? I'm not sure you should be talking
around the baby like that."

Ms. Johnson looked at Bernadette and rolled her
eyes; "It don't matter what the hell you sure of-"

"Ma!"

"No but what is that? *She's not sure...* like
she's the authority up in here or some shit."

"I never said that Aretha. Please do not curse at me."

"I'm talking to my Grandson; the baby I watch at least once a week when these kids wanna go out and have some fun."

"So what, you watch him? I have a career!" Bernadette fired back refusing to be pushed past a certain limit. "I'm not trying to spend the little bit of free time that I do have, baby sitting for them."

"Well…" Aretha rolled her neck full of nerve and sass, "that's just too bad, now ain't it?"

-"Alright guys squash it. Leave it alone." Lakrisha's Uncle Dalvin interjected.

"Okay, no problem."

-"Shit, don't play wit' me in here tonight. I'm fit, lit and I ain't taking no shit."

Everyone in the room save for Bernadette giggled beneath their breaths. Junior bent down to plug the lights into the tree and tried to stop himself from laughing aloud with the cover of the side of the couch.

"I thought you said Gwinn was coming over Bernadette." Dalvin asked for the sake of commencing any sort of peaceful conversation.

"Yeah, she was supposed to have been here. She's not answering her phone."

"Hmm" Ms. Johnson hymned loud enough for all to hear. "I wonder why."

"I-hate-this-j-o-o-o-o-b. I-hate-this-job…"

Junior had been tossing his softball in the trailer for close to five minutes. Due to the blizzard business was exceptionally slow, even for New Years Eve. *"I-hate-this-j-o-o-o-o-b…"*

"What you doing tonight?" Damon, one of the new parking attendants asked as he flipped his hood over his head and lit another cigarette.

"Nothing special; me and Krish probably gone get a bottle of something and count down to 2007 at home." Junior shoved his hands deep in his pockets reaching for warmth. "What about you, how you bringing the New Year in?"

Damon kicked the snow from the soles of his boots, stepping back into the warmth of the office. "We going to Club Exotic and popping a couple of bottles. It's gone be mad chicks in there; HOT 97 gone be there & all that."

212

"Okay, that's what's up."

"You gave up the party life huh?" Damon asked as he started a fresh pot of coffee.

Junior laughed, "Na not even. I'm prioritized things right now. But I'm a be back in the spot light in a hot second... Right now I gotta take care of the household." His facial expression altered as he began staring imaginatively across the street, "Lakrish is pregnant again too."

11:13PM; THE SAME NIGHT

"A shootout survivor; 5 borough live wire; the Hip-Hop Siar, I spit that fire. And Motherfucker I got kids 2 feed. So if that mean, your team gotta bleed, GOD just gone have to put that sin on me. I ain't come here to play no games, homie I take my aim & spit my thang; you feel my pain? This industry strange, half my homies flip that Cain. So in the Club we could make it rain, hundreds fallin' on your dame. Raise the 8th & take yo' chain, my clique's insane, no chicks, no lames, just thugs that's quick to bust & bang..."

Junior sat in his living room writing his heart out; putting everything he had into his verse for a ten emcee remix that the B.X Bombers were doing for one of their tracks. Junior occasionally returned back to the world from the confines of his imagination by checking out the BET New Years Special on channel 43.

-*"You alright baby?"*

Junior could hear her, but couldn't see his wife yet. *"Where you at?"*

"In here."

Junior stood from his seat and walked into the bathroom a few feet away, discovering Lakrisha slouched helplessly over the toilet bowl with the lights out.

"You sound a like a straight killer in that rhyme." She said as she as she flushed the toilet from her knees and wiped her mouth.

"Baby you need anything? I'll run to the street for you." He said in pity of what she was going through in her first trimester of pregnancy.

"I could go for a ginger ale." She said as she pushed herself miserably to her feet. "Oh, and baby I forgot to tell you, a Ms. Bayless from Wreck House Records called. She said she want you to give her or her assistant a call. I'll give you the number when you get back."

"When I get back? Girl if you don't give me that phone number."

"What, your pending record deal is more important to you than your pregnant wife?"

"Ain't nobody say all that. Just get the damned number Krish."

JANUARY 4TH 2007

Junior got off the 6 train at 110th and stopped by his Mother's house after he got off of work on Thursday, the day after his meeting at Wreck House Records. As he walked up 112th street he couldn't help but thank GOD that he'd been fortunate enough to make it out of Harlem. The same cliques were sprawled about, the hood was still dirty; it was as if nothing had changed. He puffed up his chest and toughened up the look on his face as he walked past the hustlers in front of his old building.

"Fuck you, you little punk that's why I'm a get my Brother to fuck you up!"

One of the elevators was out and consequently Junior was waiting for over five minutes in the lobby watching a pack of bad ass kids run around and play fight.

"Fuck you, you dirty bitch!"

In many ways Junior felt exempt from the ghetto. The possibility of prosperity that he got after his brief meeting with Ms. Bayless, senior A&R at Wreck House, put Junior in a better place mentally. It was as if he had renewed faith. Junior was careful with himself, or at least tried to be. He had an eerie feeling that something bad was going to happen to him before he came into his riches.

"Eww Tyrek got a booger on his nose!"

The group of kids ran through the A staircase and out the backdoor as the elevator arrived. Junior got in and pressed the sixteenth floor.

"Who is it?"

"Junior, Ma."

Bernadette removed the two deadbolt locks and the chain and opened the door.

"Have you seen your Sister?" She asked in place of greeting him. She was still in her work clothes and seemed highly disturbed and concerned.

"No, I haven't seen her."

Bernadette exhaled with disappointment. She picked up the phone resting idly on the kitchen counter. *"No, he ain't seen her either Sandy... Okay call me if you hear something."*

"What happen?"

216

Junior asked as his Mother hung up the phone.

"Gwinn friend Maria just got stabbed in front of 1695."

"The little Puerto Rican girl Gwinn always be with? Did she come in from school?"

"Yeah, she was here like an hour ago; she said she was going to the store. I ain't hear from her since. She left her cell phone in there so I can't call her...*Oh my GOD.*"

Junior got his Mother to calm down in the near two hours that it took for Gwinn's key to hit the front door. She walked in reeking of alcohol and marijuana, with a blue bandana hanging out her back pocket, barely able to keep herself together.

"Where have you been young lady?"

"I was w-"

"What the hell is this?" Bernadette grabbed at her bandana and flicked it. Gwinn instinctively swatted her Mother's hand away as the older Sisters would give her blows if they seen someone, anyone touching her flag.

"What the hell is wrong with you?"

"Oh, Ma, I am so sorry. I ain't mean to do that."

Rendered speechless, Bernadette waived her hands around the aura of what used to be her innocent little girl; "What is all this about?"

Gwinn didn't have full command of her eyes or legs. She was looking at her Mother from the chest down and hadn't looked at Junior at all.

"You alright Sis?" Junior asked.

Gwinn looked at him then tried to look into her Mother's eyes. Guilt seized her; she covered her face and abruptly ran into her bedroom and slammed the door shut. Bernadette looked at Junior, her face rid of understanding *"Did you just see that shit?"*

9:58PM; THE SAME NIGHT

"Thank you for dinner baby, that was excellent."

"Why don't you eat your salad Junior? It's good for you."

"Aight, I'm a wrap it up and eat it later." Junior said as he began digging into the chocolate cake on the table.

"Yeah right, you aint gone eat that salad. You might as well go 'head and throw it away." Lakrisha rubbed her belly as she took a well deserved seat at the dining room table. "I'm a be fat for the winter."

Junior chuckled as he stood and began running water from the sink. "Go lay down baby. I'll clean up in here and do the dishes."

Lakrisha pushed herself up, grateful to have one less burden for the night and headed to the back room. *"I got the best husband in the world!"* She said as she vanished.

Junior washed the dishes and wiped down the counter. He got the garbage ready and cut off the lights in the kitchen. He took a Moment to overlook his small, peaceful living quarters. He was about to address GOD, and thank him for the first time in weeks when his cell phone rang.

"Hey ma, what's up?"

"Nothing, in here gettin' ready for bed. You're crazy Sister in there still knocked out from whatever she drunk."

"Oh okay."

"I know she gone be hung over tomorrow, so I'm probably gone call in to work."

"That's actually what I wanted to talk to you about earlier ma."

"What's that?"

"Yo ma, I don't think you gone be working much longer... I got signed today."

"Get out a here Junior! You got your record deal?"

"Yep, with Wreck House Records; they talking bout giving me a million dollar advance and all that."

"What? A million dollars! You signed the deal already? Did you get a Lawyer to look the paper work over?"

Junior heard a beep from a call coming in on the other line. He looked into his display screen.

((Incoming Call Renee))
(646) 555-0827

"Hold on ma. I got a call on the other line."

Before he pressed the talk button to click on to the other line Junior peeped to the back room to make sure the door was still shut. *"Hello?"*

"What's up Jay?"

He could feel the beat that his heart skipped drop to the pit of his stomach, then further south.

"Hey, what's going on?"

"Nothing; you know who this is?"

"Come on Renee you know I ain't forget your voice; cut it out."

220

"Oh...I was calling to see how you and your baby was doing."

"We good; we good. My little man is coming along, thankfully."

After a brief, overly comfortable pause she exhaled deeply into the receiver, *"I miss -No forget it; I'm a go."*

"Why? What you was gone say?"

She breathed sensually, deliberately pushing Junior's buttons *"Na, I was going to say I miss your dick."*

It was Junior's turn to exhale, *"Chill Nene."* He superficially pleaded, now fully turned on and she knew it.

"Like, I miss how it get all hard and fat right before I let you slid it inside me."

Junior's body became unsettled. He tapped one of his feet with loose energy as his testosterone and basketball shorts began to rise. He turned to make sure his wife wasn't behind him then reclined in his seat by inclining his pelvis.

"You alright baby?"

"I'm good."

"What you doing? You got Mr. Big in your hand?"

"Na; not yet."

He was lying, he couldn't control himself. He laid back and his ex talked him through an organism that felt better than live action with most others.

6:48AM; THE NEXT MORNING

"Junior get up!"

As soon as he became conscious he could hear Lakrisha yelling at him and Anthony crying. He stretched his sore, exhausted body before turning around to get the time off of the cable box.

"Oh shit Nene, why you ain't wake me up sooner?"

"What did you call me?" Lakrisha asked as she looked around the kitchen wall at her husband who slept in the living room last night.

"Huh?"

"What did you just call me Jayson?"

"I ain't call you nothing, I said baby. Oh shit *ba-by*."

"Hmm… That didn't sound like no *ba-by* Junior. That sounded like *Ne-Ne*." Lakrisha said as she went back into the kitchen to tend to the food and the baby.

"Looks like it's going to be a few months before you get that advance check Mr. Jordan."

"A few months?"

"Yeah, I didn't like some of the terms they'd outlined in the contract, and I wanted to push for more ownership of your material..."

Junior stopped listening mid-sentence. He had to repeat it at least five times before letting Phil, his entertainment Lawyer go, *call me as soon as the meeting is done.* Now he'd heard enough out of Attorney Price already.

Yesterday at his follow up meeting with Ms. Bayless, she seemed pressed for time. She explained to Junior that she thought he had commercial viability and that she wanted to introduce him to Wreck House CEO Johnny Myers. Three and a half minutes later, Junior was in a meeting with Johnny Myers. Johnny asked to see Junior's teeth, demanded that he lift more weights and told him that if he gained twenty pounds he could be a marketable Hip-Hop commodity. Mr. Myers looked Junior over one final time and agreed to sign him to a single record/digital recording deal. Johnny tried to push Junior to sign his contract on the spot but Junior decided to let Phil look things over.
"They wanted to give you a $25,000 advance but I think we can get that bulked up to around 50K."

"Oh, that's it?"

"How much did you think you were going to get?"

"I don't know. Okay, thanks Phil."

Junior hung up the living room phone, sat back in his seat and fell into despair. He had big plans that needed big money to manifest and he had already started making plenty promises to plenty people. *"What the fuck?"* He asked aloud.

8:30PM; THE SAME NIGHT

"Why you can't ever just be straight up about shit? How you gone give me a record deal then let me quit my job, then don't give me the money? Why would you do that? Now money is crazy tight, think about how I'm gone a look! Give me the deal, the advance money and let me do what I gotta do, damn!"

Junior walked over a mile during his monolog with the Lord. He walked all the way up to Boston Road, then up Boston Road to Eastchester Road before finally heading back home. When he got back Lakrisha and Anthony were already sleeping. He warmed up the plate that his wife left him in the microwave while he checked his e-mails and Myspace messages.

Junior spent the night in the living room, but he didn't get much sleep. He tried to visualize the life, the stardom, the love and the better days. He couldn't tame his adrenaline enough to sleep. He envisioned his look, his soon to be famous disposition, answers to questions from imaginary reporters, the women, the power, the lights, the cameras, and the action.

MARCH 7TH 2007

Yo, yo what's going on New York City? This ya girl D.J Chase E; Power 105.5 on your radio dial for the top five at noon...

Junior turned the volume up on his car stereo as he breezed down University Avenue.

The number five joint of the day is coming from N.Y.C's own J3. I don't know if you guys know this but J3 is actually the oldest child of incarcerated Rapper Architekk from the N.Y.C.M.C clique. Remember them Ralph?

Yeah Tekk got caught with a trunk full of that good greenery; Stacky rest in peace, Buck from Wagner.

No doubt, big shout out to the whole eastside of Harlem; Taft, Jeff, Foster, lets see um...

-Metro North, Clinton-

-Johnson, Lehman, Douglas; yeah all that! This is the number five song of the day New York; J3 Pop goes my 9...

It was easy; it was all too easy Junior thought to himself as he turned the volume up all the way. He was only nineteen and already cruising around the B.X in a drop-top. Junior put up a lot of cash and Lakrisha's credit at the Mercedes of Manhattan for his ride, but this feeling made it all worth it.

As he crossed Fordham Road, he tried not to smile. Johnny Myers warned him that the streets would be watching him, and to never let the streets see him feeling himself too much. With that in mind, Junior sunk into his leather seat, kept his foot on the pedal and hid behind the protection of his Ray Ban's as he smoothly rolled on.

Junior pulled up to in front of building five and turned his stereo down. He sat in the driver seat in sweet, serene silence as he looked around the apartment complex where he spent many lustful nights during his High School years. Today he was clean, he felt fresh and confident. He stepped out of his luxury coupe and the sun illuminated his new shirt as well as the gold chain around his neck. Junior felt as if he had been delivered by GOD. He walked into the building lobby and pressed the intercom for apartment 17C.

"Who?"

"Jun- J3!"

"Oh, come in!"

The electronic buzzer for the front door activated. Junior stayed put and pressed the intercom again.

"Yeah?"

"Come downstairs!"

When Junior saw her walk out of her building he could no longer justify his being there. Part of him wanted to run back to his family as quickly as he could. But this day had been a long time in the making, and the stronger side of him produced a welcoming smile and open arms for his other High School sweetheart. "What's up Renee?"

"Hey Baby." She returned his smile and embraced him. At first sight Renee appeared to be the same way he left her. She was wearing a black sweater, blue jeans and tough leather high heals. She still had acme bumps on her face, and by the way she was switching from side to side, Junior could tell that her biggest bump was still behind her.

"That's your car?"

Junior puffed up with pride looking at his newest sweetheart, his Benz. "Yeah, that's me right there."

He could see delight in her smile; and he could feel his plans to keep things between them nonphysical slipping away. He deactivated the car alarm via a single key remote. "Hop in."

12:11PM; THE SAME DAY

"…How's the grilled Salmon?"

"Oh, it's actually quite the delight. It has just a wee bit of orange flavoring to give it a little extra jazz; delicious."

"Ok shit, let me get that." Renee said as if impressed.

"And for you sir?" The waitress turned to Junior, who was still staring at Renee.

"What?" Renee asked.

"Come on Nene, you can't be saying shit like that to the lady."

"What?" She asked with her face screwed up.

"Cursing and sh- whatnot, damn."

Junior adjusted his shades and smiled at the waitress, "Can I have the chopped steak with the Luger sauce please?"

Renee unrolled her utensils to the table and threw the embroidered napkin that they were tucked in at Junior.

"I'm sorry Miss; you gotta excuse her, she straight out the ghetto. She don't know how to act." Junior facetiously explained to the waitress.

Renee smiled sarcastically, not feeling the need to explain herself. The waitress took their menus and went about her business. It was that Moment that Junior looked into Renee's face and realized that he never got over her; he never shook her. She still had that heightened sense of style that attracted him. She was still exciting to be around and she was still a sweetheart in her own Boogie-Down Bronx way. Her body was still tight and the things she'd been saying over the phone combined with the way she was now rubbing on him with her foot underneath the table ensured him that she still had that *down for anything* freak in her.

"I- I..."

Even in her failed attempts to locate Mr. Big Renee got Junior going to the point where he could no longer put together a meaningful sentence.

"What you said?" She asked as she slid lower in her seat to give her curious foot better leverage. "Baby you wanna get out of here?" She suggested in her after hours voice.

"Right now?"

She squeezed his erect penis with her toes and he pulled out his wallet and placed a hundred dollar bill beneath one of the candleholders. "Let's go."

"…and last but not least I want to thank J3 for that killer performance tonight at Club Home. This is going to be a great year for Wreck House records!"

Johnny Myers held up his brut Rose Ace of Spade bottle and toasted with Kevin Anderson, his new R&B soloist. The B.X Bombers crew, Club Home staff and Wreck House staff all toasted then sprawled into separate groups conversing amongst themselves. Through all the commotion Red Out pulled Junior aside.

"Yes." Junior said with an arrogant grin before taking another sip of champagne.

"Yes what?"

"I already know what you gone ask, and the answer is yes."

"You sure you know what I'm a ask son?" Red Out asked skeptically.

"You gone ask if you can get in the Studio with me to finish recording your demo."

"Actually, well, yeah. I want that too. But right now I got more pressing issues than that my Brother." He lowered his voice and leaned in, "I need you to let me hold a lil something to invest with. If you know what I mean." Red Out inched in closer and grabbed Junior by his shoulder; "Right now the price is right, I can get

230

that good, good white for like thirty cent a gram. And we can bring that back to whatever the fuck we need to, ya heard?"

Junior looked deeper into Red Out, seriously considering. Red Out knew Junior was on the brink and so he pushed on. "We can start making big money right now. You don't gotta wait for them checks from these clowns ass record execs to get paid; us nigga."

A few extra dollars coming in regularly was what Junior needed to get his budget back on track and link up his finances smoothly. He damn sure wasn't going to get a job, not with his new image at stake and the responsibility to be in so many places to promote his music. Furthermore, a move like Red Out was purposing would allow J3 to gain more credibility on the streets, which in turn would appreciate his value as a Rapper. "Let's do it my nigga."

"No doubt son; that's what I'm talkin' bout!"

Red Out was enthused as he embraced his new best friend. "Life is good! Life is good! Yo bring us another bottle of champagne over here yo!"

Almost everyone under twenty five left the office and made their way through the jam packed club toward the dance floor.

"We doing it big in this bitch tonight fuck that!"

Junior gave Red Out a pound before hoping on some ass and throwing his hands in the air. D, Jeff, and the rest of the B.X Bombers were on the dance floor bouncing around in their own circle of self-celebration. Junior had a bottle of Petron clutched by its' neck. Red waived his hands, he had blood red bandanas tied to both of his wrist and manicured stacks of single dollar bills in each of his hands.

"B.X get the money, long time no cash. B.X get the money long time no cash!"

D.V.D recorders were rolling. The ladies and the player haters alike were looking as the Bombers flashed their jewelry and other testaments to the good life. They were having a ball, high off of life. For Junior the feeling was surreal, he had dreamt of this his whole life and here he was, writing his name in the pages of the game. He had a rented platinum and diamond tennis necklace laying on a $300 shirt, a crisp Yankee fitted laying on his silky waves and he had the confidence that he could lay down with whichever one of the on looking freaks he chose.

"B.X get the money, long time no cash. B.X get the money, long time no cash!"

3:41AM: THE SAME NIGHT

"Junior I feel like you don't talk to me anymore."

232

"*Oh boy*, here we go with this." Junior kicked off his sneakers, getting ready for bed.

"Here we go what? Am I annoying you by trying to keep our lines of communicating open?"

"Baby listen, it ain't nothing to say; behavior is the truth. That's the one thing my Father taught me, behavior is the truth. I'm doing what I gotta do for my son right now."

"Well you not spending no time with me, or even him for that matter!" Lakrisha raised her voice as she followed him into the bathroom.

"Right now this is what it is Krish. Things ain't gone be this way forever. Let me take care of what I gotta take care of without all the stress."

Lakrisha's attitude was written all over her face. "Junior I hope you ain't letting that little fifty thousand dollars go to your head. You living way above our means right now. You looking at that check like its fancy car and jewelry time. You can't look at it like that."

"Oh yeah, how am I supposed to look at it then?" Junior asked as if mocking her as he ran water in his hands and began scrubbing his face.

"Like…like it's, like let's run the A.C. all we want this summer money. Let's take a few extra days off, not let's quit our damn jobs money. You not even sure how the album is going to sell yet."

Junior became enraged; "Fuck you! How you gone say some shit like that? My album is gone sell." He pushed her gently out of the bathroom door, "Get out please."

224

"Oh boy, now I done heard it all.
I'm going upstairs!"

Date: May 13TH 2007

"Where's your Father?"

Hollis pointed across the field a few yards out.
Junior looked and saw his Father sitting in front
of the small steam with his head hung.

*"This is boring yo. I'm bout to have my Mother
come get me."*

Hollis looked at him with intense eyes, as if she
were on the verge of rising up from the garden
swing to which she was seated. *"His Father just
died Junior."*

"Oh word?" Junior looked back over the green
pasture at his Dad. *"Dag; I hope he be alright...
I'm going to call my Mother."*

Junior opened his eyes to Renee's dormant face,
all the glamour was gone. In a post orgasmic
state, her mouth was pressed against the bare
mattress, as their physicality had ripped the
sheets off the bed. Junior felt like he'd been
sleeping for many hours, but he knew it was still
early in the day. He pushed himself out of the
bed and quickly began collecting his belongings.
He needed to move, fast or slow, left or right. If
he didn't start moving the haze of depression

would seize him with the realization that he and Renee's rendezvous had nothing to do with his work.

"Yo get up. I got a go! " Junior said loud enough to wake Renee from her slumber as he tossed the bottle of Citron that they killed earlier into the garbage.

"Damn J," She whispered as she rolled over wiping the side of her mouth. "I'm tired."

"Na, get up! I got a meeting with Johnny. It's check out time."

1:24PM; THE SAME DAY

"...Amber I don't feel like dealing with that shit right now. That's why I hired you. You figure it out and get back to me, thank you." Johnny Myers was yelling into the speakerphone on his desk from his elliptical machine across the room in attempt to work off his lunch. "What's the use of having a secretary if she gone ask me what to do all the damn time?" Johnny rhetorically asked Junior who was behind the leather couch trying to figure out the proper way to grip the golf club in his hand.

"Okay so this is what we do know thus far; it's going to be seventeen cities, New Orleans, Houston, Boston, Philly, Vegas, and L.A are certain. Tracy is going to send you an email with the complete itinerary by the weekend."

Although Johnny was exercising and indoors, he was still sporting his rhinestone encrusted sunglasses and trying to preserve his stardom. He took a swig from his water jug then stuck it back in its holster on the side of the digital read out on the elliptical.

"And when's my album release date?" Junior asked he ripped a swing through the air.

"The album'll be out some time late summer, maybe even early fall, young blood."

Junior felt it necessary to stare Johnny down Momentarily, to express his dismay none verbally. He was beginning to feel like there was some sort of conspiracy preventing the release of his album, which was initially set to release last month but had been pushed back for the second time. Junior hadn't heard anything from Ms. Bayless or Art Clay, the Wreck House co-founder, therefore he rightfully questioned why his project was in limbo despite his extensive collection of songs and his eagerness to get them out to the world. "Come on Johnny, this album is important to me, man. When we gone get this joint out?"

Johnny took a few last decelerating strides before climbing off of his elliptical. "We got you covered, don't worry bout nothing. You ready for life on the road youngin?"

The church was packed from wall to wall. Everyone was looking good and apparently feeling just as well. Junior was hot. The only thing he could think about was getting out of his hard bottoms and cracking open a beer in front of his big screen later. He loosened his tie and readjusted himself in his seat.

"Junior give your Sister another two dollars to put in the plate."

"They sending the plate around again?"

"Junior!" Bernadette shoved him in his leg; *"Stop talking nonsense and give your Sister two dollars."*

Bernadette searched through her patent-leather hand bag then turned back to her son, "And let me hold a five till later..."

And it came to pass that Junior got settled into his new life as J3 the Rapper; his upgraded social status, the money, the attention, it all quickly became habitual, like he was born to do it. He had cash money coming in left and right from Red Out and consequently he was able to take care of most of his miscellaneous expenses without pulling out plastic and breaking his budget. Junior squashed his beef with GOD; no longer yelling at him in times of adversity, challenging his authority or foolishly questioning his reach. When he was faced with hardship nowadays, he looked at the cup as half full, and gave thanks because he understood that things could be much worst.

Jayson Jordan Junior found himself still unable to shake what he and Renee had. His good fortune allowed them to live out the fantasies they dreamed about as kids. Renee was giving him head like *she* needed it; unbuttoning his pants in the middle of conversations, making craving noises and slapping it on her face. Without failure, Junior wished to GOD that she'd disappear off the face of the earth orgasm after toe curling orgasm, but in reality she didn't; in the real world he was hooked.

As a testament to his current circumstances the songs J3 wrote were…different…different from what they started out as. The melodies of humble beginnings and respect for the game were replaced with songs of self-celebration and anthems of love for money. He titled his debut album *One in a Million* as a testament to the rarity his success.

"So what you want to do?"

P Dun, the Atlantis studio in-house engineer asked as the energy departed the room as D failed to lay down his verse properly after his ninth attempt. Junior flopped down in the chair next to him and wiped the sweat from his forehead. "In all honesty, I feel like calling this a wrap and picking it up from here tomorrow."

"This L.A heat ain't no joke. We need to go to the Beach." Red Out said to no one in particular.

-"Don't yall need to have this finished by Friday?"

"We'll get it done. Worst come to worst, I'll write something at the Hotel later." Junior stood to his feet and began walking around the state of the art engineer room. "I ain't come to L.A to be sitting in no hot ass studio all day though." He waived D in from the recording booth and looked at Red Out, "Yall trying to make moves?"

"We going to the Beach?" Red Out employed a corny imitation Jamaican accent. *"Yeah Mon!"*

3:29PM; THE SAME DAY

The B.X Bombers and J3 could hardly take a few steps without being stopped by someone who recognized them. Junior's second single and video were in heavy rotation on B.E.T and had gotten its' fair share of spins on Hip-Hop radio stations across the nation. His spirits were particularly high as he was confident that his new single *This is for the Ladies* would make him a household name. Between the shows he was doing and the revenues being generated off his ring-tones and internet downloads, moving his wife and child out of New York City would be feasible by the end of summer.

"Oh snap; that's J3!"

A teenage girl pointed Junior out to her Mother before running up to him, "Can I have you autograph?"

He smiled at her and took the pen she was holding out for him, "What you want me to write it on?"

She turned to her Mother for direction, she handed her a t-shirt that read *Venice Beach U.S.A* across the front and reached in her pocketbook and pulled out a stick of eyeliner. "Here use this, that pen not gone write on that shirt."

Junior signed: *2 Keysha Flood from Buffalo New York. Thanx 4 the love.*

"Say thank you Keysha." The girl's Mother instructed her.

She smiled adorably in Junior's face, as if she thought the world of him. "Thank you."

The boys from the Bronx posted up atop a low rise brick wall across from the Ocean Shop and checked out the west coast scene. The boardwalk was live; Junior saw a couple whiz by on incline skates, a man juggling glass mugs on a bicycle and fine women were everywhere. There was one woman in particular that Junior hadn't noticed until he turned at random and saw the beauty looking at him from afar. She seemed to be walking in slow motion between her two friends and she continued to steal glances at Junior as they advanced up the boardwalk. The members of the Bombers crew hopped off their post and approached the ladies to put their bids in. Junior stayed put and looked on.

"What's good shorty? I know you ain't gone let this opportunity pass me & you by." Red Out said, hawking the brown skinned girl with the braids and curiously long legs. She kept stepping, visibly disinterested in a conversation with him.

"Oh so you don't recognize me with my clothes on huh? So last night ain't mean nothing to you?"

-"Hey, how you doing?" The young lady who was staring at Junior walked straight up to him and introduced herself. "I'm Alyson." She said with a surreal aura around her and the smile of a princess. She was unreal Junior thought to himself. Her lip gloss was shinning, her skin was like golden candy and her body was proportioned to a tee. He felt the need to look away to reserve a certain level of marital dignity. "I'm good; how you?"

-*"My bad shorty, I thought you was cute."* Red Out hollered, as he was having his share of trouble with the other girls.

Alyson exhaled and fanned her tempting bust line in front of Junior. "I'm hot."

Red Out finished insulting the California Beauties and walked between Junior and his new friend. "Excuse me. Yo, matter of fact, break out shorty. Stuck up ass bitches; yall ain't ready for no real niggas."

"Fuck you."

"Fuck you bitch!"

Junior grabbed Red Out by the waist as he tried to charge forth.

"I'll spit in your fucking face. Don't play with me!"

JUNE 13TH 2007

"Ah man how much yall want for them Gucci loafers?" D asked the salesman who'd been following them around since they walked through the door.

"Those shoes start at $525 Sir."

"Word? My man gimme like three of them joints and let me see some more stuff. What yall got in the back?

JUNE 13TH 2007

"You up?" Red Out asked as he peeped into the car that pulled up in front of him.

"Yeah; give me whatever you can for a hundred."

Red Out looked up and down the strip then dropped 5 bundles in the passengers' lap.

"Hey dude, if you wanna make some extra cash, a few of my buddies from college are having a party on North Citrus."

"Yeah?" Red Out inquired, astutely checking out the people packed in the backseat.

"Dude, at least three people came up to me and asked me if I knew who had some good soft."

JUNE 13TH 2007

"...but you can't work it like she can baby."

"Na hold up, hold up. See, cause I got this skirt on. I can't move the way I usually do."

She pulled her denim skirt over her juicy hips and wiggled her thick black ass.

"Ah!"

-"Ah!"

"Oh shit; chill, she won. It's over. I take my vote back."

She walked over to Junior and began shaking it in his face.

"Ah!"

JUNE 13TH 2007

"No he's not! No he is not!" Lakrisha insisted. "I know my Husband, he out there doing what he got a do for the fort. He ain't worried about them little scally-wag groupies."

"So what you think, they gone go to the Strip Club, get they dicks all hard and get all roused up so they can go back to they Hotel and be horny and without…every night? *Shiiiiiit.*"

JUNE 13TH 2007

"Two more days huh?"

Jason turned and smiled at Donald from Florida, most of his attention was still channeled in to the war report on the Morena T.V.

"So what you gone do when you get out Black? You got that look in your eye."

Jason didn't bother to disturb his peace by speaking. He continued to massage his rugged beard; his face barely visible behind his wool-like ropes of hair.

"...I don't believe they still over there killing innocent people for a profit." Donald said turning back at the television. Jason leaned forward in his chair and looked Donald square in the eyes and nodded as if he had a deep understanding of the situation, still no words came out of him.

"Make sure you fight the good fight when you get out there Brother."

JUNE 19TH 2007

Junior had a calm enthusiasm about him as he rode through the streets of downtown Houston on his way to his in store appearance. Ms. Bayless ejected the Usher CD that was playing from the stereo and J3's *Pop Goes my 9* single greeted them from the FM radio.

"Oh, wow!" She turned around and smiled at Junior, "You can't beat that."

Junior sat in the back of the S.U.V wondering if the pedestrians they were rolling by knew that today was his album release date. He wondered how many people were going to show up at his in store signing. He wondered if they loved him yet...

"You here kid, you here! You made it! I know this shit gotta feel good!"

D enthusiastically slapped Junior on his shoulders from the backseat as they arrived at the record store. A mild melancholic wave fiddled Junior's inner sanctum as he thought about Harlem and her interest; the hustlers, the ball players, the fly girls and the listeners back home and their acceptance or lack their of for his music. Bitter sweet was this victory as J3 came to the realization that he would have to do a better job on his next project in order to make a run at the crown of the New York rap game, therein was the respect that he secretly desired.

"Just give us one second. We wanna make sure everything is alright before we escort him in."

Force, Junior's friend and bodyguard said to Ms. Bayless before proceeding to back up the hyped crowd out front.

"Here put these on. And take this." Ms. Bayless handed J3 his sunglasses and a guest

247

pass to hang around his neck. "I told you our marketing techniques are on point." She said smiling through the tinted windows at the pandemonium outside. When Force opened Junior's door he got out waving at the camera phone wielding audience and local media. His security staff paved a clear path to the front door.

"...They just arrived; the crowd is going crazy here. I think I see J3; yes there's J3 looking quit fashionable might I say." A local reporter annexed herself into Junior's entourage and positioned herself to share the microphone with him. She placed a hand on his back as if they'd known each other for years. "So J3, tell the people out there how this feels. You're one of the hottest Rappers in the game right now. You just renegotiated your deal with Wreck House Records and you have one of the hottest videos in the country. How does it feel?"

"I love it. *I love it!*"

Junior hesitated to dial his house number; he still didn't have much to say. But he knew he had to call and say something. He dialed the phone number and fell to the bed in preparation for the drama he was certain his wife had in store for him.

"Hello."

"What's up?"

"Nothing." Lakrisha answered sharply, saying nothing further.

"What's wrong with you?"

"Nothing... I'm glad you found time to call."

"Oh boy, here we go with this."

Junior could hear her dismay over 500 miles away. He continued, *"I am busy Lakrisha. I got a hundred different things to do at any given Moment, chill out!"*

He did stop calling as much as he should have, and he knew it. He buried himself in his dealings. At some point, the nature of his work took on a form than was initially expected. He needed to do it without sleep because there was no time or place where he could get more than four or five hours at a time. He was drinking more alcohol because he didn't sleep, and the alcohol was a reward and fuel to get by. He needed his hair cut every other day, he needed the newest sneakers, he needed to party just about every night, the latest phones and an occasional blow job to stay at the top of his profession.

"...Whatever. I keep telling you, I ain't sign up to do this alone!"

"Yo, tell my son I love him. I'm a call you tomorrow. I love you, bye."

"Juni-"

He hung up the phone and fought against his sinful human soul as best he could, but less than a minute later he was on phone with Renee. Junior let the guilt go in his conscious regarding his thing with Renee; it was what it was. First he told himself that he would limit their friendship to conversations and occasional phone sex, and only when Lakrisha was acting up. He threw those vowels out a few weeks later after having live, rolling round butt-ass naked, sleazy motel sex with Renee. Then he promised himself that he wouldn't spend any money on her, eat her pussy or spend any meaningful time with her; broken, broken, broken. But Junior hadn't gone completely insane. He was beginning to see past Renee's bullshit. She was doing too much pretending with him for her intent to be pure; pretending to care about his every need. The sex was good, but she was just pretending to crave his body, and the performance that Junior kept nearest to his heart was in regard to his child at home, whom he conceived with Lakrisha during the pretended height of he and Renee's relationship. Renee was pretending that none of that matter.

Since Junior couldn't trust Renee with his prize possession, his son, there was no degree of trust that she could earn with him; therefore Junior was doing some pretending of his own. With so many lies and new people around him, only GOD himself knew the reality of all that was going on. Junior did run things past GOD... well, what he did was tell GOD that he knew he was wrong; the dirty money, the other woman, all the times he went in the recording booth and missed the mark, but that it could be worst. He thought since he was still getting paid and since GOD hadn't sent any major calamity his way that somehow that meant it was all good.

Promise after lustful promise from Renee got Junior so horny that he made catching the Red Eye flight to New York for a few hours of sex make sense to him; it would enhance the music. Five hours after his decision his plane touched down in Queens New York. An hour and a half after landing Renee had already made him leak like a faucet; seconds later his better judgment returned and he realized that he fucked up again.

Junior got dressed and left Renee sound asleep in their mid-town Hotel room. He sliced and diced through the humid, forlorn Manhattan blocks. This was the first time he'd been out by his lonesome in public in over a month. A certain fear of the unknown was present in his heart.

When he hit Lexington Avenue he saw a homeless woman sleeping in front of a shopping cart, which held all of her belongings, save for the sundry articles of clothing covering her. Junior felt the need to thank GOD for delivering him and his family from such circumstances, but he wasn't going to run the risk of someone getting a snap shot of the famous Rapper talking to himself and becoming a public mockery. He thanked his maker in his head and told GOD that if he remembered and had time, he would get on his knees and pray later.

Junior glanced at the woman several times and tried to find something in her that could explain her misfortune. When he couldn't, he simply shook his head and kept walking. Junior was shaken by the New York rats, bleak, anonymous faces, the speeding traffic, the winos and the sheer darkness of the streets. To him, his life was more significant than that of the others around him. So he sought to be extremely careful.

Junior went back to the Hotel and began cleaning the room around Renee's dormant body with a near humorous intent. When he was done he went into the bathroom with his book of rhymes and wrote a full three verses to a song for his next album which he titled *This strange life.*

"Yo fam, let me holler at you for a second."

Red Out pulled Junior aside as the rest of the entourage was greeted by the restaurant hostess who took them to their tables.

"Lets go in the bathroom real quick."

"Whoa; you wanna see me in the bathroom?" Junior playfully mocked.

"Come on man!" Red Out screwed his face. "No homo. I just need to holler at you real quick."

Red Out didn't bother to check the bathroom for privacy after they entered. He pulled a wad of money from his cargo shorts and slapped it in Junior's hand.

"Chill my dude; it ain't no rush. Take your time paying me back." Junior insisted as he reached to put the money back in his friend's hands.

"I'm good on that fam."

"You sure? I know you got your kids and all that. I'm not starving."

"Trust me." Red Out insisted as he wrapped an arm around Junior and escorted him out of the bathroom. "Trust me."

JULY 1ST 2007

The cup of rum and coke that Junior put on the floor a few hours ago suddenly toppled. He looked out of a window on the left side of the tour bus and saw Newark International Airport. Although he snuck home for a night a few weeks ago, Junior was terribly delighted to be rolling back into his hometown due to homesickness. They seemed to be hitting every pothole on the road. Junior made his way to the front of the bus and looked through the large windshields.

"Oh snap, we here."

"We'll be in Penn Station in about thirty minutes." Their driver Tony said.

Junior walked back toward the rear and cut off the video game he was playing. He removed his travel case from the side of his mattress and took off his Wreck House Records chain and put it in a compartment between two of his watches. He collected his CDs and packed them away, along

with his Bible and the sonogram picture of his
second child who was due any day now.

Junior grew anxious by the Moment, and
consequently paced back and forth throughout
the entire duration of the Holland Tunnel. *"Get
me off this fucking bus."*

8:33AM; THE SAME DAY

"You know your Daddy love you? Huh, you
know your Daddy love you?"

Anthony smiled, revealing his newly grown
teeth as he turned and tried to crawl away from
his Dad.

"Come here" Junior pulled him off balance by
taking one of his little legs from him and sliding
him gently across the silk sheets. *"Come
heeeere."* He tickled his bare potbelly. During
his endeavors Junior looked up and caught a
glance of Lakrisha's image in the closet mirror
and he turned to acknowledge her. "What you
doing?"

"Junior you ain't have sex with none of them
stripper bitches on tour, did you?"

"What? No!"

He looked up at her then took his eyes away
only to look once again to appear trustworthy;
all of which made her more suspicious.

"I swear to GOD I didn't."

"What's this?" Red Out asked Arty while
slapping all the Brothers fives who were sitting
on and around the benches in the back of the
building. Junior followed suite, dapping Harold,
Mick, Mack and Kenneth. Arty didn't bother
answering Red Out; he looked at him with lazy,
spacey eyes as if to say *try that*. Red Out took a
sip from the plastic cup and screwed up his face
completely; "Oh, yall out here drinking that
brown liquor this early. *Ooo-wee*."

These were Junior's peers while growing up.
The differences in their lifestyles kept them
distant over the past few years, mainly because
Junior was trying to excel in school and move
out the neighborhood, and they simply weren't.
Furthermore, when they were kids, Junior's
Mother made it public knowledge that the values
and disciplines she instilled in her children were
somehow better than that of the typical the
ghetto kids. Therefore Junior was somewhat of
an outsider in his own Projects, and no one
around here was rushing up to him for an
autograph. He laid low and hung alongside Red

256

Out as they got caught up on the politics of the day.

"Yo would you tell this nigga that S.P is the best mix-tape Rapper of all time. This nigga talking bout some Little Wayne. I should smack you."

"Yo, Little Whizzey is doing his thing right now, I can't front." Red Out said as he smoothly released a cloud of weed smoke through his lips.

"Thank you!"

-"Thank you."

"Oh my GOD; so you saying Little Wayne could go with Styles P? Please don't tell me you saying that Blood."

"Homie it depends on who you asking. Now me, I'll take Big L over all them niggas."

"I second that." Sasha from the fifteenth floor added.

"Yeah but still, you got a respect longevity. That's like one of the only ways to measure a good Rapper nowadays; how long he's been doing it and doing well, kn'-I-mean? The boy S.P been killing mix tapes since we was in 101. You can't just come put some nigga past him cause you like what he doing this year." Mack turned and pointed to J3 without looking at him, "That's like coming out your face saying this nigga is better than Tekk. Come on."

Whistles ripped through the Projects; Red Out stood alert, to see what was what.

"Wait, wait, what you mean by that?" Junior demanded.

"What you mean, what I mean?" Mack shot right back. His body leaned off the Paul Mason he was drinking, his hat tipped to the side.

"I'll rip my Pops apart lyrically; you buggin."

Mack threw his Kansas City Chief's fitted hat off his head and walked away, *"Oh boy, now I done heard it all. I'm going upstairs."*

8:19PM; THE SAME NIGHT

"Junior can you take this garbage out for me; help me scrub the floors or something, dang."

"Look, would you leave me alone about some fucking trash!"

Junior was formulating his toughest battle rhyme to date in his head. He was so upset Lakrisha interrupted him that arguing with her was now

258

worth it, as she had completely disturbed his groove.

"Shit, you want me to be the bread winner and the damn maid too?"

"Well excuse the fuck out of me!" Lakrisha walked into the living room from the kitchen. The hollering woke Anthony from his sleep, he began moving around on his pallet on the couch.

"You just sittin' up here on the computer, doing your own thing. I don't get to take those types of breaks around here. Anthony always needs something and something always needs to be done around the house!"

The baby finally opened his eyes and he began crying. Lakrisha dropped the dust-pan in her hand and flopped on the chair near the window.

"What you doing?"

"I'm taking break." She said rolling her neck and attending to her fingernails.

Junior rolled in his chair from his desk to the couch and picked up Anthony to comfort him. "Aw don't worry about it lil man. It's gone be alright."

-"I see we playing by a different set of rules now?" Lakrisha said folding her arms like an angry child.

Junior popped a pacifier in the baby's mouth and lowered him into his crib.

"When I was making the money I never made you feel like some type of a servant or some shit. That's that bullshit." Lakrisha added.

Junior grabbed his car keys off the desk. "Krisha look, I'm going to the studio. I got some real shit I need to get off my chest tonight. When I come back I'll help you." He grabbed his sunglasses and his wallet. He stopped in his tracks to look her in the eyes before walking out; "Mop, cook, clean, whatever you want baby, for real. Ok?"

11:35PM; THE SAME NIGHT

"I get G stacks for my freestyles; hmm, Ironic. Be in the Club leaned off vodka & tonic; rare like diamonds & Onyx, & my girls blow the homies then the chronic, leave you without an alternate option, fuck with us or vanish like the Loc-Nes, monster. Streets is our sponsor, yall phony's is actors & imposters, frontin' like a righteous Rasta. So why you got locked up? Only the fuck-ups go & get boxed up. The best, we stay out fresh, from our Nike Shox and up

fella. Your team aint ready for the Bombers'
brigade; we got pawns where you laid, get you
closer to Allah and your grave. Peace be with
you from the pretty thug with the creamy waves
& we got slugs in the 8 don't fuck around boy,
come cleaner than Cascades."

When J3 finished his verse he stared at the
microphone like he wanted to smack it. D and
Jeff were going berserk in the engineering room;
Junior could see them through the glass divider.
He laid his headphones on the mic dock and
walked away feeling like a bigger man.

"He just ended his pops career! He's finished!
He's done!"

Junior stepped in the room and received love
from every which way.

"Yo son, I ain't know you had that in you." D
said as he turned the master volume all the way
up and prepared to bring the track back.

"He's done!" Jeff yelled again not trying to
hear anything from anyone. *"Done!!!"*

"Hey Brenda, how's it going?" Denise greeted
her co-worker and continued gracing down the
main corridor for the office of admissions, her

hard high heels pronouncing her every step. They walked into her office, Junior took a seat and she folded into her leather bound chair and picked up her desk phone.

"You got your transcript with you right?" Denise asked as she dialed an extension.

"Yeah, I co-"

"Hi Bob?" She raised her hand to silence Junior. *"Hi this is Denise Knox. My stepson is in my office right now. He would like to know if he could borrow a minute of your time to speak with you about enrolling..."*

Junior looked around at Denise's vacation pictures, a picture of Hollis mid-stride in her F.D.A uniform, another picture of Hollis and her Grandmother hugging at a family cookout.

"Ok...Ok... Alright, so I'll send him down."

She hung up the phone. "Alright, so tell him that you're interested in studying part time and that your first priority would be taking classes online and over the summer. You got your transcript, so you should be straight."

NYC was in the middle of a heat wave. The Puerto Rican Day Parade was coming up, the number of fistfights were increasing, and so was the price of gas. The Projects were getting restless, the Police were getting aggressive and the hustlers were getting paid. Summer Jam, Greek Fest, and the neighborhood block parties were right around the corner. These were the annual yet ever unique circumstances from which the rap King of New York usually emerged...summer time. And New York, albeit one of the most populated cities in the world, has never been big enough for two Kings.

The Hip-Hop heavy weights were all taking this summer off, as every one who mattered had already seen their fair share of fun in the sun. The only emcees that Junior felt could challenge him lyrically were all underground Rappers who most people would never hear. He on the other hand had two hit singles, one of which went platinum and the other made the number one video on nearly every Hip-Hop video countdown, his album sales were hovering around gold, he even recorded a song with Lina Leslie, the newest industry R&B star, J3 was major.

Junior could see him from down the block. He was conversing with a homeless woman in front of the location were Magro's Sporting Goods used to be. Laronda was a few feet away standing idly looking up and down the block. Junior parked his sports car. Laronda spotted him the second he stepped on to the curb, he could see her point him out to his Father who quickly ended his conversation and made his way over.

"Peace."

"What's up?" Junior responded flatly as if he'd seen him yesterday.

Jason laughed to himself then at Laronda, "Well as the Gza so eloquently put it; *survival got me buggin' but I'm alive on arrival.*" He looked at the diamond cross hanging from Junior's neck. "Ah let me hold a few dollars. I'm hurting up right now."

Jason had on an expensive, attention grabbing watch and he and Laronda were both sporting new white sneakers and sweat-suites. Junior found some way to look past all of that, as pulling out a wad of money and breaking his Father off a little something would allow himself to shine even brighter. "How much you need?"

Laronda pushed Jason in his broad back; "Don't give him no money Junior. He just playing."

Jason gave her an uncertain smile then turned his attention back to Junior. "So what's going on, how you?"

"I'm good, can't complain."

Junior was still in extra cool mode, nonchalant, hiding behind his expensive shades.

"I guess not; you must be busy. I see you ain't respond to none of my letters."

He shrugged his shoulders as he broke eye contact; "You know how the life is right?"

"Yo my dude, you ain't been insinuating anything me in those little raps of yours have you?" Jason's sharp alteration of the conversation caught Junior completely by surprise.

"Yo, I'm saying-"

Jason interjected, "Cause you know that's a problem you don't want on no type of level right?" His face became stiff with tamed force as he easily stepped into Junior's personal space.

"What you mean?" Junior asked timidly, careful to check the bass in his voice.

"I mean I'll tear your head off kid. Lyrically, physically however you wanna do it. You understand me?"

Jason riled himself up to a point that Junior seriously thought he was going to attack him. The energy that usually propelled him had eluded him. He was emotionally stunned, in disbelief that his own Father was pressing him so hard in public.

-"Come on Jason you going too far."

Laronda tried to intervene; laying an affectionate hand on Jason's pumped up shoulders. Jason squared Junior up as if poised to pounce on him. His voice ascended to that of a sheer roar, warranting the attention of every bystander in the vicinity, *"You understand me?"*

UNIT 3

Hollis *Honey* Jordan

252

"I don't give a fuck about your graduation, you know that."

Date: August 10TH 2007

"What's up? My name is Hollis Jordan, my friends call me Honey. I just turned eighteen last month. Ummm... I'm at S.B.U on a full athletic scholarship for track; yeah, I be killin' them out there."

The room became unsettled with laugher and sneak comments. Hollis crossed her long, honey brown legs and sat forward in her chair, searching her head for more basic information about herself. "Um...I have a famous Bro- well a somewhat famous Brother."

"Oh yeah, who's your Brother?"

"J3, the Rapper." Hollis said to the curious blonde in the back of the room.

"Oh, I never heard of him."

"Yeah, that's why I said somewhat famous. But anyway, I have a thirteen year old Sister. I hate eggs, and I have a boyfriend back home named Reggie."

Hollis could feel the ease of some of the fellas in classroom sitting back in their seats. The Professor looked Hollis over, admiring her athletic physic. "Wow look at those arms, and those shoulders." She jovially mocked Hollis by flexing her weak, pale arm. "My GOD; maybe you can give me some pointers on how to get these old bones back into shape." Professor Maldonado joked.

"Uh oh, girl power." Hollis encouraged her and they busted out laughing.

"That's right, girl power!" Professor Maldonado jumped on the cool train.

"Don't have me go get my jump rope and dumbbells. We could do it."

The professor giggled as if Hollis had tickled her soul. "Alright, if I show up at your dorm room in my spandex and my jogging shoes, you remember you said that."

Hollis flashed her affable smile that was sure to make her a winner at Swanson Bryce University when the regular semester began in three weeks. She had much to learn about the world Hollis thought to herself. She didn't know old white women could be so chill.

Professor Maldonado looked at the Korean girl next to Hollis, "Ok who's next?"

"Hi, my name is-"

-"I'm sorry, one Moment." The Professor addressed the class as a whole once again, "You see guys, ice breakers can be fun. You never know what you'll discover or who you'll meet."

Hollis silently nodded her head to concur. She had her business face on as she looked the Professor in the eyes, etching herself in her memory to ensure that she wouldn't be just another anonymous face in the small lecture hall. *I'm a get an A in this class* she thought to herself as she sat back and continued listening to the Korean girl introduce herself.

After class Hollis got a smoothie from the Student Union then walked over to the S.B.U outdoor practice track by her lonesome. It was only orientation week, yet Hollis already began to stand out as a social butterfly among her peers. Consequently she already had to start going out of her way to duck people whenever she needed some Hollis time. Ever since she began training with her Father at the tender age of five, Hollis desired to hear only her own voice in the minutes and hours before running. She took a side exit out of the Union and walked along a dirt road behind the main campus library where there was no one around to bug her and there was also no shade from the scorching sun.

Hollis studied the campus during her walk to the track, taking mental note that there was a public computer room in a remote building off of Swanson Road, a sleeping lounge for commuting students in Kelly Hall, next to the school of law, and a chicken joint was in the Student Activity Center.

9:16AM; THE SAME DAY

She went through her stretches and intervals in a corner by herself and scared the shit out of anyone who dared to look into her fiery competitive eyes. She was the new girl on the scene and she knew her teammates would be checking to see if she was worthy to run the anchor-leg, an honor which Coach Drexler bestowed upon her before she arrived on campus.

"Ms. Jordan you wanna join us for this first 400?" Barb the S.B.U Lions assistant coach yelled. "Come on. I think it'll be fun. We're only paying your full cost of attendance for you to run with us."

Hollis made her way to the starting blocks and positioned herself in the fourth lane without saying anything to anyone but herself.

271

"I'm gone leave me a bitch in the dust today."

She commenced her trademark self motivating tactics; flexing her lean, well toned leg muscles, shaking out her arms and talking to herself. Barb stood next to Coach Drexler and summoned the runners, *"On your marks!"*

Hollis aligned her hands on the track bed and looked at the open lane ahead of her. Unable to keep her right leg still she bounced it from the ball of her foot, fully prepared to explode out the blocks.

"Set!"

She stared at the runners in the lanes ahead of her. *"Food...these bitches is fooood."* She laughed at her own sentiments before dropping her head and finding her peace with the Lord.

"Go!"
_____

Hollis looked into her diamond clustered watch dial, growing more impatient. "He said be at the door at a quarter to twelve. Were the hell he at?"

"You know Junior probably in there somewhere on his superstar shit; forgetting about the little people." Renee said as she popped the gum in her mouth and folded her arms.

"He need to hurry up; got us out here standing on line with these lames." Dominique said looking at the girl in front of her on the line with red hair and a matching one piece. "Matter of fact, come on; cause I'm not waiting on line. I am *way* too fly for this shit." Dominique pulled Hollis by her wrist and marched to the front of the line like a bull dressed in Baby Phat. Her thick, oversized ass seemed to be having its own party beneath her black jeans, turning every masculine head that they breezed by and even some females stared at her rump and the exposed tattoo on the small of Dominique's back.

"There he go right there."

Hollis spotted her Brother behind the security personnel on his cell phone at the door.

"Yo that's my Sister right there. Let her and her peoples in."

Hollis let Renee and Dominique go in before her to ensure their free admission. Hollis clutched her purse and eased her way past one of the enormous bouncers at the door.

"I would've let you in, sexy. You don't need to be waiting on no lines nowhere."

"Thank you." She smiled and kept it moving.

"We got a few tables reserved upstairs. Whatever yall want, whatever yall need for the night, just let one of my people know and they'll take care of yall."

Junior was wearing a deep purple button down and blue True Religion jeans. A mountain of muscle in a black suite followed him everywhere he went. Hollis peeped her Brother's gaudy jewelry and had to comment. *"Damn, what you got the 50 Cent record deal?"* She asked speculatively.

"We did alright, we did alright." He responded conservatively, barely looking at her.

Oh this boy on his superstar shit

The music grew louder as they approached the main dance floor. Hollis saw Junior and Renee whispering back and forth to one another. Renee was so mellow from the bottle of E&J that they downed before getting on the 2 train that Hollis couldn't read her face. She figured it best to mind her own business anyway.

I never got the chance to tell ya, how much a playa really felt ya...

Hollis and Dominique waived their hands in a celebration of freedom. The new J-Bzy single had the dance floor at Club Midis jumping.

Hollis' joyful spirit was renewed as the energy in the club somehow reminded her that she had just graduated High School. The girls sang along and got involved in the party going on around them.

I never got the chance to show ya, how much a thug'll roll out 4 ya...

Hollis rolled her waist and shook away the responsibilities and pressures of her life for the night. A tall, dark fellow eased up on her and smoothed his way into a dance. Hollis handed her purse to Dominique and gave him what he was looking for.

"Ooooo, work em you lil freak bitch!"

Dominique and Hollis laughed and slapped each other fives, mocking a boy from Dominique's Projects who took Hollis' rejection of his phone number way too seriously earlier.

...I never got the chance to tell ya...

7:57AM; THE NEXT MORNING

Hollis stared at Renee and Dominique as she laced her jogging sneakers on the other side of the room. Renee's head was facing Hollis' window and Dominique's was toward the closet. Hollis wondered to herself if the guys from the

club would've brought them so many drinks last night if they could see them this morning.
Renee rolled over, placing her face inches away from Dominique's plumped yet cute feet. Hollis grabbed the white jeans that she wore last night and removed her cell phone from its' carrying case attached to her belt. She took several pictures of Renee's open mouth next to Dominique's lime green toes then crept out the room slowly, careful not to wake the girls.

Hollis was silent and as focused as a laser, anxious to get out there. She began stretching her neck and loosening her shoulders as she walked down the stairs and through the living room where her Mother was having a private cup of coffee.

"Hey."

"Good morning. How was Junior's party?"

"It was good."

Hollis was brief; the more she said would lead to her Mother saying more, ultimately blah- blah- blahing training time away. Hollis' switch was turned on and she was ready to go.

"Your crazy ass Father on his way over here."

"Mm…" Hollis faintly acknowledged while flipping through the mail on the counter in search of a letter from S.B.U informing her of her room assignment for the semester. She set the stopwatch on her wrist then headed for the front door.

"Wait, Hollis did you hear what I said? Your Father is on his way over here. He's coming to see you."

Quickly agitated, she snapped at her Mother. *"So what I'm supposed to switch everything I'm doing when he decide he wanna come around? I gotta go."*

The girls had been drinking all night and Hollis didn't get much sleep. She didn't realize it until she was a few paces into her morning run, but she felt lousy. As she breezed across Union Street, she could feel her stomach resettling. She pressed her fingers deep into her washboard abdominals as she felt a cramp on-setting. To a light jog she trotted, springing herself forward solely from her strong legs, employing bad form before finally giving in and stopping. She turned her head to see if anyone was witnessing the state champion in her less than normal state and was taken aback as she saw her Father.

"Peeeeace!"

Jason was leaning out the passenger side of a silver car with his muscular, vein stricken arms and turban wrapped head hanging out. The driver stopped the car and he stepped out.

"What you got in there a bomb?" Hollis asked looking speculatively at the black duffel bag in his hand.

"Why you say that?"

"You look like a terrorist right now Daddy."

Jason looked at her as if surprised she would let her mouth give way to such ignorance. Hollis tried to stare back before sucking her teeth and turning away. "I don't believe you missed my graduation Daddy."

"So what, you mad?"

"*Daddy of course I'm friggin' mad, yes!* Any normal person would be."

Jason declined a response, he just looked her over and after a few Moments, he held an affectionate arm out; "Come here."

She gave him a half hug and he pulled her in further. "You know I love you right?"

"It don't hurt to show it sometimes Daddy."

"I don't give a fuck about no graduation baby. You know that."

"Oh my GOD, I don't believe you just said that."

"Alright, alright I'm sorry." Jason said seemingly feigning his sympathy.

"No, Daddy cause you don't care about nothing but what you doing and I hate that!"

"*Ah, ah cut that shit out!* First Junior with his shit now you. Yall kids better recognize, especially you! I went to fucking war to help maintain your little fly girl image and to get your punk ass to college. What, I need to look like one the Dads on T.V to make yall happy?"

Hollis looked at her Father and saw his frustration mounting and therefore pumped her breaks as he carried on. "I'm a simple man on ordained path, Hollis. Some men teach, some men are Lawyers; I rhyme in the name of GOD. And sometimes my Father enlarges his provisions and sometimes he restricts them. When I complete a task that he sets before me, when I have excess time or money, you are the first person I holler at."

Jason forced his mouth shut for a Moment; Hollis could see that he was formulating more in his mind. Just as she made out who his driver was her Father found his next talking point.

"Allah's law are that of seedtime and harvest; seedtime and harvest." He pounded the fact home with a fist into his opposing hand. "When it's seedtime, when I have to create an album and be in the studio all day and all night, that is what it is. When the harvest come around, yall three, all three of yall, have consistently been the ones to reap the benefits. But e'rybody wanna look at Dad funny. You was right there when your Mother left; what crime did I commit?"

"Daddy, Mommy ain't wanna leave you for no reason!" Hollis snapped. "You had a gun and drugs in the house. You was getting arrested."

"And? So fucking what? Those are the tools of my trade; getting arrested was a risk that came along with what I was doing. I knew the price and the risk, shit; you knew, your Mother did too. But nobody was mad when we was in Chucky Cheese eating them soggy ass chicken wings and shit."

"Daddy, what are you talking about?"

"Jason!"

Laronda climbed out the car and called out for Jason. He looked over and seemed to level his raging energy off.

"I been getting money here and there on the streets since before your ass was born. Them jobs don't always come in where we from kid... You...You know what?" He apparently changed his mind about convincing her to see things his way. "We gone see what course you take; cause your time is coming. I've been teaching you your whole life about being a leader, about being uppermost and the principles of adherence to GOD's path; about not following stupid ass men, supporting them and their corporations that thrive and stay two steps ahead of your poor black ass with your purchase of their goods and with the time you spend pedaling for them...I tried to keep my time and my money for yall. Now I got the time and a little bit of money and yall mad at how I got it. So now you in search of Allah's bounty; we'll see if you follow his path or the path I dedicated my life to showing you, proving to you, isn't there."

Jason stood up, leaving the duffel bag behind for Hollis. "So you go to college. Go mingle with the world. I know GOD! You find him. See if you feel the same way about me when you do."

"I guess *Allah's* plan included a jail sentence and felony conviction too huh?"

Jason slid on a pair of black on black sunglasses that were resting in his collar and mellowed out. "You know how many trips I took, borough to borough, state to state; *dirty*. They could've gave me football numbers, you think I'm trippin' off that little year. I went to Jail and did the same shit I would've been doing out here. I told the Brothers that GOD is the truth! I'm a talk to you later though."

Laronda spun the car in a u-turn and sped off. Hollis sat and wondered how her usual Sunday morning jog had turned into an emotional and physically disturbing roller-coaster. Her stomach was still turning. She peaked into the bag her Father left for her and among its' contents she could see a large tube of coco butter, a pair of flip-flops, a English version of the Holy Qur'an, perfume, a plastic accordion folder, a laptop computer, a few CDs, dental floss, a chessboard, and a Swiss Army knife.

AUGUST 28TH 2007

"...She ain't show up yet; but I ain't gone sit up here and leave all my stuff packed up for a

whole 'nother day waiting for her, no I'm setting my shit up."

Hollis slid out of her flip-flops and climbed onto her mattress, trying to keep her cell phone balanced between her shoulder and ear as she hung her Bob Marley banner over her bed.

"Babe hold on." She said after dropping a thumbtack. *"Actually can I call you back Reggie? Let me finish setting up in here."*

Hollis situated her bed with a red and white sheet-set that she got from the Mall the day before. She had Jay-Z's *Blueprint* Album blasting from the silver compact radio on her desk. Her refrigerator was stocked with Hawaiian Punch, milk and stew chicken that her Grandmother sent down with her. Jackie Joyner Kersee posters, a beautiful red and gold toned throw rug, a Tweety doll and a small plastic fan that clipped on to the side of her desk were some of the things that made Hollis feel as close to home as possible being nearly four hundred miles away.

Out of her window she could see group after group of students trekking across the walkway between Cameron and LaSalle Halls. They were on their way to the Student Association's freshmen mixer at the Swanson-Bryce Basketball arena on the other side of campus.

Hollis would be taking the same hike soon, as Jessie and Jennifer, two girls she met at orientation in July as well as a few of her teammates would be knocking at her door at any Moment.

The sound of nylon scratching against the wall a few feet away summoned Hollis' attention. She turned around then jumped off her bed to help relieve her apparent roommate of one of the large bag suspended from her shoulders.

"Oh, thank you."

"No doubt."

Hollis placed the bag on the bare mattress on the other side of the room. "Damn girl, what you got in here, a body?"

"No; that's my tennis rackets." The girl smiled brightly, revealing her beautifully white teeth, she extended a welcoming hand, "Diane Jendrowski."

"Hollis Jordan."

Hollis went back to her side of the room and flopped atop her mattress and began tossing around one of her teddy bears. "So you're a Tennis player huh?"

"Yep; since I was four years old my Daddy saw to it that I had the best training." She held both her hands out, as if to say *alas*, "Now I'm here about to play for my College. Isn't that something?"

"I bet I could take you."

"You play tennis?"

"No, but I'm an athlete. It can't be much to it."

"Well when you're ready we'll grab us some rackets and take it to the courts. I got a serve that'll put you on that cute little behind of yours."

Hollis laid back, still playing with her Swanson-Bryce Lion and thought to herself this may not be that bad. She liked Diane's personality, and the fact that she was a fellow competitive athlete. She knew she'd be able to learn something from her.

"I'm into rap music too. I got that new J-Bzy CD; it's sweet. He's originally from V.A you know?"

"Na, I didn't know that."

"You're not from Virginia huh?" Diane asked in her deep country accent.

"I'm from New York." Hollis said as if offended that Diane didn't know.

"Oh, well, cool. Don't worry girl, I can get you caught up. I know all the latest stuff." Diane sat on her bed to relive her aching feet and looked at the red, yellow, and green banner above Hollis' bed. "Who's the guy with the dread locks?"

"Jo shawty what it is? I know you got a minute to holler at a real playa."

Hollis dropped her head and kept making her way toward the campus shuttle as if she didn't hear him.

"Well keep walking then. New York bitches acting like they GOD's gift to da damn world."

She couldn't resist; *"Fuck you, you lil short ass punk!"* She yelled at the boy before boarding the bus. Hollis was on her way to her 2:30 chemistry course in Charlotte Hall. Monday, Wednesday and Friday were her heavy days; she had a 9 o'clock, a 12 o'clock and a 3-6:40 class on the west wing of the campus. Tuesdays and Thursdays were light. Her earliest class on either day was at noon, then chemistry at 2:30.

"Don't worry bout him. He just mad he been here six years and still ain't graduate."

"Fuck him, I'm not thinkin' bout him. If he get out of line again I'm a put that phone call in though. That's nothin'."

Her rough edge, confidence and style pushed the gym bag toting, fair skinned fellow forward. "Let me guess, you from Brooklyn?"

She finally looked him in the eye, "I'm from Harlem." She said as she plugged in her mp3 player earphones and pulled out her notebook to review her notes.

Hollis had team breakfast everyday at 6:15 before practice at the S.B.U Alumni Arena. Coach Drexler had her running the 4X4 this indoor season and consequently Hollis had been running 800's to train since she arrived to campus.

Between the breaks in her classes Hollis sat in the Student Union, where she socialized and eat her way toward the freshmen fifteen mostly with chicken fingers and burgers. By and by, the Union is where Hollis became further acquainted with Swanson-Bryce and college life. During homecoming week she was introduced to the Black Student Union, NESBE, and the Sisters of Pi Sigma Mu from the concession stands they all had set-up in the middle of the Student Union.

SEPTEMBER 12TH 2007

"So...any comments?" Mr. Neives asked as he cut off the V.C.R and cut on the lights, waking about half the students in the room.

"That scene when they captured Kunta, and he was trying to break the chains, that was so vivid, so inspiring...it, it-"

-"Inspiring? That 'ish was scary. He was trying with all his strength to get out of those, those fetters." Hollis reinforced her choice of words as if disgusted. "He knew it was a wrap for him; that he was going to be subjected to a life of turmoil, pain and oppression. That was..." Hollis looked off to the side in her own world of thought, "...that was crazy."

Mr. Neives leaned over the station from which he was controlling the film projector and massaged his long salt and pepper beard. "Yes, Kunta was a proud warrior and an accomplished young man in his own rite. So for him to be subjected to, as Ms. Jordan said, to a life of servitude for a people who systematically raped their woman, separated their families and forced them to work under harsh conditions; yeah, that was crazy."

Mr. Neives checked his wrist watch and saw that the class had run past its designated time. "Okay so I'll see you guys next week. Don't forget, you have a two page response due."

8:55PM; THE SAME NIGHT

The third floor lounge had become a nightly hang out spot for Hollis. She usually sat on the couch in her S.B.U sweats after a day of taking it to the max. The third floor lounge is where she ate dinner, reviewed her notes, and watched mostly *Flavor of Love*, *House* or the S.B.U movie of the week with the girls. Tonight was one of those nights.

"You don't like Jarell? That boy is very well put together. I could see potential in him."

-"Or what about Calvin, wit' his chocolate ass. That boy be coming to campus knowing he look good." Jennifer threw her two cents in.

-"He live off campus?" Hollis asked as she lifted her eyes from her economics textbook.

"My homegirl told me he live in the frat house. You know he a Alpha?"

"Oh, no I didn't know that."

-"You know he was looking to get a little Honey in his diet too." Fatima said while staring facetiously at Hollis.

"*Anywaaay*; I have a man alright? Yall so bad." Hollis said, glowing with temptation as she tried to hide back in her textbook.

Fatima was from East Flatbush in Brooklyn, Joy and Jennifer were both Virginia natives.

-"*Oh shit. This my jam!*"

That's Talisa, from the Bronx, who just turned to B.E.T., which was playing J3's *This is for the Ladies* video. Talisa turned her firm thick backside to the television and bounced it up and down as the chorus instructed.

"*Nasty.*" Hollis mocked before tossing her highlighter in her book and sitting back.

"*Bring your Brother up here for the weekend and I'm a show you how nasty I am.*"

"*Listen…*" Hollis got serious for a Moment. "I'm gone either have to go upstairs or we gone have to cut that T.V off and get some studying done. I got two response papers due and I got a read twenty four pages for my economics exam."

"Aight come on, let's focus." Jennifer, the usually quiet one encouraged the ladies.

After eight minutes of dead silence the girls felt as if they'd been studying for at least an hour. Alicia Keys' *Unbreakable* filled the room as it screamed from Hollis' cell phone. She had that ring-tone reserved only for one person. Everyone in the room turned their attention to her as she lifted her phone off the cushion beside her. "That's Reggie, I gotta take this." She stood to excuse herself from the room. *"Yo why you ain't been picking up my phone calls?"* Hollis yelled into the phone as she shut the lounge door behind her. Fatima waited for Hollis to leave before she closed her Intro to Calculus textbook.

"Talisa cut the T.V back on."

"Come on girls. This shit ain't gotta be interesting. If yall feel like blowing these wack ass broads out then let's go do it. Lions on 3; 1! 2! 3!"

-"Lions!"

Hollis glanced at Coach Drexler who was looking back at her optimistically as she concluded her pre-race prep talk with the relay team. Hollis went through the some final stretches. A substantial crowd was in attendance at the Hofstra gymnasium for their annual invitational indoor meet. Shania, the S.B.U lead leg was secure in the starting blocks with her backside sticking straight in the air. The starting gun fired and the pack was off for the first heap of the 4x4.

Shania came out of the first turn fighting for third place, a good start considering that she was coming from the sixth lane. She was kicking, but Hollis could tell that she didn't have what it took to stay stride for stride with the herd. Hollis continued to pump herself up, as she knew she was going to have some collateral damage to repair at the anchor. Shania held on to pass the stick off in third place to Candice. Candice ran the second leg from Brown University down on the straightaway out of the first turn. Hollis took a deep breath and closed her eyes commencing her ritualistic *blackout* process; the calm before the storm. She wasn't thoroughly pumped; she did indulge in her infamous self talking to and she went through all of her usual intervals, yet her intensity wasn't at its' normal day of the race, through the roof level. She didn't feel laser sharp. She stretched, but she didn't feel thoroughly warmed up. Even her traditional blackout was off, as she had gotten lost in some other thoughts instead of envisioning a victory. When she opened her eyes she turned around and quickly spotted Brandy, the Lions third leg from her thick braids and royal blue and white uniform. Brandy was tied for fourth place entering the second turn on the 200 meter track. Hollis could only watch as the Trenton team exchanged the baton to their anchor leg, easily ten meters ahead of the pack. Brown University exchanged, then the University of Columbus. Hollis moved to the inner lane and took her lead for the exchange with Brandy furious that her team couldn't put her in a better position. Hollis employed the raw power that she usually reserved for the final thirty meters in attempt to close the gap. Her lean body ripped through the first turn and left the anchor from Columbus therein. She effectively opened her stride and put Angelica Coleman from Brown in her wake as well. Hollis could see the runner in first place and she could hear and feel the crowd going berserk, edging her on. Hollis had the inner ambition to stare the young lady in the eyes when she caught and passed her, which she was vehemently closing in on doing. In the middle of a stride, Hollis pulled back in an ambivalent state of extreme pain and anger. *"Shit!"* She came to a hobbled stop and limped off of the track onto the shot-putters station, unable to put any weight on her left leg. As the field ran past her she dropped to the ground. She roll on to her stomach and realized that she was unable to fully unfold her leg. *"Shit!"*

And it came to pass that Hollis became even more popular on campus; adored by the guys and sought by many of her female friends for advice. It came to pass that Hollis and Reggie, her boyfriend of over two years, completely grew apart. It came to pass that African American studies became the course of highest interest to Hollis. Although A.A.S 100 was only a two credit course that met once per week, Mr. Neives and his perspective left lasting impressions on young Ms. Jordan. His required readings broadened Hollis' perspective on the inner workings of her old neighborhood in Harlem, and how it related to the world abroad. He showed films on America's brutal conquest of the Hawaiian Islands, the transatlantic slave trade, the Abu Grad torture prison, the Prison Industrial Complex, gentrification, the *racialization* of laws, and Mr. Neives made sure to keep his students abreast on the tragic unfolding of the war in Iraq... It also came to pass that by midterms, Hollis' continuing education advanced her to a point where she began to view nearly everything around her differently; to see the reality of things. It came to pass that her intensity effectively shifted from the track to the classroom as she made rehabbing her strained hamstring a secondary issue. The word went forth.

OCTOBER 5TH 2007

294

"He wants us to submit them to him online, no later than 9 o'clock every Tuesday."

"So basically we summarize the reading, offer five pros and five cons about taming the Everglades and that's it?"

"Yeah, and don't forget to use facts from the E.P.A's website to support your opinion."

"Cool." Hollis pushed her backside off the bed from the palms of her hands. *"Ahh."*

"Sit down, beautiful. We can show ourselves out." Gillian, one of Hollis' Environmental Studies group members demanded in his deep Nigerian tone.

"Okay; thank you guys for coming. I appreciate it."

Hollis laid down and tried to ingest as much of the pain as possible before taking two more aspirins. She set her alarm clock to allow her enough time to catch the dining hall before they stopped serving dinner. She propped her bandaged leg onto two pillows and got situated for her power nap.

"Why, why, why?"

Hollis fired her fist into her bedding as she raised her frustrated eyes to the Lord. *"Why now?"* She asked as she looked down at her leg.

The luster of college life was gone, and trying times fell upon her. Hollis already had more on her plate than she felt she could handle. She couldn't understand GOD's reason for taking one of her hamstrings and make things that much more difficult on her. Her angered, machine gun questioning, along with countless other stream of conscience visualizations eventually calmed her into a deep sleep.

She woke up at a quarter to 10pm. Diane still wasn't in. Hollis wiped her eyes and pressed the alert button on her clock to see why it didn't go off like she set it to, and discovered that it was set for 7AM instead of 7PM. She lethargically grabbed her phone off her nightstand and dialed her Mother's number.

"What's up ma?"

"Nothing, you okay?"

"Yeah I'm okay I-"

"Okay cause I'm at dinner with a friend of mine right now. Let me call you back tomorrow."

Hollis looked at her phone as if she were expecting it to explain that to her. After a few moments she felt a strong urge to call Reggie, which meant breaking a promise that she made to herself not to call him until he called her first. But her temptation and boredom overcame her. She pressed the 1 key on her phone and held it until the speed-dial connected her.

"Hello."

"Yo, what's going on with you? Why I got a call you all the time? You can't call?"

"...Shit been crazy in the hood sweetheart; and our schedules is conflicting."

"Our schedules ain't never conflict before."

"What you talking 'bout? You ain't never been to college before."

She sat and waited for him to take the conversation whichever way his will decreed, the two of them sat in silence for a few Moments as Reggie was apparently waiting on her to do the same. Hollis felt like something needed to give. *"So who you fuckin'?"*

"Yo Honey I don't feel like doing this right now. I gotta go." Reggie snapped at her.

"Yeah you do that. And don't call me back!"

11:57PM; THE SAME NIGHT

Hollis stared into her open closet at her rows of
shoe boxes and hanger after hanger of designer
jeans and shirts. On the bottom of the closet to
the left was the duffel bag that her Father gave
her this past summer.

She grabbed one of her wooden crutches and
placed her weight on it to push out of bed
without troubling her injured leg. Midway to
the other side of the room, she put the crutch
down and walked the rest of the way delicately.
She removed the bag from the closet and opened
it on her bed. The first thing to catch her eye
was the gold and green bound Qur'an to the
side. She removed the book and opened it to
page 1338 at random.

*My devotees! No fear shall be on you that day,
nor shall ye grieve, being those who have
believed in our signs and bowed their heads to
our will.*

Hollis closed the book and admired the beautiful
cover for a Moment before putting it down and
digging into the bag and removing the CDs
within; Tupac's *Makaveli* and *All eyes on Me*
double disk, B.I.G's *Ready to Die*, Nas's
Illmatic and *It Was Written*, a few Jay-Z albums

and copies of Architekk's two albums. She figured she'd indulge in the album she never heard for the night, and so she put her Father's first album *Terminal Velocity* in her radio. She dug back into her bag and removed a box of chocolates before zipping it back up.

Maybe I could wake up and sell all these dimes, and re-up by the P.M, maybe things'll be fine. Still something always comes up baby time after time. Still we gone link up soon, shorty you gone be mine, short you gone mine...

She turned her radio to a level loud enough for her to hear while she moved around and got her life organized. She was still tired; her eyes were hazy and her mind was drained at the thought all the work she was backed up on. She laid back across her bed and listened to her Father's lyrics. Some object poked at her back and she reached around her to pull it from beneath her; the Holy Qur'an. The good book was calling her, and since she didn't really feel like doing anything else, she opened it and read.

280

"Yo, yall bitches better fall back."

Date: February 2nd 2008

The ladies of Phi Mu Sigma took center stage,
the nine woman step-team were all wearing
Ottawa Senators jerseys representing their red
and gold sorority colors. The crowd settled
down as the lead Sister took command.

*"We are the Sisters of P.M.S... Your girlfriends
hate us- cause they know we are the best...
We're number 1 and I know- that you hate it.
We are the Sisters of P-Mu-Sigma inn-
corporated."*

"Lets go ladies!" The Sisters sitting in the front
row of the auditorium yelled in conjunction with
their girls on stage.

The crowd gathered at the Student Activity
Center roared louder than they did for the 1-12
football team this past season. Fatima and Joy
stood up out of their seats as the people in front
of them stood up, blocking their view.

Fatima and Joy were considering pledging
P.M.S this summer, and getting involved with
the world of Greek drama around them. Late
last semester they convinced Hollis to attend an

interest meeting with them, and Hollis, to her own surprise, actually found interest therein. According to Fatima, Joy and a few other people Hollis spoke with, apparently on GOD's green earth, one was either Greek or not. Hollis initially laughed the notion off, but as she got further involved with extracurricular activities on campus, those sentiments proved credible. Brenda Watson from Res-Life was a member of a Greek three-letter organization, so was Aretha Patterson from Student Services, and even Mr. Neives was a Zeta man.

"...We work harder than these fake- little-girls... running 'round in them fake cultured pearls."

The section of ladies in pink and green protested; the crowd went wild.

After the step show Hollis and her girls went to the basketball arena for the Winter Jam music festival that the Student Association was hosting as a part of S.B.U spirit week. When she returned to her room that night Hollis talked to Dominique for a few minutes then she called her Father who she'd been talking to on almost a daily basis for the past few months.

"...I'm an out of state student too. I'm a have to take out mad loans. But they saying I won't be

*able to register for classes if they pull my
scholarship; so I gotta do what I gotta do."*

*"I just feel like you worked too hard to just walk
away from the sport like that. You not just no
ordinary chick; you was the state champion,
baby."*

*"It's not in my heart no more Daddy...I feel like
I was doing that more for you than me."*

Jason took a deep breath into the receiver.
Hollis figured it was no better time to knock him
out than while she had him on the ropes.
*"Daddy I'm thinking about pledging for a
sorority."*

"...Mm..." He faintly acknowledged, keeping
his cool and reserve.

"Come on Pops, say something."

*"What's that Greek; a Greek sorority? What,
that was them dudes that made up all them
myths about Allah's creation right?"*

"Yes Daddy."

*"The dudes who invaded and stole knowledge of
civilization and self from the Africans; the
polytheist?"*

"Yes."

"Mm...let me know how that work out for you."

"Daddy?"

"I thought you said you been reading the Koran I gave you."

"I have. I'm ju-"

"Well what does it instruct you about lettering, and private councils, and people who accept only a part of the book even after they've been given clear signs, and the ten-percenters? It says leave them and their inventions alone right?"

Before Hollis could utter a word Jason spoke again. *"Okay bye."*

"What, you're hanging up on me?" Hollis asked baffled and mildly humored.

"I already know what you gone do, it ain't nothin' to talk about."

She laughed to herself in disbelief that her Father was acting so childish.

"There's three hundred and sixty degrees to a circle of knowledge, not thirty three and a third, bye." He said before hanging up the phone.

"Keep your legs movin'. Come on!"

Her Father yelled at the side of her face and pushed her in the back. *"What you retarded or something? You can't keep kicking your legs cause you feeling a little discomfort and pain?"*

Hollis fell to her backside and began unleashing the training weights tied to her ankles and the rope around her waist. *"I want my Mommy."* She slammed her small fist into the ground and began to cry.

"Come on Hollis, cut that shit out. You want your Mommy. You got a be able to accomplish a mission under duress sweetie. So what I'm yelling at you and pushing you? What that gotta do with your legs? You not focusing."

"I wanna go back to my Mommy!"

"No! I know you better break 35 seconds on the next 200 we run or you ain't getting no Mommy, no allowance, and no T.V. Cause you not trying. You searching for the road of least resistance."

Hollis cried out as if she was being tormented, she threw one of her ankle weights at her Dad and yelled as loud as she could, *"I'm only seven years old!"*

-*"Honey."*

"I'm only seven years old!"

-*"Honey."*

Hollis looked up into Diane's concerned face.

"You don't wanna lay down girl?"

"Oh my GOD, how long have I been sleep?"

"Well it's 6:30-"

"6:30!"

Hollis pushed her hair back and sat up. Although she was awake, she took a Moment to gather herself and seriously figure out where she was. She saw her laptop and her memo stickers posted along her study desk, it was then that she realized she had been dreaming. She grabbed her backpack and skated out of the room, as she was late for office hours with Mr. Neives.

6:42PM; THE SAME DAY

"So what do you think would be the most effective thing for someone like me to do to try and change things?"

"First, learn your history. Learn as much as you can so you could have a full understanding of how your ancient fellow man crept from the bowls of Africa and advanced, and how it all led to you sitting right here at this very Moment. If you don't know where you came from, where can you go, right?"

Hollis nodded in comprehension, as she often did when Mr. Nieves spoke.

"And make sure you get registered to vote, and actually go do it. I do believe we could get this senator from Chicago elected as the first Black President of the United States if you young people just go out and vote."

"All due respect Mr. Nieves, but to hell with voting." Hollis said while getting her backpack ready.

"Excuse me?"

"Well you taught us yourself that during slavery and all the way up to the mid-20th century, institutions like the courthouses, police percents

306

and the political system in general were all facilitators of inequality and our degradation. I'm not trying to play around with America and her facades of democracy. All the politicians and leaders of this country do is lie."

"Easy young lady, you're too intense. In order to change the system you have to understand it, and break into it first; you can't ignore it. Whatever you do, you're going to pay taxes, taxes that support government; which means you have a vested interest in government, which means not voting isn't smart."

"I guess." Hollis sat back unconvinced and unmoved. She looked at her wristwatch more so to let Professor Nieves know that she was ready to leave than for the time; "Unless you make a living off the books. You know, like on some crazy gangster type ...you know?" Hollis decided to have a little fun with Mr. Nieves as she stood up to leave. She could tell that he already thought she was a little criminal minded, and she thought it was cute to shock his poor old soul every now and again.

"Goodnight young lady." He said with his flat South African voice as he escorted her out. "Stay away from rap music for a while."

After office hours Hollis walked over to the financial aide office and picked up a FASFA form. She walked through the school of Architecture buildings as a short cut to her Residence Hall. She saw individual students sprawled throughout the corridors, some reading, some were putting the final touches on models they'd designed, some were fighting exhaustion to finish other projects, but all of them were putting in work, on what was, for the most part a barren academic campus at this hour.

11:23PM; THE SAME NIGHT

Hollis pushed open the heavy fifth floor Girls Bathroom door and slid herself past it careful as to not disturb the towel wrapped around her body. She placed her bath bucket on the counter above the sink and ran to faucet to brush her teeth. While she waited for the water to heat up she looked at herself meticulously in the mirror. The definition in her body was giving way. She held her right arm out with her toothbrush in hand and shook it gently. That which was a well toned tricep muscle range just months ago was now a soft mass of flesh, which she had minimal control over. She grabbed her stomach and for the first time ever, she could pinch excess fat between her fingers. She looked in the mirror horrified. She cut off the water, grabbed her bucket and rushed back into her room.

"You okay?"

"Yeah, great." Hollis said as she scattered through her closet. She slipped into her Pepe sweatpants and a fleece, and searched through her collection of footwear for her jogging shoes.

"You seen my gray New Balance Dee?"

"Na, I haven't." Diane answered looking suspiciously at her possessed roommate. "Your leg is better?"

Hollis found her sneakers beneath her bed and sat down to lace them up, "No..." She grabbed her stopwatch off of her desk and headed for the door; "But I gotta go."

11:48PM; THE SAME NIGHT

"Ahhhh-hhhhhh-hhhhh!!!!!!!"

Hollis released a deaf defying holler as she shot up the small dirt hill like a bullet, for the fourth time. Her adrenaline fueled her, as it did in years past at Penn Relays, States and the East Coast championships. *"Lets do this! Lets go Hollis!"* She clapped her hands as she made her way back to her makeshift starting point.

Hollis established a training post in a remote area behind the parking lot of the football field, where she ran a few straight-aways, did ten repetitions of incline sprints and she did over a hundred sit-ups and calf rises. When she got back to her room she felt somewhat back to proper form. She showered and stayed up until close to 4am studying for her upcoming test; fully focused and fully acceptant of her life of hard work. She was working on A's in her advanced African American studies course, her introductory level Sociology course and Woman's Studies 224. Her other two courses; Intro to Computers and Calculus 2, she was sitting on solid B's, with A's in reach if she took care of business on the final exams.

Against Resident Hall policies Hollis covered her smoke detector with a plastic bag and lit a incent. She sat at her desk playing *Who is Jill Scott?* on low and stayed in the books until she couldn't take anymore.

MARCH 7TH 2007

"Welcome to the 49th annual meeting of the ladies of Phi Mu Sigma Incorporated Alpha chapter. For those of you who do not know, today is the first day of our Founders week."

-"If you don't know that you really shouldn't be in here." Abby, the ace of the spring 99 line said.

-"As a matter of fact..." Leyla, Abby's line Sister looked through the crowd of approximately twenty interests and pointed to Hollis; "You, name our six founders."

Hollis responded quickly and arrogantly, "I have no idea who your six founders are."

"You didn't read up on the organization after the first time you showed up here?"

"No not really. I've been reading for my classes. I'm trying to get a 4.0 this semester."

"Well good for you." Persilla, a Sister from Virginia A&M said as if smiting her. "Do you still run track?"

"No." Hollis responded flat, not as upfront as she previously was.

"Why not?"

Persilla was dwelling in sort of a *no fly zone* with Hollis. Since she stepped away from the sport she'd been answering questions about why for long enough. It was a personal issue that was not up for public discussion.

"I got injured and…I don't know, I…"

"You quit?"

"Quit?"

"Yes quit; did you quit?"

"Yo…" Hollis sat up in her seat and looked beside her at Fatima whose face seemed to be desperately pleading with her not to ruin her chance to pledge. Hollis controlled herself and kept quiet until…

"Are you crazy or something?"

The question came from among the panel of P.M.S. Sisters seated at the front of the room.

"Yeah, I am crazy; but I ain't no fucking weak! I don't quit. I train-" Hollis pounded a fist into her open hand producing a loud smack of flesh, "-*hard* for what I want!" She sat back content that she said what she had to in order to convey her point, which eased her nerves. "And I get what I want."

-"Well do you want P.M.S.?"

Hollis was grilling Persilla, who was staring at her. She reached down and grabbed her Dior bag from under her seat. "Na I'm good. Fuck this."

APRIL 9TH 2007

Hollis finished packing her small refrigerator and turned around to find Joseph standing behind her with a silly look on his face. "I brought this for you."

She prayed that she wouldn't look down and see a ring box in this boy's hand. She looked, and sure enough, it was a ring box. Hollis huffed visibly; not in the mood to spare his feelings. "What the hell is that?"

Joseph removed the gold lid and looked at her with a naïve smile, "A friendship ring."

"What you brought me this for?" She removed the ring as if it were ill-infected and took a seat on her bed.

"Just for you to have; dag, sorry."

Hollis lightened up as she realized she'd been treating Joseph too cold for the past few days. He had been kind enough to walk with her to the supermarket earlier and almost killed himself trying to carry all of her grocery bags back himself. Furthermore, since she first spoke to him on line at the dining hall in the Grixby Complex, Joseph always made time listen to her. When she needed to vent about Reggie, classes, work, anything, he always went out of his way to lend an open ear and be supportive.

She placed the two-tone emerald ring back in its box and kissed him on the cheek. "Thank you."

Joseph exhaled deeply and closed his eyes, as if Honey's kiss melted him. "

What?" She asked in curious admiration of her influence over him.

He leaned into her neck and inhaled her sweet scent, *"Hollis you are…"* He closed his eyes. His reaction to her sheer presence flattered her. Joseph was weak for her, mentally and physically. Hollis knew she could control him and for the first time that fact turned her on. She caressed the side of his face and leaned in to plant a second, gentler kiss.

Joseph grabbed at her shoulder and pulled her in for a bold, equally passionate kiss on the lips. Hollis let herself go, allowing him to do as he pleased. He moved closer and caressed her breast. He lowered her to the bed and kept his mouth occupied. And the word went forth.

7:24PM; THE SAME DAY

Hollis could barely open her eyes. She rolled over and answered her room phone when the answering machine failed to answer after a fourth ring. *"Hello?"*

"Yeah!!!"

"Daddy, wh- what are you doing?"

Her Father was over zealous about something. He raised the pitch of his voice; Hollis could hear him clapping his hands through the receiver. *"Yeah!!! It's finals week baby! Time to pull all the tricks out the hat; crunch time, you ready?"*

Hollis felt human flesh brush against her leg and became intensely frightened. She rolled over in her bed to find Joseph fast asleep. *"Oh shit!"*

"What?"

She sat up quickly, leaving her sleepy haze behind. *"I'm sorry Daddy. Look, I'm very happy for you. I gotta go."*

"Happy? Wh-"

She dropped her phone and eased her body from the side of her bed. Without a second thought, she ripped the blanket off of Joseph and began sweeping the bed with it. *"You got a go. Look at this place! My parents would kill me; my Father would kill you! Come on, you got a get out of here right now!"*

"Damn, can I at least put my pants on?"

"No, no; my Dad is coming up the stairs right now. *Get yo' ass out of here!"* She shoved his clothing into the pit of his stomach, *"leave 'fore he get you!"*

Hollis spent the next three hours reading as much as she possibly could in preparation for her Sociology final, which constituted thirty percent of her grade for the course. She made flash cards to identify keys terms after class last week, so she had that much less to cram into her brain. When she needed a break from reading she either twisted her hair or typed away at her comprehensive paper for A.A.S which she'd been working on for over two weeks now. Hollis looked at any time spent on the computer during finals week as downtime, as she would often play her music and/or surf the internet at random. As for her Calc 2 final, she wasn't so worried that. Hollis hadn't missed one calculus class this semester, and she'd been receiving extra help from her G.A, so she decided to walk in the lecture hall pretty much as is with all intentions on smacking Mr. Chin's final.

Hollis stayed in her room for the rest of the night, no lounge, no hanging in Fatima's room in Franklin Hall, no dining hall and no boys. Most of the spots where students gathered were dead. Everyone was preparing themselves for judgment time; no more procrastination, no more excuses. Hollis and her peers were capping off their first year at Swanson Bryce. They were either getting ready to go into their respective majors or punch their tickets and head back home defeated by academia …finals week.

12: 17PM: THE NEXT DAY

Hollis stepped out of the Lions' Den Café after an hour long solo lunch. She was casually walking toward the Bus Stop when she suddenly, changed directions and ran across the walking path toward the back of Townsend Hall. She stopped and superfluously retied her shoes, in attempt to not seem like she'd completely lost her mind to anyone that may have been watching her. She calmly changed her direction yet again and headed back to the Bus Stop. And just as she thought, the Volvo she'd been watching from window at the Lion's Den drove off. She saw the same car in Franklin Hall parking lot this morning. The same car was in the Law School loop when she left out after checking her e-mail in their lab, and now this.

Who the hell is following me?

Hollis looked around then continued walking in vain as avoid being reported to public safety by her fellow students, taking note that the car made a right turn onto Swanson Rd. Swanson was a one way conduit that was going to swing the Volvo around to the back of Townsend Hall. She hurried to the side of the building, where she knew she could get a better look into the car.

Hollis took cover alongside the edge of a brick column near one of the back exit doors. Within seconds she was able to see clearly into the sedan that parked, apparently because they'd lost sight of her.

"Ain't this about a bitch?"

She marched across the manicured spring lawn fuming, straight up to the driver side window and she pounded on the glass. *"Daddy!"*

Jason froze in apprehension, spilling the binoculars he was looking out of into his lap. He lowered the window. The smell of fresh marijuana escaped the confines of the interior. *"Shit; Honey, where the hell you come from?"*

Hollis was on the verge of blowing her lid, *"Daddy what, what, what could you possibly be doing on my campus smoking weed with binoculars and Stump?"*

"I'm, I'm glad you asked that question baby." Jason massaged his goatee, stuck on stupid. "Get up." He slapped Stump on his large pot belly to stop him from snoring.

"Hm? Oh what's up Hollis? You found her boyfriend yet?" Stump asked in a low degree of consciousness before rolling on his side and falling immediately back to sleep.

318

"Daddy you did not come down here looking for my boyfriend!"

"Huh?"

"Daddy listen to me…" Hollis leaned into the open window.

-"Hollis-"

"No, no listen to me Daddy." She spoke at him like he had some sort of hearing impairment. "This is too far. Okay? This is way out of bounds." She looked into his face and saw that her words had a minimal impact, as if he were taking her for a joke. So she turned and walked away.

"Honey come here." Jason jumped out of the car and ran after her.

"Daddy! This is Virginia okay, not the 126th street. You can't be sitting on my campus staking out, watching me with binoculars & shit. *You can't do that!"*

"Aight, alright, I'm sorry. You just sounded a little bugged out on the phone yesterday that's all baby, I'm sorry. He opened his arms, "Come gimme a kiss. I don't wanna fight no more."

319

"No Daddy." Hollis said in attempt to get him to take her more seriously as he squeezed her.

"My beautiful baby; you look just like my Mother you know that?"

"Daddy why don't you buy me a pair of sneakers? I don't have no spring sneakers." Hollis said, still scrunched in his arms.

"And then we even?"

She simply smiled. Jason turned his attention to Yolanda, one of Fatima's Graduate Assistants as she walked past and they exchanged smiles. They both turned to continue flirting and checking each other out.

"And don't be afraid to introduce Dad to none of these young girls around here either Hollis." Jason removed his sunglasses and took a sip from his plastic bottle, trying to do the smooth thing. *"Can I talk to you for a minute?"* He yelled at Yolanda.

Hollis buried her face in her hands and shook her head clueless. *What am I gone do with him?*

"Yo, hold this for me." Jason handed Hollis his bottle of water and trotted over to Yolanda who apparently gave him her approval.

They all had on black and white N.Y.C.M.C t-shirts with pictures of the late Robert "Stacky" Reid on the back. They all laughed deep and passionately, seemingly at anything, and they all had positive energy exceeding them. Hollis was actually thinking about not going to the Phi Mu Sigma party as she was having so much fun listening to war stories from Stump and listening to the music that her Father was playing from her computer.

"So what you trying to do?" Hollis asked Jason as her laughter settled from a joke that Diane made. Jason was sitting at Hollis' desk with Laronda seated on his lap; he looked to Laronda. "I don't know; what you wanna do?"

"It's up to you. I'm not in want." She answered emotionless, now checking her e-mail.

Laronda looked completely differently from the last time Hollis saw her in St. Nicolas Projects beating a defenseless boy over the head with a champagne bottle. She seemed confident, focused and peacefully exempt from the need to speak.

During the past week Hollis and her Father talked about everything from her walking away from track, to Reggie, to the fistfight she almost got into with Persilla from P.M.S, even the mistake she made with Joseph. She confided in him and he proved to her that he wasn't there to judge her, but simply to listen to and help guide her. They didn't get to spend too much time together however, as Jason was running around on business in nearby D.C. and spending a significant amount of time at the campus' Islamic center. All of which was perfect because Hollis was busy testing and studying.

Margo returned to the overcrowded room with Fatima who rode with him to Herndon Parkway to get food for everyone.

"Ah Blackman, they ain't have none of that shrimp, pasta shit you wanted. I got you some fried chicken."

"Fried chicken?"

It was a Friday night; most students were done with their finals and were hanging around campus for the infamous S.B.U weekend of partying that capped off each semester. Several students had come through to meet Tekk and buy copies of his new underground single *Survivor.* Hollis was sitting on Diane's desk in a gold Roberto Cavalli dress, sipping on a peach schnapps-lemonade mix, getting into party mode. Diane and Fatima were sitting next to each other on Hollis' bed. Everyone was just chillin'.

"How this fool go from shrimp alfredo to fried chicken? You ole country bama ass ni-"

-"*Yo what's up man?*" Margo dropped the bags in his hands and snatched at his jeans before throwing up his hands. "*You been talking that shit all day; what's up? I ain't no punk. I done put boys twice your size in the sand, chump. What it is cuz, what it is?*

Force busted out laughing at Margo's mocking of the natives. Margo couldn't help but laugh himself. "Yo Tekk when I was locked up in Attica, I knocked a boy 6-11 straight out. Hit him with the boom-" Margo took a lightning fast jab inches away from Forces' chin. As Force threw his guard up, Margo shifted his body weight and hooked each of his fists into the sides of Force's torso, "*boom, boom.*" He stepped back, floating like a butterfly, ready to sting like a Bee. "See that boy? That size don't mean nothing; you soft as pudding." Margo said as he cut the antics and went for his carton of food. "Yo Tekk I'm telling you Bro, when I was locked up, up north, I was a absolute problem. You heard me Black? A problem."

Jason stopped rubbing on Laronda's thigh as the spotlight shifted to him. "Shit, not me. I was in there reading my Koran, lifting and watching Tyra."

-*"Watching Tyra?"* Diane and Fatima asked simultaneously and laughing.

"Hell yeah; Brothers wanted to be in there watching football & shit. I seen enough big sweaty ass men during rec. Everybody knew, 4 o'clock came, Tekk gone wanna see his Boo, no ifs, ands or buts."

-"That's your boo?" Laronda asked Jason on the low.

Talisa, who Hollis felt had been playing her Dad a little too close whenever she got the chance placed a hand on one of his shoulders, "I know you had to get these muscles doing something."

Laronda turned and looked at Talisa's hand, then at Jason's face without saying a word. She continued reading from the computer monitor breathing steam through her nostrils.

"Here, let me get up." Jason said as he slid from Talisa's grasp to avoid a conflict. "This is my proof that I can channel my energy; designed and built under adversity." He said flexing his right bicep. "I spread the word of Allah in Prison; fought the good fight."

Hollis was enjoying the scene until that Moment. She could feel a sermon on the horizon as she noticed her Father beginning to smile at the thought of GOD and she didn't want him to start preaching to her friends, who for now thought he was at least half way normal.

"O-K! So, Daddy; we gone go to this party at the Sigma Shack okay? I love you."

"Wha-" Jason tried but Hollis wouldn't let him.

"Okay good. Lock my room door when yall leave please. Okay? I love you."

1:25AM; THE SAME NIGHT

Hollis and her girls were enjoying themselves at the final P.M.S. house party of the year. Fatima was talking to a few of the Sisters near the kitchen; her and Joy along with six other underclassmen got the okay from nationals to pledge this summer. All things considered, this would be the last night that the girls would be hanging out like this for at least a few months.

Hollis was grooving by her lonesome in the dining room where the stereo system was set up. Joy was next to her dancing with Barry. The DJ put on J3's debut single *Pop goes my 9*, which mostly everyone at the Sigma shack sang along with word for word. Hollis smiled with secret pride and continued dancing.

Hollis wasn't exactly sure how the Sigma Sisters felt about her after she almost came to blows with Persilla at their last interest meeting. A few Sisters she never met had been looking at her funny on campus. She looked at them funny right back, but that was the extent of that. The Sisters that she knew from classes and the Union beforehand were still cool.

Through her peripheral Hollis could see more Hockey Jerseys around her than she cared for. Fatima and Joy were nowhere in sight. Sharee from Virginia A&M suddenly stopped pretending to be dancing next to Hollis and turned in on her. Hollis knew it was on. She backed up swiftly and threw her hands up. "Yo, yall bitches better fall back."

Sharee continued advancing, trying to get an angle. Hollis could see Big Deidrea, the 200 pound plus Sister from Manassas taking off her jewelry. Hollis jabbed at Sharee's face, barely missing her mark. She turned her head and saw the side door and made a move for it.

When she got outside Hollis threw her hands back up and squared Sharee up. *"Yeah, what up now?"* Inspired by what she seen Margo do earlier, Hollis shot another jab to Sharee's face.

As expected, Sharee raised both her arms to guard the decoy punch. Hollis cocked back and brought a left hook to her stomach, and Sharee went bye-bye.

"Yo Deidrea get that bitch!"

-"Let's jump her!"

The jerseys began to swarm again. Hollis kept her guard half way raised, her heart pounded. A razor sharp whistle broke through the drama.

"Ah yo!"

Hollis looked to her left and saw Margo stomping across the yard. *"Yall fucking with the wrong person! Go 'head, I'm telling yall."*

The 6'4" Bodyguard Force came rushing in from the opposite direction. Tim, the muscle bound Theta Bull Brother approached Margo. "What's up? You old ass Grandpa lookin' nigga. What the fuck yall gone do?" He yelled in his deep southern accent before pushing Margo in his chest. Margo quickly gathered his balance and moved in on Tim. Every Theta Brother in sight stepped up. Margo stepped back to gather a new game plan. Through all the drama, Deidrea was walking around Hollis trying to decide how she was going to attack.

She chose her strategy and charged at Hollis from a few feet away.

"Ahhhhhh!"

Roaring machinegun rounds ripped through the Virginian night, commanding everyone to hit the deck. The former party people were suddenly fleeing targets. By the time Jason finished firing into the sky, the only people on their feet were all from Harlem, save for Hollis who was still in the dirt.

The Dread rested his smoking barrel in the ground and leaned some weight on his hefty assault rifle before addressing the people in a mild degree of humor. *"We come in peace!"* He said with a hint of a smile across his face. He opened the back door of the burgundy car that he was standing in front of and looked at Hollis; "Come on baby." He addressed the crowd once more, *"But if you fuck with my family, I'll kill you dead."* He grinded maliciously and raised his barrel and jolted it to and fro, *"Any last one of you."*

Force backed up with great care, watching the every move of the Theta Bulls as they returned to their feet. Margo followed suite, retreating to the convoy on the curb as Jason shut Hollis' car door.

"Don't forget to go support my new single in stores or on the internet at www.onthebooksent.com" Jason said before they peeled off.

"After your TAP, PELL and your scholarship from Harlem Learns…"

Mrs. Harrington, Hollis' financial aid advisor punched a final set of numbers into her calculator then handed it to Hollis, "That's what your student account balance is going to be heading into the fall, once they pull your track scholarship."

She sat back and looked at Hollis wishing there was more that she could do for her. "Take out loans, as many of them as you need to finish. Get your parents to co-sign. You said your Mom is an academic counselor in New York right?"

"Yeah." Hollis said trying to regain her spirits after the discouraging news.

"What about Dad? He has a stable job right?"

Hollis scratched her head and looked away at nothing in particular. When she looked back Mrs. Harrington was still eye balling her and waiting for a response. Hollis looked back down at the calculator.

"What about your Father?"

"Huh?"

308

"Thelma, Louise, yall have a nice day."

Date: June 1st 2007

"That boy, or man or whatever been looking over here for like five minutes."

Hollis looked up from her magazine, down the subway platform, "Who?"

He couldn't have been any younger than thirty; posted against a column on the Uptown side grabbing at his crouch and apparently talking to his friend about her and/or Gwinn. Hollis flashed her million dollar smile and waived him over. *"Come here."*

Grinning as if he'd won whatever game he was playing in his mind, he whispered something to his partner and strolled over with the swagger of a star athlete.

"Eww no." Gwinn said as if her skin were crawling.

"Don't worry Sis; I got this."

-"What up shorty?"

Hollis screwed up her face and rolled her neck, "I'm taller than you. How you gone call me shorty?"

"Yeah, you know, it's a figure of speech or whatever. Who cares?"

Hollis motioned her head toward his friend standing beneath the 110th street sign, "What did you say to him before you came over?"

"What?"

She began to speak condescendingly clear, "What-did-you-say- to him before you-came over here."

"I, I-"

She turned to Gwinn; "Bullshit Brother."

Gwinn busted out laughing then covered her mouth as if she felt out of order.

"Yo hold on shorty, I'm from Bed Stuy, I ain't no bullshit Brother. Fall back wit' all that. I told my homeboy to watch me bag this *bitch* number, that's what I said. But fuck it; I don't think I even want that shit no more."

She smiled, standing stern and in command of her near six-foot stature as she continued to manipulate the conversation whichever way she chose, "You don't want my number?"

"Yo shorty, you like Jeopardy on the train or some shit. You trying to give me your math or what? My train coming."

Hollis turned to her younger Sister, "What you think? Should I give him my number?"

Gwinn's face was barely visible beneath her white K-Swiss baseball cap. She held her tender hand up and pointed her thumb downward.

"Na; sorry, my Sister isn't feelin' you."

"I can respect that. Thelma," He turned and looked at Gwinn, "Louise, yall have a nice day."

Hollis was in NYC for the month long intermission between the end of the spring semester and the beginning of her summer classes. She was taking three business courses and working a summer job with an insurance company that promised to have her promoted to Manager and opening her own office within a year. Gwinn kept her Sister abreast to the latest Uptown styles and all of the drama in the hood. Among other things, Reggie, Hollis' ex-boyfriend was in jail for an assault charge he caught on 125th after someone tried to snatch his gold chain. Junior had a flock of player haters in the Projects due to the fact Harlem hardly saw him and his musical content had gone from hard to sweet. The J.E.S.I.C.A gang had been increasingly terrorizing the neighborhood as they were now controlling the loose cigarette and P.C.P dipped hustles and banging on innocent people as an initiation rite.

Hollis and Gwinn were taking the 2 train to Hoyt Street in Brooklyn so Hollis could pick up as much cotton fabric as she could for $200. They rode and talked away.

And so...it came to pass that through all the trouble in her life, Hollis not only held on to, but grew in her faith. When financial trouble lurked, Hollis continued praying at both ends of the day, before each meal, and in the shower. It came to pass that the loose flimsy twist in her hair kinked up and grew livelier, stronger. It came to pass that Hollis met the best financial aid advisor at S.B.U, who stopped her panicking and got her planning. After all of his secret loan and grant hook-ups got processed, the financial aid office was sending money back to Hollis. It came to pass that Hollis transformed a drawing that she made while bored in class and teachings from her Father into a small idea, and that idea into a strand of ideas. And Hollis Jordan was about to bet her natural ass on those ideas.

9:03PM; THE SAME NIGHT

When Hollis and Gwinn got back to Hollis' home in Hicksville they found an unusually packed, lively household. Aunt Simone and Denise were sitting in the living room talking. Dominique, who Hollis barely noticed due to her new haircut, was sitting in the dining room with Renee messing around on the computer. Aunt

Simone embraced Hollis whom she hadn't seen since she left off to school.

"Hi Auntie!"

"Hey baby, how you?"

"I can't complain, can't complain."

"What's this?" Aunt Simone asked after hugging Hollis and grabbing a section of her nappy, plotted hair.

"That's my hair Auntie." Hollis answered as if she didn't feel like entertaining people with her appearance.

"Hm, that's what you call it?"

- *"Where's my girl?"* Renee snuck past Aunt Simone and reached out to embrace Hollis.

After greeting everyone Hollis took Gwinn, her girls and shopping bags to the privacy of her bedroom upstairs.

"Okay, so guess who's pregnant." Dominique said as she shut Hollis' bedroom door.

"Who?"

"Khalia from Foster."

"Get outta here. It's Rick baby?"

"Yep…and she not the only one pregnant either." Dominique said as she eye balled Renee who took a seat on Hollis' dresser.

-"So, how you did in school this semester Honey?" Renee asked.

"Your girl got four A's, and a B+ in calculus."

"That's my girl." Renee gave her a five, sincerely happy for her. "You settin' the right standard for the next three years."

Hollis walked over to Gwinn who took a seat on the bed and handed her a sneaker box from out one of the shopping bags. "Actually, next semester is probably going to be my last semester there."

Hollis' words seemed to rile the room with curiosity. Renee hoped to her feet; "Why?"

-"What you transferring?"

"Na…" Hollis looked into the mirror and began taking off her jewelry. "I'm starting my own business."

Hollis grabbed her bathroom bucket and towel before opening her room door. The shower had become sort of an asylum and a place of solace for Hollis. She didn't have to say or do anything and she was in a perpetual state of cleanliness, which she understood was next to Godliness.

On this particular morning the apartment that she was subleasing for the summer smelled like tobacco, marijuana and sweaty feet. Hollis peeked in the living room and saw Jeremy asleep in a foldout chair against a wall. She walked in further. Derek was sleep in the loveseat with Tiffany, her suitemate passed out on his lap. Empty bottles of Devil Springs, Hennessey and Belvedere were scattered across the table. She turned to go back to the bathroom before noticing what seemed like every cup and plate in the house used and scattered about in and around the kitchen sink.

7:51AM; THE SAME MORNING

"What's up Honey baby?"

Gay Jeff greeted Hollis as he stepped into his freshly waxed car. She waived from across the parking lot, *"How you doing?"*

"I'm good and yourself?"

"I'm blessed."

"I heard that girl." Jeff snapped, crackled and popped his happy ass into his Jetta.

Hollis walked along Bryce Road to the academic center for her 8:40am Macroeconomics course. It was over ninety degrees in Northern Virginia and Hollis felt every bit of it on her near half hour walk to Mosley Hall. The students that were fortunate enough to have their own cars passed her by. She stayed strong as she knew they were watching. She was a former track star and popular among her peers. Although she increasingly sought not to be seen, Hollis had an undeniable attractive force, and at nearly six feet tall she was a standout presence, people couldn't help but look. Those who chose to stare were frequently mistaking her nowadays; judging her as passive, weak, and/or weird, as her mind often drifted to some far off place to ponder on the advanced endeavors of her life. It came to pass that Hollis attained knowledge of her self, her history, and the ability to distinguish that which is truth from that which is false. And so it came to pass that Hollis could understand nature and the nature of certain objects, and therefore Hollis' mind may or may not have been in her body or in this world. This because Hollis understood that nothing is new under the sun, so she allowed herself to wonder beyond. It came to pass that Hollis' understanding of GOD became clearer, her Moments of sharpest clarity came when she was prostrated before her Lord, with her face to the earth in sincere humility before Al-Khaliq which means *The Creator* or Al-Musawwir which means *the fashioner of shapes*. She prayed in the morning, early and late afternoon, and toward the coming of the night, no matter where she was or what she was doing. GOD, Allah or Al-Matin which means *the invincible* reached Hollis through inspiration and his wondrous signs and symbols, and alas, the previous lost soul had guidance on the earth.

9:17 AM; THE SAME DAY

"...and once the company has reached its' breakeven point, then it can become truly profitable. The business has its' capital assets, liquid assets, uh...working capital, and there is demand for the product and or service. This may take a couple of years, but for the company, it will be well worth the wait."

Professor Wong was a clean cut, handsome Chinese gentleman who Hollis came to find a mild attraction to. He was a sharp dresser, witty and had a smooth way of conveying his business wisdom, all of which helped make his 120 minute lecture a little easier.

"Is it necessary for the business to switch up any of its strategies at that point, in order to continue to grow?"

Hollis made sure to sit in the front row and to ask at least one question per class. That was her third for the day.

"I'm glad you asked that. That's actually going to depend on the nature of the business and the consumer demand as well as a few other dynamics..."

"Tell me what you see."

"I see the sky... and stars."

"What else?"

"Um…"

She found discomfort in not following her
Father's line of thought. She lifted her eyes
from the telescope lens to the ceiling. *"Uh…"*
She tapped at her honey brown chin, *"I don't
know."* She said dropping her head, growing
disappointed in herself.

*"Here, look again. Don't get upset. GOD will
enlighten you by degrees baby. Right now you
have to trust your eyes… So…Tell me what you
see."*

She looked through the lens and tried to focus
again, *"Stars…Outer space."*

"Okay, good. What else?"

"…Light; there's light over there."

"Goooooood."

Hollis indulged in the comfort of her sheets,
cooled by the air conditioner. The woods
outside of her window were pitch black and
crawling with insects and the unknown. She
knew it was well after midnight because she laid
down a few minutes after 10pm.

She went into her closet and pulled out a black t-
shirt that she was using as a canvas to create a
signature design for the clothing line that she set
her mind to birthing. She laid the shirt across
her bed still draped from the hanger. Before she
took her nap she stitched one of the Honeywell

Urban Outfitters patches she ordered over the internet across the front. Hollis stood over her project and tried to think of the hottest complement possible. She looked around her room and grabbed a whiteout stick out of her S.B.U Lions cup and wrote across the front:

FROM HARLEM 2 HOLLYWOOD

She stood back and looked at her creation and it failed to move her. She put the whiteout stick back and left her room. The apartment was void of light. She walked into the living room and took a quiet seat on the couch and peacefully contemplated on what she learned in a year of college. It was as if GOD, for reasons only known to Him transcended her soul from the backwoods of Virginia to the hustle and bustle of New York City; the filthy concrete of the Projects and the multitude of people without. She was mentally there with them.

In college Hollis witnessed her peers, the near future leaders of the world and the intellectually elite, dismissive of the problems of the poor and those without. She wondered if they knew. She didn't know, until she found herself on certain trains late nights leaving Reggie's house. That's when the homeless crept from the bowels of the city in search of a place to sleep. Until studying with Mr. Neives she didn't understand the depth of the effects of the trans-Atlantic slave trade, or the manifestation of mental slavery and mental inferiority among her Brothers and Sisters, but it was all starting to make sense.

Hollis came to see academia's outline for the enhancement of society as too bureaucratic in nature, too ignorant of the people on the ground and ultimately upholding a system that was brutally built on the backs of her ancestors. Hollis Jordan now stood as a woman who saw herself as behind enemy lines, but she knew that no matter where she stood, she was on GOD's green earth and so she wasn't afraid to go.

She sat in peace, trusting her eyes and judgment to distinguish truth from lies as she bore witness to GOD's magnificence in the moonlit sky through the open venetian blinds. The Devil was no where to be found. In her heart she desired to keep him away, so she got off the couch and went in the shower to clean her body and pray.

2:57AM; THE SAME NIGHT

Hollis stood over her designs trying to twist some better thoughts out of her hair. Ideas were coming to her at an infinite rate, she felt like she could just reach into the sky and pull anyone out and it would be the one.

She went back into her closet and pulled out a white t-shirt that was folded on the top shelf. She removed a metallic gold felt pen from her Lion's cup and tried to write across the front. The instability of the cloth forced her to search for a platform to write on. She turned around and grabbed her copy of the Old Testament off of her desk and slipped it under the bottom of

the shirt. In an elaborate penmanship she
transcribed across the front:

HONEYWELL URBAN OUTFITTERs
est. 2007

She stood back and looked at her creation, and
she was pleased. And the signature design for
Honeywell Urban Outfitters was manifest, and
the word forth.

Within two weeks of the start of the fall
semester 2007 Hollis had close to $11,000 in her
bank account. She received two loan refund
checks from Swanson-Bryce, totaling over
$5,000. She also had another $2,400 remaining
from the money she saved working at Harlem
Learns in High School and her summer job.
And she still had more than half of the money
that her parents gave her for graduation.

Hollis had her eye on a pressing machine at JC
Penny that would gobble up about 800 of her
dollars. She brought her blank t-shirts from
23rd street in the garment district of NYC, $28 a
dozen. The studio apartment that she was going
to lease in the Bronx, $900 per month;
trademark, vendor I.D license, registration
numbers and building her own website,
$2,163.13. Starting a female owned and
operated sole proprietorship with the Lord's
blessing…priceless.

Hollis sat alone at the campus bus stop
observing the day that the Lord made. It was the

last day of September; seventy-two degrees with the ever slightest breeze. She was sporting a pair of Hugo Boss shades to protect her eyes from harmful rays, chillin' almost to a criminal extent.

Most people around were rushing to get here or there. The campus shuttles were dropping loads of students off every few minutes. There was stress and confusion all about; freshmen trying to find their lecture halls, others running late or chatting their freedom away on cell phones. Hollis had little concerns, her heighten state of calm exceeded her like an aura, compelling stares of perplexity, admiration and discontent from people who couldn't understand her.

It came to pass that Hollis began to sacrifice in the name of the Lord; continuously prostrating herself in the shower and keeping GOD ever present in her heart. It came to pass that her unattractive twist grew into beautiful, strong, ropes of human hair. It came to pass that GOD or Al-Wahid, which means *the one unequalled* restored her soul, and removed the Devil from within her. GOD or Al-Haqq, which means the truth, exposed her to the flawlessness in his designs, the infinite sustainability in his ways and he inspired her to fuel herself with the good things on the earth.

Hollis folded her Elle Magazine and kicked back and observed her fellow classmen rushing through life. She felt exempt from mundane drama, content with herself, content with the Lord's path for her and her positioning… she was resting. She looked up to the sky, humble and gracious as she took another sip from her mocha latte. "All praise be to you."

NOVEMBER 26TH 2007

"It's that damn gentrification. Property value went through the roof, cost of living went up. You know the Pizza Shop done moved into the same building as the Fish Market? I go in there for a slice, I don't know what the hell line to stand on. I'm confused... You know what it is?"

"What's that?" Hollis asked looking up from writing in her notepad.

"The game's fucked up." Said Margo, before pulling out another cigarette; "The game is fucked up."

Hollis laughed for a second then swiftly brought the conversation back to its' course. "So, essentially your storefront is on the internet now; that's what you telling me?"

"Yep; it has its' pros and cons. But for what you're doing I think it could really work."

"Cool. So what you need from me to get the website up and running?"

Margo spilled some of his coffee on his wool sweater. *"Damn it. Shit!"* He excused himself from the table. "I'm going to need your information so you can accept credit cards

payments online. You got a business account?"
He asked as he dabbed at the stain with a rag.

"No."

"Okay, what you gotta do is go downtown, to
the Country Recorder's Office. Tell them you
want to register your business name and get a
D.B.A certificate. You take the paper they give
you to the bank with two pieces of I.D and you
in there. The whole process can be done in one
day."

Hollis checked the time on her wristwatch then
stood up and grabbed her leather briefcase,
which she began toting around religiously. The
intensity in Hollis' eyes seemed familiar to
Margo, as he'd seen her Father do some strange
things with that same seriousness in his eyes.

"I'll be right back."

DECEMBER 4TH 2007

Hollis approached finals week the same as she
had in semesters past, with discipline and
diligence. She made flashcards for key terms
with definitions on the back, she took frequent
study breaks and she removed herself from all
forms of communication… grind mode.
Although she was set in her plans to leave
school at the end of this semester, in pursuit of
happiness, she wanted her final grades to reflect
her capability, to show that she could, but she
was choosing not to.

Her bags were packed, more right to say her everything was packed, save for her toiletries, laptop and her books. She had four final exams, two on Monday and the other two on Wednesday. Hollis was sitting at her study desk reviewing all of the highlighted sections in her Micro-Economics text book, beneath that she had a spiral notebook and her Africans in America text. She was twisting her hair and every few minutes she would get up to stretch a different part of her body. She was waiting on an instant message from Dominique to let her know if she liked the shirt designs she e-mailed her earlier, and she was slowly eating her dinner. Multitasking had become a necessity for the deliverance of Hollis' clothing line, as for now, Hollis was her company. She used superset excising routines that her Father designed for her to work twice the muscle in half the time. She maintained her hair while she contemplated issues, she read up on the industry while stretching, and she talked to GOD while jogging late nights; efficiency manifest.

DECEMBER 9TH 2007

Hollis looked to either side to see if it was safe to cross the street and a white minivan cut in front of her to make a sharp turn.

"You need a perm baby!" A fair skinned Sister shouted at Hollis as the car sped off.

DECEMBER 9TH 2007

*"...So I guess what I'm asking you Denise is...
is, will you be my wife?"*

DECEMBER 9ᵀᴴ 2007

"Strip it." Jason said, gasping for oxygen as he
racked the barbell. "Take...take off the 10's,
I'm a do another six reps."

Force and Ronnie each removed an iron plate
from their respective side of the Olympic bar
while Jason rose from the bench and flexed his
lats, showing off his massive upper body. Force
secured the collar on his side and stood clear.
"There you go Boss!"

DECEMBER 9ᵀᴴ 2007

"Uno."

-*"Uno!"*

"Out."

"No, I said Uno before you Gwinn. You gotta
pick your card up and draw two."

"No I don't. I'm out; don't tell me what I gotta
do."

"I said it before you. You are such a cheater!"

Gwinn stood up and stepped over the pile of cards in the middle of the 6 train and slapped Jocelyn across her face. *"Who the fuck you talking to?"*

DECEMBER 9TH 2007

"I never said I wanted an abortion that was you! You ain't want your *family* to know about us and mess up your whole little perfect world. *I hate you!"* Renee used most of her strength to lift the brass lamp off the nightstand and sent it airborne at Junior's head. *"I fucking hate you!"*

DECEMBER 12TH 2007

Hollis sat next to a middle aged white man on the 9:30AM bus to New York. In the bus station she managed to get four items on her to-do list checked off; e-mailing her Brother, ordering a dress for her Mother's wedding, putting the finishing touches on a hat design that she was working on and she checked her grades over the S.B.U automated system.

She took in the trees and the open space, and the sense of peace that one could find on the Baltimore-Washington Parkway. However, Hollis didn't let herself get naive about this. She understood that she was heading back to the belly of the beast. New York was going to test her. The Devil ran rapid through the streets where she was going to solicit business. People were chastised for following the straight way and preaching the word, which Hollis found herself increasingly compelled to do as she got closer to GOD. She was ready though, Hollis was ready. She had developed a work ethic that was uncanny, not likely to be matched, yet and still she was ever mindful not to underestimate what the next woman could be doing. She was from the Mecca of urban style, Harlem, which she made sure to keep in mind at the drawing board. Hollis had been piling up her righteous deeds and she had Psalms: 23 written on a scroll that she kept in her wallet for especially trying times... She was ready.

As the bus stopped to make its Baltimore exchange, Hollis looked around and saw that most of the passengers, including the man seated beside her were sound asleep. She sunk deep into the confines of herself and she closed her eyes to make a quick prayer. She remained in a meditative state until the bus began moving again. When she opened her eyes there was a green interstate sign out of her window.

INTERSTATE   NORTH
95
NEW YORK
KEEP RIGHT

Hollis brought a fish tank to spruce up the apartment and to provide a sort of visual stimulus in her humbly boring abode. Her computer station was the focal point of the room as she didn't bother getting a television set. She had a pair of small gray speakers to either side of her Laptop, a fax machine, paper shredder, scanner and her lan-line phone all situated on the only desk in the apartment.

On the opposite side of the room was her sleeping quarters. When Hollis informed her Father of her business plans and that she was getting her own place, he wished her well and warned her vehemently of the detriment of sleep while on this journey. Subsequently, Hollis brought a sleeping bag to which she could only get but so comfortable on her hardwood floor. She set up a candle visual for her late Uncle Ernest and best friend Trisha near the head and kept an egg crate turned desk at the foot, with her perfume, a reading lamp and other miscellaneous items atop.

Wherever she went she hung her posters; Bob Marley, a S.B.U Lions banner, a black and white portrait of T.I from his King album, the George Washington Bridge at night, and new to her collection a 30x40 of Angela Davis.

Hollis ate oatmeal because it was filling and cheap. She drunk a lot of water because it cleansed her body, cleared her skin and it was cheap. She brought her toilet paper, soap, and paper towels in bulk because it was time saving and cheap. She budgeted every penny and watched her money like a professional accountant. Her days were spent sowing, pressing, stitching, drawing, e-mailing and researching. But none of her chores felt like work, or at least work as she had previously known it. There were no arbitrary deadlines. Her projects were subject to the public, which meant that her work manifest, defined her. All of which made diligence and proficiency a necessity. In a sense…there was no more Hollis Mekada Jordan, only Honeywell Urban Outfitters, only the businesswoman. Her thoughts, feelings and emotions, one would need to analyze one of her complicatedly beautiful design schemes to understand.

"Come on, pull-up."

Her Father pulled down on her folded legs, adding torturous extra resistance. Hollis cringed her face and tightened her grip on the frost bit bar. When she cleared her chin over the top, she exhaled in brief relief as Jason released his stronghold. She lowered herself to do another rep.

After their last set of pull-ups they jogged from the monkey bars to building 51 and through the back door.

"You ready to do this?"

Jason asked stretching his neck and loosening his shoulders at the landing of the first floor steps.

Hollis was jogging in place, "I keep telling you, I was born ready."

Without so much as a word, Jason darted up the first flight of steps.

"Cheater!" Hollis yelled before chasing after him. She finally passed her Father on the seventh floor and separated herself so that she had almost fully caught her breathe by the time he met her on the roof.

"What you thought, I was gone be your Rabbit?"

Jason's palms were stuck to either side of his waist. He wasn't concerned with responding in the least, he dropped to the surface of the roof.

"I ain't no Rabbit! I'm a Lion! I eat slow-pokes like you for breakfast."

He was finally able to speak after a couple of failed attempts. "You got a be…you gotta be humble baby…"

Hollis laughed; filled with pride, "Oh now I gotta be humble cause I'm at the top of the food chain?"

Jason smiled and looked at his growing daughter who he could no longer beat in a foot race to save his life. Hollis looked over the railing to Amsterdam Avenue, "GOD's green Earth… Boy do I feel good."

Hollis swept down 125th street with grace and a glow. She had on a brown three-quarter length leather, and a pair of Cole Hann boots. Today she couldn't help but smile. She was glad to be back home, back in the midst of fly Harlem girls and New York hustlers with style; she felt apart of the world again.

"Oh my GOD, you are such a beautiful person."

The woman draped in rags stopped dead in her tracks and stared at Hollis like she'd seen a ghost. "You look like an angel."

Hollis was compelled to stop, although stopping for such a woman made no sense at all, at least on a superficial level. Still, Hollis was in no position to judge the woman who had gave her the most sincere complement of the day. "Thank you." She said glowing further.

"Let me just say this to you. I know you're a busy woman. I know you have many things to do. But let me say this..."

"Uh huh." Hollis uttered as she looked up and around her to analyze the renewing pedestrian traffic on Lenox Avenue.

"You ever watch the Wire, that show that come on H.B.O?"

"Well I don't really watch T.V like that. I've seen the show though, I know of it."

"Mm...You know that boy Omar is bad. He just be ripping and running. And they can't get to him."

Hollis looked up out of attention once more, growing inpatient and beginning to second guess stopping to converse with the homeless.

"You know he about to go to war with that boy Marloe?"

"Okay lady, I got a go."

"But you didn't hear me out."

"Yeah but like you said, I'm a busy woman." Hollis began walking away.

"Just hear me out."

Hollis turned back around rolling her eyes, agitated and just about maxed out on patience.

"You know that song they play at the beginning of the show? *Gotta keep the Devil, down in the hole.*" She dipped into a drunken lean and snapped her fingers.

"Alright miss, enjoy the rest of your day."

"That's it! You got a keep the Devil down in the hole!"

As Hollis got to the corner she began to wonder to herself how a homeless woman would be in tuned with a cable television show and its' storyline. She kept walking, but her mind hadn't settled on the issue and she began to search her mental for possibilities. There was no cable in shelters nor in most other public places. The

woman was clearly homeless as she was lying
on the ground when Hollis passed her. Hollis
turned around to see if the lady was bothering
any other pedestrians and she was no longer
there.

9:38; THE SAME NIGHT

"Peace Black woman."

"Hey Daddy what's up?"

"How you?"

"I'm blessed; can't complain in the least."

"I hear that." Jason sounded happy. He paused
as if expecting her to elaborate but she didn't.
"So things is coming along huh?"

*"The Lords' promises come to pass, all of them.
You know?"*

Hollis sounded enthused and he wanted a part of
it. *"Oh I know, trust me I know. The question is
to what extent do you know? Cause Allah is
stern, he's strict; he is forgiving, the oft
forgiving, most merciful. But he has his laws,
his ways, prescribed periods and he smiles upon
righteous deeds, sacrifices in his name..."*

Hollis kept quiet. Ever so often her Father's
words were passionate and relevant enough to
warrant her full attention and she would give it
to him. When they were face to face she would

356

stop everything she was doing and look directly into his loving eyes. In recent years, circumstances changed but not the bond and the respect. Hollis muted the volume on her computer and turned up the volume on her cell phone.

"...you trying to fast with N.Y.C.M.C this Ramadan?"

"Fast with N.Y.C.M.C?"

"Islam is a Brotherhood, and a Sisterhood. We are commanded to help one another in righteousness. GOD has prescribed for us, a period of self restraint and enlightenment."

Hollis did some quick pondering then waived her hand as if her Father could see, *"I don't know if I'm ready for no fast Daddy, maybe next year."*

"Next year?"

She shook her head knowing that he was about to blow things out of proportion as usual and she didn't feel like getting into it with him. *"Daddy let me call you back after I finish doing this thing real quick."*

"Whatever."

She put her cell phone down and Moments later the glass on her table began to tremble to the vibration of another incoming call. She looked at the display screen. Although she deleted his contact information out of her phone after she convinced herself that he was cheating on her, there are some phone numbers you just don't forget.

"Reggie..."

She missed him, and she was sure to let her voice reflect that.

"How you doing sweetness?"

His voice forced her to sit up in her seat and smile. *"How you Bunny?"*

He laughed, *"Bunny...I ain't heard that in a minute."*

"My baby, you okay?"

"I'm good. How you been?"

"Blessed; tremendously blessed."

"Blessed?"

"Blessed." She repeated with certainty.

"Why blessed? Why not good, or fine, why blessed?"

"I'm blessed because..." She second guessed herself, then she decided to speak her mind, as Reggie would need to understand that she wasn't the same person that she left to college as; *"Because I know GOD."*

336

"I fuck wit' you. You be on some other shit, but I fuck wit' you."

Date: February 16TH 2008

Hollis sat at her kitchen table and looked out of her window on to 167th street. Thick heavy snow was falling on the Bronx. She had to go out there, she wished to GOD that she didn't, but she had a mission for the day. She needed to pick up three dozen in-seem labels, she was meeting Reggie on his lunch break and she had to go to the Post Office. The distinct ring of the lan-line phone summoned her.

"You want me to get that?"

She rose up and placed her cup of peppermint tea on the table. "No I got it… I gotta answer that phone like a professional." Hollis said as she smiled at her Sister, lifting the cordless handset.

"Hello, Honeywell Urban Outfitters, how may I help you?"

Hollis lent an open ear to the phone as she watched Gwinn scroll through her extensive Art Library mounted in her wall-unit. She checked her watch to see how much time she had before she had to leave out. *"Oh yeah, how much was I approved for?"* She said into the phone. *"Okay, well send me the information in the mail*

and I'll certainly take a look at it." Hollis crept
up behind Gwinn and played with her curly hair.
*"No I don't handle business like that over the
phone. Send me the info in the mail and I'll take
a look at it okay? Okay thank you."* She hung
up the phone.

"What happen?"

"I was supposedly pre approved for a business
line of credit." Hollis took a look at the book in
Gwinn's hands, "The Da Vinnci Code. You
read it?"

"Na, I seen the movie though."

"Okay, Cool." Hollis turned to her wall unit
with a certain degree of pride. "These are some
of the works of art that helped me understand
GOD. You should take some time to go through
it."

Gwinn examined the covers of Mos Def's *Black
on Both Sides* album then Jezee Monet's *Most
High* single, then a psychology textbook before
she removed the beautifully decorated black and
gold Qur'an. "What's this?"

"Girl, how you Jason Jordan's child and you
don't know what that is?'

Gwinn opened the book at the section reserved
by an elaborate bookmarker; "Daddy wasn't
there for me like he was for you."

Hollis looked at her, but Gwinn's eyes were conveniently in the book. Hollis looked away before dismissing whatever she was going to say. "Aight, I got a go. You wanna spend the night tonight?"

"Can I?"

"Of course you can sis."

Hollis ran her errands then took the 3 train to Chambers Street to meet Reggie. He clocked out for his lunch break and pretended to be nice for the first few minutes after they left his office building. They were walking down the Avenue of the Americas on the Westside of Manhattan when Hollis popped the question; "So, what you wanna eat?"

"I don't know, it's up to you swee-" He caught himself, as to not refer to Hollis by the pet name he gave her in High School.

"It's okay; you can be nice to me." Hollis said working her way toward softening him up.

And it came to pass that GOD delivered on his promises to Hollis, perfecting that which concerned her. Honeywell clothes were selling well on the streets and in a few small retail stores throughout N.Y.C. and Virginia. The company website was averaging close to 4,000 hits per week, and about five percent of her visitors were buyers. It came to pass that Hollis found herself living out visions that she had as a young girl, or as she often put it, she was living her dreams. It came to pass that Hollis struck what was at the time, the prefect harmonizing balance between business and pleasure. It came to pass that Hollis was approved for a Vendor I.D. license from the city and she established a business center via her 6x2 table on 125th street. Now Hollis was turning her attention and energy to getting the love of her life back.

"I missed you." Hollis said out the clear blue sky. She could tell that his silence was a testament to his lack of clever, harsh repartee so she beat him to it, "What, you thinking of the meanest way to tell me to go fuck myself?"

"Yep."

His response was sharp and firm, as if he was on the verge of exploding. Reggie always had a fiery temper. To bring the situation to a harmonizing balance Hollis turned up her level of sweetness. "Come here." As if moving on a chessboard, Hollis employed her seductive, concerned voice. She reached out in every sense of the word, extending for a hug and putting her pride aside, as if she were silently saying that she was sorry, and she was reaching out for a new beginning.

"Yo Hollis what you want from me? I feel like you got an ulterior motive or something. What the fuck is up?"

"First I want you to stop being so mad. I don't like to see you so upset baby."

Reggie stopped dead in his tracks and threw his hands in the air, "*Oh my GOD!* Why you talking all sexy & shit?"

Hollis could tell by the weakening in his voice that he would be folding soon. She simply smiled, careful not reveal her entire hand. Reggie deflated.

Check

"...But what do you want? I don't see why you checkin' for me again. What, you fucked up in College or something?"

Hollis placed a tender hand on his shoulder, "Can you stop cursing please?"

He sucked his teeth as they crept past the entrance of Battery Park. His hands were sunk into his forest green Parka. He could only look at his former best friend. Through his eyes she could still read him like a book. His anger was diluted. He was ready to hear her out, ready to submit.

"I missed you too sweetness."

Checkmate

"Every time I come up with an idea, he find something wrong with it. It's too expensive, we don't know nothin' about it or something. It's always something."

Although Rosy wasn't talking directly to Hollis, Hollis could feel her trying to reach out to her. Rosy's body language and antics were directed toward Amanda, who was sitting in the entrance of building 55 on a dirty leather office chair firing up another blunt.

"So now, I'm like fuck it. I'm a just fall back, play my position and let him run it like he see fit."

"I hear that." Amanda said between sharp inhales of smoke.

-"Well why you need his approval to manifest the ideas in your head?"

Rosy looked at Hollis who was standing near the mailboxes looking out the window and timidly shrugged her shoulders. "I don't know."

It was in the mid-30's in New York City but the sun was out; and its glare seemed to be locked on to Hollis' face through the lobby window, complementing her gold tone. "I mean, what were you thinking about doing?"

"I don't know…Like that Nutcracker shit."

-"Yep." Amanda quickly recalled as she passed the blunt to Rosy and exchanged places with her at the door.

"I been told Gary we could get money selling liquor in the hood. He was like *naaaa*. He rather go out there, play hardball and risk it all."

"Yeah but Sister you know where the liquor store is. You can go buy your own blender and count your own money. You don't need him."

"Yeah Hollis, but everybody needs help."

"Then come see me, fuck that. Let's get together and I'll help you develop whatever plans you want to develop. I'm in the business of getting shit done."

Rosy smiled and passed the blunt to Hollis. "I fuck with you. You be on some other shit, but I fucks wit' you though."

10:44PM; THE SAME NIGHT

Hollis rose from her deep sleep to discover that the sun had set. She tried unsuccessfully to find some source of time before burying her face back in her pillow as she realized that despite the time, she would be pulling another all-nighter. She unraveled herself from her sleeping bag and gathered herself before standing and baring witness to the streets outside of her window. The poverty stricken city and her inhabitants hadn't gone to sleep.

Hollis could see a Brother pushing a shopping cart full of bottles across the street, a Nurse in green scrubs and white sneakers waiting for the street light to turn her favor, visibly exhausted from her days' work. Hollis gave thanks that she was exempt from the realities of the cold world at least for tonight. For this night at least, Hollis' path was smooth. She was charged with stitching thirty patches on the sleeves of a line of worker shirts she designed. She also had to finish the outline of her official business plan for her meeting with a local S.B.A representative on Thursday.

Hollis put a pot of water on the stove for her tea then she went to her desk to power up her computer. She pulled out her briefcase, while she waited for her Laptop to boot up and got to work.

"You ain't even that tough you know that?"

Jason looked over the top of the computer monitor at his Daughter like she was crazy. "Say what?"

"You heard me. I been hitting the gym hard body, I think I can take you." Hollis said bouncing around from side to side with adrenaline.

He laughed; seemingly convincing himself that she was just playing and went back to reading.

"I'm serious. I may not be able to throw the hands with you like that. But I think I can hang a few minutes in a tussle with you."

Jason was tickled with laugher. He sat back in his seat and folded his arms, "Aight now, you feeling froggy gone on and take a lil leap."

Hollis ran at him and punched him in his back. "Come on."

Jason met her on her feet and flashed his fist; "Hollis you better sit yo' ass down. You gone get dropped. I'm tellin' you." He reached behind him and squeezed his back muscles, *"Ah that shit hurt."*

Hollis figured it to be the perfect time to charge him as his guard was down. She bolted forth like a woman gone mad. Jason planted firmly in the floor as if prepared to meet her head on. As she came rushing in he took a sharp step aside. Hollis crashed violently into her wall unit, knocking several shelves and their contents down before falling herself. Jason looked down at her, "Allah loves not the aggressor. You remember that lil dude."

Hollis rolled over on her backside and looked up at her Father who decided to use her folly as a teaching point. "It's not me against you. It's you against your enemies. And you attack only after measures of peace have been fully exhausted. Not because you been out there doing pull-ups every other morning and you feeling strong & shit."

Hollis returned to her feet and left her adrenaline on the ground. "Daddy you play too rough." She said as she rubbed a swelling knot on her head.

"Come here." He wrapped his arm around her and kissed her on the forehead. "You know your Daddy loves you?"

"Yes."

"You don't have a clue child. You don't have a clue." He kissed her again and looked her square in the eyes. "You like my Pit-bull."

"Daddy you say such sweet things to me." Hollis responded sarcastically still visibly in pain.

"You know how niggas be walking round the hood wit' they diesel ass dogs, knowing they can't be touched. That's how I felt walking around wit' you when you was a kid. You were a shining beckon of peace. It was like we couldn't be touched."

Hollis' studio apartment was dim, lit only by means of nature. It was close to seven o'clock and the sun had just completely set, indicating that another spring in New York City was on the horizon. Hollis began to stare blankly at the area rug that she got from Target. After several silent Moments she looked up at her Father who was looking at her computer monitor with an easy look of astonishment on his face reading her screen-saver.

PERSEVERE

APRIL 2ND 2008

For as far back as she could remember Hollis was sitting in some boring classroom at this time of day. She'd been waiting to see what goes on in the free world on the first warm day out of winter. She showered quickly. When she finished in the bathroom, she threw on a white and purple Armani Exchange outfit, slapped on her sunglasses and sprayed a dab of Burberry Brit at the top of her chest and wrist before floating out the door.

2:00PM; THE SAME DAY

"Damn baby." A heavy set boy in a white tank top stopped and gazed at Hollis as she sassed past him on Frederick Douglas Boulevard. "You look like a tall glass of good. What I got a do to get a taste?"

Hollis smiled by accident. She looked over her shoulder and saw him jogging up behind her.

"What's good; I know you trying to give me your number."

Hollis laughed again, "No, I ain't wanna mislead you but you made me smile."

"Yeah but that ain't gotta stop you from giving me your math. That sound like two positive things."

"No, I can't." Hollis said still giggling. "I just got back with my boyfriend last month. I can't do that."

"Damn Ma, ain't nobody ever teach you about spreading the wealth, distributing the wealth?" He asked, now laughing even at himself.

"No. But if you need a custom t-shirt to complement those broad shoulders visit my web-site or you can check out one of our friendly locations." Hollis gave him a business card, smiled and walked away.

- *"We got cell phones. I got them new T-Moblies, we got Sprint, Boost, we got them I-phone for you. Come check us out."*

- *"I got DVDs; one for five, two for eight, three for ten."*

Hollis removed herself from the pedestrian flow when she reached 8th Avenue, placing her back against a Department Store's display window.

-"Get your Honeywell Designs gear right here; support Black business. Spend $50 and get a free gift basket."

Hollis spied on Dominique and her cousin Ashley for a few Moments, using the multitude of people on 125th as her cover. Hollis sought to verify that they were putting their maximum effort forward.

"Get your Honeywell Designs shirts here; newest styles and designs on the streets yall. Free gift basket with a $50 purchase."

Hollis didn't wait one minute before walking up to Dominique who was flipping through a magazine and chatting away on her phone at the table.

"What's up Honey? Where you coming from?"

Hollis didn't bother answering Ashley. She stood in front of Dominique and folded her arms, "Hello?"

"Oh hold on." Dominique said into her cell phone. "What's up?"

"Dee I thought we talked about this. If you gone be manning the table then you need to be out here on your shit, not on the phone."

"Relax yo; I was just taking a break."

"Dee, I was just watching you from over there and I seen you on the phone chillin' for like five minutes. Yall just got here an hour ago, how you taking a break already?"

Dominique raised her phone; *"Yo let me call you back. People out here tripping like this a fortune 500 company or somethin'."*

Oh no she didn't, Hollis thought to herself. She let her body language temporarily convey her dismay as Dominique listened to whatever the person was saying on the other end.

"Okay...Okay. Aight girl I'm a go."

Dominique looked up at Hollis, "Now what's up?"

Hollis clapped her hands with energy as she spoke. "This ain't the place for breaks. It's prime time in Harlem. You see how many potential customers is out here?" Hollis pumped her breaks as she realized that she was in a state of self perpetuating anger. She looked away from Dominique who didn't seem much affected anyway and stopped wasting her time. Hollis collected the bank from Ashley and advised the girls that whatever they sold for the rest of the day they could keep 50% commission on and she left them be.

Hollis walked over to Grant Projects, which was about a ten minute walk away. Rosy and Amanda had migrated from their winter spot in the lobby to the park in front of building 50 where they were sitting with a few J.E.S.I.C.A Sisters. The kids were out of school, some were gathered at the Ice Cream truck on the curb, some were running on the playground and others were just doing their own thing.

Hollis had grown to view her old Housing Projects as its own little ghetto world of manifested lessons. There was drama throughout every fragment of concrete. Every issue that came about seemed to be a matter of highest regard to each individual. Everyone was feeling the economic decline of America and making due however they could. Everyone was a character in a chapter in the beautiful story of Harlem.

"They gone tear these Projects down in a few years."

"Hmm...then were we gone go?" Mrs. Ella asked while twirling her old cane on the ground in front of her.

"I know my Cousin talking bout moving back down south; either Atlanta or North Carolina."

-"Shit, it seems like everybody trying to do that."

"That's why I'm telling yall, yall need to go out and vote for Barack Obama. He's the answer." Mrs. Ella said pointing an adamant elder finger at Amanda. Hollis could no longer keep her reserve. She'd been listening and learning for the past half hour, keeping what was real and laughing past and occasionally challenging the fake.

"Barack ain't the answer; GOD is the answer. Black people been running from here to there for too damn long. Didn't we get up here running from the oppression of the south in the first place? We gotta fight wherever we are. Lightly or heavily armed, we gotta fight."

"Fight who? It is what it is, economics. It's..." Amanda snapped her fingers trying to find her word of choice, "...what's that word? Profitable; yeah profitable, it's profitable to push us from here to there so they do it, and they gone keep doing it until-"

"Until our Black asses take a serious stand and push back until we get our fair share. You live on GOD's green earth, not some fucking man's.

You don't gotta move your ass cause they want you to, or when it's profitable for them. That's not the way. GOD created the earth for just ends; you entitled to life, liberty and the pursuit of happiness, just like them. What if we needed to move them from their neighborhoods for our profit?"

Mrs. Ella was smiling, Hollis had her undivided attention; "I heard that."

-"But you saying fight like you talking bout some damned Jihad or some Black Panther shit or something. A Black man or woman can get whatever the hell they want in America. All that oppression, slavery shit is a thing of the past."

"Shhhiiiit; take a look at where we live, and how you got there. You been in Grant what twenty years? Your Mother another twenty on top of that; another twenty, what, five for your Grandmother? It's fucked up here, and it's been fucked up. Barack ain't gone change that shit cause Barak ain't from here. We from here, so it gotta be on our agenda to change our hood... And I am talking about Jihad, which means struggling in the ways of GOD. We gone a have to persevere through some shit, side by side, *together*. We gone have to stop wearing the enemy's clothes *together*, we gone have to patronize Black business *together*, and the wealthy among us are going to have to give the poor among us some sort of authentic opportunity."

- *"Uh oh, she on her Assata Shakur shit today."*

"Whatever." Hollis responded to Amanda and kept it moving; "We need to negotiate peace talks between our Brothers out here killing each other over nothing every night. We need to inspire them with the word and let them know who and what they really are. We need to clean *our* own neighborhoods and our own homes, and take responsibility for the mischief that *our* young are spreading. We need to be civil and fair, honest and accountable. I mean what the fuck, we can plant anything in this ground and it'll grow; it'll grow in Harlem just like it grow in Idaho, just like it'll grow in China. But we'd rather kill and steal, and hustle, then take the money we make and go spend it with the first person that don't look like us."

The Moment Hollis realized that she had the full attention of everyone around, her fountain of articulation ran dry. She looked over to Rosy, surprised to discover that she was listening. Mrs. Ella and Ms. Brown, who Hollis knew since she was a child were listening along with Lenee from building 57. In her heart Hollis wished that the Lord would remove the spotlight for a second, to allow her time to gather her thoughts, so that she could hit her mark. There

376

were too many eyes on her for her liking, but she understood that the Lord was watching her, testing her to see how she was going to proceed now that she had understanding. Hollis prayed for attention, which would drive in more sales, and more sales meant achieving her goals… getting in harmony with the infinite, the elite, attaining access to the resources that she watched being squander in college and using them for good. No one else chose to speak during the brief Moment of silence, unusual on this side of town, so Hollis continued. "You seek from GOD's bounty, not some imaginary white man in a tie who controls the whole world. GOD is our sustainer, he provides us with water, meat, grain, and fruits and the best, excuse me, the only resources."

- *"That's definitely Architekk's Daughter right there!"*

The small crowd laughed in harmony, finally easing the tense rigor of the situation. Amanda pushed Hollis in her best attempt to show her some love. Mrs. Brown raised her left hand and Hollis slapped her a five. Rosy squeezed Hollis' shoulder, "Come on girl, lets go smoke. You getting too serious on me."

MAY 11TH 2008

"Can I speak to you for a second?"

Hollis put her nephew Terrell back in his crib and followed Lakrisha out the room. Hollis could feel an unusual negative vibe from Lakrisha since she got to the house and was interested in what she had to say. She followed her through the hallway. Lakrisha turned around when she got to the front door, "Is your friend fucking my Husband?"

Hollis' heart skipped a beat, though one couldn't tell by her face. "Lakrisha you asking the wrong pers-"

"Is your friend-" Lakrisha interjected waiving a single finger in front of Hollis' face, with a short fuse, not in the mood for bullshit, "fucking my Husband?"

"Yo, let me tell you something; I'm stronger than you, faster than you and I'm probably crazier than you. So if you wanna *box*, we gone get it in, you understand me?"

Lakrisha folded her arms, leaned back and looking into Hollis' eyes as Hollis continued. "Now as I already told you, you askin' the wrong person. If you want to know if Junior is having an affair with Renee, then…" Hollis stopped speaking midsentence as she seen Lakrisha's demeanor harden at the realization that Hollis knew Renee was the suspect without Lakrisha ever saying so. Lakrisha stepped back

378

as if she thought about it first, then she cocked back and punched Hollis in the face. Hollis stumbled backward into a set of plastic storage bins behind her. Lakrisha advanced to finish what she started. Hollis' raised one of her powerful leg and kicked the wind out of Lakrisha's chest. Her body fell to ground with such force that the thud of her head pounding on the floor was the final evidence that there had been a skirmish.

"Stupid bitch!" Hollis yelled over Lakrisha as Gwinn and the baby sitter Amanda came rushing in from one of the rooms.

"That's what happens to aggressors! Look at you...laid out."

Dominique, Ashley and the neighboring vendors could tell that Hollis was frustrated and left her alone accordingly. She'd been sitting on the trunk end of Dominique's car for the past 10 minutes listening to her mp3 player in her own world. She snatched her earphones out and decided to get back in the game.

"Yall wanna take yall lunch?" Hollis asked Dominique as she handed her $20 and began tidying up. "I got this."

Dominique and Ashley walked towards Popeye's. A trio of teenaged girls approached Hollis' table as she was straightening a pile of t-shirts.

"How yall doing?"

They declined to respond, preoccupied with skimming through the designs. The young lady in the middle grabbed one of the white camouflage hats and held it up for one of her girls, "These shits is ugly right?"

"Excuse me?"

"Look at this shit it, look like she made these shits herself."

Hollis snatched the hat from her grasp; "Gimme my fuckin' hat."

"Bitch I'll slap the shit out of you, you ever do some shit like that again."

One of the girls walked around the side of the table. Hollis took a step back apprehensive to throw the first punch and commence a three on one fistfight. One of the other girls began to close in on her from the opposite side of the Honeywell table. Hollis took a few steps back before bumping into Dominique's car behind her. Her

Momentum dropped her over the hood of the vehicle. She looked up before coving her head from the blows to come; all three of the girls were closing in. She curled herself up and waited. She tightened up so vehemently that the few seconds of waiting had become more agonizing than the possibility of a tussle. Hollis looked up hesitantly through her forearms and saw no immanent danger. She lowered her guard and she found two Brothers in front of her using their bodies as a human barricade.

"Yall not harming this Sister while we here."

"No, she wanna be getting all jazzy & shit let that bitch fight."

"We were watching the situation. This woman instigated no problems with you."

Hollis stood to her feet behind the Israelite Brothers whose bookstand she patronized from time to time. She fixed her hair.

"Yo forget that bitch Dashiqa. Let's get out of here. I'm telling everybody I know not to buy these weak ass shirts."

Hollis packed up early and walked over to Grant. Today it wasn't about business or learning. She just wanted to chill out with the family of friends she had rediscovered in the Projects. She needed reassurance not to take things too seriously, lest she should forget why she became an entrepreneur in the first place.

Hollis bared witness to the beautiful brown people and their dealings in the heart of Harlem; 125th street. She found discouragement in the carelessness and unrestricted freedom on the streets. She had troubles that she was facing; website fees, a decrease in sales and creation ideas weren't coming along so easily nowadays. Nevertheless Hollis found encouragement in the same faces; if her Brothers and Sisters could keep moving through their troubles then she had an obligation to.

Hollis could see at least four Police cruisers on the curb of 126th & Broadway. She saw yellow Police lines marking off the walkway in front of building 57, holding back a crowd of onlookers. The light rain seemed to mesh in a state of mellow reality with the Police lights. From about fifty feet out Hollis was able to make out Rosy's head lying on its' side, void of any life with her eyes and mouth open. Hollis' chest sunk in, her legs stopped and she stared into Rosy's eyes. She could only hope that she made it;

that somehow, someway Rosy made her peace with her maker before whoever got to her got to her. She walked up behind Ms. May from the 13th floor of her old building and continued to stare in silence.

For the next few days Honey stayed locked in her cave in the Bronx. Although consistent over spending had jeopardized her savings and livelihood, she went shopping and brought a bed, a television and a bagful of DVDs. She got caught up on sleep and Hollis time. She watched music videos, talked on the phone with Reggie and played solitaire on her computer. She took a break from exercising, stretched and running. She didn't speak to GOD much; she didn't know how to address him. In her heart she wanted to question him snatching Rosy away just when she felt like she was beginning to have a positive impact on her. But she had been vehemently warned against such behavior, and therefore she just sought to ignore GOD's presence and guidance until she cooled off. Tonight, she laid in front of the television with frustration and grief pulling at her chest, reexamining the authenticity of her path and purpose.

When the infomercials, Law Firm ads and get rich quick commercials that dominated the post midnight air waves became depressing, Hollis cut off the TV and made her way into the kitchen. She grabbed a pint of Butter Pecan ice cream out the freezer and went back to flop across her bed, bored out of her mind perceiving nothing for her to do.

Hollis sat in the first row next to her Grandmother who was dressed in an elaborate peach and white dress. She tried to remain congenial and was doing well, so long as she didn't look at George, who she didn't know and didn't trust with her Mother.

With her Uncle Leon by her side, Denise came strutting down the aisle to the praise of the church organ. Hollis stood among her family and friends and played her role. She peeped through Denise's lace veil and wondered to what extent her happiness ran. She wondered to what extent she would go to adhere to the oath she was about to make before GOD. Her Mother's physical being was a testament to the sheer elegance of a woman. She glided with grace further into the church, her hips swayed to either side and her postured was without flaw. Denise looked directly into her only child's eyes as she passed her and spoke under her breath.

"I love you too." Hollis said now beginning to tear up. She excused herself as the dogmatic service began to take pictures for her personal collection. When the memory on her digital camera filled, she searched through her flicks to see which ones she could delete to free space on her memory card. When she was ready to resume she looked around the back of the church to see where she could get her next unique shot. Her blood flow plummeted when she saw her Father leaned against a wall in a white suite. She turned her camera off and hurried over.

Jason smiled at Hollis, obviously aware of her presence then he went back to observing the ceremony. Before she reached, Hollis saw her Dad turn his head to the other side of the pillar he was leaned against to address someone.

"Yeah, she's a beautiful woman." Jason said to Stump who was slouched in a fancy chair in the hallway. He reached out to embrace Hollis as she got close. "How you doing?"

"I'm good. How you?" She asked as she wrapped her arm around his waist.

"Oh, peace is with me, peace is with me."

The two stood and listened to the union taking place before them. Stump walked over and stood behind them in silence. Stumpy, Hollis and Jason each looked on lost in their own thoughts. Hollis was taken out of her zone when she heard her Father exhale in a faint laugh which he probably meant to keep to himself. He looked at Denise as Hollis looked at him; he laughed again then excused himself from the premises.

-"That was a beautiful testament." Hollis said as hit got up to eject the disk from the DVD player.

"Testament?" Gwinn asked looking for an explanation.

"Yeah; those people were on that mountain for over 70 days, no food, nothing to drink. And they made it; they lived. GOD saw them through. That's a testament to the strength of the will of man, and the mercy of GOD."

Gwinn tossed another handful of popcorn in her mouth and looked at her Sister strangely; "If you say so."

"Shut up." Hollis pushed Gwinn, toppling the bowl between her legs.

"See what you made me do." Gwinn threw a fistful of popcorn at Hollis. "Shoot, I worked hard to get those kernels popped just right, the perfect mixture of butter and salt. You a hater."

They enjoyed in a mutual laughter. Hollis stuck the *Alive* movie back in front of the *AZ Pieced of a Man* album in her GOD Library. "Shut up and get dressed. Let's go get another bag of popcorn before the corner store close."

Gwinn stood from the bed, put on her sneakers and pulled her curly brown hair through the back of her North Carolina Tar Heels baseball cap. Hollis cut off the television and changed into a new t-shirt and they headed out.

They brought popcorn, milk, butter, a loaf of bread, soda and a couple of bags of chips. Although the sun had set it was still well over 80 degrees in the Bronx. Hollis stopped to open a can of soda she brought to quench her thirst. Gwinn walked on, she was staring at a makeshift wall on a construction site that served more as a poster bulletin than whatever its intended purpose was. Hollis walked up to her holding her grocery bag between both her arms and looked on.

THE CRITICALLY ACCLAIMED NEW ALBUM FROM NYC'S OWN

*******ARCHITEKK*******

THE DREAD

07/21/2008

www.ONTHEBOOKSENT.com

UNIT 4

Gwinn *Lil E* Sessoms

364

"You know they calling me the black Kate Moss out here."

Date: June 24TH 2008

"What the fuck you doing?"

Gwinn sucked her teeth and rolled her head away from her Father who she hadn't seen since her birthday last year. She didn't even try to hide the alcoholic beverage in her hand.

"What you said?" Gwinn asked Tyshena who was sitting in the passenger seat of Shanequa's car in attempt to dismiss her Father who was approaching the parking lot.

"You know your Pops behind you?" Tyshena asked.

"Whatever."

Jason seized Gwinn by her wrist and spun her around, "Yo what you doing?"

"Can you leave me alone please Mister!" Gwinn yelled as she snatched her arm back. "Thank you."

-*"Somebody's sleeping on the job."*

Gwinn shook her head as she awoke from her alcohol infused coma and saw Dina and Iesha from 115th street looking at her. She quickly tried to gather herself.

-"Uh oh, that's blows." Iesha said as she counted out the cash that Candice handed her on the opposite side of the terrace. Iesha was blued up, wearing a pair of number 8 Jordans and an air brushed tank top that read *J.E.S.I.C.A. SET BITCH* across the front and *Jefferson Projects* on the back.

"How many in?" Dina asked as she approached Gwinn.

Gwinn wiped her face and cleared her throat; "Nine for the day."

-*"How she gone know? She probably been sleep her whole shift."*

"Na, I just finished speaking to Ms. Shelly, I couldn't have been sleep that long. Nine in; nine out."

"Shut the fuck up." Iesha put Gwinn back in her place for correcting a Superior. She approached Gwinn and began staring her down, trying to intimidate her. A sharp knock on the window dividing the terrace from the hallway demanded the focus of all four ladies.

Gwinn waived, *"Hi Ms. Drummond."*

Dina and Candice waived. Iesha looked in the opposite direction through the plastic coated fence out to 112th street.

"Am I dismissed?"

"Yeah youngin'; get your ass home before your Moms be out here looking for you."

Iesha grilled Gwinn once again as she passed her to get to the terrace door. "Yo Dina, don't she got blows?"

"Oh yeah," Dina confirmed to Gwinn's dismay just as she reached for the knob. Gwinn wished that she could be anybody but herself for the next few minutes. Her heart beats raced as she tightened her stomach and turned to face the music.

"Come on bitch, you know what this is," Iesha said to Gwinn then turned to Candice, "Yo get the fuck out of here, shop closed for the night."

Iesha made her way to the B staircase looking at Gwinn like she was something to eat. "Step into my office." She said as she pushed the door

392

open. Gwinn followed her up the stairs, Dina trotted up behind Gwinn.

Iesha's sky blue bandana bounced in her back pocket as she scaled the steps. Gwinn made sure to walk quickly as to avoid giving Dina another reason to hit her. She focused on chewing the gum in her mouth as a means to help her remain calm, a tip that Box Cutter Keisha gave her after a two hour session of blows in Lincoln Projects. Iesha turned around as she reached the 10th floor landing. "Spread your fucking arms."

Gwinn held her breath and reached each of her arms out to either side. Iesha wasted no time wailing into her stomach; "Fuck you doing sleeping on your shift?"

Gwinn folded in agony. She tried to answer but simply could not catch her breath. Dina kicked her in her hip, dropping her to the ground. Gwinn covered up as she hit the staircase floor. The lingering pain from the initial two blows made all the stomping that her big Sisters were engaged in tolerable. She waited the beating out in a protective fetal position, mindful to pretend to be more hurt than she actually was, thankful that it wasn't Amanda and Jaliqua giving her blows.

9:59PM; THE SAME NIGHT

When Gwinn walked into her apartment her Mother was in the kitchen preparing Gwinn's lunch for tomorrow. She kissed Bernadette on the cheek before she put the deadbolt on the front door.

"How was your day at Camp?"

"Huh? Oh it was okay. We had crazy fun today."

"I told you you'd end up liking it there. After all that fussing you did."

The top of her blouse was open and so was her brown leather belt in her pants. Bernadette sealed Gwinn's sandwiches in a large zip lock bag then cut off the water boiling on the stove and removed her yellow #1 Mom mug from the cabinet.

"Yeah, I guess it's not so bad…Well, I'm gone a go take a bath. I fell today while we were playing kick ball and I feel a little sore."

"Alright, well I'm gonna see you in the morning. I'm a go try to steal me a good night's sleep."

"Okay ma, goodnight."

The next morning Gwinn woke up before her preset alarm went off. She rolled over in her bed to check the digital read out above her television set.

8:03AM

She closed her eyes and listened carefully to the apartment to see if her Mother had left for work. She daydreamed about all the things she wanted to do with Justin on the bus trip to Dorney Park next weekend. When she opened her eyes she looked back at her alarm clock.

8:11AM

She got up and opened her room door.

"Good Morning." Bernadette was in the bathroom applying a coat of blush to her face looking in the mirror. "I left breakfast in the microwave for you. Don't be late for your bus to Camp."

"I wont."

Gwinn said as she made her way to the living room. She snuck open the glass door on the entertainment center on the wall, turned on the stereo and forwarded her 50 Cent CD to track number 19 and pressed pause.

"Okay Gwinn, be good, I love you. Talk to you later."

"Alright bye ma. Have a nice day."

"You too." Bernadette said as she shut the front door.

Before blasting her new morning song Gwinn gave her Mom what she assumed would be enough time to return for anything she may have forgotten by going to brush her teeth and running the water for a cold shower. If she got caught listening to 50 again it was certain punishment. She rinsed her mouth out and made her way back to the living room. She pressed play and tuned the volume all the way up.

"GOD gave me style. GOD gave me grace..." She sang along with her favorite Rapper as she laid a pair of new Nautica sweatpants and a Moschino tee across her bed along with her 95 air-max shoebox.

"God put a smile on my face..."

She showered and stepped out of the building fresh, with Uptown splendor. She knew she was going to be the center of attention wherever she chose to go today. She popped in a stick of chewing gum and went forth.

"Sister!"

"What's poppin'?" Gwinn dapped Candice and Tyese from building 1690 then slouched down next to them on the benches. The Projects were humid, it was going to be over 90 degrees today and the slow, mid 80 degree morning was somewhat indicative of a day full of drama to come.

"We bout to go to Barkim house." Candice said as she looked through a bag of goodies that Dollar, a neighborhood hustler had for sale. "Some East River Sisters supposed to be there. Barkim got some new Sub Zero DVDs & shit."

-"Justin supposed to be there too."

Tyese threw in her two cents and tapped Candice on her leg to watch Gwinn's reaction. She gave them what they were looking for as she blushed, allowing herself to act her age for a change. Gwinn tried to turn her face away.

"Look at this punk ass bitch blushing and shit." Tyese said.

Candice pulled out two dollars to pay Dollar for an Ipod charger and a bottle of coco butter. "Yall ready to get outta here?"

10:AM; THE SAME DAY

Since she was a toddler Gwinn loved to stroll down 3rd Avenue. As they crossed the intersection to 103rd and 3rd Gwinn became lost in the trafficking of goods and services around her. The African Brothers were selling sunglasses and bootleg watches on their vendor tables. An older Spanish Brother was slinging ice cold bottles of water for a buck, Icee vendors, dope boys and department stores. 3rd Ave was manifest proof that East Harlem was the best; the reason Gwinn represented her set so vehemently at school and the reason she didn't plan on following her Mother to her American dream in the suburbs next month.

Candice turned to Gwinn who was lagging behind, "You better keep up Sis. You know we got beef with them G.W. bitches."

Candice tried to look into Gwinn's eyes but she wouldn't give them up. She was doing her own thing mentally.

"You alright?"

"Yeah, I was just thinking about something."

"I'm supposed to be at my summer school class right now." Candice proceeded in trying to make small talk.

Gwinn chuckled slightly and finally looked at her, "Yeah? I'm supposed to be on the bus going to camp right now."

Their trek to Stanley Isaacs Projects finally came to a head. The girls got to 93rd street and abruptly cut through traffic to get across 1st Avenue.

"Sisters!"

A J.E.S.I.C.A Sister whom Gwinn never met flung the front door to building 1349 open with a careless shove. She greeted each Sister individually with crew love and introduced herself as Bladder, a 6th round true-blue, two ranks above Tyese and one above Gwinn and Candice. The girls had a silent understanding that they were probably going to have to comp the bigger Sister somehow.

"Where yall going?" Bladder asked Candice.

"My nigga Barkim crib in 1353."

"Aight, I'm a roll out with yall."

"You ain't know Sisters was getting together up there?" Gwinn asked speculatively.

"Na, I been out of the mix lately. But come on let's go."

Bladder was as animated a Sister as Gwinn had ever met. She couldn't keep still and she walked like she had something to prove. All she did was talk about fights that she almost got into on their way to Barkim's. They got on the elevator and Candice pressed for the 8th floor. Gwinn popped the gum in her mouth and leaned against a wall and watched Bladder pace to and fro rapping to herself. Out of nowhere the pumped up Sister fired her fist into the hallow elevator wall. The force shook the elevator car Momentarily, threatening to get stuck.

"Yo homegirl what's your problem?"

"What you mean what's my problem? You got a problem?"

"A yo go 'head with all that. Walls don't hit back but I got something for that ass." Gwinn stepped into Bladder's face meeting her with equal aggression and readiness.

"Oh word, you set tripping on a superior now?"

The elevator door opened. Candice called out to Justin who was shooting dice on the terrace straight ahead, *"Jus you better come get ya girl. She bout to transform to lil E out here."*

"Na fuck all that; I asked you a simple ass question and you jumped in my Motherfucking face like you bout to do something, so pop the fuck off!" Gwinn crunched her soft yet menacing hands into mighty fist of rage; *"Pop off!"*

-"What happen? Chill; chill." Justin said wrapping an arm around Gwinn and pulling her off the elevator. "Who that you beefing with?" He asked in his ever-mellow voice.

"Some fucking bird I'm a have to smack if she get out of pocket again."

Justin laughed before taking a sip from his beer and leading Gwinn into the terrace.

"Yo this my girl right here son; she bad right? And my nigga, she younger than me!"

Justin was drunk and high. Gwinn could tell by how he was stumbling clumsy and speaking recklessly.

"How old are you?" One of the fellas asked.

Gwinn readjusted her stance, fluffed the bun in her hair and popped the gum in her mouth, "Thirteen."

"Daaaamn!"

-*"Daaaamn!"*

"But I'm a be fourteen this October so..."

Justin took his arm back. He picked up the multicolored dice resting atop a flipped box and began shaking them, "That's why I need to get my money back from you nigga. So I can take my shorty out this weekend." He looked at Gwinn and pointed at Barkim, "Baby this nigga cracked me for $200 earlier."

Barkim pulled out a wad of crumbled bills and began manicuring them, "What's up then? I'm down to take some more of your money."

"Baby go inside, they watching DVDs and eating and shit. I'm bout to win my money back. I'll be in there."

Gwinn walked around the nobodies gathered in the hallway and into apartment 8F.

We got the bar, we got the bar. This is Bird Gang money...

Jim Jones was blasting from Barkim's desktop computer. Porsche was sitting in the living room with Terrence, Chris, tall Douglas and Twin, Jamilia's Sister, they were all looking into the screen on a portable DVD player on the table.

"This nigga be having the baddest bitches on this shit yo. Look how fat her ass is."

Arianna, Terrence's girlfriend, who normally didn't hang out with them, was sitting quietly through the ruckus watching television with no sound.

"You alright?" Gwinn asked as she popped open a wine cooler and sat down next to her on the couch.

"Yeah, I'm okay."

"What you thinking about?"

-"I made that bitch say Auntie!"

Arianna was startled from the yelling; she spilled some of her cup of soda in her lap. Gwinn turned to the direction that the shouting was coming from. Bladder came busting out of the back room with a swarm of blued up J.E.S.I.C.A Sisters.

"Had her like uh, uh!"

"Yo what's wrong with that bitch?" Gwinn asked loud enough that only Arianna could hear her.

- "Sister!"

Gina from 119th recognized Gwinn as they got to the living room, Monica from the Johnson Set and Sadia also walked up to Gwinn and dapped her up.

"Yo you know her?" Gwinn asked Monica as she nodded in Bladder's direction as Bladder reenacted a fight she'd been in.

"Na, I just met her. She bugged out." Monica said around her laughing.

- "Bitch give me one of those fucking gums." Bladder snatched the pack of gum that Arianna pulled from her pocketbook, frightening her yet again to a standstill.

"Uh uh see something wrong with this bitch."

Bladder heard Gwinn's sentiments and approached her a second time, "Yo you been trying to come at me sideways-"

Gwinn cocked and popped her fist right into Bladders big mouth, knocking her off balance. Gwinn dove her entire body into her ex-Sister's stomach and pummeled her to the floor. She mounted her and began wailing to either side of her head relentlessly until Monica and Gina finally dragged her off.

"Bitch!"

Gwinn leaned over the railing in front of the building and began visually sweeping through the streets to see what was out there. She saw drunk Calvin talking to and falling over himself as he entered the Projects via the parking lot on 112th street. Through his lightly tented windows Gwinn could tell that Nemar was sitting in his car with a passenger, smoking. She looked along giving no intimation that she saw them. Freddy Mack was talking to Jaliqua in front of 1695 across the street. Gwinn figured the silver Volvo that she saw at the end of the parking lot was a Detective car.

When Gwinn spotted the Detective car she casually walked in the building and keyed up Dina on her cell phone *push-to-talk* as she hurried to catch the elevator before it shut. She snuck in a groove between three bodies; she turned her head and asked a man to press the 14th floor.

Dina hadn't responded yet. Gwinn pulled the bandana from her back pocket and wiped her forehead with it. She saw her friend Samantha's Grandmother through the corner of her eye. "Ms. Ruiz you need help with those bags?"

"No baby these few little bags ain't troubling me much. I sure do appreciate it though."

"Yo?"

Dina finally responded to Gwinn's alert, coming through on her speaker. Gwinn waited until the last person was off the elevator before she picked up the conversation.

"Yo I think the boys is sitting in the parking lot."

"Oh word? What it look like?"

"I can't really call it, but they been sitting out there for a minute. Look like two DTs, a male and female in a silver Volvo."

"Aight shut everything down for now. Let me see what's up."

Gwinn flipped her phone and pushed open the elevator door. She knocked on the first door on the left hand side of the hallway of the 14th floor.

"Who that?" A deep raspy voice demanded from the other side of the door.

"Blue's hot. Shut it down." Gwinn said then she made moves. She opened the terrace door and looked down the fourteen flights at the silver car in the Lot. Her vision was limited from the distance but she could see that the car was vacant, which meant the Officers had probably came into the building. She made her way to the A staircase and darted downward, wanting to get in the house and off of the radar. Gwinn didn't know the ins and outs of the Sisters stronghold on the cigarette and Angel Dust Dippers trade, but she put in enough work as a lookout to get wet if it should happen to rain. She made her way past the eleventh floor and began to slow down as she heard people speaking a few flights below. She began to creep. She considered switching to the B staircase but her curiosity propelled her.

"...and all that's still in there?"

"Yeah."

"Start breaking that down into a liquid budget so we can make whatever moves we got a make. That fifty thou is what I'm gone use to buy the land."

"...That's peace. That's definitely peace."

Gwinn turned the corner of the staircase wall that divided her from the conversation and immediately was caught in her Father's eyes as well as the eye of former J.E.S.I.C.A Superior General Laronda. Gwinn waived a hand as she tried to find some comfortable spot for her eyes, "Hi."

"Hey beautiful." Jason turned and grinned at his baby. Laronda smiled as well, standing in front of Jason who was sitting on a newspaper on the bottom step.

"How you doing Lil E?" Laronda asked still smiling brightly.

Gwinn scampered past them; uncomfortable and looking to converse no further.

"You wanna go get something to eat?" Jason asked.

"No." Gwinn said as she ran away.

"Mommy I'm leaving!" Gwinn yelled from the kitchen as she finished the last of her fruit punch and placed her cup in the sink. Bernadette appeared from the hallway half awake.

"I'm sorry I can't go with yall. I'm just gone stay in my bed and chill out today."

Gwinn could already tell what her Mother's plans were for the day. She heard Rodney come in late last night and Bernadette was in her silk robe, which she never wore unless Rodney was there.

"Hold on Gwinn!"

Rodney yelled from the master bedroom. He exited the room with a bare chest and glowing. He pulled out his wallet and handed her a $10 bill.

"Thanks Rodney."

Gwinn pressed for the elevator then flew into the staircase to change out of her white tank top into her sky blue BCBG halter-top. She added the $10 Rodney gave her to her wad of over $400 and went downstairs to board the Dorney Park bound charter bus.

9:26AM; THE SAME DAY

"Tupac."

-"50 Cent."

-"BIG; it's BIG I hate having the conversation with people cause it's BIG. He was the best Rapper ever. Like, stop talking about it. Biggie Smalls was the fuckin' illest."

"Ah yall watch yall mouths back there!"

"Sorry Ms. Jamerson!" Troy apologized and just as quickly went back to making his point.

The Taft Project kids and many adults spent the entire day at Dorney Park in Allentown Pennsylvania. Gwinn didn't bother with much play and games, she was too busy being cute and trying to escape here or there with Justin.

The sun was beginning to set. Gwinn laid her head back and partook in the fireworks and the light breeze coming off the lake. Justin's head was laid across her lap. He was so relaxed that Gwinn wasn't sure if he was still awoke. She continued to graze the waves in his hair with the tips of her fingers. She knew they had to be at the bus soon and she tried to check the time on her cell phone without disturbing Justin when the phone exploded in her hand.

I-don't know what you take me for. I- really don't play that shit...

Gwinn's ring tone woke Justin and pissed her off, as she knew that particular tone was reserved for the *not so important* people.

I- ain't got to get you hit. I'll get out myself & spray this shit...

"*Hello?*" She answered as if she were on the verge of cursing someone out. "*...No I'm not on the block. Don't call me no more tonight.*" Gwinn disconnected the call and placed her soothing hand on the side of Justin's head and pushed him back to her lap.

"Who was that?"

"Stinkin' Alize' wit' her bullshit."

Justin chuckled and relaxed. Gwinn kicked her feet out and scooted down to a declined position. Her and Justin both were on the verge on falling asleep when a voice from the hood hollered through the line on her Nextel; "*Lil E! Where you at?*"

"Oh my GOD!"

Justin sat up again, "Come on baby. We gotta be back at the bus soon anyway."

"So you prepared for this right? You got him beat?"

Junior laughed at his baby Sister who was scrolling through a display of blouses on the second floor of Bloomingdales. "Of course. I ain't come this far to loose to some old timer."

"Big Brother can we hit up the Macy's on 34th too?"

Junior looked into his diamond infested watch dial. "I don't know G. I may slide you a few dollars and let you roll down there yourself; traffic gone be crazy by the time we get out of here."

"...Yeah but anyway, I think something is wrong with him. He call his self trying to come around and talk to me now. I'm like *please*; too little too late."

"What you mean he be coming around?"

Gwinn pulled out a $350 Gucci blouse and held it up and across her chest. "He be showing up out of the blue trying to...I don't know, I don't know what he want. He gave me $30 the other day and told me GOD loves me."

Junior's face became hostile; "Don't take no money from that nigga. Don't take shit from him! We good now, we don't need him."

6:01PM; THE SAME DAY

When Gwinn got out of her Brother's chromed out S.U.V. in front of her building she was smacked with the reality of East Harlem. She toted her *Big Brown* Bloomies bags in sheer arrogance as she click-clacked up the walkway in her Via Spias short heals seeking to keep the filth away from her.

"Yo lil E bleep Chante for me."

Gwinn didn't even look at Sabrina; she just held up her bags and kept walking, not looking to have her mood spoiled. "As you can see, my hands are all little preoccupied."

"Oh my GOD, I'm about to kill this bitch. Please call Chante for me G."

Gwinn removed her Leopard print shades and gave Sabrina some attention; "What happen, it's beef?"

"Yo this bitch Dana and that *bitch* Jasmine is in back of the building right now."

"Wh-aat?"

413

Box Cutter Keisha walked up to them in front of building 1694; "We gone get they asses, they ain't going nowhere. I made them bitches feel comfortable." Keisha pulled her blue rag from her back pocket and swiftly snuck her orange box cutter therein. "Oh my GOD, I'm putting one of those bitches in the Hospital."

Gwinn saw Amanda's car pull up on Madison Avenue, across the street she could see Chante walking up Park Ave from Johnson Projects.

"Yo let me go drop my bags upstairs real quick. Yall don't move on them without me."

Not wanting to engage in small talk with her Mother and/or risk the possibility of not being able to go back outside, Gwinn left her bags with the Set look-outs posted on the 11th floor terrace. When she got back downstairs none of her Sisters was where she left them. Amanda's Honda was peeling off; Money Makin' Monica was hanging out the passenger side window laughing and waiving her sky blue flag in the wind. Sisters were hoping over the barricades and scattering through the Projects. Gwinn made her way up the walk way toward the back of the building. She could see Dana and Jasmine. Dana was beaten to a pulp, no movement. Jasmine was trying to pull herself to her feet, holding the side of her torso. Gwinn spun around and went back upstairs.

After the sun set Gwinn went back downstairs to get a can soda and a snack for her lunch tomorrow. She changed into a yellow and blue Polo t-shirt that matched her nails; Antique Boutique jeans and she capped her evening attire off with a Yankee fitted hat.

Iesha and Amanda were in the lobby with Kenneth and Trevor, the twenty-five and older crowd. They were drinking bottles of Rose and talking at the top of their voices over the radio, which was blasting a Wendy Williams Hot 93.3 interview with Tekk.

...I mean, first of all, I wanna say that this is a completely ridiculous situation. I wish it ain't have to come down to this, but it is what it is. So... I'm a have to air the boy out...

"What up lil E?" Trevor asked when he seen Gwinn get off the elevator.

"What's up Trev?"

"You hear your Pops on the radio? He talking about the battle. That nigga Tekk ain't no joke!"

Okay so tell us a little bit about how you guys ended up clashing to the point where you got a take it out on each other in front of the whole tri-state area at this year's summer jam.

Na, he been coming at me sideways through the media, and mutual friends and family, saying this and that. Everybody got they limits Wendy.

Right, right, no I feel you. So fifty thou' on the line, winner takes all. I know you excited; fifty thousand. You can get a whole lot of pounds of weed with fifty thou'.

Tekk and Wendy both laughed over the airwaves. *Ah, ladies and gentlemen Architekk is in here giving me the finger right now...*

Amanda was all over Trevor who was trying to converse with Gwinn as he'd been a friend of the family for many years. "Your Brother gone do his thing though."

-"Yeah but he can't go with Tekk." Kenneth said as he placed his cell phone back in its' holster.

"It's gone be a good battle; lets' leave it at that."

"Get the fuck outta here. With fifty thousand on the line? Tekk gone spank that boy." Kenneth chuckled to himself, "Daddy gone give lil junior a spanking." He said before going into an all out laugh.

-"I'm GOD!"

416

All eyes in the lobby turned suddenly to Chauncey who jumped on a car parked in the lot out front and shouted near the top of his voice, *"I-am-GOD!"*

"This nigga done lost his mind."

Iesha pushed open the front door and the crowd in the lobby crept out to witness Chauncey make a complete fool of him self on an Angle Dust trip.

"Repent your sins Motherfuckers! Din-Din-in-in!!!!! I-AM-GOD!"

"His fat ass found him some money last night. He brought four Dippers off Candice."

Gwinn looked off to her right for some odd reason and saw a familiar silhouette entering the parking lot. "Is that my Sister?" She asked no one in particular.

"Which one?" Amanda asked as she overheard and was now looking the area that Gwinn was looking in.

"No I mean my Sister, Sister."

Gwinn excused herself as she jogged down the few steps in front of the building and through the parking lot entrance past Chauncey.

"Come to your Master." Chauncey said to
Gwinn as she walked by, igniting the laughter of
everyone who'd gathered out front.

"Hon-ey!"

Hollis extended her arms for a hug before
Gwinn could reach her; "Hey Sis."

They embraced; Hollis looked her Sister over,
under a street light in the parking lot. "What's
up my lil fly girl?"

"Nothing, I'm 'bout to go to the store."

"Come on I'll walk with you." Hollis said.

"Where you coming from?"

"Reggie house." She answered as she double
took Chauncey's antics. "Hey, when the next
time you gone come spend the night with me?
You need to get away from here more often."

Gwinn smiled like an innocent child, "I'll come
up there anytime. I love chillin' at your place. I
just don't want to crowd you, with your business
and everything."

"Na your welcome Sis; you're welcome.
Business been at damn near a standstill for me
anyway."

They walked into the bodega on 111th. Gwinn gave Poncho, the storeowner a five and walked to the refrigerators in the back.

"You should give me a few shirts. I can get business poppin for you. If people see me in your stuff, I guaranteed you they gone want it." Gwinn placed a box of Crunch & Munch and two 20-ounce bottles of Hawaiian Punch on the counter; "You know they calling me the black Kate Moss out here?"

Hollis laughed, but she already begun seriously considering; "Alright, we gone work something out."

"So what you think about this whole rap battle thing between Pops and 3?"

Honey's face soured up, "Honestly, I think it can get ugly. I don't know… as long as Junior stay strong he'll be alright though. He could at least hold his head."

"Hold his head?" Gwinn looked at her Sister; "So you think your Father's gonna win?"

"Oh…oh, you, you think 3 is gone win?" They exchange identical looks of confusion, each staring as if the other had lost their mind.

"He's going to win." Gwinn said.

392

"...make sure your Father don't walk out of these Projects with $50,000 worth of weed."

Date: July 22ND 2008

"How was camp today?"

There was something in her eyes that suggested that Gwinn should've been honest about it. Gwinn removed her key from the front door then guided the door shut. She knew her Mother wouldn't have been waiting near the door and slamming her with questions as soon as she got in for no reason, but she decided to push the envelope anyway.

"It was good. We-"

Without the slightest hesitation Bernadette smacked the taste out of Gwinn's mouth; *"Get your ass in the room!"* She followed behind Gwinn, who was holding the side of her stunned, stinging face. *"Gone sit up there and lie right to my damn face! Three weeks they said it's been since you been to camp! Get in there & don't come back out for the rest of the damn night!"*

In an instant, Gwinn's world seemed to have caved in. She knew a lie like this would yield her at least a few weeks on punishment. She paced between her closet and window crying with a chest full of stress. Through the thin apartment walls she could hear her Mother ranting either on the telephone or to Rodney in the next room.

"That girl is getting completely out of control. I don't know what I'm a do with her…"

Gwinn was finally able to counter her hurt with anger, giving her the balance she needed to chill out after a few Moments. She flopped on her bed and grabbed her book-bag and removed the outfit that she really wore today, a Marc Jacobs short sleeve button-up and a pair of skintight Evisu shorts. She folded her shirt and opened her closet to stash it in the large trash bag where she hid all the expensive clothes that she brought with her lookout pay. She could tell that the bag was gone as soon as she looked up on the top shelf. She reached around aimlessly before the realization set in that her Mother had discovered her secret stash. She quickly checked behind her bed to see if her secret shoebox of designer shades were still there...that was gone as well.

Gwinn knew with so many offenses, she hadn't heard the last of her Mother's fury for the night. She stood completely still knowing that she would be able to get some information on the situation by listening through her walls.

"...She's going to be on punishment for the rest of the summer. And I'm about to go in there and tear her little ass up too..."

The first thing she thought about was Justin, then the Set, then Harlem, that was before some illogical reasoning seized her. She grabbed her doorknob and swung it open quickly, as she knew from experience that the door made a crackling noise if opened slowly. She carefully stepped across the threshold and tippy-toed past her Mother's closed room door.

"...Will you be able to watch her until I get off?"

A few feet later, Gwinn was at the front door where being discreet was no longer a concern. She unlocked both of the deadbolts and ran out of the house.

11:57 PM; THE SAME NIGHT

Gwinn opened her eyes and painfully twisted her body around. She was quickly brought back to the reality of her circumstances when the shoe boxes beneath her began to tear, making enough noise to completely blow her cover. Her back, hips and knees were sore. She wished terribly that she could be in her bed with a clean slate, just regular Gwinn Ella Sessoms, whose primary concern was finishing her homework and

422

household chores. She was trying to stretch her legs over an egg crate full of beauty supplies on the other side of the closet when everything supporting her suddenly gave way and collapsed. That's when she decided that she was done with this. Gwinn opened the closet door to find Candice getting out of bed, apparently to check on her. "You okay?" She whispered.

Gwinn stretched her aching limbs, "Na, I gotta go."

"You going home?"

"No..."

By the look on her face, Candice could tell that Gwinn wanted to say more, but even she hadn't figured out what she was going to do yet.

"Well, where you going?"

"I'll figure something out. You know me."

She reached down to embrace Candice. A part of Gwinn desired for Candice to beg for her to stay. But Gwinn built her reputation on her strength, and bullheadedness, all of which caused Candice to sit in her bed and look at her Set Sister with care and concern but no attempt to stop her. "Call me in the morning."

"Thank you Sister. I appreciate what you tried to do for me."

"I'm serious G, call me."

It wasn't until Gwinn got to Story Avenue that she discovered that her cell phone battery was dead. She gathered up all the scattered bills in her pocket and stopped to count them out to $158. She checked her surroundings to make sure no one was watching her, then she stuffed the knot of bills in her right sock. When she stood erect she saw a tall Black man in a blue t-shirt round the corner and her cool escaped her. She walked on and checked the man through the side of her eyes, ever ready to run and scream if need be. As he passed her, Gwinn gave it a few feet then looked over her shoulder to ensure that he was still walking away from her. The man had turned as well, apparently to check out the curvature of Gwinn's backside, which at this hour of the night she didn't mind, so long as he kept on walking.

There was virtually no one outside. The Bronx was bleak and growing scarier by the Moment. Normally Gwinn would be looking at a 5 through 10 minute bus ride from Candice's apartment to the 6 train at Hunts Point, but she knew that at this hour of the night she'd probably make it to Hunts Point on foot well before a bus arrived.

Fifteen minutes into her trek Gwinn found herself under the cover of a highway overpass along the Bruckner expressway. When she was absolutely sure that no one was looking, she spoke unto the Lord; "I know you not gone let nothing happen to your girl GOD, are you? Na, I know you not gone let nothing happen to me."

The Subway station was forlorn; it was pushing one in the morning. Gwinn couldn't stop thinking about all the trouble she was in and how every minute that passed was a strike against her. She didn't feel like being a rebel any longer, but she wasn't going home, at least not for tonight. She knew she had a hefty punishment ahead of her; that was inevitable. The little freedom that she had remaining, she was going to exert to allow herself to wake up in peace tomorrow morning; that was important to her.

She nodded in and out of conciseness as the 6 train coasted through the tunnels of the Bronx. There were only two other people on her train car; a big white girl who was wearing a t-shirt that read *I'm with stupid* and a Puerto Rican man who seemed to be just as tired as she was. As they pulled into 125th Gwinn leaned forward on her seat with the intent of getting off the train then she second guessed herself.

125th street, transfer here for the 4 and the 5.
Next stop 116th street. Stand clear of the
closing doors.

Gwinn dashed up and through the double doors
onto the platform and walked up the stairs to the
4 train, which she rode to 161st street, Yankee
Stadium. When she got off the train she walked
as quickly as possible, 167th street bound
although she did make a stop at the corner store
on Sheridan Ave. She brought a carrot cake and
apple juice which she planned on waiting until
she sat down to eat but had fully devoured
before she made it to her Sister's building.

She didn't bother coming up with a story, her
night had been long enough. She knocked on
the door and wished with all she had that Hollis
was home.

"Where you been? Your Mother been looking
everywhere for you." Hollis inquired before she
fully opened the door.

Gwinn could see her Father stumble around a
wall in a white tank top and basketball shorts, he
walked up behind Hollis.

"Can I please stay here tonight?" Gwinn broke
into tears and hung her head as she spoke.

"Come in here sweetheart."

Neither Hollis nor her Father bothered asking
any more questions, which was exactly what she
needed tonight. Hollis gave her a washcloth and
towel and warmed her up a plate of food.
Gwinn ate then went in the bathroom to wash
up. When she came out Hollis called out for
her, *"Sis come here for a sec."*

Gwinn walked past her Father who was sitting at
the kitchen table to Hollis who was sitting on the
counter near the sink. "You had enough to eat?"

"Yes, thank you."

"It's plenty more if you need it."

-"I got some left over Popeye's in there too."
Jason added.

"Na, I'm good; thank yall."

"Okay, go 'head and take my bed. I'm probably
gone be up all night anyway."

Gwinn awoke several times throughout the night
due to the whispering coming from the kitchen.

"What you thought he wasn't gone test you?
Allah will test you every step of the way...
Valleys and peaks; you gotta roll with the

427

punches. If you can't do that you ain't gone never build nothing..."

She planned on listening in long enough to grab the context of their conversation but she drifted back to sleep with ease. A few minutes or hours later she awoke again to her Father's deep voice, as he continued to lecture Hollis.

"...Shit people gone try to tell you all kind of crazy shit about GOD, but nothing is worst than a lie invented against the most high; cause that lie throws the beautiful balance of all the other shit off... Allah is beyond all restrictions, he is the infinite; you can't even begin to grasp him. You just gotta take his signs and his laws and go forth..."

When Gwinn awoke the next morning she saw Hollis sitting her at desk typing away at her laptop. Her dreads were sprawled all over her head and her long legs were folded into themselves on her chair.

"Good morning."

Hollis spun in her leather chair, "Good morning. How'd you sleep?"

Gwinn looked around and didn't see her Father anywhere. "I actually slept really good."

"I talked to your Mother last night."

"What she said?"

"I got her to calm down a bit. She just told me to make sure you go straight home when you leave here."

Gwinn slammed her head into the pillow and looked out of the window at the humid city that she got further acquainted with last night. "What you doing today?" She asked Hollis.

"I got a few errands I gotta run here and there... why?"

"Nothin'."

She got out the bed and went in the bathroom. After a twenty minute shower Gwinn became somewhat disappointed after drying herself off and realizing that she had to put on the same dirty clothes from yesterday. She wrapped herself in a towel and opened the bathroom door. *"Sis you got a shirt and some shorts or something I can borrow?"*

Hollis pushed her chair away from her desk and walked to a large wooden chester next to her GOD Library. She popped it open, "There you go. Pick out whatever you want."

Gwinn searched through the multitude of
Honeywell shirts and jeans before picking out
the best possible match to wear with the brown
on brown Mauri sneakers she had on. She went
back in the bathroom to put herself together and
stepped out looking like the fly girl she was, like
she hadn't missed a beat.

"Aight sweetie, make sure you go straight home
please." Hollis said as she got up to lock the
door behind Gwinn. "Hey you wanna come to
church with me and Daddy tomorrow?" She
asked as she snatched her hair back into a
ponytail and secured it with a rubber band. On
the other side of the threshold, Gwinn pretended
to think about Hollis' proposal for a Moment.
"...No thank you. I know I'm a be on
punishment anyway."

"I'm sure Bernadette wouldn't mind; it's
church."

"Na that's okay."

Hollis handed her a small manila envelope,
"Alright, well here's a set of keys I made for
you. Come by whenever you want."

Gwinn entered her Housing Projects by cutting
through Park Ave and up between 112 and 113th
streets, a route she hardly ever used. She
noticed the backdoor of 1695 open and dipped in

undetected by anyone who knew her. She took the elevator to the 14th floor and went on the terrace to examine the hood. It was politics as usual on Madison Avenue; moderate traffic in and out of the buildings, no Police in sight, save for a few beat walkers who were walking down toward 110th. Just as she turned to walk off the terrace Gwinn saw her Mother step out of her building across the street. She was wearing a t-shirt and a pair of sweat pants that were hugging her hips. The guys in front of the building followed her with their eyes as Bernadette made her way to her car. Gwinn figured she must be going to her new Saturday morning yoga class and Gwinn was struck with an idea to buy her some more free time. She waited until her Mother's car was out of seeing distance then went downstairs and across the street.

"Oooo, you gone be in trouble Lil E."

Tyrone, Annett's little Brother attempted to tease Gwinn as she walked by him in front of the building.

"What you talking about little boy?"

"Your Mother called my house like three times last night looking for you. Where you been?" He asked in his light, raspy voice which Gwinn found cute any other day except for today.

431

"Anyway." She waived him off and walked in her building.

"What up lil E where you been?" One of the girls in the building lobby asked.

"*Damn* everybody all up in my business. Excuse you." Gwinn pressed for the elevator. Bones and Trevor came bouncing out of the staircase with a fiend not far behind them.

"Aaaah, that's my lil fly girl right there."

"What up Trev?"

"Oooo you got the Mauris on?" Trevor asked as he scoped out Gwinn's sneakers. "Check that out Bones."

"Yeah, I see shorty be crushing it with the gear. Where you get that shirt from?"

"Oh this right here, this is kind of exclusive out here. I don't know if you ready for this."

Bones and Trevor checked out the design and tried to read the front. "What that say, Honeywell Urban Outfitters? Who make that?"

"It's a hot, black owned company. Just get some of they stuff when you get a chance."

Gwinn knew it would take her Mother at least an hour to get in from Yoga. She went upstairs and threw a pair of raytheon pants her Mother brought her from the Gap and a white J Crew top in her book-bag. Then she pulled out a metallic silver shirt that read Fendi across the front and pair of crisp V2 jeans that her Brother brought her. She grabbed her white Polo Sport flip-flops and went to the bathroom to change. Before she left out she slapped a note on the kitchen counter.

GOING TO CHURCH WITH HOLLIS TOMORROW

WILL BE BACK STRAIGHT AFTER SERVICE

8:19 PM; THE SAME NIGHT

Shelby walked up to Sandy and cut in on her conversation with China, "Let me get a cigarette."

Sandy snapped at her customer who obviously forgot what she was about, "Who you talking to bitch? Let me get some money."

Gwinn was on 106th street with some older Sisters from Clinton Projects; Sasha, Sandy and China were 3rd round Sisters who liked to, as the

433

Sisters in the set would say *turn it up.* If the hood wasn't popping, one of them, usually China took that personally and got on a mission to perk things up. Gwinn planned on getting on the 6 train at 8 o'clock, but Sisters came through with drinks and stories and subsequently Gwinn set her new departure time for 8:30.

Shelby pulled out some loose change and began to count it out.

"I hate when Motherfuckers do that." China said. "Gone come up to you knowing they gone get somethin' but don't got the fucking money ready." She shrugged her shoulders at Gwinn who reciprocated. "Matter fact, here take this and go on 'bout your business." China gave Shelby a cigarette from a pack that she pulled out her back pocket and brushed her off.

"Yo Sasha let me hold your crack-berry." Gwinn said as she thought about Justin and all the news developing on 112th street. "I got a get on my AIM flow real quick."

"This one of them 8th floor cigarettes or one of them 19th floor cigarettes?"

"Go 'head Shelby." China waived her off again. "Fuck you think?"

Shelby lit up and took a drag as Gwinn began texting frantically into Sasha's phone. China grabbed Sandy by her shirt and began pointing at the customer she just served and began laughing, "Look, look."

"Ah man, what the fuck did yall give me?"

Sandy began laughing before she was fully aware of what she was laughing at, "What happen?"

"I gave her a Dipper." China said.

Shelby began walking questionably slow and was visibly disturbed and beside herself. China and Sandy cried out with laughter.

"Oh no what yall done gave me!"

9:20 PM; THE SAME NIGHT

Gwinn pressed her ear against the front door and heard music coming from inside. Although she was happy Hollis was home, her Moment was short lived as the possibility of her Mother and Sister speaking about her whereabouts for the entire day, and Hollis discovering that she'd been used in a lie could've landed her in more trouble. She took a few Moments to get a story together in her head then opened the door.

"And I'm saving all my love. Yes I'm saving all my lovin! Yes I'm saving all my love…"

She wished terribly that he was only joking. No one could seriously sound that bad. He held each of his arms out and balled strong fist as he prepared to blow out the final note of the Whitney Houston classic, *"For yooooooooou!"*

Gwinn couldn't help it, she tried and she tried, but she busted out laughing as she walked past her Father who was sitting in front of Hollis' computer singing. He turned with what seemed to be a mirror image of his youngest child's face and smiled. Gwinn didn't intent on smiling back and breaking any ice, but her grin was still settling from Moments ago. Jason suddenly snatched the headphones off his head and turned and asked Gwinn, "Yo what you need extra money for?"

"Huh?" She asked as she flopped on Hollis' bed and began emptying her pockets.

"Money…" Jason said as he took a giant bite from a sandwich he had wrapped in a napkin, "Why do you need it?" He muffled.

Gwinn turned her sass and defensiveness back on, "You need money to live; food, clothes, everything…Why you asking me that?"

"Your Mother called here earlier looking for you."

Gwinn became visibly unnerved. She looked at her Father demanding more information without saying it.

"I told her you went to Church with Hollis."

"Church Daddy?" She instinctively pounded her hand into the mattress, "You couldn't think of nothing better than that?

"Your Moms wanna see your little ass locked to your bedpost. Church is the only thing she trying to hear right now. Don't worry, Ms. Lilly from the 16th floor be having Saturday night programs at Madison Avenue Baptist, it's half way believable."

Gwinn threw her head to the pillow behind her and squeezed both sides against her head.

"Yo what the fuck you got yourself caught up in out there?"

10:40 AM; THE NEXT DAY

"Jesus is the answer! I said Jesus is the answer!" The Pastor let the hymn of the organ behind him speak to the congregation for a Moment, then he was back at it, *"Jesus! Jesus!"*

"Boy, they love them some Jesus in here don't they?" Jason said in a not so low voice as he looked on. "And what the hell is your pastor doing with a silk shirt on?"

Hollis tried to ignore him by turning her attention to Gwinn, "You okay sweetie?"

"Yes." She answered without the slightest thought, as if overcompensating for not being tuned in.

"What's going on here? I thought we were here to praise GOD." Jason smiled and facetiously shook his head. Gwinn laughed then covered her mouth as if she made some sort of mistake as Hollis looked at her.

"Yall done paid admission three times for a Jesus concert." Jason cracked himself up with laughter and continued, "And they sending that collection plate around again. Oh believe you, me, they sendin' that plate around again."

Gwinn laughed with him once more.

"Listen, I don't wanna hear anything else out of you till the service is over okay?" Hollis said then turned and addressed Gwinn exclusively as a bigger Sister, "And you cut it out. You probably gone need a prayer or two when Bernadette get a hold of you later."

438

"Cool." Jason said then remained silent for a brief Moment before turning back to Hollis, "Yo let me ask you one more question."

Hollis grabbed her Sister by the arm and escorted her to a new plot of seats. One pass of the collection plate and nineteen boring minutes later, the church was standing and singing again. Gwinn was reluctant to get up this time. She was bored and had been ready to go home a half an hour ago. She noticed that her Father didn't bother to get up this time, which helped in her decision to sit down midway through the hysteria.

4:01 PM; THE SAME DAY

Gwinn was fully stretched out on Justin's bed trying badly to hold on to herself. Justin was grazing the side of her rapidly maturing figure and tenderly kissing the side of her neck. He forced the tips of his fingers beneath the opening of her shirt and abruptly squeezed on of her nipples.

"Ouch."

"Oh my fault." He tried to bury his head back to obscurity but Gwinn pushed him off.

"What happen?"

"That shit hurt."

"My fault let's try again Boo."

"No, I got a get home." Gwinn said as she stood to her feet and collected herself, "I just came from Church too. Uh uh."

4:49 PM; THE SAME DAY

She exhaled deeply then stuck her key in the front door of her apartment. In many ways she wished to see her Mother as soon as she got in. Too much time had gone by and she was ready to know what her fate was. Bernadette had brown plastic storage bins all over the house in preparation for their upcoming move. The wall unit in the living room was gone, the stereo, and just about everything that was previously in the hallway. Gwinn crept into her room and closed the door. It wasn't too long afterward before her Mother came pushing in.

"I was going to pack your stuff up but I'm scared I'm a find a gun in here or something."

Gwinn knew Bernadette already looked through her stuff thoroughly anyway and therefore she kept her mouth shut.

"Find you some of those plastic bins and get all your winter clothes and things you don't need right now together…" She pointed to the huge banner of 50 Cent, "These posters and whatever else."

"Alright."

"You're going to stay with your Aunt Nailah until the school year begins." She said then shut the door. Gwinn breathed in relief that her Moms didn't seem too concerned with what had happened over the past two days. She was especially relieved that she hadn't found out about all the extra hanging out she'd done this weekend. Bernadette busted the door back open; "Give me your cell phone." Gwinn hung her head, scared to look her Mother in the eye as she slapped her phone in her hand. "Girl don't make me smack you out upside your head." Bernadette said raising her free hand. "And no TV, no computer, no outside, until…" She said as she slammed the door. *And take that trash out to the incinerator!*"

AUGUST, 11TH 2008; SUMMER JAM NIGHT

Gwinn spent the past ten minutes looking for scotch tape to no avail. She finally opened one of the kitchen drawers and pulled out a black marker and the duct tape instead. She ripped off a small piece of tape and saturated the back with black ink. Gwinn knew she was pushing it, but

441

she didn't care much for playing it safe nowadays. She had an entire two weeks left on her punishment, which put her under until the beginning of the school year. So she figured what the hell. She gave it at least an hour before Auntie Nailiah would be back, but in case she was wrong, she had a back up plan. She pasted her plot of tape over the power light on the computer in the den and typed in www.onthebooksent.com in the address bar on the internet explorer.

Welcome to the live broadcast of this year's Summer Jam, live from the Meadowlands Arena in New Jersey. And yo, yall know it's time for the main event right? Yall know it's time right? Let me hear yall make some noise.

When Gwinn heard the roar of the crowd at the Meadowlands her soul became jittery. She would've given a pair of her designer frames to be in attendance tonight.

First coming to the stage, out of Harlem New York, Mix tape legend and...

The video feed began to freeze as Aunt Nailiah's computer was nearing Gwinn in age. Over the Momentary silence Gwinn could hear the latch on the front door turn. She cut the power, grabbed the first book she could reach and flopped down on the loveseat.

"Gwinn!"

"Yes?"

"I know you not in there on that computer."

Gwinn slammed the book into the cushioning and got up as if she decided enough is enough. Nailiah met Gwinn half way in the main corridor of the apartment. "What you was back there doing?"

"Eww, why it gotta be like Rikers Island in here?"

"Excuse me young lady?"

"Auntie Nailah I want to leave!" Gwinn hollered, then she pouted her hardened, beautiful face in a failed attempt to stare her Aunt down.

"That's your problem now; you think it's all about what you want. Get in the room."

Gwinn headed straight for the front door of the apartment, opened it and slammed it behind her as hard as might allowed.

Gwinn caught the 101 bus across the street and rode it all the way through Harlem, down

Broadway, up 125th, then down Lexington Avenue where she finally got off at 114th street. She took her lay-low route to her old neighborhood and she crept into building 1695.

Gwinn chose the 11th floor terrace tonight. One of the first things she noticed was a Narc van on the corned of 112th and 5th Ave. Gwinn figured they were probably snapping pictures of the Bloods getting money in front of King Projects. Trevor, Kenneth, Bo and Mack were all standing on 113th in front of what used to be Margo's Sporting Goods, all in N.Y.C.M.C t-shirts. Horse, Bryan, and Orian all pulled up in and hopped out of a black car, likewise for Margo, Stump, Laronda and Jason and Margo's Jeep. Everyone was smiling and joking, talking loud. Jason had a bottle of champagne in the hand of the arm that he had wrapped around Laronda's neck. Laronda was apparently telling a joke of some sort to Stump as they were chatting and laughing away. Orian reached in the trunk of his car and wrestled out a box, Horse grabbed the opposite side and they waited for Margo who walked up to the entrance of his old store and unlocked the door.

Gwinn pulled out her cell phone and dialed her Brother's number. She watched the entourage across the street file into M.S.G. one by one as Junior's phone went straight to voicemail. She made her way downstairs. Convoys of first and second round J.E.S.I.C.A Sisters were arriving on the block as Gwinn stepped on to Madison Avenue, everyone heading into M.S.G.

"Yo, why's everybody going into Margo's old spot for? I thought that place was shut down." Gwinn asked a Sister who was standing in front of 1695.

"I don't know. Tekk ripped J3 at Summer Jam, maybe they going in there to celebrate." Tamara said without taking her eyes off the streets. She finally looked at Gwinn, "If you working tonight our orders are to be on the lookout for Police in unmarked cars. And they paying us tonight."

Gwinn had her sights locked onto M.S.G. and wondered what the hell was going on. "Who gave those orders?"

"Laronda."

-"Here."

Asha, the set General from Johnson Project's tapped Gwinn on the arm and handed her $200 for what Gwinn took to be for last week's pay. "You been briefed on everything?"

"Yeah I guess so."

"Oh yeah," Tamara called back to Gwinn, "And we ain't got no more Dippers... We supposedly out of that business."

Asha posted Gwinn on the 17th floor of her old building, 1694. She'd been up there by her lonesome, alert and watching the streets before the elevator door behind her swung open. Stump stepped out as calm and cool as could be, both his hands were shoved in his pockets and he was whistling a light tune as he stepped selectively through the hallway. Laronda followed in his wake and finally the Architekk.

"What's up lil E?" Stump greeted her as he entered the terrace and looked out through the fence.

"Hey, what's up?"

She became uneasy, she wasn't able to figure them out by looking at them and that make her uncomfortable. Jason didn't bother speaking, he joined Stump in looking down onto 112th street, they both focused on their mutual thoughts.

"So G, you know what's up right? I mainly need you-to-..." Laronda began eye balling a green Benz that pulled up in the parking lot, completely dismissing Gwinn, "...*Well look at this shit here.*"

Gwinn noticed her Father and Stump sharply focused on the same vehicle.

"What think they gone park right in our hood and we ain't gone see them?"

"You sure you wanna put that order in Bro?" Stump asked Jason all the while looking at the Benz. Jason forfeited a response, he finally decided to look at his Daughter and he smiled at her.

"Who is that Daddy, what you doing?"

-"That's the Hip-Hop Task Force...They wanna make sure your Father ain't gone walk out of these Projects with fifty thousand dollars worth of weed." Stump said as he laughed and turned away pulling out his Nextel to chirp someone. *"Aight it's a go; tomorrow night."*

SEPTEMBER 11TH 2008

Gwinn saw Honey through her window, as she pulled up in Bernadette's newly paved driveway in a yellow cab.

"Gwinn!" Bernadette yelled from the living room. *"Come downstairs!"*

Gwinn hugged her Sister who was sporting a new short hairstyle. The girls took seats next to one another on the opposite side of the room from Bernadette.

"So…you guys really think you can do this?"

"Yes."

-"Yeah Ma."

The Sisters both answered promptly. Bernadette turned exclusively to Hollis, "Honey?"

"Yeah Ms. Sessoms. Gwinn is very respectful of me and my things. I'll make sure she sticks to whatever curfew you feel is appropriate and make sure she goes to school everyday. I think it's going to be all good."

"That's what worries me." Bernadette said as she sat back in her chair.

- "Ma?"

"Alright, alright."

Gwinn sat by her lonesome at her lunch table. The school year began a few days ago, but she hadn't eaten in the lunchroom until today. She popped a French fry in her mouth and looked around to check out the scene. Just as she was beginning to regret choosing to go to High

School all the way in Brooklyn, a group of girls walked past her.

"Them shoes is tough, shorty. Where you get them from?"

"Scheme on 25th." Gwinn said as she popped another fry in her mouth.

"Oh aight." The apparent leader of the crew put forth a friendly hand, "Ebony."

"G."

"Aight." Ebony nodded in respect and the girls kept walking through the lunchroom.

Gwinn looked down at her blue Prada shoes and smiled.

420

"Tell them to bring it, we ready for war!"

Date: October 25TH 2008

Jayson Jordan Junior laid across his bed with his legs fully stretched and the remote control pointed at his 57-inch plasma screen. Both the kids were in the next room napping.

"…Well…I could always go back to work if need be." Lakrisha said before Junior got up and left the room. He went to his studio in the basement where Red Out was smoking and playing video games with D.

Junior played an instrumental and nodded his head in imagination and all intentions on ripping the beat. He stepped into the vocal booth and put Red Out to work on the controls of the track-board. The opening bars passed by but nothing creative was flowing his way. Red Out held his hand up and began counting down with his fingers for J3 to jump in on queue. 3,2,1, nothing…

OCTOBER 25TH 2008

"Well you know what Rodney? I think it's time for you to do your thing then."

Bernadette slammed the master bedroom door and stormed into the private bathroom and took a look around her. The large sunk in bathtub with jet streams, her vanity mirror and the huge yard out back. She took a seat on the basin and wondered what she was going to do now.

OCTOBER 25TH 2008

Jason sat in silence on his prayer mat with his legs folded and his dreadlocks resting on his shoulders. He was staring out, across his self constructed deck in mellow contemplation when Laronda's image appeared in the glass in front of him. He turned around; she smiled at him holding a large object covered in a sheet of black plastic. He stood to his feet as Laronda pulled off the plastic revealing a gold plaque for his album *The Dread*. "We did it!"

OCTOBER 25TH 2008

Gwinn strutted past the group of seniors who she noticed had been paying her a particular degree of attention and talking about her behind her back. She continued listening to 50 and texting on her iphone as she walked right past the losers, to her 8th period class. *"GOD gave me style. GOD gave me grace..."*

OCTOBER 25TH 2008

"Hi Jake, I want to introduce you to the new rep we have coming to the floor today. Her name is Hollis but she says all her friends call her Honey. And by looking at her I don't think we need a Board meeting to see why."

"Excuse you."

"Whoa darling I was just kidding."

And it came to pass that Gwinn and her Sister began to share Hollis' small living quarters in harmony. It came to pass that with time invested, Gwinn began to confide in her Father and she allowed him to do the same. It came to pass that with the change in the weather there were changes in the lives of the people. Gwinn found a place and purpose, with the challenges that came along with her first year of High School. It came to pass that she gained greater knowledge of the world and the people around

452

her with the help of her required readings such as *Brave New World, Things Fall Apart,* and *The Da Vinci Code*; she was reading Flyy Girl on the side. It came to pass that Gwinn changed the station on the music she was listening to, becoming more appreciative of different styles of sound, less hardcore. And would you believe, the soon to be fourteen year old lady even had one of Architekk's entire albums downloaded on her mp3 player?

OCTOBER 30TH 2008

Mr. Bower stood from his chaotic desk and pulled his trousers up along his protruding waist. "So you guys obviously know that the Presidential election is next week right?"

"Go Barak!"

"Oh, ok thanks for that Tyrell. Okay, so-"

-*"Hell yeah Barack gone win yo!"*

-*"Barack ain't winnin'. They are not gone let a Black man run the whole dang on country, yall bugging."*

"Well we'll see, we'll see. But listen guys-"

-*"I bet you if he do get on, he gone be getting head in the Oval Office like my G, Bill Clinton."*

"Guys!"

The class finally quieted down enough to not give Mr. Bower a stroke. "Thank you… Okay, what I decided I'm going to do is, since you guys didn't care for the Great Gatsby too much, I'm going to let you hand in a paper on what the significance of having an African American as the President of the United States would be."

- *"How many pages?"*

"Give me four typed pages, double spaced."

The bell signifying the end of the 5th period rang from the loud speaker.

"And no that doesn't mean hit the space bar twice after every sentence you type Jomar! Have a good weekend guys."

After school Gwinn took the 2 train uptown and stopped by her old Projects to see what was good. It was slow, no Sisters were out and the Police had all the hustlers scattered about. She decided to go to Kim's apartment in Johnson Projects when she saw a mob of Sisters walking up Park Avenue. They were on the prowl, blued up and at least twenty deep, looking for trouble. Amanda, the set General was among the girls in front, China and Iesha were rolling as well. Gwinn knew whatever they were about to get into they were going to get deep into, and she knew whether she liked it or not she was going to be tagging along. Two girls who were walking between Gwinn and the Sisters crossed the street in obvious search of solace.

"Yo G tap one of them bitches pockets?"

Gwinn initially pretended to not understand, then feigned stupid as the girls walked out of her reach. Iesha jogged across the street and a few Sisters followed. Gwinn could see Iesha grab the charm on the gold chain of the taller girl. She pushed Iesha's hand away and Iesha punched her in the face. The shorter girl grabbed Iesha's hair and dragged her to the concrete. Several Sisters bombarded her with punches, yet several Moments went by before Iesha was out of her grip. Box Cutter Keisha grabbed an empty bottle out of the trash can on the corner and busted it across the shorter girls' head yet she still continued fighting off the mob.

Gwinn knew she was in enough trouble with the older Sisters as is; that pretending to be deaf shit wasn't going to rock with Iesha. First and second rounders liked to give blows after rumbles anyway. Gwinn knew the harder she went in right now, the easier they would be on her in the blows cut later. She threw her jacket to the ground and grabbed the tall girl around her waist and wrestled her to the ground, where she held her with her arms locked. *"Listen to me, just stay the fuck still."* Gwinn whispered into her victim's ear as she kept her pressed indefensibly against her body.

It took four Sisters but they eventually beat the shorter girl down, bleeding and swelling in the face. From her seat on the ground Gwinn could see Iesha tussle her jaw to remove the razor blade from her mouth. Iesha clutched the gem star with a wave of her hand and swiftly carved the side of the unfortunate girl's face spilling her blood.

"And you bitch."

Iesha addressed the girl Gwinn was holding on the ground. "I'm a carve my name in your fuckin' face. Come here."

7:12PM; THE SAME NIGHT

"I told you this bitch ain't no beast, she ain't J.E.S.I.C.A. This bitch is Sarah or some shit; Sarah Lee. Go bake us some pies or some shit."

The first round J.E.S.I.C.A Sisters took a pause from smoking and drinking to laugh at Gwinn who was sitting off to the side. Gwinn's dismay became evident in her face, which was growing sharply with anger.

"She gone act like she ain't hear us. She a fake bitch."

"Well then pop off then!" Gwinn said with the gull of an Eagle. They were going to beat her down when they finished smoking anyway. She figured she might as well have an excuse to dish some blows back. Iesha always seemed to have had some special interest in making Gwinn's life difficult. She was a second rounder and as thorough a Sister as the set had, Iesha couldn't have thrown her hands up quicker after Gwinn's challenge.

Gwinn hardened her fist and strengthened her legs. She knew she was in for quite the dance. She tossed her hands around with energy as Iesha moved in. Gwinn figured she'd fight a smart fight, as she knew Iesha wouldn't respect her strength and try to rush her. Through her reasoning, Gwinn was caught with a right cross to the side of her face, setting off the fight.

"Yeah, what up?" Iesha asked with confidence all over her devious smile.

Gwinn stumbled back but caught her footing soon enough to dissuade the rush. Iesha tried to throw Gwinn off with a fake of a punch and a release from the opposite side. It was a risk, but Gwinn gambled on Iesha making such a move, she shifted too heavy and there was no cruel intent in her face when she made the move. Gwinn weaved out of the way as Iesha threw a hard jab harming nothing but the air. She planted firmly and swung a vicious elbow to Iesha's nose. One could feel the air deflate out of the Sisters gathered around as Iesha flimsily dropped to her defeat.

The fire that fueled Gwinn was ousted as she took a look at one of the realist girls from the set on the 1st Avenue concrete, done for. She knew this was a long way from over, but by the way Iesha was stretched out, Gwinn knew she had tucked her in at least for tonight.

"I'm leaving yo, I don't need this shit."

On the train ride to the Bronx Gwinn made a decision not to go anywhere this weekend. It was beginning to drizzle and old man winter was beginning to show his face across the tri-state area. She thought her fight and her general disposition would be written all over her face when she walked in, but her Sister was too occupied to notice.

"You seen my big door knocker earrings?"

Hollis barely acknowledged Gwinn when she walked in to their tight apartment, she was wondering about frustrated.

"No, I haven't seen them." Gwinn said as she sat down and tried to stay out of Hollis' way.

"Damn I'm supposed to be going out with Reggie tonight and I can't find the earrings I want to wear." She continued to toss things around in manifest aggravation; "I guess they just grew legs and walked away."

Gwinn's chest sunk in. She willed herself not to respond for a Moment as she wanted badly to avoid being confrontational, but her nerve pushed her, "What you trying to say, I'm stealing from you or something?"

"I don't know Gwinn, a few things have been missing around the house, I don't know." Hollis grabbed her keys and started for the front door, "And I see you been watching those videos of your little gang on the internet. I don't think your Mother'll like that."

Gwinn sat in the same spot for nearly a half an hour and tried to figure out what Hollis coming at her sideways was about. When the tension of her day finally peaked, Gwinn went in the bathroom and closed the door.

"GOD what I do to have you messing with me like this?"

Warm tears ran down her teenaged face
unrelenting. She tried to pick herself up
Moments ago but she wasn't done letting it out.
The thud of the slam of the front door made its
way to the bathroom. She wiped her face and
ran the water from the sink to drown the sound
of her getting herself together.

*"...Get there early; that way yall ain't gotta be
rushing & all that..."*

Gwinn pressed her ear to the door and was
somewhat relieved when she heard her Father
and not Hollis.

*"...Aight Bro, I'm a holla at you later though.
I'm beat, man."*

Gwinn ran two hands full of cold water on her
face and checked herself in the mirror before
walking out.

"What happen baby?" Jason noticed something
not right with her immediately. It was as if his
words had hit a nerve, Gwinn's tears began to
flow again.

"What happen?"

"Nothing." She said as she covered her face.

Jason sat back and gave his daughter some time, keeping his head down and his mouth shut for several minutes until, "You know how I started rapping?"

She looked up from her seat on the edge of the bed to her Father who was hunched over in the desk chair.

"I was writing you a suicide note."

Gwinn squinted her face in confusion. Jason sat back in the leather bound chair and spun it away from Gwinn as he commenced a long overdue talk.

"It was important to me to explain to you how I got to where I was in order to try to prevent you from ending up there; at the very least, you know? While I was writing... I don't know man, it was like GOD took control...He took me to my past and helped me understand it, he enlightened me along the way, he explained mysteries to me, and he, he took care of me."

Gwinn sat staring straight ahead in a mellow trance. She could see her Father turn to see if she was paying him any attention.

"I'm listening."

10: 56 PM; THE SAME NIGHT

461

"…You gotta know how that sounded to us when we first heard it. We couldn't talk; I couldn't speak."

Gwinn laughed and took a sip from her can of soda, "He was that good?"

"Rakim was the truth. Nobody could go with him. It was the R then everybody else."

"You think he was the greatest of all time?"

"I don't know, I always favored Pac there personally. But I think when you look at an Artist's body of work you probably gotta go with Jiggaman."

"Na… 50."

"50?" Jason asked as he gave Gwinn a paternal smile. "Well you a real chick, and real recognize real, you entitled to your opinion. I'm just glad you ain't say Vanilla Ice or something'."

"Who?"

"Don't worry about it."

11:48 PM; THE SAME NIGHT

462

"...That almost drove me to murder...yeah, I wanted to kill her ass...I fucks with Bernadette though. But ain't no getting around that; I mean if you was gone kill a Motherfucker you was gone kill a Motherfucker...I cut your umbilical cord though; ain't no getting around that shit either. You think all these so called deadbeat Dads out here running around don't care about they kids? I don't think so." Jason blew a cloud of smoke out of the kitchen window and ashed his blunt on the window seal before carrying on, "And trust me, I've put some time into thinking about it. These niggas either got some beef with they baby mama that they not man enough to over look, or they on some all or nothing shit with they kids cause they see in between as weak, and they not strong enough to be weak until they get strong."

Gwinn thought about it, then she decided to figure that out later; "So what are you?"

"Shit...All praise to Allah, now I am strong." Jason smiled and tried to hide his teeth with his big lips. "I'm 34 years young, I got my own record company; I just got my own home. Allah set me up so I have free time when I want and need it. I aint nobody's slave... I got knowledge of self... How you want it?"

463

He took an arrogant pull from his Dutch all the while looking Gwinn straight in the eye. "What you wanna do?"

1:59 AM; THE SAME NIGHT

"You apart of a Brotherhood of Human Beings that gets better with time. GOD created you and bestowed upon you from his grace, his liking and in his image. You ain't evolve from no fucking Ape. If that was the case you'd see Apes transitioning into people everyday; the caterpillars didn't stop turning into butterflies." He removed the Immortal Technique disk from the stereo and loaded Styles P's Gangster and a Gentlemen album from Hollis' GOD Library; Jay-Z's Kingdom Come was apparently on deck. "You don't have to go out and kill your food because the Brothers and Sisters before you built upon on a body of knowledge, and eventually set up a system of agriculture that would allow Motherfuckers to get fat without doing no work…And you could do shit like buy sunglasses." He smiled at Gwinn then continued, "One should ask themselves however, where would we be as a human race if everyone did exactly as you do, contribute like you contribute, or not."

Gwinn shook her head as she contemplated. Jason got up and walked over to the window.

The sky seemed to be a shade of white; it began to snow.

"So you trying to live among the righteous?"

Hollis' key rattled from the front door warranting the attention of Gwinn and her Father. She strutted in chatting on her cell phone in skintight denim jeans, gaudy jewelry and effaced make-up. She lowered her phone when she saw her Father and Sister sitting in peace. She looked around mildly perplexed, "What's up?"

NOVEMBER 1ST 2008

Gwinn could see her set Sister coming up the walkway apparently rapping to herself and staring down random objects with sharp beady eyes. When she noticed Gwinn standing in the lobby she scampered over. When Candice got close enough Gwinn put her hand out for the customary set dap but was pulled into a hug instead. She screwed her face and tried to hold her breath; "Damn Candice when the last time you took a shower?"

"I smell bad?" Candice grabbed her dingy bubble coat and sniffed it, "Hmm."

"Yo what's up with you?" Gwinn asked aggressively as she pushed her back.

"Nothing; chilling. You don't got a couple of dollars I can borrow do you?"

Gwinn just got hit off from Amanda, who was paying her personally now that Gwinn and Iesha was at war. She pulled out two twenties and gave them to Candice.

"Thank you." She pulled Gwinn in again and embraced her before walking off into the Projects.

-"I wouldn't have done that if I was you."

Box Cutter Keisha said from her seat on an egg crate on the other side of the lobby. "That girl gone take that money and smoke herself good and dead, watch."

"What you talking about?"

"Crack-heads don't know how to budget, that's what I'm talking about. They smoke crack. Crack, crack, crack, that's all they looking for."

"Candice is not getting'high."

Keisha chucked and looked away. Gwinn excused herself and stepped out in front of the building. She watched her friend of nine years as she spoke with Kenneth up the block before walking in the back of building 1690 with him.

Trunk thumping music was coming from one of
the flashy luxury cars that pulled into the
parking lot. All of the windows on both cars
were tinted but Gwinn figured whoever they
were, they would be alright with her as they
were blasting music from her Brother's
upcoming album. Through the corner of her eye
Gwinn saw a mob of heads cut around the corner
of 111th street. She turned to make sure her
Sisters were still behind her in the lobby.

"Who them niggas?" Box Cutter Keisha
demanded as she pushed open the front door.

The passenger side door opened on one of the
BMW's and Junior stepped out.

"Hey Big Bro!"

The mob of fifteen or so foreigners rounded the
black railing outlining the Taft houses and
marched down the walkway obviously on some
sort of mission. Junior's people began to
emerge from the confines of their automobiles in
the parking lot. Oneisha, Rosy, Tyese, and
Nelcia filed out of 1694.

"Who did it?"

On the front line of the mob was a stocky light
skinned boy of eighteen years or so in age. He
pulled forth a girl who had a face full of fresh

stitches, who didn't seem to care for being there. She looked through the girls in blue and turned back to the enraged boy. "I don't know Jo-Jo! All of them are J.E.S.I.C.A, any one of them could have did it."

He pushed her aside, "Yo one of yall bitches better tell me who did this to my Sister face or I'm fucking all yall up right now. Fuck that."

The girls remained silent. Each one of them was there when it went down. Gwinn remembered vividly pinning the girl to the ground like it was yesterday. She tried not to look her in the eyes.

"Yo homie what's the problem?" Junior asked as he shut his car door and made his way over.

"What the fuck you mean what's the problem! Nigga you see this big ass scar on my Sister face?"

He grew more excited by the Moment. Unable to control his nerves, he began taking steps in any direction, pounding his hands as he spoke his next words. "Somebody gotta pay for that shit. It's that simple."

Junior's entourage, Shock, Big Verdict and Red Out approached to the J.E.S.I.C.A Sisters' relief.

"So what, you was gone come over here and beat up on a bunch of girls?" Red Out asked in his rough deep voice.

"With GOD as my witness, *somebody gone pay for this shit*! These bitches jumped my Sister and her friend for no fucking reason! My Sister don't bother nobody!"

His voice began to give way to emotion, he put his hands up to his face then in a swift shift of intent, with fire in his eyes, he quickly reached into his flight jacket.

- *"Whoa, whoa chill out Motherfucker!"*

- *"Don't move nigga!"*

Red Out and Big Verdict both drew handguns and froze the revenge stricken Brother in his place. Both parties of onlookers stepped back. Red Out approached with his pistol at the face of his target. He reached in his jacket and removed the pocketknife stashed therein.

"Oh this nigga came to cut some shit didn't he?"

THANKSGIVING DAY 2008

"Can you say Auntie, huh? I know you can. Say Auntie Gwinn."

469

Terrell began to glow with a smile that never failed in brightening Gwinn's day. Gwinn caught a strong whiff of the macaroni and cheese from downstairs and was reminded of how hungry she was. She stood to her feet and noticed the headlights of a car pulling into the driveway through the nursery room window. She lifted Terrell from the bed and carried him down the stairs.

Hollis and Denise were sitting in the living room watching the football game with George, Red Out, Frederick, Pastor Daniels, Uncle Terry and his wife Susan, and Grandpa Sessoms.

"Aw let me see my little man."

Hollis stood and fixed her long suede skirt before taking Terrell from Gwinn. "I ain't no you was up lil man."

Gwinn handed Hollis his pacifier then walked out the front door. .

"Guess whose coming to dinner, knotty Dread Lock."

Jason slammed his car door and Laronda did the same. Jason continued singing aloud as he walked through the small garden on the side of the house. His head was wrapped in a black turban with extensions of his hair sneaking

470

through and he was wearing a camouflage jacket. *"Guess whose coming to dinner..."*

"Hi Daddy."

Laronda fell back to allow Jason to go in front of her. He walked straight up to Gwinn and kissed her on her forehead, "Let's go eat!"

Bernadette didn't seem much interested in speaking to Denise and her Husband. Denise's husband George didn't seem much interested in speaking with Denise, Gwinn couldn't figure out if it was because the football game was that interesting or if there was trouble in Paradise. Junior and Jason didn't seem to have too many words for one another, but then again Jason barely said anything to anyone other than Hollis and Gwinn. That was before Laronda went to the bathroom leaving Aunt Nailah and Jason alone in the dinning room.

"You still rapping Jason?" Nailah asked as she placed a bowl of collared greens at one end of the luxuriously extensive table.

"Yeah I'm still rapping."

"But you still don't have a record deal huh?"

Jason stopped texting on his phone for a Moment and finally looked at Nailah, "I don't

471

need one; not getting fifty thousand dollars winning battles & selling on the streets."

- *"That little 50 thou wasn't nothin' my man."*

Junior yelled from the kitchen as he overheard their conversation a few feet away.

"Well put another fifty up. I sure would appreciate it." Jason said looking at Gwinn but addressing and laughing at his son.

- *"Alright everyone yall come eat. The food is ready!"*

Ms. Johnson, Lakrisha's Mother called for the fellas in the living room watching the game. Ms. Johnson took a final sip from her Heineken before grabbing Lakrisha and Aunt Nailah's hands, "Pastor you gonna say grace?"

"How bout I say grace, huh? Alright, thanks."

-"Why don't I get this one Jason?"

Gwinn could see the muscles in her Father's forearms work and he gripped Pastor Daniels hand, "No not today. These are my children here."

Gwinn joined hands with her Mother and Brother; she didn't bother closing her eyes as she'd been getting paid for over a year for keeping her eyes open. She witnessed Ms. Johnson, Laronda, Red Out and the children quick to bow their heads. Hollis and the Pastor exchanged a strange look before lowering their heads.

"Father, thank you for gathering us here today. Thank you for your infinite blessings and mercy. Thank you Father for creating us in your beautiful image, thank you for keeping true to your promises and thank you for guiding us on the way that is straight. And before we indulge Father, we want to kindly ask that you allow your kingdom to come Father; on earth as it is in heaven. Bestow health, wealth, independence and peace upon your devoted servants. Father go 'head and send down calamity, and your wrath and punishment among the constant rejecters of faith. Separate those of us who have worked deeds in your name, those of us who have given to the poor, who practiced equality with our Brothers and Sisters, those of us who spoke fair to the people and uplifted. We ask you to judge between us Father; that we may have clear proof of right from wrong."

Gwinn looked up and saw her Father getting deeper in his prayer.

"We ask for a speedy punishment for those of us have not strived and persevered in your ways.

We forfeit our respite from the fire of hell and we ask you to take us right here and now Father."

"Alright Jason."

"A yo I'm praying. What the hell is wrong with you?" Jason checked the Pastor.

"Can we eat please?" Denise said as she released her grip on Grandpa Sessoms and Hollis.

Aunt Nailah took her seat and half of the people in attendance followed. Lakrisha ordered most of the dinner from an upscale catering service, therefore Gwinn was especially happy when she looked on the smaller kitchen table and saw that Grandpa had made his signature sweet potato pie with toasted marshmallows. Lakrisha began serving her guest. She started with Laronda, reaching a large spoon of Ham hocks over her plate.

"Mm mm; I don't eat that."

"Excuse me young lady." Aunt Nailah said.

"Oh, I'm sorry I don't eat pork." Laronda said apologetically.

"Hm. You know I never understood that. They been raised on pork they whole life, they Brothers and Sisters been raised on pork, then all of a sudden pork is so bad for you. Where's the proof?"

"Proof?" Jason demanded with a heightened level of seriousness in his eyes. "What she need to present proof to you for, you the one on the offensive. Just like in a court of law, the burden of proof is on the Plaintiff."

Aunt Nailah laughed and looked away.

"This woman sitting up here in peace, trying to hold on to her values and disciplines. You the one fucking with us."

"Us? No I was asking *her* a question-"

"Well that's my wife."

Each individual present seemed to have their breath escape them. Junior looked at Laronda who was wearing a D&G hoody and blue jeans, more casually dressed than any other women in attendance.

"I don't know, this just seems like an epidemic, all these young black thugs are supposedly Muslims now. I see it a lot in my neighborhood." Aunt Nailiah said as she loaded Denise's plate with the ham hocks.

"An epidemic?"

-"Leave it alone." Laronda insisted.

Jason smiled as he locked eyes with Aunt Naliah, "An epidemic?"

"Yeah that's what I said."

"What's an epidemic is your damn life. What did you gain like fifty pounds in the last four years? You sit up there in that big for nothing ass apartment with that ugly ass cat; no man, no friends outside the family. You completely suck." Jason said with a mixed look of disgust and arrogance across his face. "Talkin' 'bout my Brothers and Sisters out there struggling in the name of Allah is an epidemic. We have guidance in life; guidance that yo' ass obviously need."

-"Tekk chill."

Jason turned and looked at Red Out who was giving him a look as if he understood, and an easy hand as if to say this wasn't the time.

-"You are a very disrespectful person, you know that Jason?"

"Fuck you. We came here in peace. You started fuckin' with us. And the question is why. Why did you feel the need to start fucking with us? Cause you fuckin'-"

-"Yo you gone have to stop cursing at my Aunt; you stepping way out of bounds now." Junior decided it was time for him to assume his man of the house position.

"What the fuck ever." Jason expressed as disrespectfully as possible while helping himself to a serving of yams.

Junior stood up as Jason sat down, "Take a look around you homie; you in my house! I don't wanna have to kick you out... But that'll probably be doing you a favor. Gwinn was about to get into some shit in the hood the other day. Where was you at; who the hell knows? Me and my niggas had to handle that."

"Oh you mean with JoJo? You know JoJo just beat a murder right? Nigga fresh out; and he want your head on a stick for that shit yall pulled out there. You better tell your fake ass gangster friends; the next time they pull a gun on somebody they better use the Motherfucker."

Junior rammed his fist into his expensive china; "Tell them bring it! Anybody can bring it; you,

JoJo, Danger Manger, whoever. We ready for war!"

Jason wiped the sides of his mouth gently with his napkin; "Boy sit your little ass down, you ain't ready for no war. You ready for war like I thought I was ready when they killed my man Stack. You got a record deal, not knowledge of self or wisdom. Before you got signed you was on the road with me in search of Allah's bounty. Now you got signed and some money and you supposedly some tough guy or a boss? Fuck out of here boy, there's people out there that really hit the block and got it in for theirs; all that shit you claim to do in your fancy little songs." Jason chuckled to himself, "*Pop goes my 9*; fuck outta here. You never poked nuttin' never popped nuttin' nigga stop frontin'." Jason glanced over at Gwinn to see if she noticed that he quoted her favorite Rapper.

Junior looked at Red Out seemingly for instructions, which Jason took special offense to.

"What the fuck you gone do?"

"Get out my house!"

NOVEMBER 30TH 2008

Gwinn heard the apartment door open and the fear set in her stomach that she prayed that GOD

478

would remove. She started coughing, as she had instantly created her excuse for Hollis as to why she wasn't in school. She diluted the strength in her eyes and held her stomach as apart of her act.

"Why you not in school?" Jason asked as he stepped into sight.

"I ain't wanna go today." Gwinn answered not looking to deceive her Father as she had grown in confidence that he was beginning to understand her.

Jason looked at her hard and critically but didn't say a word. He stuck the duffel bag he was toting in a space between Hollis' desk and the wall.

"Daddy, what do you do all day?"

Jason smiled and took a seat as if too exhausted to respond.

"I wanna roll with you."

"You wanna roll with me? You know I'll never hear the end of it if your Mother find out you cut school and was hangin' out with me all day." Jason visibly reconsidered the notion as if the idea didn't sound so bad. He stared off into space for a brief Moment, "…Come on."

They caught the 4 train to the 6, and took that to 96th street. They walked down Lexington Avenue; it was cold outside, but bearable. Jason kept her close, either to help keep her warm or for protection. Gwinn had her face tucked behind the fabric of her ski coat. They stopped at the Papaya's on 86th street before Jason took her to buy a few new outfits. They caught a matinee' and they ate again.

"I want to show you something." Jason said looking at his daughter seated on the stool beside him.

"What's that?"

"You finished?" He asked looking down at her chicken basket.

"Yeah, let's go."

They walked up 3rd Ave, back toward Spanish Harlem. When they got to 96th street, Jason looked up at the elaborate dome on the Mosque across the street while they waited for the light to change. They crossed the intersection and Jason grabbed her hand and stirred their path toward the front door.

"Where we going?"

448

"You know this nigga?"

Date: December 9TH 2008

No one ever could understand Gwinn's attraction to Harlem; the magnetism between her and the streets, between her and her Sisters, and the Projects. Gwinn found her solace on the concrete terraces under the cover of obscurity, watching the nature of things. She was no longer profiting from looking out for the Cops, most of the older Tru-Blues had recently abandoned the Angel Dust trade to help one of the founding members make some legal money.

Gwinn didn't make it to Taft as much as she used to when she first moved out. Her Mother was gone, as well as Junior, Candice moved to the Bronx last year, and Gwinn's life went on, the word went forth. She moved on past Justin, past her twenty city block radius of life, and past the perpetual state of hate she used to have to stay in, in order to be on point. Gwinn made the honor roll during her first marking period at Brooklyn Tech, she engaged in battles with her Father on the chessboard and she began jogging around the south Bronx with Hollis…A new day.

Friday's Gwinn stole for herself. After school she hung out with her new friends from Bed-Stuy at the Junction Station in Brooklyn, where all the cool students got together. That was before making her way to the 6 train and heading home. Hollis worked a late shift on Fridays, giving Gwinn liberty to do as she pleased until a little after 11. This particular Friday rendered Gwinn homesick and she returned to Taft to check on the hood.

She sat on the 15th floor terrace, just looking, just watching. Kenneth and Trevor were still in front of 1694 pumping whatever they were selling this week. Fiends were still wandering to and fro void of direction. The children were still trying to camouflage their poverty with fashion and words. Gwinn crossed her legs and kept watching…still Harlem.

8:42AM; THE NEXT DAY

Gwinn could smell winter in the air as she awoke. She rolled over in her bed and saw Hollis scrambling to get things together. "Good morning." She greeted Hollis in an especially good mood.

"Hey sweetie." Hollis spoke without taking her line of sight from the television. She was dressed in her gray and black pants and a black cardigan, her work clothes.

"How are you today?"

"Late."

"You gotta go on a Saturday?"

"Yep; we supposed to be getting the bulk of our calls this Saturday."

"We?" Gwinn asked as she sat up on her backside and removed her silk head wrap.

"Yes, we; my company, well the company I work for."

"Mm…that seems like a jip."

"Gwinn please." Hollis waived her younger Sister off and leaned in to kiss her on the cheek.

"You're not coming to Daddy's house today?"

"No, I'm not gone have time. But I'm sure you guys will have lots of fun together." She said before leaving out. Gwinn wasn't certain what her Sister's problem was but she didn't let it bring her down. She got up and pulled a pair of black jeans from her side of the closet along with her Yves Saint Laurant sweater.

Gwinn took a quick shower and got ready for her Father, who would be by to pick her up soon. She packed her book-bag with her World History textbook, the laptop that her Mother bought her last Christmas and her five subject notebook then went to sit by the window.

Gwinn could see a group of children throwing snowballs at each other and playing freely, a Dominican Brother in a tan worker jacket changing a tire on his car across the street, a young couple walking up the block in one another's arms. She felt forced to look away from the happy couple into the kitchen, then down at the floor. There was no place of comfort for her eyes. Her ex boyfriend Justin was on her mind and she couldn't deny it. She pulled out her cell phone and scrolled through her phonebook until she got to his number.

"Yo G!"

Gwinn scooted up in her seat and looked out of the window to see her Father looking up from the sidewalk.

"Yeah, I'm coming!"

12: 40 PM; THE SAME DAY

Gwinn did a lot of sleeping and staring out of the window on the drive up the 99 interstate. In her inner thoughts she reconsidered her dedication to New York City. Traveling along the expansive highway, she got a better feel for how spacious GOD's green earth is; large farms, open roads, she wondered if perhaps the happiness she was seeking was somewhere out there.

Laronda and Jason were engaged in a friendly political conversation in the front seats, the smooth jazz station was flowing. Gwinn figured she'd let them know that she had awoke from her second nap by jumping in the discussion. "Daddy did you vote for Obama?"

Jason turned in his seat and smiled at her. He reached back to wiped face; she pulled back instinctively.

"Come here you got something on your face." He licked his thumb and began smearing whatever she had on her face. Gwinn tried to sit still, yet the force in his hands pushed her about. When she relaxed, she felt a degree of love in his hands that she hadn't felt in years.

"I gave Barack some support."

Laronda looked at Jason and smiled, finding amusement in an obviously personal joke.

"But you didn't vote?"

Gwinn could see Laronda peep at her through the rear view mirror in mild amusement. "That girl don't play." She said as she glanced at Jason.

"Unfortunately ex-cons can't vote in this country baby. Our voices don't count after we mess up. Fortunately however…" He looked at Laronda, "I sold over half a million records that contained a track in which I encourage Brother and Sisters to go out and vote for what it's worth, and I even gave President Obama some encouraging words, if he still listens to the voices from the gutter."

"Well I voted for the both of us baby; and we won!" Laronda said as she caressed Jason's scalp through his hair, partially minding the road.

3:26 PM; THE SAME DAY

Gwinn could see her Father and Laronda smoking and conversing on the other side of the large bay windows at the east wing of the home. Although it was freezing outside, the sun was shinning in its full majesty over the snow covered hills afar through the home. Gwinn looked around the living room and continued to try to make sense out of her Father's humble yet complex abode. Stacked alongside the marble topped island in the kitchen was bag after bag of seeds, large, clear, and labeled across the front. There were Rosemary seeds, cucumber, spearmint, thyme, watermelon, strawberry, tobacco, cotton, wheat, barley, sugar cane, carrots. Sitting atop some sort of unique gardening container were uniquely packaged bags that read Northern Lights and Purple Haze across the front.

A large photo posted on a wall afar caught Gwinn's eye. She walked across the ground level and into the entrance to the basement staircase where large vivid photos lined both walls. She was staring at a life size portrait of her Dad's debut album; younger Jason Jordan leaning over the side of a balcony and turned away from the camera. Next to that was a portrait of Architekk's second album. She turned around, a black and white image of Hollis in her High School track uniform with her hands planted on her hips staring at the track bed beneath her. Adjacent to that was a portrait of Junior shaking hands with Mayor Gulliani after receiving an academic achievement award. Gwinn took a few steps, mindful of the drop in the stairs in front of her and took in the last picture on that side of the wall; a picture of her Father holding her between his arms in the hospital on the day she was born.

Several Moments had gone by, yet Gwinn couldn't take her eyes off the picture. She was so little, so pale, wrapped in a soft white and yellow blanket. She wondered what her Dad was thinking as he looked into her face so deeply. She was still lost in the rapture of her visual history when she heard the screen door shut and Jason's strong voice. She made her way over.

"Aaaa, look at my little girl."

His eyes were like red clouds of fire and joy as he reached out to Gwinn, exceptionally happy to see her. "You know how much I love you?"

"Yes." She smiled mildly embarrassed.

"You don't have a clue; not a clue." He said as he squeezed her around her shoulders. "Come here."

-"So I'm going to be back around 6 or so, okay baby?" Laronda said as she removed her keys from her leather purse.

"Yeah, yeah." Jason said as he walked off with Gwinn who could smell the fresh marijuana scent on his fleece. "I heard Sheek Louch say one time on one of his album skits, he said to one of his mans; it's easy to go out there and bust your gun and do this and that wild shit for me. He asked him; what would you give up for me though? What would you do without for me?" Jason's heavy construction boots slammed into the carpet with a melody as they began to scale the spiral staircase in the living room. "For you I went without a home…without stability, without, well you get the point." He got to the top of the stairs and huffed in exhaustion; "You don't know how useless I felt as a man when your Brother and Sister was born. Two kids in two years, two different women." He caught his breath and continued as they walked through the second floor corridor; "When you was born that was the start of my path, my trek of 1,000 miles, towards making myself the Father that I wanted to be. I had to say to hell with what your Moms think, to hell with what the people around me think…I even had to say to hell what you thought. But I kept you ever present in my heart, and I continuously asked the Lord to give me a fair shot one day. To give me my own home where my kids could come and grow to their uppermost potential." He stopped and stuck both his hands in the pockets of his baggy army pants as the first of another ensemble of huge portraits caught his attention. He was staring proudly at an image of a younger, skinnier version of him in the lobby of his old building in Grant. "Come her let me show you something." He said as he moved on.

"A Pastor in Norfolk said to me one time, he said; GOD will perfect that which concerns you." Jason pushed open the last bedroom door and stepped aside to allow his little lady to enter first.

The first thing that Gwinn noticed was the posters and pictures of her favorite Artists sprawled across the walls. There was a large bed with an elaborate white canopy between windows with white ledgers and white nightstands. A picture of Gwinn in her 3rd grade dance class hung from the far wall. She walked to the center of the room, under the ceiling fan, which was twirling lightly and held her hands to her face speechless.

"So now I do believe it is our time. I am here right now, telling you I want you in my life, everyday, every step of the way…And I love you greater than that which you understand love to be, greater than what your Mother and Brother, and the world thinks love should be. And I'll love you always."

Gwinn hurried over to him and wrapped her arms around his waist. He caressed the top of her head and leaned to look into her face, "But you gone have to figure out if you can handle the pain, and the rain that comes along with being with Dad." His face grew serious. "Cause it's gone rain when you with Dad… The rain is essential for the seed to grow. We observe all the seasons that the Lord made and we seek to achieve higher degrees of knowledge year-round. Now you might not know exactly what I mean, but at the end of what I'm saying to you is, we don't play it safe. Allah is your only protector; if he decree a course for you there's nothing that I can do except for guide you and hopefully strengthen you along that course; and only that be by his will. GOD may ordain you to be a Doctor, a Judge, a Dentist. Or our Father may have intended for you a life as a bus driver, a telemarketer or a drifter. But only he has the secrets and the keys to your happiness, filling your inner heart's desire; only through He. Don't doubt that; it's the maturation of your doubt that will crumble the entire empire; the empire which the Lord has architected for your advancement…Faith, you must have faith. I'm a telling you; I am telling you! GOD is real, he is the creator of the heavens and the earth and he is the giver of peace, or as we say in Islam; As-Salam! I'm telling you this as clear as I know how to baby, but even still I know you will doubt. The deception of the world has found a home in you. But Allah loves the man and woman who fight against their sinful soul. So fight your doubt, know that you are created weak in the flesh; just make sure you don't die in doubt. Or else I'll never get to show you how much I truly love you on the other side."

Jason stood up and left Gwinn in her room by her lonesome where she pondered extensively on her Father's words. She went through many questions in her head, but all things considered she felt good, positive; as she stared out of her window and wondered what in GOD's name her Dad was doing with a flock of horses.

"What do you guys think will be a good research paper for you to do over the winter break?"

-"Let us do a paper on this season's So You Think You Can Dance. That's my favorite show."

Another student mimicked from the rear of the class, *"That's my favorite show."*

"Shut up Jomar! That's why your breath smell like a thousand asses."

Gwinn slammed her pen on her desk frustrated at her classmates who were joking her education time away. She turned her heated face from the back of the room back to Mr. Bower sternly; "We should do a follow up on the Barack Obama paper we did a few months ago."

Mr. Bower acknowledged Gwinn with a certain level of attentiveness and respect, as Gwinn didn't seem like she was in too much of a playing mood.

"We could demonstrate how Americans stood up for change and how that change is now manifest with a Black man as the President elect of a Country in which he would've been a slave less than 200 years ago."

"You mean manifested."

"No I mean manifest; it's life, it is. It is not the words. It's bigger than the words. So I'm speaking to the unfolding of the life, the current situation; the actualities."

Gwinn noticed Mr. Bower turn away confused and therefore she astutely got back to the point; "We could also present arguments on what Americans need to do in their own private lives to make the world abroad a better, more equitable place; since they were at the forefront of destroying it."

A stark silence fell upon room 202. Gwinn glanced over her shoulder and witnessed nearly every eyeball planted on her back, including Jamal, whose attention she'd been trying to get for over a month. She no longer needed the attention. She felt extra comfortable in her kinky hair, her brown skin and her sweatpants. For Gwinn Ella Sessoms-Jordan had come to know GOD; and she felt particularly strong in him.

"O..k…Alright ,write your papers on what she said."

4:22 PM; THE SAME DAY

Since Gwinn stepped off of the 2 train she had a strange feeling in her heart. It was as if her eyes weren't as sharp as they used to be. East Harlem was moving too fast for her to grasp; she felt weird. And it certainly didn't help when she got to 112th street and saw her Father yelling at her friend Candice in front of her old building.

*"It's not meant for you to be out here in
constant want, a perpetual state of scheming,
plotting in the name of stimulation. You need
proper nourishment Sister not high after high.
You need a clear line of sight to allow the
Lord's light to shine on you."*

Jason followed Candice in circles, unrelenting in
his effort. Gwinn walked up and stood beside
Laronda who was watching with sharp intensity
as Jason stayed on Candice.

*"What you don't want to hear the truth? You
don't want to hear the truth? What you think
these people see when they look at you? The
truth is there whether you want to hear it or not;
you're fucked up! You aint what you used to be,
you cannot deny that, you can't... "*

Through her peripheral vision Gwinn could see
Hollis and Reggie walking down 112th street.
They were involved in a conversation, oblivious
to their surroundings. Gwinn dug her hands into
her blue bubble coat and watched them stroll
past the midway point of the block where she
caught a glance of Detectives sitting in the
parking lot in a green Mercedes paying
particular attention to Jason's evangelistic
efforts.

*"...You should be uppermost! Allah ain't make
no mistakes when he created you! Your saving
grace is right here, right now! Shake that shit!
You following a path of the Devil's deception, a
path of anti-reality, a path of nothingness, it's*

not there! That's why it's never enough, that's why you're always in want..."

Candice grew weary, her legs became visibly weakened, and she fell to the floor.

- *"Oh shit!"*

- *"Sis you aight?"*

"No leave her there."

Jason said to Box Cuter Keisha who gave the diesel Dread none of her usual bullshit. He had a heightened level of seriousness exceeding him as he turned back to Candice, "GOD has a path for you! And it did consist of you hangin' around these Projects getting high and fucking around your whole life. This is a new day, people are standing up and fighting the people who put the crack in your neighborhood; they the same Motherfuckers responsible for your poverty and lack of understanding of yourself. Join the fight at least. Stop being a weak ass bitch!" He yelled at the height of his capacity then walked away with his people.

"I'm ready!" Candice professed from the seat of her pants.

Gwinn along with the bystanders around were stunned. *Only in Harlem*, Gwinn thought to herself, *only in Harlem.*

Jason turned around, he took a deliberate glance to the sky before he reached out to her, "Come on then; let's get you back on your feet."

Gwinn could feel her feet planted firmly in the earth as she tried to register what was going on around her. It was as if GOD was lurking, as if he were right here, right now. The feeling was immense. Gwinn was certain that there was a surplus of energy around her, but she couldn't see or identify its' source; mass, mass, vivid, clear energy. There was a sense of heightened familiarity here; there was tremendous freedom in the energy. Gwinn squeezed her eyelids shut and when she opened them the power in the surrounding buildings and the streetlights were out. She could hear residents complain to and question one another. Gwinn returned to the world, it was only then that she realized that her mind had transcended the physicality around her. She was depleted of any want, feeling no desire to move, nor speak, an unprecedented state of peace. But she knew she couldn't stay there. She was alone in the middle of the Projects, not scheming on getting money; she wasn't looking out or watching her back, or trying to get ahead or running her mouth, and she knew Harlem wouldn't let her get away with that. But she couldn't move, not until the force of the energy was completely gone.

A few Moments later, GOD left. When Gwinn realized that he had come, she wished to herself that he never do that to her again. She was nauseated and at a loss of understanding. Still stuck, Gwinn watched her Father and his

congregation walk around the corner toward
M.S.G. For some odd reason she turned around,
and when she did she saw a swarm of men
coming from around the side of the building.
She identified them quickly then turned to check
on her Father who was now out of seeing
distance around the other side of the building.
She turned swiftly and darted in the front door
of 1694. She raced up the staircase and her heart
raced faster, seized by fright. She ran to the 8th
floor and banged on apartment 8Q. Gwinn
could hear Samantha taking the chain and the
locks off of the door.

"What's up girl?"

"What up Sam I need to kick it here for a
minute, if you don't mind."

"You better get in here. What you mean if I
don't mind?" Samantha stepped aside; "Our
electricity is still out but we'll be alright."

Gwinn felt safe, and therefore switched her
entire demeanor the instant her backside hit Ms.
Ruiz's couch.

"You duckin' blows from your Big Sisters?"

"Na, that boy JoJo and his crazy ass crew."

"JoJo? What he want with you?"

"I held his Sister down while my homegirl sliced
up her face."

"Eww…" Samantha squinted her face tightly,
"…Well you good over here girl. I'm a be back
here with the baby. Help yourself to anything
you want."

Gwinn watched JoJo and his crew prowl the
Projects for nearly ten minutes from one of the
dining room windows. The electricity in the
building was still unstable as the lights had
flickered off and on a few times and Gwinn
could hear the emergency alarm scream from the
elevator as if someone was stuck. She began
gathering the few things that she left at
Samantha's when she moved out of the building.
She sat at the kitchen table and scrolled through
her bag of pictures; flicks from Junior High
School, Dorney Park, Block parties, 125th street.
There were pictures of her showing off her cute
outfits, drinking with Sisters, snowball fights
with Junior…Gwinn looked at every picture she
had and felt a sense of satisfaction as she already
had enough memories to last her two life times.

After she got her things ready Gwinn checked
back out the window and saw the Detectives still
parked out front. The car's headlights switched
on just as she began to look away and the Benz
slowly rolled out of its' parking space. That's
when her phone rang.

"Hi Daddy." She answered as her Father's name
appeared on her called id.

"Where you at?"

"At my friend Samantha's in 1694. You still out here?"

"Come to M.S.G; go in through the back. I'll see you when you get here." Jason said before hanging up the phone.

- *"You calling him Daddy now?"*

Samantha appeared from behind the kitchen wall and opened the refrigerator. "Things must have really changed since you moved."

"Yeah, somethin' like that." Gwinn said as she stuffed her phone back in her pocket, "You gone be here? I planned on taking my stuff now, but my Pops asking me to meet him at M.S.G. for some reason."

"Yeah I'll be here."

Gwinn walked downstairs and out the back of the building. She could see no light through Margo's storefront and the gate was shut. She walked around to the back were there were two young ladies posted at either side of the door. As she approached, one of the girls stepped toward her with her arm extended, "Whoa-"

"No that's Architekk's Daughter." The other girl said. She looked Gwinn over again then stepped to the side and allowed her the rite of passage.

"...Our brains, our mental capacity has exalted us above the hunt and kill for food, we have

*established homes and places of business,
institutions; man can live in peace and
harmony. So long as that man has knowledge of
himself and can embrace his harmony with the
infinite. "*

Jason cracked a warm smile and turned toward
Laronda who was sitting to his right, "*...The
infinite; harmony with the infinite. The elements
that GOD used to create the heavens and the
earth, those same elements are in you; calcium,
oxygen, hydrogen. And I say that to
demonstrate to you that there is so much more
out there for you than death, and betrayal, and
deception, and loss, lack of. The ways of GOD
are clean, straightforward, upright, they feel
right. We care about community, so long as that
community is built in the name of GOD, we care
about family, so long as my Brother is my
Brother in the Lord, the same holds true for
political processes, Policing, and the general
governing of man...So long as it is all in the
name of GOD...Anything not in the name of
GOD, we fight to the death against..."*

Gwinn stopped listening for a Moment and
started looking around. All of the original set
Sisters were there, N.Y.C.M.C was there and so
were various residents from the neighborhood.
Although he didn't speak from a podium, and
there were no distinguishing settings, it was
clear that Jason was in command, wearing a full
camouflage suite with his dreadlocks sprawled
all over him.

"You particular young ladies are the descendents of slaves, living in the land that your parents-parents were beaten and terrorized for hundreds of years to build; kidnapped, cut off from their history, their religion, language, from the knowledge of themselves. I am talking about Al Jihad!"

Gwinn could feel and hear the people in the room become unsettled and apparently so could Jason. *"Don't get scared Motherfuckers. Al Jihad which means struggling in the way of the Lord, is the war fought by man against his sinful soul. Man has to persistently fight against his sinful urges, and temptations; and it never stops... So we enjoy our Moments of peace as they come, and we stay ready for war. And we stay mindful of our enemies."* He shut the books in his hands and looked analytically through the congregation, *"We got a get our shit together first. When we got our shit together, if our enemies still don't wanna let us be free, then we engage in the other war; so we'll see. Okay so we're all on the same page? We know what we're doing?"* No one had anything further, and so he concluded, *"Okay, Peace be with you all, I will see you next time."*

The Sisters on the floor stood to their feet. The Sisters who were standing along the walls began greeting one another and exchanging small talk. Margo was whispering something in Jason's ear that was causing him to smile. Gwinn could tell when her Father recognized her by the alteration of the expression on his face as he caught eyes

with her from across the room. He left from his
entourage and walked over to his daughter. He
greeted her with a kiss on the cheek and he
wrapped his arm around her. "You got your
things together?"

"Yeah, everything is ready."

"You alright?"

"Yeah I'm good."

He took her by the hand; "Come on."

It was a dark, rainy Friday night. The hood was
quiet, and the street lights seemed to illuminate
the filth scattered about. They walked around
the side of the building to Madison Avenue
where Sisters were filing into cars and Jason's
close friends were waiting for him.

"Sweetie I got a speak at one more conference in
Grant. It should only be about an hour or so.
You wanna come?"

"Na, I think I'm a go hang out with Samantha
until your done. Just come back for me."

Jason looked her straight in the eyes as if he
were looking for something, she turned away.

"Yo Dread, we out?"

Gwinn kept her eyes to herself. Jason backed off from his silent investigation as if he'd unfortunately found what he was looking for.

"Yeah we out."

9:33 PM; THE SAME NIGHT

Gwinn walked to 110th street and got a bag of onion and garlic chips and a ginger ale soda before going back upstairs. She banged on Samantha's door and dug into her bag of chips as she waited. Gwinn could hear Samantha speaking to someone on the other side of the door before opening up.

"Oh hello… Junior? Junior?"

She opened the door; "That was your Brother, he said he just got out of class. He on his way over here to see you."

"Oh okay." Gwinn grew excited as she hadn't seen her Brother a while. She walked in the kitchen and disposed of her empty potato chip bag and soda bottle in the trash can. "What you up to?"

"I'm about to go drink with Dotty on the 3rd floor. Sal back there with the baby. You tryin' to roll?"

11:38 PM; THE SAME NIGHT

Gwinn, Samantha and Dotty sat in the dinning room on foldout chairs with enough liquor to fuel a small party. Each of them had a plastic cup in their hand and sloth written across their faces. Dotty stood up for no particular reason, "The block is crazy dead. Ain't nobody outside." She did a double take out of the window that she just turned away from, "There your Brother go right there Lil E."

Gwinn took another sip of Hennessey and slammed her cup on the window ledge, "Aight; let me go."

Samantha dug into her pockets and pulled out her house keys, "He meeting you at my crib?"

Gwinn inadvertently took steps in a circle and smeared her hand across her face, "Oh I forgot. I called him and told him we down here."

"You aight girl?" Dotty looked at Gwinn as if she were about to erupt in her trademark hysterical drunk laughter. "You looking a little saucy over there." Dotty went off, laughing so hard that she almost fell off her chair; Samantha had no choice but to join. Even Gwinn had to laugh as she contemplated to herself; *damn, why did I just walk around for no reason?*

503

Samantha gained control of herself, "Be careful, that's the Hen Rock. That'll put you lightweights to sleep."

"Oh shit yall heard that?" Dotty turned toward the front door, "Sound like gun shots."

"Yeah I heard it too." Samantha said before standing to her feet. "This nigga JoJo been out here for a minute."

Gwinn hurried over to look out of the window with Samantha, to the front of the building where JoJo was rushing from. Gwinn shifted her focal point from JoJo to the Volvo that pulled up on the curb on Madison. "Oh shit, my Father's back."

Dotty walked over. "Your Pops be looking like Sergeant Slaughter & shit." She bussed out laughing and fell over Gwinn's shoulder. "Look at that nigga; hut 1, 2, 3, 4, hut."

"Shut up… I wonder where my Brother went."

-"And look, Laronda is the Lieutenant; them some crazy niggas."

Gwinn suddenly became sick to her stomach and took a seat. There was a feeling in her that she didn't want to leave Harlem, not tonight. Not to go to some quiet farm in Pennsylvania, away from the action, away from the drama and the comfort of familiarity.

The activity on the street was beginning to pick up. Yvonne or Big E, Gwinn's parental Grandmother made her way to the front of the building, Trevor and Kenneth were out front talking to Mr. Paige who was leaning against the handicap railing.

"Oh, this my jam! Baby don't leave me, don't ever desert me…" Dotty turned her radio up and sang along, *"I promise my life to you and I love you always."* Dotty apparently heard a knock at the door that Gwinn didn't; *"Coming!"* She walked over. *"Baby don't leave me…"*

Gwinn grabbed the bottles of whiskey that they'd been drinking and quickly swallowed them in a throw blanket that was laid across the top of the coach.

"Hi Mr. J."

"Oh yall in here partying huh?" Jason asked as he smiled and walked in the living room. "You ready to rock & roll?" He asked Gwinn smiling.

She frowned and spoke reluctantly; "I think I'm going to stay here just for one more night Daddy."

"You're not ready to go?" His demeanor became hardened with attitude.

"No."

"Aight man, well I guess I'm a see you when I see you then."

"Bye Daddy."

11:57PM; THE SAME NIGHT

"Aight G, we about to do shots!"

Samantha yelled from the kitchen as she finished mixing up another blender full of Nutcracker.

Gwinn's phone began to vibrate on her hip, it was her Father calling.

"Hello?"

"G meet me at the elevator. I wanna give you something."

"Aight."

Gwinn went into the kitchen and took the cup that Dotty was holding out for her.

"Alright now." Dotty said using her free hand to wrestle her unbuttoned jeans back up her thick booty, "1, 2, 3." The girls swallowed the full contents of their cups, each in one shot. Gwinn rammed her cup into the counter with such force that the cup tore apart. She stumbled backward, back into the living room, where she saw her Father walking back toward the building out of the window. "Aw shit, I forgot. I gotta go."

"Where you going?"

"Nowhere, I'll be right back."

Gwinn opened the apartment door and grabbed the edges of the threshold as a balancing act before crossing out.

"You know this nigga?"

Gwinn let nature shut the apartment door and looked down the hall where she saw her Father standing with and a man she never saw before. Jason's eyes had a certain rigor, like lasers, staring into the elevator that he was standing in front of.

"Tekk you knew that nigga?"

"What yall looking at?" Gwinn asked walking toward them from down the hallway.

507

"Gwinn go back inside."

Gwinn could see a large handgun in her Father's hand as he raised it to waive her back. But there was no way that she was going back. She walked quicker to confirm what was going on.

"Gwinn!"

She leaned to get a visual around the corner of the cement wall where the elevators were. "Oh my GOD, who is that?" The green and brown leather boots hanging out of the elevator froze Gwinn with apprehension. Her Brother was the only person she'd ever saw with those boots.

"G go back inside sweetie."

"Oh my GOD! Junior!" Gwinn squeezed her fist and her legs locked, rendering her stuck.

"Fuck that I'm out of here." The man with Jason made up his mind and jetted off into the staircase. When Jason swung his head around and caught eyes with Gwinn she ran back toward the apartment that she came out of.

"Gwinn! What the hell you doing?"

She came to a halt by violently smashing the side of her fragile body into the steel threshold of Samantha's apartment. Her adrenaline carried her in and she slammed the door shut behind her. *"He killed Junior! He killed my Brother! Call the Police! Call the Police!"* Gwinn paced to and fro uncontrollably; *"Oh my GOD, oh my GOD."*

"What happen? The Cops are right outside." Samantha said.

Gwinn tried to catch her breathe.

-"Oh shit look at Tekk!"

Gwinn rushed over to the window with Dotty and Samantha.

Jason was standing in front of the building, barely. He was slumped over himself still holding his gun and stumbling about.

"Drop that fucking weapon now!"

Several plain clothed Detectives closed on Jason with their weapons drawn. Without wavering, without a second or first thought for that matter, Jason raised his handgun and fired at will. Gwinn felt like life was unfolding before she could process it; and for that reason she found brief, very brief relief in the possibility that none of this was happening; that this was all a dream.

"I fuckin' hate yall! I fucking hate yall bitches, bring it!"

There were a few more isolated shots after the hail of gunfire settled. Gwinn turned and fell dumbfounded to the floor, thinking there was no way; this couldn't be real.

"I wouldn't say I'm Nino at the Carter,
I'm more like the plant at little shop of Horror."

Cam'ron

C

This books is dedicated to Leyla R.
Williams and Nailah K. Smith...

2744170

Made in the USA